HERE & ELSEWHERE

HERE & ELSEWHERE

The Collected Fiction of Kenneth Burke

Introduction by Denis Donoghue

A Black Sparrow Book

DAVID R. GODINE · *Publisher · Boston*

This is
A Black Sparrow Book
published in 2005 by
David R. Godine, Publisher
Post Office Box 450
Jaffrey, New Hampshire 03452
www.blacksparrowbooks.com

The contents of this book were selected and arranged by Christopher Carduff of Black Sparrow Books in consultation with The Kenneth Burke Literary Trust.

Book design and composition by Carl W. Scarbrough

LIBRARY OF CONGRESS CATALOGING-IN-PUBLICATION DATA
Burke, Kenneth, 1897–1993.
Here & elsewhere : the collected fiction of Kenneth Burke /
introduction by Denis Donoghue.
 p. cm.
Includes bibliographical references.
"A Black Sparrow Book"
ISBN 1-57423-201-0 (softcover : alk. paper)
ISBN 1-57423-202-9 (hardcover : alk. paper)
1. Burke, Kenneth, 1897–1993 — Selections. I. Title.
 3503. 6134 15   2004
813'.52 22   2004017236

First Edition
PRINTED IN CANADA

Contents

Introduction

It is a standard assumption that a writer, having something to say, looks about for the best means of saying it. The something to be said is deemed to come first: it waits around, biting its fingernails, till the writer has found a satisfactory form to express it. W. B. Yeats wrote some of his best poems by first knowing, more or less, what he wanted to say. He started by jotting down his argument in ordinary, rather commonplace, sentences; later, he revised them, rhyming word with word, into decisive poetry. But that is not always the case. Some writers have a gift for certain styles, distinctive flourishes, biases of language: the something to be said seems to come later, and is chosen because it enables the particular style to be fulfilled. A style is a gift, but it is also a limitation. Presumably, many things such a writer might say don't get said because these things don't lend themselves to his style or styles. If a writer has a gift for the jeremiad, he or she is unlikely to write tender passages of love. I should not aspire to Wagnerian amplitude if my native gift is for the sonata or the *lied*.

In the later years of the 1920s Kenneth Burke tried to write a novel along customary lines of plot and character, set in Greenwich Village. The American economy was at that time taking a crash course in self-destruction, so there was plenty of reality to be apprehended. Conditions were favorable for writing a naturalistic novel in which the hero, a deserving fellow, is defeated by external forces: another *American Tragedy*. Such a novel would require many external details, density of background, an apartment or two, furniture of convincing seediness, bouts of bohemian excess. Nothing wrong with that, unless you disapprove of realism, as Burke's Herone does in "The Anaesthetic Revelation of Herone Liddell":

> In any case, nothing could be farther from realism, in its essence, than the kind of thinking now called Real-politik (which is a materialistically toughened brand of idealism, idealistic sentimentality in reverse). The problem of cooperation that Herone's tentatively imagined Ur-Realismus could not solve, and that accordingly called for the death of realism in its purity, was signalized perfectly in the Spanish proverb "When two share the same purse, one laughs and the other weeps." True realism can't long survive the ability of language to observe that, when the cream has settled, one can "by sheer oversight" grandly pour himself the thick and leave the thin for others, in their role as mean, justice-mongering grumblers.

With whatever misgiving and reluctance, Burke kept the realistic narrative going as long as he could, but he was disgusted with the result. At some point he threw the typescript away and decided that he must change his procedure. He had written short stories, poems, and essays, but none of these called for the observances of a standard novel. He was devoted to the little magazines, especially to *The Dial*, where editorial inclination favored avant-garde practices. In short: the realistic or naturalistic novel did not allow Burke to use the styles he wanted to use. So he changed his direction, consulting his gifts rather than the public conditions on which they might be employed. He decided that he did not want to deal with external situations; nor was he interested in furniture. He wanted to write passages of "lamentation, rejoicing, beseechment, admonition, sayings, and invective." These seemed to him "central matters, while a plot in which they might occur seemed peripheral, little more than a pretext, justifiable not as 'a good story,' but only insofar as it could bring these six characteristics to the fore." As he said in justifying this decision: "*Facit indignatio versus*, which I should at some risk translate: 'An author may devote his entire energies to rage purely through a preference for long sentences.' "

Burke maintained that his six modes of expression marked, "in a heightened manner, the significant features of each day in our secular, yet somewhat biblical, lives—and what I most wanted to do was to lament, rejoice, beseech, admonish, aphorize, and inveigh." Note that none of these gestures takes its character from the external world or acknowledges it, except indirectly as incentive or provocation. Burke's claim that they mark the significant features of each day in our secular lives is dubious. I find that I spend little time on any of them. The claim, as I understand it, is Burke's defense against a possible charge of subscribing to "art for art's sake," or Decadence. Each of his six gestures releases an internal motive or capacity, a gift or an impulse. Burke beseeches, I infer, not necessarily because he wants anything in particular but because beseeching is one of his favorite styles; he is good at it and therefore likes doing it. Not incidentally but explicitly. He found that "whereas these [six] characteristics can readily be implicit in the realistic, objective novel, one cannot make them explicit, one cannot throw the focus of attention upon them, without continually doing violence to his framework." So he changed his tack. Several of his early writings were on musical themes, and he learned from old-style opera that it was crucial to get fairly quickly to the arias, "whereas the transition from one aria to the next is secondary." The aria delays the drama, but "once the delay is accepted, we may pursue the development of the aria's theme into other aspects of itself."

The logic of Burke's gifts might have suggested that he should commit himself to the essay and write essays, on Montaigne's authority, in each of the six modes. But he evidently thought that, while abandoning realism, he could still devise a gnarled form of fiction in which a few rudimentary characters, sketched rather than imagined in depth, would have experiences corresponding to one or more of the six modes of expression. The principle of his conviction is given in a rhetorical question he ascribes to John Neal, hero of *Towards a Better Life*: "If one seeks new metaphors, will he not also find new

Introduction

women?"—a lively notion which, if valid for metaphor, might facilitate equally fruitful correlations with the other available figures of thought and speech. This device would enable Burke to practice his gifts as a rhetorician, one who has "an interest in formal and stylistic twists as such" along with, as a secondary inclination, an interest in "their entanglements in character and plot."

It follows that Burke's sentences must be internally eventful, composed with so much stylistic *élan* that the absence of newsworthy events passes unnoticed. They are exciting as a good sonnet is exciting, by offering a profusion of verbal events sufficient to engross the most demanding reader. Thus the author hopes to enchant readers who would normally be satisfied only by images of mayhem, and to send them back to ordinary life with their lust for excitement somewhat stilled. *Towards a Better Life* and Burke's short stories are therefore in a strict sense verbal and stylistic, to begin with. Once they are under way, the possibilities of invention are nearly limitless, there being no known end to the figurative resources of the English language. But because words and figures can't be prevented from suggesting forms of life, Burke trades on certain incongruities between style and action. In the second chapter of *Towards a Better Life* he has John Neal, twisted as always, making a painful telephone call to his beloved Florence from a public booth: ". . . and while Florence listened to words as desolate as my talent and my predicament could make them, I was grinning into the mouthpiece that the man beyond the glass, waiting to speak here next, might not suspect my condition." Later, at a social gathering of low voltage, John feels compelled to denounce his rival Anthony in a style of formal complaint: "This ideal is facile and meaningless . . . You may advocate much, and thus ally yourself with goodness, through being called upon to do nothing. You need face no objective test. Under the guise of giving, you are receiving."

So the story is managed not according to the usual laws of resemblance and probability that govern realistic fiction but according to devices to achieve variety in the sentences. If a certain mood has persisted for a while, it is time for a change. This may seem a puny consideration, but Burke is immensely resourceful in divining when the reader has had enough of a good thing. The essence of stylistic appeal, as he notes in *Permanence and Change* (1935), is ingratiation: gaining favor by saying the right thing. "A plainspoken people will distrust a man who, bred to different ways of statement, is overly polite and deferential with them, and tends to put his commands in the form of questions (saying 'Would you like to do this?' when he means 'Do this')." An example from real alcoholic life:

> I have seen men, themselves schooled in the experiences of alcohol, who knew exactly how to approach a drunken man, bent upon smashing something, and quickly to act upon him by such phrases and intonations as were "just right" for diverting his fluid suggestibility into the channel of maudlin good-fellowship.... I should have hated to see a Matthew Arnold tackle the job. He would have been too crude—his training would have been all incapacity.

Style is the gift of saying the right thing at the right time to the right person or people, a theorem announced at the end of *Towards a Better Life*: "speech being a mode of conduct, he converted his faulty living into eloquence. Then should any like his diction, they would indirectly have sanctioned his habits."

I should quote a fairly lengthy passage to show Burke's resourcefulness in making a trope or a formal paradigm develop into an image of life. Think of the movements of a minuet or a choreography of partnering, then think of giving the form an ironic twist:

> Dare I go further among this uneven lot? No further than to mention briefly a beautiful and even picturesque woman, a Madame Durant, loved by two men. Through letters, telegrams, sudden visits, and the intervention of relatives, she carried her drama tumultuously across many states. With her arms about Joseph, she would cry out that she loved Josephus and thereupon, misled by a desire for too literal a symme-

try, would cross the room to embrace Josephus and
protest her love of Joseph. For to be alone with one of
them seemed far greater impoverishment than to be
with neither, and whichever she lived with, she thought
herself conscience-stricken for leaving the other,
though in reality suffering most from a drop in the liveliness of her situation. She wept in contentment, insisting that she was degraded—and friends, stopping to
rebuke her for her inconstancy, would become her suitors. On one occasion I drank a toast to her elopement,
using for the purpose glasses given prematurely as a
present for her prospective marriage to the groom now
temporarily abandoned though on hand to bid her and
his rival farewell—and I left in complex cordiality,
loving her, her two men, her dog, and the darkening
inhospitable sky which matched my lonesomeness.

We read this prose as if it were poetry, perhaps eighteenth-century
couplets in which the outside stays the same while the inside changes
from syllable to syllable. Every detail in Madame Durant's emotional
life is contained "in principle" in the formal resources of language,
not forgetting such items as rhyme, alliteration, and assonance. If
finding a metaphor suggests finding a woman, would it not be possible to think of human relations equivalent to simile, rhyme, or oxymoron; as we commonly say that a particular situation is ironic, a
certain relationship is paradoxical or tragic or comic, moving from
tropes to lives without stopping to reflect that that is what we are
doing? In the passage I've quoted, Burke's narrator starts out as if he
were a disinterested witness or a choreographer of transits—Joseph,
Josephus—until we find him a participant in Madame Durant's
comings and goings, a victim, a sad sack, committed to loving not
only her but her appurtenances, stopping not short of the sky.

In "The Anaesthetic Revelation of Herone Liddell" Burke has a
paragraph that brings these considerations down to one simple fact,
that a word is not the same as the thing or non-thing to which it
refers. Herone has been trying to sum things up:

"First," there is man the "economic animal," in the strictly biological sense, such a creature of ecological balance and geophysical necessities as he would be even without his "reason" (that is, without his ability to find words for things and non-things, though frequently, by misuse of his "reason," he puts himself geophysically and ecologically in jeopardy, at the same time victimizing many humble "lower organisms" that don't quite know what happened to them; but somehow, as the result of human improvising, they ceased to find life lovable, or even livable). Here would prevail, basically, the aims and behaviors that make for growth, self-protection, and reproduction.

Now add *language* (the "grace" that "perfects" nature). Henceforth, every "natural" movement must be complicated by a *linguistic* (or *symbolic*) motive—symbolic not just in the general sense that an animal's posture may be symbolic of its condition, but also in the more specific sense that the word "tree" is symbolic of the thing it names, and this word can undergo developments, such as declensions, syntactic location, grammatical and phonetic changes, that are quite independent of the nature of tree as a thing.

He means the word "tree" in English, of course: "*arbre*" in French and "*albero*" in Italian are just as independent of the nature of a tree as "tree" is, but the possibilities of their development, each within its own language, differ—grammatically, syntactically, acoustically—from those of "tree."

To enjoy the difference between "tree" and a tree, Herone must love "the sheer jingle of words," and here he finds companionship in the poet Keats's letters; Keats, who even in the throes of dying keeps fiddling with words. "Yet I ride the little horse," Keats reports, "and, at my worst, even in quarantine, summoned up more puns, in a sort of desperation, in one week than in any year of my life." On which Herone comments that "whatever fragment of a damned outraged monster there may be, howling deep down in a chasm, there is the possibility of this pure exercising whereby essences are suggested by an engrossment with the sheer accidents of words."

I am not suggesting that Burke's fiction is just fiction like anyone else's, only different because of its verbal inventiveness. Nor that his "In Quest of Olympus" and "The Death of Tragedy" are much the same as "Ivy Day in the Committee Room," the best story in Joyce's *Dubliners*, except for a few oddities of language. It is a different kind of fiction from the kinds we are used to. In ascriptions of this kind we do well to consult Northrop Frye's account of the several forms of prose fiction. Then it appears that Burke's fiction is not a freak, a sport of Nature, but an instance of a distinguished tradition, the anatomy. It answers in every respect to Frye's description: it deals "less with people as such than with mental attitudes," its characterization is "stylized rather than naturalistic," it presents its figures as "mouthpieces of the ideas they represent." The anatomist sees evil and folly "as diseases of the intellect, as a kind of maddened pedantry." The narrative is "loose-jointed." The writing "relies on the free play of intellectual fancy and the kind of humorous observation that produces caricature." The anatomy presents "a vision of the world in terms of a single intellectual pattern." The major works in this genre include *A Tale of a Tub, Candide, The Anatomy of Melancholy, Headlong Hall,* and *Brave New World.*

An anatomy of what, then? Burke's fiction is an anatomy of dissociation. John Neal, riveted to language, is as detached from Nature as from us: "the weather's metaphysical whisperings" do not sing to him. His human relations are never more than provisional, tentative flurries in a doomed genre. He is so conscientious in husbanding grimness that, buffeted beyond endurance, he is never surprised in principle. He is our little scapegoat. At the end of the book the quality of personality has drained away from the people he knows, collecting itself only in lampposts, streetcars, and gutters. His last event is a fixation on a wooden policeman outside a cigar shop. This stage in his anatomy is conveyed by unmailed letters to his dead mistress, the style a tissue of quotations from a favorite poet, William Blake. (Keats has much the same provenance for Herone Liddell.) As he sits in his room in New York ("this inexorable city"), John says: "Watch the mind as you would eye a mean dog. Wait. Die as a mangled wasp dies." Thereafter he delivers his testimony in fragments of aphorism. There comes a time, he says, when one must abandon his vocabulary, "for the rigidness of words, by discovering a little, prevents us from discovering more." Time to be silent. The book ends: "Not only not responding, but even refraining from soliloquy—for if we tell no one, the grave burden accumulates within us. Henceforth silence, that the torrent may be heard descending in all its fullness."

Denis Donoghue
New York, New York

TOWARDS A BETTER LIFE

Being a Series of Epistles, or Declamations

Preface to Second Edition

The first ten chapters of this novel (or should we rather say, in current cant, "anti-novel"?) were written and published as "work in progress" during the fatal months that were urgently on the way towards the "traumatic" market crash of 1929. The book was completed in the "traumatic" months immediately following that national crisis. And it was published in 1932, when the outlook was exceptionally bleak. Though several competent critics were friendly to its experimenting, the author found that the figures of its sales (or, more accurately, non-sales) were also "traumatic."

Originally I had intended to introduce each chapter by an "argument," but at the time I was not able to write those pieces. They were done eventually—and a version of them is included in this edition. Their insertion is advisable because the plot, being told somewhat obliquely, emerges little by little from a background of aphorism, lamentation, invective, and other such rhetorical modes. Particularly in the early chapters, where the narrative strand is being slowly extricated from this somewhat "sermonizing" or "attitudinizing" context, the brief summaries help to point the arrows of the reader's expectations.

The mention of "expectations" brings up another likelihood. I have found that the title of this work can be misleading, if the words are read without ironic discount. I recall, at the time when the book was first published, being invited by Horace Gregory to read portions of it to a poetry club in which he then officiated. The now-deceased poet John Brooks Wheelwright, who was in the audience, told me of an elderly lady who sat next him. After a while, she had turned to him and asked: "Young man, just *what* is the title of that book?" He answered: "*Towards a Better Life*, Ma'am." Whereupon she: "Hm! I think it's getting worse and worse." This was a necessary part of the development.

On the other hand, there is also a sense in which an ironic discounting of the title must in turn be discounted. My later study of various literary texts, viewed as modes of "symbolic action," has convinced me that this book is to be classed among the many rituals of rebirth which mark our fiction. And though I did not think of this possibility at the time, I noticed later how the theme of resurgence is explicitly proclaimed, even at the moments of my plaintive narrator's gravest extremity.

In the last analysis, a work of art is justified only insofar as it can give pleasure. Somehow it must contrive to convert the imitation of ethical liabilities into aesthetic assets. Yet writers often symbolize modes of "purification by excess," designed to "seek Nirvana by burning something out," to call forth a "Phoenix out of the ashes," or to get things entangled in a "withinness of withinness." (I am quoting from one of my later critical books, *The Philosophy of Literary Form*, 1941.) To this end they may utilize "some underlying imagery (or groupings of imagery) through which the agonistic trial [that is a bit pleonastic] takes place, such as: ice, fire, rot, labyrinth, maze, hell, abyss, mountains and valleys, exile, migration, lostness, submergence, silence, sometimes with their antidote, sometimes simply going 'to the end of the line.'"

Often, a closer look at such texts will make it apparent that, however roundabout, they are modes of symbolic action classifiable as rituals of resurgence, transcendence, rebirth. Thus, in a moment of extreme discomfiture, the plaintive narrator (our "hero," query), tells himself: "The sword of discovery goes before the couch of laughter. One sneers by the modifying of a snarl; one smiles by the modifying of a sneer. You should have lived twice, and smiled the second time."

So perhaps, by the devious devices of the psyche, these solemnly grotesque and willfully turbulent pages herald (among other things) the enigmatic inception of an author's devout belief that the best possible of worlds would have the Comic Muse for its tutelary deity.

Earlier, as the reader can learn by consulting the preface to the original edition, I proffered a way of placing this ambitious effort. I'd now want to modify my statement somewhat, as follows:

In its nature as a story that speculatively carries things "to the end of the line," *Towards a Better Life* could be classed with any work such as *The Sorrows of Young Werther*. (We are talking of literary *kind*, not of *quality*. And even when it is viewed simply as a kind, we necessarily note: It differs from great Goethe's youthful piece in that it by no means called forth a wave of spellbound suicides.) Also, as is most clearly indicated in the chapter called "Despite them all, in their very faces," the book was written by the sort of verbalizer who had taken particular delight in the "pamphleteering" style of Léon Bloy (who was pleased to pose for a photograph of himself among his pigs, and who wrote, as early as 1897: "*Que Dieu vous garde du feu, du couteau, de la littérature contemporaine et de la rancune des mauvais morts!*"). Nor should we forget, as regards the pleasurable accents of gloom, Ricarda Huch's *Erinnerungen von Ludolf Ursleu dem Jüngeren*. (I still keep trying to recall books that had somehow got me.) Then add the fact that the tone of the fourth chapter in particular stems directly from the author's love of St. Augustine's Latin, in the *Confessions*. Later, in *The Rhetoric of Religion* (1961), I returned to that text by a quite different route—and so it goes.

In any event, the book itself is here born anew, as attested by the brute fact of its being republished, after having languished in an O.P. state for thirty-five long (long!) years. Whereupon the retrospective quality of the author's experience has suggested to him some verses that, though they were composed with different thoughts in mind, can be adapted to this benign occasion:

HEAVY, HEAVY—WHAT HANGS OVER?

> At eighty
> reading lines
> he wrote at twenty

5

The storm now past

A gust in the big tree
splatters raindrops
on the roof

By paring a decade or so from the top figure, and adding it to the bottom one, you bring the span of years close enough to the present situation. And whether these early stylistic exercises are storm or bluster, they are of a sort that, for better or worse, their author could not now contrive to unfold again.

And so it goes . . .

Kenneth Burke
Andover, New Jersey
August 1965

6

Preface to First Edition

The first six of these chapters were published in *The Dial*, the seventh, eighth, and ninth in *The Hound & Horn*, and the tenth in *Pagany*. They appeared under the title of Declamations; but though they now have another title, the present version is substantially unchanged. The remaining eight chapters are here printed for the first time.

Originally I had intended to handle this story in the customary manner of the objective, realistic novel. To this end I made a working outline of plot, settings, incidental characters, and the like, before attempting to write any of the chapters in detail. But when I sat down to follow my outline, a most disheartening state of affairs was revealed. Three times the expectant author began, with two men talking in a room, an illicit "dive" in Greenwich Village. These men conversed for a fitting period, telling each other a few things which it was very necessary for the reader to know; a bell rang, the waiter's steps could be heard going down the hall, a peephole was opened; next the slinging of a bolt, then the unlatching of the iron grate; the newcomer, after low-voiced words at the door, could be heard striding along the hall; he entered the room where the two men were talking; "Hello," he said—and for the third time your author tossed Chapter One into the discard. Thereupon he decided that he had best read the signs. And if, with Chapter One barely started, the thought of the projected venture became appalling, the signs very definitely indicated that some fundamental error in procedure was involved. For I had by now written enough to know that, were this to turn out the most amazing book in the world, it could not, as so written, serve as a vehicle for the kind of literary experience which interested me most and which I was most anxious to get into my pages.

Lamentation, rejoicing, beseechment, admonition, sayings, and invective—these seemed to me central matters, while a plot in which they might occur seemed peripheral, little more than a pretext, justifiable not as "a good story," but only insofar as it could bring these six characteristics to the fore. These mark, these six mark, in a heightened manner, the significant features of each day in our secular, yet somewhat biblical, lives—and what I most wanted to do was to lament, rejoice, beseech, admonish, aphorize, and inveigh. Yet I found that the technique of the realistic, objective novel enabled one at best to bring in such things "by the ears." Or rather, I found that whereas these characteristics can readily be implicit in the realistic, objective novel, one cannot make them explicit, one cannot throw the focus of attention upon them, without continually doing violence to his framework. Thus a different framework seemed imperative. So I reversed the process, emphasizing the essayistic rather than the narrative, the emotional predicaments of my hero rather than the details by which he arrived at them—the ceremonious, formalized, "declamatory." In form the resultant chapters are somewhat like a sonnet sequence, a progression by stages, by a series of halts; or they might be compared to an old-style opera in which the stress is laid upon the arias whereas the transition from one aria to the next is secondary. However, much emphasis is placed upon the transitions within this static matter itself, as one follows the ebb and flow of a particular sonnet though this sonnet "interrupts" the story in the very act of forwarding it—or, as in the case of the aria, the aria delays the drama, but once the delay is accepted, we may pursue the development of the aria's theme into other aspects of itself.

I have described my changing of the framework as a decision reached by logical steps, but the process was really much more confused. In the books I had especially admired, I had found many desirable qualities which threatened them as novels—and in liking these qualities unduly I had already betrayed my unfitness to write a novel. I could readily remind myself, by considering the world's arcanum of prose, that the conventions of fiction as developed in the nineteenth century have enjoyed prestige for a very limited stretch of time; and I would not have to look far in search of precedents which gave both a guidance and a sanction for radically different concepts of what constitutes desirable prose. And if I could always, when a writer had contrived some ingenious mechanism of suspense, if I could always, when he had thrown equal suspicion upon nine different people, the heroine among them, if I could always at this point find it quite natural to lay down the cunning volume and never think of it again, what good would it do me to attempt writing in a form wherein this aspect of appeal naturally flourished? I would not dare speak ill of discipline, but to discipline oneself in a field wherein one was so hopelessly outdistanced not only by lack of ability but even by lack of interest, would have been an absurdity. Clearly, I was entitled to read the signs, confining myself to the club—offer of my Six Biblical Characteristics, the Six Pivotals as I conceived them, and rearranging my work accordingly, always recalling, for my encouragement, the more declamatory manner in which prose was written before (and even after) our first great journalist, Defoe, showed that if one thinks of people enough dying horribly enough in a plague one can get effects enough out of simply saying so.*

But there is a further step to be considered. I must impress it upon the reader that many of the statements made in my story with an air of great finality should, as Sir Thomas Browne said even of his pious writings, be taken somewhat "tropically." They are a kind of fictive moralizing wherein, even though the dogmas are prior to the events, these dogmas are not always to be read as absolutely as they are stated. What is right for a day is wrong for an hour, what is wrong for an hour is right for a moment—so not knowing how *often* or how *long* one should believe in the dubious aphorisms of my hero, I should say that there is more sincerity in their manner than in their content. *Facit indignatio versus*, which I should at some risk translate: "An

---

* It should be noted, however, that Defoe points in a direction, rather than taking the direction in which he has pointed—and the work of those who learned from him is quite different from his own, which largely retains the formal characteristics of his times.

9

author may devote his entire energies to rage purely through a preference for long sentences." And if, like a modern painter painting a straight-legged table crooked to make it fit better into his scheme, I had to distort my plot, expanding it or contracting it, accelerating or retarding, giving undue consideration to some minor detail only to elide a major one, and all for the purpose of stressing my Six Pivotals—I had further to select as the most likely vehicle for these outpourings a hero so unpleasant that the reader could not possibly have anything in common with him. He laments, rejoices, beseeches, admonishes, aphorizes, and inveighs, to be sure, but always in a repellent manner—and thus, though he could lay claim to pursuing, in a heightened form, a set of experiences common to many, his way of experiencing them may be too exclusively characteristic of himself alone, particularly as he lacks that saving touch of humor which the reader wisely and deftly summons to sweeten his own personal dilemmas.* He is a very frank, a very earnest, a very conscientious man, in whom one should place slight confidence. He has an enquiring mind, which he converts into a liability, or at best employs industriously to arrive at zero. I can say nothing in his favor except that he is busy, and busy in ways that will add not a single car to our thoroughfares. It is perhaps this predicament he has in mind when referring vaguely to his "insight." I have further chosen, for the purposes of the fiction, to give him a kind of John the Baptist quality, allowing him in his extremity to think of himself as a "forerunner," though I should be hard put to explain what sort of salvation he foreruns. He is an outsider, an ingrate, a smell-feast, and who could possibly see the burgeoning of a savior in such qualities?

By changing the proportions of a very average man, we can obtain a monster. We make him a monster if we minimize, let us say, how he feels when patting his little daughter on her curls or when hurrying to some address with a round of presents, and stress how he feels when fleecing his partner or when, like a male mosquito, he cannot eat, so that his only hunger is for the female. That is, a mon-

---

* The reader may summon it here also, as he chooses. For if my hero lacks humor, he does not lack grotesqueness—and the grotesque is but the humorous without its proper adjunct of laughter.

strous or inhuman character does not possess qualities not possessed by other men—he simply possesses them to a greater or less extent than other men. Fiction is precisely this altering of proportions. The fictions of science alter them by such classifications as Nordic, capitalistic, agrarian, hyperthyroid, extravert. The fictions of literature alter them by bringing out some trait or constellation of traits, some emotional pattern, and inventing a background to fit. So science and fiction alike make monsters, though adults have agreed not to call an anatomical chart morbid, confining their attacks to the monsters of art. These monsters are constructed partly in the interests of clarity (as is shown in classical drama, where the depiction of violence, disease, excess, coexists with the ideal of clarity, strongly unbalanced characters more readily displaying the mainsprings of conduct). But there is a second factor which leads us, whether scientists or artists, to evolve monsters. A reptile must consume another reptile to become a dragon, says a Latin saying (*serpens nisi serpentent comederit non fit draco*)—and who would not make himself a dragon?

If one could pay homage to a living master without implicating the master to whom one pays homage, I should pay homage to Thomas Mann, whose work has always and in many ways astonished and gratified me. Whereas Milton was concerned with passion as tempered by reason, perhaps we could say that a basic dichotomy of Mann's work is hypochondria as tempered by reason, hypochondria serving as the impulse to discovery, and reason as the means of revising hypochondria's first excessive statement of the discovery. In this, it seems to me, the author of *Death in Venice* and *The Magic Mountain* offers a very profound modernization, or secularization, of Milton's theology-encumbered pair. It is a naïve habit of some critics, when noting that an author's hero ends in bewilderment, to complain that this author has only bewilderment to offer—but the works of Thomas Mann stand as a sturdy refutation of their claims. His works end ever in a hero's bewilderment (may the critic's deathbed be uniquely otherwise), yet the stages by which the author brings his hero to this point offer something very different from bewilderment. He charts a process, and in the charting of this process there is "understanding."

Each sentence of this short work may strike the reader as an error—and I can make no answer. But should he question the "aesthetic" behind it, I dare protest. Whatever the failures may be, they cannot be attributed to the underlying "aesthetic," but only to my ways of exemplifying it. In considering the past of English prose, and in realizing by comparison with the present how much of the "eventfulness" of a prose sentence is omitted from our prevalent newspaper and narrative styles, we are furnished with authority enough for a "return" to more formalized modes of writing. There is no reason why prose should continue to be judged good prose purely because it trails along somewhat like the line left by the passage of a caterpillar. Why should an author spend a year or more on a single book, and end by talking as he would talk on the spur of the moment? Or why should he feel impelled to accept as the "norm" of his elucubrations that style so admirably fitted for giving the details of a murder swiftly over the telephone and rushing them somehow into copy in time for the next edition of the news? The two billion such words that are printed daily in the United States (to say nothing of the thousands of billions that are uttered) would seem to provide the public with enough of them—and if only through modesty, an author might seek to appeal by providing something else. As for what this "something else" might be, the arid stretches of monosyllabic words and monosyllabic perceptions which, partially engaging a sluggish corner of the mind, pass today as the major concern of fiction, would seem to justify anything unlike them, even to the extent of that *Zopfstil*, that "periwig style," that incredible jargon of nonspeech, which the German scribes once so zealously cultivated in their legal documents. Quintilian warns us against orators who, in quest of inspiration, rock back and forth with great assertiveness though they have nothing to assert. By striking such postures as would befit a weighty message, he says, they hope to conjure up a message weighty enough to befit their postures (*corporis motuum non enuntiandis sed quærendis verbis accommodant*). The risk of absurdity here is obvious. But is not the contrary practice of today as ripe for distrust—that easy wording, that running style beloved of evaders, a method without risk, since it is imperceptible, like a building ordered by a merchant who wants it devoid of character, knowing that any trait, if too pronounced, might earn it enemies and thus alienate his customers, so the modern precept is to write as one would write a laundry list, shunning any construction likely to force the mind into a choice where there need be no choice. On the virtues of my method I can insist, since the method is not mine; and I should like to be more emphatic in defense of it, but I cannot without embarrassment grow very militant in behalf of a neglected cause which I have only too fragmentarily embraced (having taken too few steps towards the re-erection of the "structural" sentence, the "Johnsonese" if you will, as opposed to the "conversational" style which enjoys current favor). I must be content simply to offer the present volume as practical evidence of my faith in the forthcoming "turn," away from the impromptu towards the studied, while we leave the impromptu to our barroom discussions and our accidental bumping of shins, where it most delightfully belongs.

Kenneth Burke
Andover, New Jersey
September 9, 1931

Part One

Nunc serpens, nunc taurus erat, nunc cygnus et arbos.
St. Paulinus: POEMA ADVERSUS PAGANOS

I.

"My converse became a monologue"

General statement of the narrator's antinomian philosophy. And his corresponding discomforts. Reference to a trip with a friend to whom these "epistles" are addressed. Concern with death (as the narrator meets a man "while traveling south alone"). Foreshadowing: thoughts on destitution. Attack upon friend to whom he is writing, and in whom he sees the lucky antithesis of himself. Close: statement of antinomian ars poetica.

I had become convinced that, by the exercise of the intelligence, life could be made much simpler and art correspondingly complex; that any intensity in living could be subdued beneath the melancholy of letters. And I tried to realize that we should all be saviors of mankind if we could, and would even slay one another for the privilege. I felt that the man who strove for dignity, nobility, and honor should have his task made as difficult and as hazardous as possible, and that in particular he should be forgiven no lapses in style. The day was long since past when I drew moustaches on the pictures of pretty women, though I still warmed to find that a new generation had arisen to continue the tradition, to carry on the torch which we had handed down to them. When finding that people held the same views as I, I persuaded myself that I held them differently. And as for bravery: dead upon the fields of glory are millions who would have feared to wear a hat in inappropriate season, so I judged that brave warriors were dirt cheap as compared with untimid civilians. We create new ills, I thought, and call it progress when we find the remedies. Yet I was not without wonder, the nonbeliever finding a legend of miracles itself a miracle.

On looking back upon one's own life, one may sometimes feel that every moment of it was devoted to discomfiture, marked by either pain or uncertainty, and he may worry lest this day be the very one on which he snaps under the burden and, if not talented at suicide, becomes insane. Yet it is possible that by a constant living with torment, we may grow immune to it, and disintegration will fall only upon those whom adversity can overwhelm as a surprise, making little headway against those others who would accept even prosperity with bitterness. For when I have heard much talk of the world's growing worse, I have known that this was indulged in by persons who had thought that it could grow better. And in any case, the belief in human virtue is no cause to neglect the beating of our children.

I finally came to hold that one cannot distinguish between friends and acquaintances—and from then on, my converse became a monologue. I sought those who would listen, when I could not go without them, and did not scruple to avoid them if ever I became self-sufficient, believing that in these unnecessary moments they would be most likely to do me harm. It is obvious that I came by preference to talk most intimately with strangers, and to correspond with my friends on postcards. I discovered that in confessing a reprehensible act, I would sometimes add a still more reprehensible interpretation—and whereas I might forget my own judgments upon myself, those in whom I had confided would carefully store them against me.

Not as by accident, but rather as though some voice had called me, I would awake in the night, and thereafter there was no sleeping. Could vigilance, under these circumstances, be an advance retribution for some yet uncommitted act? Though not by earthquake, people are driven into the street, pawing at one another, gentle and even courteous when necessary, but in the absolute crude, direct, revolting—and it is this panic, or should I say this glacier movement, that must be considered. Did not we two go on a premature search of an already premature spring—and did we not find the skunk cabbages well thrust up, and brooks temporarily crossing the road from every field, while the same Eumenides still rode upon the shoulders of us both? Who, seeing us munch chocolate, would have thought us dangerous? As a precaution, we carried not pistols, but rum. Feeling our flasks against our moving legs, we were assured, aiming to protect ourselves less against the malignant bite of snakes than from the benign mordancy of the season. Oh, tender psychopaths—if you be young and one of us, and it is spring, you suffer beneath the triple proestrum of climacteric ("if you be young"), personality ("and one of us"), and calendar (that is, "spring"). I the while being condemned as an apologist; as though he who speaks were more goaded than he who must remain silent! We know there has been a major ill in every stage of the world's history, since we know that in no age were all men sovereigns—but one must sing, though it be but to praise God for his boils. And if I have invited death, calling upon death to take me, I likewise avoided traffic with agility.

Recently, while traveling south alone (and I cite you the episode as evidence of my newly discovered patience), I met a man who attracted me by the obvious disquietude of his movements. As he sat facing me, we were finally able to talk with each other, though the conversation was an unsatisfactory one; for between long pauses, while both of us looked out the window, he would sigh and say, "Death is a strange thing," or "I should not fear to die," remarks which seemed to demand an answer as strongly as they precluded it. The real meaning of this, I came to understand in time, was that he was hurrying to a woman who was near death. After he had spoken at length, and in particular had talked with much penetration concerning suicide, at my suggestion we went to the back of the train, where he explained to me that he was religious, and believed firmly in the process of the Eucharist. Then, as we stood swaying with the car, and watching the tracks untwist beneath us, he said that he had prayed, and that he was sure this much of his prayer would be granted—that he would arrive at the woman's bedside either while the life was yet in her, or before the animal heat had left the body. This, he insisted, would be solace. In circumstances like these, I answered, we may feel the divisions between us: for I could be certain from the way he spoke, that he had thought a great deal upon the matter, and that his preference was a strong one—yet for my part, without the assistance of the death to sharpen my imagination, I did not see how he could feel so niggardly a concession to be the answer to a prayer.

I talked with him further, asking him questions as though he had come from some strange region. And upon my enquiring as to what he feared most of the future, he answered: "Destitution. Destitution of finances, destitution of mind, destitution of love. The inability to retort. The need of possessing one's opposite in years, sex, and texture of the skin; and the knowledge that by this need one has been made repugnant. The replacing of independence by solitude." His reply, I said, suggested that he must be well versed in this gloomy lore. I was sure that had I instigated him further, he could have discoursed with authority on many aspects of fear and undemonstrative disaster, though every conclusion would have been drawn solely from the laboratory experiments of his own biography. With him, surely, each adversity would have its parallel in thought, its ideological equivalent, its sentence. And I knew that the world would hear no more of him. And God pity the man or the nation wise in proverbs, I told myself, for there is much misery and much error gone into the collecting of such a store.

Need one, his eyes shifting with humility, need one who is uneasy on finding himself in two mirrors, need one whose pity of mankind is but the projection of his own plight, need such a one relinquish however little his anger with those who cross his interests? Would a gifted daisy, from thinking upon his crowded slum conditions in the fields, find thereby any less necessity for resisting the encroachments of a neighbor? We must learn to what extent our thoughts are consistent with our lives, and to what extent compensatory; to what extent ideals are a guide to behavior, and to what extent they are behavior itself. We would not deny the mind; but merely remember that as the corrective of wrong thinking is right thinking, the corrective of all thinking is the body.

You moralistic dog—admitting a hierarchy in which you are subordinate, purely that you may have subordinates; licking the boots of a superior, that you may have yours in turn licked by an underling. Today I talk out to you anonymously, not because I should fear to tell you this to your face, but because my note of scorn would be lacking. And I would have you perceive the scorn even more than understand its logic, being more eager to let you know *that* I resent you than to let you know *why* I resent you. I would speak as a gargoyle would speak which, in times of storm, spouted forth words. Further, I have many times changed my necktie to go in search of you and explain to you my resentment, meaning to give you at once an analysis of yourself and an awareness of my hatred—but when I found you, lo! we were companions, exchanging confidences, congratulating each other, and parting with an engagement for our next meeting. I have watched you each year come to consort more irresponsibly with God; I have seen you take on ritual dignity, as the impure take on ritual cleanliness by laving the hands or by spilling goat's blood with the relevant mummery. I have seen you grow brutal under a vocabulary of love. If you wanted to thieve, your code would expand to embrace the act of thieving. Feeling no need to drink, you will promptly despise a drunkard. Nor do you hesitate to adopt such attitudes. Yet he who flicks a weed unthinkingly is heinous, while a crime brewed in protracted spite is pardonable—for the doer, had his equipment been directed otherwise, would have been capable of great pity.

It is true that you are absolved of guilt through your disinterest in these matters, where I am guilty through too much husbandry of my despite. That a stranger, asking us each about the other, would receive from you a kindly, regretful account of my errors, and from me an explosion of venom against you, a credo of vindictiveness which would turn him from me in loathing. This third person, this "disinterested party" (and I already contemn him like yourself) would further think it significant against me that, for every item of good fortune which has been bestowed upon you, he may find in me a corresponding item of failure. But since even humility too consistently maintained becomes a boast, how could I expect otherwise than that my accusations against you should redound upon their author? Yes, I have shouted in still places that this aversion is beyond our clashing interests, that it is not rivalry, but *ars poetica*, and as such would necessarily entail rivalry as a subsidiary, but far subsidiary, aspect.

For all such reasons, and primarily because of my difficulty in finding such an account of my position as would serve also to justify me, I have been silent, until I can be silent no longer. I have waited, trusting that from somewhere would come a formula, which I could point to, saying: That figure is you, and I am this other. But despite much persistent praise of patience, I feel forced into a choice. And I have remained apart from you, that I might not be weakened by your good nature.

Yet there are times, in the very midst of such preoccupations, when my retaliation is of a different order. Our unavowed conflicts, and even my recurrent melancholy memories, seem separated from me, as I find myself busily at work upon my utterance. I would, on such occasions, deem it enough to place antinomies upon the page, to add up that which is subtracted by another, to reduce every statement by some counterclaim to zero. Did each assertion endow with life, and each denial cause destruction, at the close the message would be nonexistent; but, by the nature of words, after this mutual cancellation is complete, the document remains.

II.

"If life moves with sufficient slowness"

Opening complaints on life and its injustices. Narrator's envy of his friend. He recounts an incident at a farmhouse, where his friend had become intimate with a girl. Peroration of complaints.

When people are both discerning and unhappy, they tend to believe that their unhappiness is derived from their discernment. For how may we dare solicit the kindliness of Providence, we who in fields and on roadways have killed many bugs? In seeking causes to exist, one should not scruple at the choice of allies, and if noble motives seem weak, let him be quick to hunt out ignoble ones. We may be encouraged to continue purely by the thought that our death or default might give too great satisfaction to our enemies—and the strength derived from this attitude may later be turned to wholly praiseworthy purposes. Life is most difficult for those who are gnawed by the morbidity of justice, particularly if their own ambitions and appetites force them into unjust actions. (Yet I knew a man who was secretly committing crimes against the state, but though conscientious he did not greatly suffer at the thought of treason, for being a magistrate he could discharge his debt to society by the harsh

23

penalties he laid upon even the petty offenders brought before him.) We must be content to possess only as much of nobility as resides in the contemplation of it, while yet remembering that such an equipment will not enable us to live on better terms with our neighbors. The world is made more tentative if all sagacious things are said by despicable people, and all stupid things by the lovable—and wisdom, in becoming a kind of self-appointed martyrdom, constitutes the sage's one claim to coxcombry. Could we, by deliberateness, by refusing to do otherwise, come in time to imagine a less defensive kind of living, and even to acquire something of that geniality which is most intelligently advocated in the books of the sick? Or could we call despair a privilege without implying that mankind should show it preference over happiness when the choice could be settled by a toss? No one's discomfitures are above suspicion, for those who possess neither a great man's power nor his torment, record their own maladjustments at length in the belief that they are somehow displaying the rest of greatness. I mean, by what I have been saying, that knowledge is undigested knowledge; that anything can be contemned, and for good reason; that only those exhortations are of worth which a community could not live by, for he is a shabby moralist who does not outrage the law; that nothing is blunter than a wise rule of conduct obeyed in situations which it was not designed to handle; that the builders of a new continent will learn ways of thinking which serve them well, but which become obstructive once the continent is peopled.

I have considered the highly selected breeds of cattle which are most prized when grossly overweighted with beef, or so hypertrophied and distorted in motherhood that the naturally brief sparing flow of the mammæ is prolonged and made excessive, as women in certain regions of Africa are deemed beautiful whose thighs and buttocks have become enormous from disease; and I have realized that men beneath the same sky, with the same readings of thermometer and the same averages of rainfall, are bred to vastly differing environments, so that frailty may be but the outward aspect of exceptional vigor and tenacity. The apparently weak are merely schooled to other strength and may be easily enduring hardships which are intense and even still unnamed, while the man who triumphs has done so by acting in accordance with other rules, like one who would win at tennis by shooting his opponent. Why! when a great philosopher goes mad, pedants of the opposing schools promptly seize upon his misfortune as a proof of their doctrines—and the people will be convinced, for the world is made logical easily when we link an outstanding trait of a man's character with an outstanding trait of his career.

If life moves with sufficient slowness, or is relentless enough in its consistency for us to awaken day after day upon the same issues, we may contrive to keep our terminology abreast of it, at least to the extent of being able to avow, in written, spoken, or meditated speech, any surrenders which were forced upon us in actuality. What we have been compelled to do, a continuance of the same compulsions makes it easy to admit. Accordingly, it costs me little effort to tell you that I have many times cherished details of your life as though they were my own; that not only in the loose talk of barrooms, but in the solitude of my thoughts, I have used such transferences, saying "I" where I should have said "he." I have knelt as you would kneel, though aware that you yourself did not put sufficient content into the posture to find it difficult. On one occasion, when I had overstayed myself, and suddenly realized that the two of you were waiting for me to leave, the abruptness of this disclosure made me feel as though I had committed some overtly unpleasant act; and I remained still longer, as though to bury it in further sociability. And I have since (by imaginings) stood in that room, and seen the door close behind me, heard my footsteps diminish in the hall and, in your person, turned smiling to my companion. Yet though I have thus drearily mimicked you, I can say with authority that your enviable condition arose from absurdities unperceived, from your failure to hamper your own life by certain self-questionings (self-questionings which insufficiency alone can enable one to neglect, though they usually bring more powerlessness than quality). We were in no outward peril, such as earthquake, attack, or flood, which would have justified your instinctive manner.

Oh, were I to leave some heritage of good counsel for the young, my code would advise the striving after such privileges as are not obtained through deliberation or discipline, but could only be bestowed by hazard. "Go thou, young man," I should begin—and those things which I should tell him to go in quest of, would be such as no quest had ever yielded. By watching you, I learned that blessings fall as manna, which feeds the trivial because the great have prayed. And by unescapably living with myself, I learned that when rewards are commensurate with efforts, they find us already too exhausted to enjoy them and too dispirited through the practice of long patience to feel assured that they will not be taken from us. You drew forth the good things of life like a magician pulling rabbits out of a hat. They came to you, that is, regardless of your character.

But I, who should have considered it my mission to make life more difficult for both of us, labored instead to continue your good fortune. On seeing you so far entrenched in ways which I myself should have chosen, I was led by a kind of moral pedantry to make those aspects of your career over which I had some influence, remain consistent with those aspects which were independent of me. And nothing so much as the thought of my own unreasoning collaboration confirms me in my conception of you as one unjustly sunned upon and favored.

Among those times when I lay sleepless, I should mention first our night at the farmhouse. I had not wanted to stop here, yet you insisted. Did you spontaneously know that this was the place for your purposes, or could you have turned any other equally to advantage? I was prepared to go with you to the river, when I observed that plans of your own were already under way. I wandered through the barn alone—and later, coming upon the hired man, I asked him questions about the crops and learned the parts of a harness. It was also at this time that I made friends with the collie, whom I called old Fritz and buffeted into growling good humor. You were now well along the shore, and the hired man explained to me that your guide had returned recently from a convent which, I gathered, she had attended less in the interests of religion than of delicacy. As evening came on, I sat waiting for you in our room, smoking in the dark by the open window. It was a long vigil, preponderantly a period of sound. The clock in the hall struck deep and sluggishly—and after each hour had been thus solemnly proclaimed, it was repeated in a hasty tinkle from the parlor. Our room too possessed a heartbeat, sometimes in the ticking of my watch, and sometimes in my own pulse. "I am waiting," I thought, "like a wife," with the exception that your return would comfort me purely as the cessation of your pleasure. With this girl, I had noticed, there was a slight convulsion of the nostrils, a suddenness of breathing, when certain words were spoken. Yet in so short a time I could not perceive anything in common among these words but their effect, and I took them to betray a state of mind which in its deeper aspects was closed to me by unimaginativeness or the need of longer acquaintanceship. It seemed to indicate a conflict between eagerness and retreat, as though she had included much within her scheme of the repugnant and the illicit, yet by a strong gift of sympathy was made constantly prone to weaken her own resistances.

At last you entered, bearing your disturbance like an emperor. I turned away, that no more might be conceded you, that your expressions should go unseen. "We must leave," you whispered, "leave quietly—not by the hall but through the window and down over the porch." Now we were allies, if not in our adventures, at least in our escape! As I sat up in silence you added, "She is hysterical." We left money by the unlit lamp, and in the yard I proved that I too had spent a profitable evening by having made friends with old Fritz who, at my whispered assurances, permitted us to go unmolested. And as we walked in the grass by the roadside, doubtless even the girl did not know that we were leaving.

Thus the two cronies trudged through the night, while you tossed me the crumbs and bare bones of your evening. But eventually you grew critical, and proved to me at length why this girl was inferior to Florence, why she could not make Florence seem any less desirable, your talk becoming in time one enthusiastic pæan to Florence; until, as we arrived at the next village, and learned that you could telegraph there, at your suggestion we sent her our joint compliments and expressed the hope that we would soon be with her. Though I concealed my anger, I tried to make it clear that I was doing so.

There are many now who talk of so standing that the waves alone are in front of them, and the very vessel on which they advance is behind the rim of their vision. And I recall the words of a man (I did not like him!) who saw a great poet, now dead, hurrying along the city streets, suffering from physical pain, and through thinking of other things allowing himself to act as though the stresses of his mind and body could be outpaced. Travelers looking to improvement have gone long distances, changing all the outward aspects of their life, yet finding that they awaken to no new internal dawn. Despite motion, philosophy, medicaments, the one unchanging self remains, to feed upon its store of remembered injustices, of stupidity triumphant, of suicidal worth, of resentments which, though they may lead to the hilarious and the absurd, are none the less burdensome to their possessor. There was even the time when I talked with anguish in a public phone booth, and while Florence listened to words as desolate as my talent and my predicament could make them, I was grinning into the mouthpiece that the man beyond the glass, waiting to speak here next, might not suspect my condition. And on another occasion, when she discovered tears in my eyes, they had been unloosed by nothing more serious than an accidental tap against the bridge of my nose as I stood at the window twirling a curtain string. These trumped-up tears I displayed as evidence of my unhappiness, and I can assure you that they were not inaccurate. They lay in the otherwise stony eyes of one who knows that as a heavy bolt of lightning will, in its discharge, clear an entire countryside of electricity, similarly those near us who absorb good fortune must thereby detract it from ourselves.

III.

"This day I spent with Florence"

He recalls his trip through the woods with Florence, and their sitting on a rock together. Describes a play in which Florence and his friend were acting. (He notes with resentment how they flattered themselves by living a fiction, in carrying over their parts from the play into real life.) His envy of Florence and of the friend (Anthony) leads to compensatory boasts of his own, as he tells of his mastery over one Genevieve.

Coming upon the rock, we likened it to a gunboat, or to the crust of some enormous prehistoric turtle, and climbed aboard this monster's kindly back to ride statically through the woods of hickory and oak, and among the scattering of lesser boulders. I, in this early springtime, had not yet learned to distrust the seasonal promises which lead us to mistake exaltation for futurity, and which fulfill themselves not in renewals of our life's texture, not in metaphysical disclosures to correspond with the weather's metaphysical whisperings, not in the quickening sap of changed relationships, but solely in the delicacies and amenities of arbutus, liverwort, and violets protruding through the fallen leaves. I have since found good cause to

29

meet this graceful season with sullenness. Yet I am not one to turn with over-promptness against the uplift of receptivity. I can tolerate in advance that man whom I am later to call a fool; I can make allowance in general for those I shall despise in the particular. Like an earnest woman in pregnancy, I have observed beautiful forms and colors, and listened carefully to harmonious sound, in the hope that such experiences might somehow become incorporate in me and pleasantly affect my issue. And if I now refuse to consider the problematical, it is because the certainty of grimness is preferable to the possibility of disappointment—if I stickle for better prices on Tuesday, it is as one who on Monday bared his breast to the elements.

You and I had not yet taken our trip together, on this day I spent with Florence in the woods. I did not yet have reason to suspect that the subsequent months would prove so favorable to you and so disastrous to myself. We knew that you were at the theater, reciting your lines as Alcæus with sporadic energy, waving your right hand as you would later wave it before the audience, while consulting from time to time the still unmemorized script which you held in your left. Surely, of all those details which conspired to assist you, this casting in the part of Alcæus was among the most momentous. It endowed you with such a character as you could profitably project beyond the limits of the drama into your actual situation. And when on the night of the *première*, the emotions of the audience brought freshness to your repeated lines, I soon discovered that it was not you, but Alcæus, who walked among us after the curtain had fallen. Even had we not been predestined as enemies, this incident would have remained an oddity between us. I did, it is true, defend you; I could still forgive you laughingly, but with such readiness that I allowed my resentment to continue.

Long after the theater was closed, when we had carried our conventional celebrating to the point of ribaldry, you retained your vicarious dignity, tossing off your glass with the defiance of the Grecian in the play. Thus incited, Florence prolonged her part as Mary, and sat drinking humbly among us as none less than the Mother of God. The barmaids and kitchen scullions and manservants and apprentices, all those who had provided the background of obscenity to this theme of intense moral effort, were still moving about in their costumes—and this was enough, with their drunken jests and singing which they had no need of borrowing from their rôles, to repeat in reality the scene as you and she had acted it upon the stage. Here was religion for the godless, the inverted piety of distorting the sacred legends, the profane worship of those last pillars of the Faith who painted the image of Christ upon their feet that they might blaspheme him in walking.

The momentousness in the retaining of these rôles came not from the characters themselves, but from the fate to which they had been subjected. Implicit in your mimicry, was the determination to duplicate the plot as well. When the aged Joseph, with his difficult code of purity, has learned the full import of Alcæus' tirades, has learned that a different avowal of ethical convictions foreshadows a divergent scheme of conduct, and that this Hellenic poet has refused to recognize the barriers of an Hebraic household, we understand the marriage of tetragrammaton and Artemis which was transmitted to the West; like Joseph we see that Mary has been refined by something more subtle than abstention, by exposure to vacillation between opposites, by reverence for both Joseph and Alcæus at once—so that he may still, when the Wise Men appear at the incunabula of this new faith, confirm them in their worship, while himself compelled to do homage to a purely mental aspect of virginity. The playwright who could conceive devotion under this guise, could readily conceive its dramatic counterpart. Accordingly, as Joseph prophesies (a *vaticinium post eventum* in which he foresees broadly the whole of Europe's courage under the Christian exaltation), the vulgar supernumeraries enter, to begin their dalliance about the edges of the stage, while Joseph, Mary, and Alcæus stand apart, untouched—and thus the curtain may fall upon a tableau of contrasted austerity and coarseness. What more, I ask, was needed to bring together two who had borrowed their characters from these sources, what more was needed to give them that illusion of splendor which could make their idyll inimitable?

With fallen branches, as dry and brittle as chalk, and some dead leaves gathered from the crevices, I made us a bedding, where we half reclined and talked. The snow still lay about in irregular patches, like the spots of sunshine that filter through the trees in midsummer. Also, a few of last year's leaves were clinging to the oaks—and it was these leaves now which began to rustle, first far off in the valley under a slow breeze which came upon us a full minute in arrears of its own sound, so that we heard this rustling in other areas while the woods about us were still quiet; thus warned, we could observe the crackling foliage pass from its initial interrupted twitchings into a state of vigorous commotion. The crowns of the trees then yielded, each after its fashion; a few scattered pads of rain fell, visible not as drops but in the starting of dead leaves; and the woods were now beset by a miniature fury so thorough, so all-pervasive, that it even caught at the hems of our coats, suggesting to me in the general flurry the thought that I might, with mock possessiveness, act as though shielding her in some grave onslaught. We peered studiously into the vacant forest as the breeze dropped away, and everything again became silent, leaving no echo but that in our own minds.

I have rehearsed such miniature cycles as of that day, such minor episodes of ebb and flow which, if our life were a scrapbook, could be cut out and pasted upon a page for me and others to turn back upon, just as I have kept with me a picture of that boulder where we sat. Oh Florence, oh Anthony, call me Florentinus, call me Antonine, as Cato the Younger was called Uticensis for having put an end to his existence at Utica.

I have never consented to console myself with the thought that we may be rich in spirit while tangibly impoverished. Wealth—wealth in love, money, the admiration of oneself and others—is indispensable to those who would surround themselves with the flatterings and stimulations of beauty. Let any one, I repeated in self-admonition, who feels that he possesses some elect insight, make efforts to procure its material replica. As it was once said that the soul, by being enclosed in matter, could not sink below matter, so if we convert our understanding into wealth we shall have an outward form beneath which the inward cannot lapse. Were we to live sufficiently in the past or the future, or in the contemplation of remote ideas, the present could rot without our notice, so that our pretensions to order and repose would be disproved by the repugnance which we should arouse in others. In resigning ourselves to deprivations, we make philosophy another word for envy. Accordingly, I felt that I must acquire much more to retain even that which I already had, as one who would strive for millions to avoid starvation.

There was, in these subsequent months, when I watched the structure of your happiness being erected out of the timbers, the steel and marble, of my despair, one man who felt towards you as I, and we found each other with quick understanding, on our first meeting. He was a sickly and unsightly creature, a mouse-faced man who chewed briskly, and whose enmity of you was cheapened by being part of a general aversion. He hated his employer, his clients, and in particular all laughter which possessed the unthinking ebullience of health. His hostility, despite its constancy, was a blunt and undiscerning thing, content with the scantest of documents. Indeed, in time it came to serve me not as a corroboration, but as rebuttal—for when he had accepted my statements against you, he felt entitled to share them with me like truths we had discovered in common, so that they lost their cogency for me and compelled me to seek new justifications for my complaints. How many weeks did I support this unseemly alliance, prompted by no motive but the fear of relinquishing it? But when, in his zeal as my colleague, he attempted to expand the field of his denigrations by including Florence as well, I found the release for which I had been waiting, and tore at him like a fiend, so that we parted company forever.

Yet I would not have you think that I have been wholly devoid of mastery. I do praise that niggardly configuration of the stars whereby I have been enabled partially to cancel my frustrations by my dealings with another. Though I shared with you but the surfaces of Florence, there is a woman, a certain Genevieve, who has gone to secret places with me, providing me some moments of brilliance and tenderness. I do glorify my fate that others have thought her lovely, and that her loyalty could thus yield me some portion of honor. What comfort to see gladness in her moist, doglike eyes; what harsh solace to feel her creeping against me in petition! Nor was it an unfair contract. In her I nurtured sinister refinements of which, since she was contented and cheerful by nature, she would have been otherwise incapable. What harm have I done in bringing anguish into a life which was so well able to surmount it, and even to profit by it? Even in trickery and neglect, I knew how to value her, never forgetting that a woman of less delicacy would have been harder to deceive, and that one of no reveries could have added nothing to replace those lacunæ in her knowledge of me which I purposely left open. That is, had she been blunter, she would have been less eager to endow me with virtues each time I concealed a vice. For though she thought of me as unyielding, I had constantly made concessions to her—never revealing the details of my difficulties, consistently relying upon her to imagine such explanations as would do me credit, and remaining vague that she might lavish her charity upon me unoffended. You, Genevieve, if at times of a summer evening, when the sun is setting beyond the orchard, and the mist and the indeterminate night sounds are arising, if you go out to walk through the greenish, sea-like woods, I know that the corrosion of your melancholy is not intense, and that it is pure of my own untiring rancors. I know that you walk in sweetness, who believe unquestioningly in moral obloquy, and believe that I have impressed such upon you. As one carves his initials in a tree, so you will bear the mark of me perpetually—and for this also I am grateful. Yes, let life be dogged and weighted down by rigid scruples, that affection, in destroying such resistances, may prove itself imperious.

IV.

"My vengeance lay in complaint"

Memory of preadolescent delight. Then: the furies of adolescence. His later attempt at cynical "calm." Further account of his resentment at the way Anthony and Florence have built themselves a gratifying myth. His confusion when he tries to attack this myth. How his attack was invalidated in the eyes of others by Anthony's statement that he (Anthony) had the money to carry out the plans for the colony. Closing grimnesses.

It is no dismal trick of the memory that there seem to have been gentler days in childhood, lived among animals, and when the fear of death descended only at nightfall. For I recall little mice, brought home in a box of cotton, and themselves warm cotton. I know that we had a parrot which had learned to say good-bye with exceptional affability, though generally by way of greeting. And there were rabbits which I had planned to have ranging about like sheep, but which the terrier could not tolerate. This terrier was obstinate, his character was hardened, he would not change his attitudes—and since he enjoyed the trip with me to the river, his interests and ways of thinking were much closer to mine than theirs were, until his antagonism

35

to the rabbits turned me also against them. When my mother at last refused to feed them, they were sold, and the terrier was allowed to scent his way nervously through the empty cage. There were also two pigeons, but though my father had felt of them as squabs, they proved in later months to be unmated, and no vast flock rose from these simple beginnings. I have since, in the city, watched pigeons resting high upon a ledge where, from their appearance, I have judged that they were cooing with a drowsy murmur, a soft flute-note. But the heavy roar of the traffic confined them to a visual subsistence.

There were still other animals, and though I owned them at different times, and in different houses, I can readily imagine them as existing simultaneously, all sitting about me in a friendly, ill-assorted circle, kindly and communicative, comfortable in a New Testament manner of living, and attentive to my preferences. In a toy-shop window I have seen tiny Swiss-carved cows clustered beneath a life-sized chanticleer—and in such simple disproportions these fellows seem to have surrounded me.

What hordes suddenly befell me? By what demonological event was I torn, transformed, plunged into stridency, with my mind henceforth an intestine wrangle not even stilled by the aggressions of external foes? I learn from the study of other records that this change was not abrupt; but to the natural memory, not rectified by documents, it seems so. As the building of vocabulary admitted me to new fields of enquiry, even the work of the philosophers became an ill-poised and unclean thing. Art, letters, the subtleties of affection and longing, the sole factors by which some whit of human dignity might have been made accessible, were surely the foremost causes of my decay. I openly identified myself with literature, and thus identified disgrace with literature. I doubtless brought disrepute upon the guild for deformations which were my own, but which, since I laid such bold-faced claim to art, have discredited in simpler minds this calling whose self-appointed representative I was.

To these responsibilities I have since become more sensitive, being careful to acknowledge as personal stigmata those vices which earlier I should have attributed to my medium. I am aware, however, that many of life's questions have found unseemly answers through being of such importance that they were prematurely asked, while art, by the greater clarity it brings to any subject, may seem to magnify the indecencies which it is enlightening. People who have focused their purposes upon other matters than speech, allowing their familiarity with it to grow by hazard, can condone in practice what would alienate them harshly if spoken. Not considering the breach between thought and action, they can brook no great speculative latitude, and will restrict the possible more jealously than the real. Thus, at least part of the blame must be shifted to my auditors.

While others were devoting themselves to some positive discipline, I made the unwitting choice of looking further into my disasters. Under the slightest of reverses, I would welcome bad weather, would go out to scan a broad, lonely sky at sunset, saying, "This I know; this is a return, a homecoming." Or would stand in places which seemed to prepare me for future misadventures, seeking a process whereby the observation of natural objects might serve as solace. Imagining myself stripped of all hope, all glory, all prospects of learning more and of being fawned upon, I tried to find some resource beneath which I could not sink. For each of the senses, I would note a corresponding external substance—the curving hill for the eye, the smell of birch fires for the nostrils—and in thus considering myself denuded, I have in glimpses understood my privileges. But that man is destitute who, to prove himself well favored, must glorify his possession of those things which all men have unthinkingly. My awe is rather for persons whose delights are too ingrained for their perception, as with the natives of Tibet whose long inhabitance in purer altitudes unfits them to notice the ringing of thin air.

Me flendo vindicabam: my vengeance lay in complaint. Until I came to practise my unlovely science even in times of greatest comfort. It was accordingly by reason of both this attitude and a lamentable situation that I did, on the night of the *première*, begin explaining my limitations, despite the turbulence and good nature all about me. For I observed how you could share your satisfactions with others, while keeping the causes of them for yourself alone.

To whoever would listen, I explained this subtler kind of injustice, pleading that you had brought them nothing, had admitted them to no real partnership. You had come among us with postures which could easily be proved absurd. Your schemes "for human betterment," your exhortations "towards a better life," were matched by an equally obvious ineffectualness. Such generosity was clearly fostered by the irresponsibility of your position. I approached you, pointedly interrupting you as you talked with Florence, and placing these matters before you. "This idealism is facile and meaningless," I challenged you. "You may advocate much, and thus ally yourself with goodness, through being called upon to do nothing. You need face no objective test. Under the guise of giving, you are receiving."

If only a few had paused to hear me, all paid attention to your answer. "I am prepared to face an objective test," you countered. And they listened without envy while you explained how these unforeseen sums had come to you, and how your plans for a colony could now be carried into effect. Looking at Florence, I perceived that in her mind your previous easy heroism had been corroborated. This disclosure of your wealth was like the sudden unfolding of a new virtue. It was received as integral to your character; coming upon you unexpectedly, it had the quality of a profound accomplishment. But how could I plead such matters, when even in my own eyes I was despicable?

I had lived many years with the vacillations of my thoughts—and these events, while they seemed new to others, were for me but the culmination of my weariness. "I accept," I whispered, though the words were inadequate to convey my wretchedness. In their lame pathos, I was not permitted even the partial relief of an adequate expression for my rout.

Henceforth the relationship among the three of us was definitely established. I, whom people spontaneously called by the surname— you, whom even I preferred to address as Anthony. I saw that I had previously done little to awaken more delicate responses in her: out of my self-questionings, I could offer as my one certainty the fact that I would very much like to have her, thus standing as hardly more than a candidate. If I was incapacitated by my shortcomings, I was made still more so by my abilities. My affection for Florence was too great to admit of caution in my dealings with her; I could not dissemble, since I sought her to endorse and supplement my character.

You had appeared among us with ambitions which I had found it convenient to ridicule. But your new resources would now, in the minds of all unthinking persons, seem a guaranty that these altruistic plans would go into effect. Your wealth immediately became engrafted upon your temperament, lending sharpness to your wit and moment to your moodiness. What reason indeed would Florence have for prying into these matters, if prompted by neither adversity nor natural bent? Hypocrisy which does not know itself is, in a gracious woman, graciousness—and the plans which you had explained to her during your time of poverty were pretext enough for her to accept you under your present flourishing. By a sweet logic of the emotions which I could look upon with impatience but not with irony, she would picture the many inducements you might now be able to offer her, and from such an inventory could conclude that you stood greatly in need of her, thus adding the weight of an imperative to what was in itself but a personal preference. I imagined with too great credence these private musings, as she sat alone before the glass, peering into her own eyes, and speaking in a gentle voice to her reflection, "When the time comes, Anthony, I will be ready."

How may one transform his failures into profit, not in the sense of those who leave failure behind them, since that change would involve a profound forgetting, but in the sense of those whose structure of existence is made of the materials of their frustration? I have walked boldly through life, head erect and shoulders thrown back in shame. And when I read of the happiness or sorrow of some one in the tombs of Egypt, when I learn that this name was a sovereign or that name a slave, a kind of silent panic comes over me—for I would not protest against disasters which I knew to be inevitable, but I am troubled by the thought that they might have been readily avoided had I known one trivial rule of conduct which would have altered all my experiences. I become afraid that I may have omitted some slight correctness of procedure, and that this omission has made my difficulties incommensurate to the offence, as with a man who is struck down by lightning through having chosen shelter beneath one, rather than the other, of two adjacent trees. Yet though I consider grimly the spectacle of my own misfortunes, I burst into mild tears at the reversals of a fiction, perhaps because weeping is less a weakness than a danger, and may be indulged when danger is absent. But whereas, through fear of death, one may desire to die, and may find all his interests converging upon this single purpose, such notions are loath to permeate the tissues, and the wish never to have been born is unknown to our organs and our senses.

V.

"Unintended colleague"

He tells of another man who, jealous like himself, killed him-
self. The incident happened while all were celebrating the
success of the play. He considers this man's suicide as a por-
tent of vicarious release. ("He died for me.") How, on the
hunch that things would turn out well, the narrator decided
to squander what few funds were still left. But in the end
he must steal from Florence. In his state of gnarledness, he
recites a catalogue of other gnarled people he has known.

We could easily retain the quality of a man's voice if his words were
uttered immediately in front of us, and but a few minutes later we
heard him cry from a distance. Though we may, as I have done, forget the very name and features of this person, we can picture him as
he swayed above us in a brilliant room, if we were soon thereafter to
see his body lying amorphously in shadows. He exists for me as a
voice and a form, since each was abruptly altered.

"We spoke of a little dog," he told me, "meaning a certain lawless
portion of her thoughts which would run ahead, or lag, or veer to
one side or the other, always experimenting, and living for the
future." To expand the metaphor, he pictured the dog as nosing at

41

trouser legs or scattering a school of sparrows. "I had intimated that there was such a dog, and she had laughingly admitted it, though we may have had different things in mind, and I did not dare press her for more accurate definition. 'You will be away from me this evening,' I would venture; 'keep the hound leashed'—all the while trying to decide how much vagrancy I was striking out of her by this method, and how much I was suggesting. Yet I groveled before her as a tribute to her purity, for in thus groveling I could better imagine her as pure."

"Such terms are inappropriate to things as they are now," I answered him, referring both to the turmoil at the other tables on this night of the *première* and to the general temper of our age, "and being inappropriate, they cannot lead to anything much more instructive than suicide or murder." When he replied, "In this instance, I can assure you, they will not lead to murder," I was minded to object on the grounds of bluntness, but instead I challenged him: "You speak as though you were here, drinking, with a purpose." So early it was agreed between us that our conversation would terminate in his death, which I took no interest in preventing, despite my sympathy with his disclosures.

He showed the dying man's tendency to summarize, defining himself as "an aggregate of downpours, tides, and crusts," meaning thereby that each sentiment or desire was a commensurable quantity of his body—speaking of the "hellish slaughter going on within me, with various favored and sacrificed populations, and much hasty rebuilding after destruction" . . . "with the sum total of it all as words," and referring to "obscure processes, the meeting point of Neanderthal ancestors and children yet unborn." Then returned abruptly to the more specific matter: "She had declared with vigor that she would rather live in poverty in Europe than in luxury in America; but by accepting me, for the time being she found herself forced to compromise with her preferences, and live in America in poverty. We did spend pastoral months, however, observing the sun set behind an orchard in a rich documentation of causality and myth. Or we walked together, our elastic shadows turning at the toes. And on cold days we sat in our little house, the smoke from our chimney racing across the fields—we sat in our house, a-sailing. Yet by the end of that season, I feared to touch her, lest it be a fishy hand I laid upon her heart, reminding her of another—I who had lifted her bodily out of girlhood." In trying, it appears, for his sake, to seem a bit more faithful than she was, she had disclosed a slight margin of falsity which he had widened even more eagerly in his fears than she in actuality. He believed himself superior to her in talent and understanding, yet found that her exceptional loveliness enabled her to paralyze him by a mere shift of mood. They returned to the city, and "it was at this time, on glancing into the awry mirrors of a shop window, that I mistook some one else for me. When the phone next door was ringing, I thought it was ours." Explosions, falling over cliffs, trampling by elephants, the birth of an idea (shooting from the head in thick red and yellow rays); a man annihilated by a rejoinder, with nothing left but a few lines to indicate the speed of his departure; the lamppost wrapped about the neck—at this time he particularly enjoyed that hilarious aspect of distress in which our cartoonists specialize.

"Yet I was not without method," he insisted. "I carefully avoided all traits that might make a demand upon her tolerance. I was not unskilled enough to attempt persuasion by weeping." Tears, he said, were like surface ore: it was readily available, but soon exhausted, so "one must learn to work more low-lying veins which, though harder to exploit, are richer." When she returned to him after a nominal visit to a school friend (and he told himself it was fidelity enough if she returned after flight), he "would sometimes talk of events which had occurred during her absence, advising her to look into certain books I had supposedly enjoyed without her, expressing the hope that an interesting symphony might be repeated, and even on one occasion attempting to suggest that our separation happened to coincide with a milestone in my own progress. I could, with a show of good humor, correct her in the use or pronunciation of a word, or protest that the cut of a garment was too modest." Such discretion served as a stay at best, for in spite of his ability to modify his conduct tentatively, her absences became more frequent. He would open her wardrobe, he told me, "and find her hanging on all the clothes-hooks—or would watch her dainty feet, twelve of them, in a row under the bed.

But the smile, and the eyes, were elsewhere." He described her in velvet tones that embarrassed me, "with her knees crossed, and the suspended foot lifting slightly to the beat of her pulse."

Later I came to understand why I connived so readily in his destruction. As he dropped from the balcony, it was like the cutting from me of some parasitically feeding thing. One may welcome defection in his friends, not through the malice of rivalry, but because their disastrous use of qualities held in common argues a greater possibility of a good outcome for these same qualities in himself, since we have learned from the study of numbers that the continued failure of a plan increases the likelihood of its success. "*Incipit vita nova*," he confided smilingly as he left the table for this Leucadian leap into the unseen litter of the courtyard. And I felt that the new life he spoke of was to be my own. "He died for me," I whispered with conviction, though he had not yet descended. And for days afterwards I found myself repeating, "He died for me."

Now I can fully understand the secular certainty which came upon me, leading me to act as though I were protected, enabling me to pattern my life in accordance with your recent announcement, and thus to top each of your expenditures by a greater outlay of my own. There were securities left me by an uncle who had shown good judgment in investing—and in the course of years I had slowly added to them by occasional earnings. They seemed to guaranty me against the last reaches of defeat; I had, when my depression was greatest, got encouragement from the thought of their support. So much, I told myself, was assured me by the organization of a great people who would protect my little in protecting their much. Yet it now seemed that by squandering these bonds I could end my essential poverty. I could look forward to some event, still undefined, which would repay me in both emotional and financial fullness. By spending showily and paying my debts promptly, before my funds had vanished I found creditors willing to trust me for almost as much again. It was several months before the falsity of my belief could be concealed no longer, and I wrote upon a sheet of paper, for my own eyes to read, among designs of cubes and crescents and little running men whose heads and bellies were made by circles, with members and neck each a line: "You are broken." If I then stole from Florence, as I repeatedly denied, I now marvel at the wisdom of this act, which placed some distance between us when I was so thoroughly subject to her. I can be grateful that my predicament forced such accuracy upon me, dictating a form of treachery which, as I now see, was the sole possible manner of rescuing my independence.

The process is now clear to me: How, having died by proxy, I felt that a new era was in store for me; how I had full confidence that the new era would be fortunate, for in being new it would be different from the past, and the past had been unfortunate; how this confidence, by landing me twice over in debt, brought me to such a state that I could steal from Florence. In this devious way I managed redemption, dwarfing the miseries of my love by overtopping them with financial chaos; or we could say that I protected myself from one illness by contracting another, as paretics are sometimes cured by the high fevers of malaria. I understand all this in retrospect, for the knowledge of living is not something to be learned in advance of the calls made upon it; it accumulates with age, matures as its utility diminishes, and under favorable circumstances dies at ninety. We must have haggled with persons since deceased, have sought the favors of the formerly ignored, and received with chill politeness those whose good opinions we once courted. Have repeated in subtler form that process of entering from the cold to stand before blazing logs, or going from the pale of this warm, humming fire into the darkness. Have seen parched ground, then heard a sky split and watched the falling torrents soaked up by myriads of organic and inorganic mouths (this not solely as a meteorological happening, but as a condition among mankind). Have kept our enquiry a little free of our behavior, that we be not too disrupted on permitting ourselves breaches of principle, since the indulgence of a minor weakness may be our surest way of attaining a major end.

In labeling the lives of other people, we may persuade ourselves that we are attempting to increase our powers by a wider knowledge of motives. But in this very defense of thought we are guilty of inaccurate thinking. One observes his neighbors, not in a search for usable maxims, but because he can best counteract the memory of past unhappinesses by adopting an aloof attitude towards them, he can best adopt an aloof attitude towards them by adopting such an attitude towards himself, he can best adopt this attitude towards himself by adopting it towards others and transferring it to himself, and he can best adopt it towards others by constant observation, since observation is from without. So I have tried to look upon people as little more than the proof of a thesis, like blackboard drawings to illustrate a proposition in Euclid. A man may have a strange preference for green satin; he may take pride in sending his family each year to the seashore; he may vote the Republican ticket because his father did; he may be doing nicely with his mortgage; by name, address, by his way of gripping a cigar, by the particularities of his experience, he may be distinguishable from every other man and is, of course, strongly aware of his distinguishableness—yet his doctor may think of him primarily as an example of a certain complaint of the liver. So I have given much thought to the surprising mainsprings of human conduct, considering among other things how a slight deflection near the center can become a wide difference at the circumference.

I have recalled, for example, a poet whose work was exceptional; but restless because he could not write better, he remained enigmatic in his habits, coming from vague places, en route for places equally vague, seen where he was not expected and offering no explanation—and by all this doubtless trying in some desolate way to make his verses still rarer by the rarity of his appearance. And I knew a lonely, introspective fellow, awaiting the pollen of another's charity, well versed in the construction of bridges, but kept ineffectual in his own eyes by reason of his humility in the presence of women. Explaining how one of them, who had forgotten some object or other, returned for it to his apartment where he was alone, "What would you say to that?" he asked me—and I answered, with regard for both the facts and his feelings: "Were five or six such incidents to occur, your two lives might become wholly different," knowing that they would not, as they did not, that his knowledge would be confined to bridges of steel and masonry alone, on which more light-hearted Leanders could keep their trysts in safety. There was a woman so assured of others' kindliness that all who knew her conspired in limiting her experiences to this simpler reality. She sat, I believe, in the shade of an arbor, or in equivalent places, learning of the contemporary through the courtesies of her visitors and the filtrations of well-modulated prose. I could mention another, so little adjustable to conditions other than those for which she was preeminently fit, that she was prized by her acquaintances when they were ill, since she could care for them so sweetly, though they found it necessary to discourage her from visiting them too frequently when they were in health and preferred the company of those who, at the time of their need, had abandoned them. Despite divergencies, she resembled a modest clerk I talked with in the West. He had leapt to a position of leadership during an earthquake, showing the abilities of a commander when his superiors were in panic—yet otherwise he spent his life as one tolerated by wife and friends, owing to the infrequency of this disaster. And once, in the springtime, amid a plethora of apple blossoms I caught on the breeze a scent that was meant for buzzards, as an old man lay on the nearby porch dying of gangrene.

My unintended colleague of the suicide had also told me of his eventual flight: how, as he stopped at a general store in the country, he was pursued impersonally, by mechanism, since a concert which he knew his former wife to be attending in the city, was recorded here on a raucous instrument. He recalled that a kitten lay asleep, its ear tickled by the rim of a spittoon; he described the crack of billiard balls, in an adjoining room, at moments foreign to the rhythms of the orchestra; he mentioned a bell which, installed at the door to announce the entrance of new patrons, gratuitously marked their exit.

VI.

"The twitter of many unrelated bird-notes"

Tells of how, by giving Anthony and Florence keys to his apartment (without telling either that he had given a key to the other), he set the scene for their union. His jealousy at the success of his own plan. His gloom as an "outsider" when he followed Anthony and Florence to the hotel on the island. The "insight" of money versus the insight of poverty. His "N'importe où, hors du monde" escape. The dog barking behind the mist, and related enigmatic portents.

We may hold that we would have not one day of our past repeated— and yet may have been brought to this view by the repetitiveness of memory. Like a dog leaping after bacon, I continue performances because of their failure. Injustice to another, we feel, is capable of payment, but our mistakes against ourselves seem beyond revision. The tyranny of even minor social absurdities is not weakened with time, though its intensity may be disguised by the addition of humor—and we suffer perennially anew a gnarling of the mind at

48

the thought of circumstances which once involved the deeper mor-
bidities of our nature.

When giving Florence the keys to the apartment, I had not
planned to give you the others. It was two hours after I had left her,
with an agreement to meet her at the theater the following afternoon,
that I thought of forcing upon you the rôle of an intruder. I found
some relief on bringing this blunt element into a relationship which
had been too tenuous. And I walked the streets in vicarious triumph,
imagining the furnace of your skin as you, to her astonishment,
dropped upon the bed, heavy and quick-breathed with drunkenness.
There was gratification in the thought that I might derive even my
defeat from within.

My plottings seemed to have given me some claim upon her—
and when I appeared in later weeks at the hotel on the island, I went
to her mechanically, offering myself, without hope, almost without
desire, but equally without vacillation. Failure, already predictable
through my lack of dignity and absence of gradation, was made
inevitable by my diffidence. Yet when I wept, confessing that I had
acted by resolve, she was sorry for me, and in her compassion even
laid a hand upon me—whereupon I attempted to pursue my advantages, dogmatically translating her caress into encouragement. Her
sympathy now gave place to repugnance, as I felt repugnance for
myself—yet through many rehearsals of this scene in retrospect, I
have come to understand my conduct better, and to see that I had not
been undiscerning. I acted through no misinterpretation of motive,
but that I might for the moment enable myself to imagine the motive
as different. That is: The hand, laid upon me in compassion, still
rested there as I touched her aggressively, and thus was given at least
a temporal relation to my embrace.

In the dismal days that followed, I hovered about you that I might
spy upon you, not by opening letters and listening at the door, as you
might think of one who stole from her, not in things secretly overheard and the bribing of the maid, but by the patient reading of
omens, by the effrontery of almost imperceptible changes, by the
unwitting expansiveness of her manner. I even found that you spoke

in a language peculiar to your own companionship—a separate idiom distinguishable not by the introduction of new words, but by the holding of expressions in common, and by the fleeting reference to many events which others could not understand without further explanation.

I watched the sweet hypocrisy of her plans for the colony. As my own funds neared exhaustion, I observed with fuller realization the powers of your wealth. You could provide material support for those delicacies of thinking which the impoverished, if they happen to possess ability as artists, must generally confine to their medium, and which are denied entirely to all others. You could purchase the elimination of the inappropriate; given your beginnings in imaginativeness and culture, you found an idyll economically obtainable, could back your caprices by ponderable objects, could counteract by external loveliness the lapses between your moments of affection, disguising flaws in the texture of your emotions by covering them with the texture of your environment. While this process was still unfolding, any loss of mutual engrossment would be undetectable.

If one would be receptive without unhappiness, he makes himself dependent upon good fortune. The dignity of great prosperity can be denied only by those who forget that a cathedral can arise out of wealth alone. Wealth and talent being complementary, neither will deem itself enough without the other—and if some men are sought though lacking either, it is only while they hold out the promise of both. Any who write beautifully or speculate profoundly in a hovel are to be commended for the excellence of their product, but unpardoned for indifference to their whereabouts—as their justification for neglecting their furniture would justify others in neglecting them. With wealth there goes a separate biology. I knew one man who had applied his wealth to carrying doubt into his very tissues. As birds, though out of danger, fly with the self-protective darts and veerings proper to their kind, so he kept his statements guarded, even among friends. And I knew another whose fortune enabled him to crowd with affirmations and denials a day which might otherwise have been devoid of both, permitting him to build an environment arbitrarily about him, to maintain a background consistent with the consistency of his own character. Equanimity came easier to you, who could now hire others to bear your annoyances, could by a kind of commercial contract buy off the influences unsuited to your temper. Add the kindred wealth of Florence's affection, and your equipment was complete.

With so much given, I watched you unerringly grasp the remainder. The plans for the colony could follow the rise and fall, not of a colony, but of your courtship. With purposiveness too deep for scheming, you employed them to your personal advantage, discussing a community of cultural interests until you and Florence felt that you shared such, outlining the cycle of a humanistic day until your excursions as lovers seemed the perfect instance of such a cycle, and through your proposals of emotional freedom preparing for her surrender. Is it to be wondered that, once these subtler ambitions were gratified, the plans themselves claimed less of your attention, that the colony should have grown, flourished, and decayed purely *in utero*? The colony perished prior to its inception, because your aims had been attained during its planning.

Oh, maddening trickery, when one may find himself so hemmed by strategy that even his benevolences have an element of cunning— while this man could be villainous under the ægis of nobility. When one may find it necessary to force the expression of his emotions purely that others may understand him rightly—while this man can walk through a tangle of inconsistencies without the scotching of his self-respect. When one, through wishing a fortunate woman ill-used purely that he may befriend her, must be troubled by his own lack of generosity—while this man can, unthinking, situate his boredom in the failure of another to entertain him. Bah! let us endure our minor reversals by inviting major calamities; let us dwarf annoyances, or even melancholy, by calling upon life's entire structure to collapse. I fear that our fate is an aspect of our character, and that even one who dies by accident dies by his own hand.

On leaving suddenly, I sought to abandon the field not only of my humiliating love for Florence, but of many subsidiary jealousies. I returned to the city, where I spent the few remaining hundreds at my disposal, attempting again to live as I had seen you living, but without the too vivid comparison of your presence. Though Florence would have nothing of me, I felt that I had done much to sharpen her interests, and that my removal would prove a disappointment to her. In the city I lived, for the few weeks my funds permitted, in a kind of scandalous affluence, awaiting the unnamable and unimaginable event which would come to rescue me. And when I could disguise my hopelessness no longer, I went to the terminal at midnight, procured a ticket to a town which I had not known, and within an hour was leaving forever. Reaching the little country station at dawn, in a valley still blank with mist, I stood on the cinders with my suitcase, in the chilly morning air, while the train continued on its way through the valley and the vibrations of the engine diminished irregularly to silence. I noticed then the twitter of many unrelated bird-notes, with the rustle of water somewhere behind the mist—and a dog was barking, imposing fresh sharp sounds upon his own blunt echoes.

Part Two

Thou preparest a table before me in the presence of mine enemies.

Psalms 23:5

I.

"I am to Genevieve permanently grateful"

He is grimly "at home," after having established himself in a rural setting. Reminiscences of Florence. Compensatory "use" of Genevieve. Peroration: his ill-natured philosophy of calm.

Rightly they cherish their nationality, for the sole distinction they possess is as members of a group. And so great is their desire for conformity, that in an environment of geniuses they might even have shown talent. They are all men of honor when their interests are not at stake—and as their indifference spreads to many areas, the vocabulary of justice still flourishes and exerts influence. On doing them a kindness, if one is too modest in accepting thanks, he finds them prompt to join in the belittling of his services. They preface a boast by avowing their dislike of boastfulness, and before saying ill of a neighbor assure you that they will say ill of no one. He would be a monstrosity among them who did not speak of frankness when speaking with caution, or who would not vaunt his full confidence in another on requiring him to warrant his promises before a notary.

For one may commit infractions of their code with impunity, but only by granting the soundness of the code itself. Yet on defending a cause unpopular with them, he will be judged capable of thievery or extortion—and were a murder to be committed they would ask where he had been before they searched for a fiend. One should not, after saying good-bye, turn from them in silence, lest they take his departure as a dismissal of them; rather, he should keep turning to face them, and repeating their own remarks, until he is beyond earshot. I went among them as one rebuked, for there are many things which, if still preserved as echoes, would condemn me. To earn their respect, I left my self-doubts unuttered—and only by keeping my work unseen was I accorded the honors due my profession. Our divergencies being total, I felt no need to reveal them; had they been less, I should have been more liable to altercation. No longer required to wrest an existence from the wilderness, their intolerance for their natural enemies is now trained upon one another. At night the dogs bark in behalf of their masters. The dogs of the different farms exchange challenges—and it is the family units of the countryside proclaiming their isolation.

Since the occasion two years ago when I disappeared abruptly, both you and Florence must think of me as lapsing into silence. Yet for me these long months have been restless with the shouting of many voices. As though housing a fugitive in secret, I have spent clandestine hours with my distress, living among people to whom I could mention nothing. Repeatedly I have speculated upon my unclean courtship, and marveled at the contrasted accuracy of your advances. Testing the evidence that your affection for Florence was abating, I have imagined the growing tentatives of separation; I have pictured your love, like the heart torn from a turtle, beating after death.

When walking through the country in early spring, you have observed a fresh-cut stump, a massive wound, bleeding its sap into the sunlight. The condition of its baffled roots, severed of purpose, could be the symbol of my predicament. Consider their inarticulate sorrow—yet despite vocabulary my own unhappiness tends to become as puzzled. I have given thought to my bodily well-being, attempting to promote by health a kind of physical certainty which, while not removing doubts, would deprive them of their maximum annoyance. During this self-imposed exile, I know that my eyes have been less eager—not through increased hopelessness, for my hopelessness was always thorough, but through absence of an object for them to light upon. I have thus felt the eagerness die out of my own eyes. Yet could I think of Florence so recurrently without some reciprocation on her part? Could such a giving-out remain unanswered? In speaking her name, I did so with no faith in magic, no belief that the syllables could bring me the reality, but solely because my preoccupations made this labeling imperative. The word did not deny the emptiness about me, though I seemed to have cancelled something by the utterance of it.

Perhaps it is to Genevieve I owe my life—at least to her I owe the fact that this evil was made bearable. In no way could she have been different and served to aid me as she did. Deeply emotional, yet lacking a medium of art in which to embody her emotions, she was compelled to seek her poetry in the disposing of her own person. A pronounced gentleness opened her to another's certitude—and as I gave deep thought to the matter, I saw that, while she was still lighthearted, she was equipped already for her eventual abandonment to my wishes. Thus, I was healed by new designing—and for this I am to Genevieve permanently grateful. There have been months when my delight in her loveliness was exceptional—when a posture or expression astonished me. "Cherish these," I have told myself, as I made efforts to fix them upon my memory. But though I still recall that there were scenes of this nature, their details have escaped me. And on occasions, during our companionship, when I have laid hands upon her, in my enjoyment I have wished that we were at liberty, ranging through a variety of cities, and that I might come upon her by hazard, meeting her in odd places, thereby multiplying this experience under many guises. Was I, in inventing the fiction of my marriage, attempting to help her despite myself, by suggesting an added cause to resist me? Or was I contriving to make her acquiescence more heinous in her own eyes, and thus more a tribute to me—for I had made this false confession previous to my demands as a lover, insisting that she keep it secret. As she did, and she believed me unquestioningly until I myself

57

told her I was not married, when admitting that I had asked another woman of the village to marry me. Had she been strengthened by lack of sensitiveness she would have exposed me, or at least rebuked me, but she received both disclosures without protest.

Can one be said to have misused a woman's gentleness who has always thought of it with gratitude, applying it for the very preservation of his life, and even serving by his praise to make her more gentle? I assured its permanency by setting an appropriate stamp upon her. Though slighting more obvious obligations, I was scrupulous in the shouldering of remoter ones, for I accepted the responsibilities I had incurred in putting our relationship upon so ambiguous a basis— and that its intensity might be maintained, I spent many hours considering it while she slept. Though she offered to relinquish me, I refused to accept this opportunity to settle the matter so easily. At much inconvenience, I still insisted upon clandestine meetings with her, to shield her from the thought that her own virtues had told against her—and only gradually, with the appearance of speechless regret, I yielded to her insistence upon separation.

During the more tentative eras of the Church, there was a sect which held that one is purified by excess, virtue remaining in the sterile ash left from the conflagration. And similarly we may conclude that there is no inducement in refraining, and all issues must be both met and mirrored, though we may regret that our life was not such as to show this contention to its best advantage. And I should hesitate to compromise a moral by drawing it from my defective living, except that I could not decide whether insight is caused by our faults or exists in spite of them. Thus: if naturally inquisitive, we may find in failure an added incentive to brood upon the norms of justice. Or exceptional wavering may end in constancy, as the waverer learns the quicker to stabilize his conduct without regard for his moodiness. And too great goodwill can lead a man to express his arguments vilely since, being too sweet-tempered to hate his opponents, he grows lax in his thinking, and gives us in one volume and for one price both a doctrine and its rebuttal. But even without this confusion, I would ask no one to believe me virtuous, holding that all virginity were best enjoyed alone.

I have sat at the window, silhouetted by the lamplight, thinking how a prowler without motive could slay me undetected. I have sought the spread of painlessness to further free areas of investigation, rejoicing that I did as the rest of mankind though preferring to do so at some remove from my neighbors, submitting to a self-enquiry maintained without assent, dwelling continually upon my own attributes—a repetitiveness which, though not solicited, is the equivalent of great industry—and by many subterfuges of thought and action bargaining to keep insanity logically submerged.

In summer, during the late sunset, I have walked my acres (for can I not call that mine which I have earned by marriage), have walked these acres, knowing myself vaguely driven, asking for much, too much, expecting nothing. Vigorous young frogs chirp, doubtless enchantingly, in the swampy portions of the meadows. The trees fringing the crest of the hill show no evidence of wind. And distantly, against the seething of my pipe, I catch a bell, shaken by the cropping of one cow, but announcing the herd. The night patiently descends, with a coexistence of sound and silence which is the quality of expectation, and thus of twilight.

Dare we, on such occasions, feel ourselves on the verge of wisdom, and melt with some kind of theoretic charity as we consider our continent passing into darkness and oceans turning cumbrously towards the sun? One's death becomes preferable to the ultimate destruction or desiccation of our planet. And even the perishing of mankind seems less abhorrent than the thought that profound volumes will lie unread and symphonies be without meaning. I would see all gathered into lore, the defunct vestiges of enthusiasm jealously collated, prizing what has been done against the tyranny of death. There is peace in a sequence of changes fittingly ordered: vegetation is at peace in marching with the season; and there is peace in slowly adding to the structure of our understanding. With each life the rising of a new certitude, the physical blossoming free of hesitancy, the unanswerable dogmatism of growth. Who would not call men to him—though he felt compelled to dismiss them when they came, communion residing solely in the summons.

II.

"How different, Anthony, are the nights now"

Continuing the era of "composure" (composure with reservations!). He contrasts with his present anchorage the earlier period of grotesquely intense suffering (as on the night when he gave Florence and Anthony the keys). We gather that he has married, and is propertied. In keeping with his new "composure" he propounds an ars poetica. *And he tells of meeting a scholar who represents an aspect of his own weaknesses.*

How different, Anthony, are the nights now, when I leave my family and walk alone, from those nights of my love for Florence in the city. How different in particular from that Walpurgis night when, without your foreknowledge, I arranged that the two of you should share the dark together. On dim, deserted streets I hurried through a city of eyes, under the surveillance of disparate objects which, as I passed, each transferred me to the supervision of the next. And there were real eyes among them, eyes of the cats that paused to note me with distrust (some of the cats stringy, others crouching in bunches

60

behind their faces). As though demons had met to decide the next step in my conduct, and as though, after much heated argument, they unanimously acclaimed a policy for me, I suddenly felt my bafflement give way to one clear desire. I would go, I told myself, and batter at my own door until you came to admit me. I would make my way as in a trance to Florence—and regardless of her attire I would kneel before her. But as I hesitated at the door without knocking, I found a packet of refuse I had earlier placed there—and in the barren hallway I lay down beside it. Such is the grotesqueness of suffering, that I lay down beside this refuse. Then I went quietly away, and all beyond the door was left silent and enigmatic.

Now that this trouble's molten fluids lie buried beneath a crust of melancholy, my walks in the night are short interims between study and sleep. I recapitulate the day, to guaranty the soundness of my investments, be they in lands, cattle, or family. I inspect the remaining centrifugalities of my character, questioning my present anchorage, and in the interests of protection attempting to foresee what possible events could again dislodge me.

This dampened moodiness, this confining of the horizon to my own hills, this blankness of the future—could I not, if differently schooled, wholly accept them as placidity? The frog from which portions of the brain have been abstracted, leaps at each prodding, and when caressed, croaks. The frog, I believe, is happy. Similarly we would drop things from us, to reach haven by a lessening. Yet I am aware that the very caution of our life adds incaution to our speculations, equips us to consider protest, disappearance, abandonment. Where there has been much gnarling of the past, we must maintain equilibrium by leaning.

Ah, one will scheme for his composure. Though none but tainted men contemplate madness and suicide, a certain immunity may result from thinking of these destinies. It is useful to have been morbid in youth, since we learn to bargain for balance at a time when hopefulness was strongest. And when later experiences threaten to overwhelm us, it is as though, having gone mad or killed ourselves before, we could profit by the skill of our past error. Few would perish by their own hand if they waited a fortnight—and surely no one will fall victim to a form of insanity which he abhors. Still, one fears destruction less when he has completed his samplings and knows that he has had a little of all that others have had in great quantity.

By what justice, Anthony, do I write these pages as though for your perusal, when in their very composition I am relieved of the desire to address you? We both share the certainty of words—and one who is at work while his neighbors slumber needs no external sanction for his trade, assured that even a philosophy of despair may, in its couching, become an ornament to living. I pursue these difficulties, knowing that what can cross the mind of one man can be the lifelong preoccupation of another, and what can be the lifelong preoccupation of one man can become the dominant concern of whole eras and peoples. I would have you join me in lauding the pressure of speech. Consider Voltaire, by nature fawning, open to any bribe, currying the favor of any despot, limiting flattery solely by the measure of his auditor's credulousness, bending to any opportunity, renouncing any principle, yet undoing whole months of sycophancy by a sudden flash of wit, for he could stifle a remark which he considered too malicious, unless he also considered it clever. Each time he retorted to avenge an insult, his words were of so pointed a nature that the structure of the state would groan. It was not his venom, but his accuracy, that aroused the resentment of the court—a splutterer might even have been lovable. It was not his bravery, but his phrasing, that made him intransigent.

A gift is an imperative; a power is a command. It is the successful at love who burn for women, and the articulate who are driven by the need of statement. I would proclaim the musculature of diction. I have seen men of practical accomplishments, harsh in their detestation of thought, who would have terrified me as monsters, and cowed me as powers, did they not proudly display some pun, sickly but of their own making, and insist that their companions show delight in it. There is not one of them but would be an adept at repartee, and withal not one of them fit to apply the sound epithet to a single item of God's universe. I will not allow these weaklings of art to enjoy a jot of self-respect beyond their skill as drudges. He who is impatient of reading, who cannot trace coexistent melodies, who perceives no vast authority in a brushstroke, is no dog, for he lacks the keen scent of dogs. Whatever our humilities, let them vanish in the presence of such opponents, who merit no encouragement until they have groveled. Yet I have often left my position unavowed, aware that the self-appointed champions of difficult causes usually display few virtues beyond their devotion, and by their raw urgency will enlist further enmity for the things they advocate.

On my score I have dared quarrel with art, regretting the effectiveness of silence, and of that trickery whereby the sentence most trivial in itself is made weightiest by the assistance of plot—as when a little girl says, "See, the red poppy is in bloom," saying this as an observation of no importance, merely out of pleasure with the flower's suddenness, though the reader knows from past disclosures in the text that the blooming of the poppy is to mark her own death. I have also, in considering art's shortcomings, noted how thinkers, in the codifying of their passions, find names which the thoughtless can appropriate to flatter their own preferences; how men of intensity, dismayed at their excess, give formulæ for its cancellation, and these formulæ are left to the middling, who needed goads rather than assuagement. However we choose to classify mankind, people must fall into at least two opposing groups, and for one of them the world's best doctrines must be subversive. So we must hold that wisdom itself remains a jungle, and that the most astute advice can fall upon the wrong ears.

Yet have not the most menacing foes of art been its adherents? For if they are not worse than other men, their greater expressiveness makes their vices more apparent. They are proud of their deformities, as an unnatural father, thinking of his child's worth in a circus, might be gratified that it was born armless and four-legged. Still, they are to be listened to, since their unwholesome manner of living brings them an advantage in style over those whose environment is less exceptional. Untouched by compromise, the most ineffectual of them will pardon no lack of greatness in his acquaintances, nor forgive its presence. Yet when they condemn a colleague, they do so not wholly through malice but partly in the effort to keep from repeating him. They are at their best when attacking their own vices in other people.

63

If, on setting out to defend a cause, they find that it impairs their diction, they will defend the opposite. Many of them, who produce little, lay all the blame to the inferiority of audiences, having persuaded themselves that if there were a good echo they would shout at it. And often, before this exile, I have heard them, fresh from their failure to write a sonnet, proclaiming the futility of all culture.

It is, rather, the scholars I would solicit, humble voyagers bewildered in that jungle of wisdom which I have mentioned, equally incompetent in life and among the archives. One I have met since coming here, with an absurdly kindly face, as in some comic drawing of a fruit or vegetable which, by the artist's addition of arms and legs and a few crude lines of physiognomy, recommends itself more to our sympathies than to our appetites. "Raised in an atmosphere of piety," he confided, "denied the correctives of vulgar witticism which are needed to keep the mind of a child wholesome while it is being taught a code of the unclean, I early possessed a structure of theological thinking which left me little desire for companions of my own years. Indeed, my life was given an unreal consistency, for my parents were too scrupulous in their upbringing of me to permit themselves those moments of anger or injustice which would have provided me a sounder schooling. One's childhood should be a closer duplicate of the adult world, should be this later world in miniature—and my parents would have done me greater benefit had they been less exemplary. For my misdeeds I was reprimanded, as neither my mother nor my father would allow themselves to relax in my discipline, and for my accomplishments I was rewarded, with the result that I faced the future with no notion of the tentative nature of our living.

"I will not pause now to explain the perilous years during which I struggled to adjust this early equipment to a world tragically different. Not only would the account of them be inessential, but also they seem by a purposive forgetfulness to have been crowded from the memory. Whereas some things are locked too deeply for avowal, others may be sunk even beyond recollection.

"After the dangers of madness had been miraculously weathered —and only weathered, I believe, by such accidents as a change of scene at the proper moment, or the failure to receive a certain letter, or the death of a dear relative under absurd circumstances—I met a quiet woman of twenty, Margaret, of pious parentage like myself, and equally timid. Though I had by now turned to the most godless of philosophies, and looked upon myself as the negation of what I had been, I soon discovered how much faith within me was still pleading for corroboration, as I had come imperceptibly to place upon Margaret the full burden of these earlier responsibilities, exalting her, and even inspiring her, with theological terms of praise.

"We had gone far in this difficult probing—and both her health and my own, I believe, were being impaired by the strain of our restrictions, when this idyll suffered the irruption of a man who had no patience with such rarity, and perhaps did not even suspect its presence. He was much older, but possessed a certain physical obviousness, and had about him such an air of the expectant as to awaken in those he particularly cared to please, strong suggestions of the future. They would not ask themselves, 'What is our relationship today?' but 'What will this relationship be subsequently?' With others I enjoyed his heartiness, his muscular manner, his willful judgments, made abrupt and youthful by good health and previous successes.

"I am not competent to describe the change which came over me. But a new factor had arisen, or something asleep was awakened. My love for Margaret, as I had known it, was gone, and in its place I experienced a kind of harshness. Painfully engrossed, yet expert with a new slyness, I watched her transformation at the call of this man. Under the guise of conversational levity, I noted their blazing eyes, their alert bodies, their flood of witty interchange. During banter on the surface harmless, I observed her, tranquil under months of our subtle courtship, now made hectic with consent. The man left soon afterwards, so there was no open crisis. But within a week I too had gone—for that undefined groping of our past could not be restored, and I was not enough the schemer to adopt the tactics of my rival. Yet the incident left me strangely envenomed, and it was many years before I could see that I myself had been at fault."

After a considerable silence, the gloom dropped from him. He faced me briskly, and I saw that he was about to speak with encouragement. "I believe the day will come," and he was prophesying, "when all these disturbances are over, when two people are no more set apart from other men by love than they are by speech, or happiness, or music. The day will come when affection is shared as we now share the elements, when universal gentleness takes precedence over the fierce predilection of one person for another. The day will come—" and at this point his voice became inaudible. Then, with a new beginning: "But will the day come? For people are set apart by art or happiness, just as one interrupts for a moment his exaltation in a concert hall to glance with scorn at a restless neighbor. One cannot feel uplifted without feeling that he is lifted above others. And we share the elements not through virtue, but merely due to imperfections in our ways of ownership. Could sunlight be deflected, the countries of the vanquished would lie in darkness. I mean thereby that we cannot have the softness of great insight, the pardon before offence—or that we can have such only in glimpses. The day, and here I would revise my statement, will never come."

He wept, and I saw that he had wept seldom, for his whole body bespoke weeping—and in its surrender was repulsive as the distorted features partially hidden by his arm. Finally, "As a test of happiness," he resumed, "imagine what manner of life one would impose upon himself were he expiating some great wrong or striving to obtain forgetfulness. Picture existence as it would be under such a theoretical burden, and you will picture the daily habits of us all."

I cherish such meetings, when each man puts his wares upon the table for the other to observe and value. Even while hearing little beyond one's own old soliloquies, he profits by the alterations which a fresh auditor demands of him. However, the two of us have since avoided each other, for both realized that in our first discussion he had brought forth everything he considered of moment, had given me the best cullings of a life which was, in its total, dreary and unpointed. I respected him for his ability to exhaust himself thus rapidly, for though a greater power of multiplication would have brought him more comfort, his aridity made him more accurate.

III.

"My exile had unmade itself"

His sudden alleviation. He recites details of his attempts at settling. How he even wrote a trivial play for a local school. How his activity with plays led him to make arrangements for a troupe of barnstormers. Among them is Florence. Their incidents together. His elation and boastfulness (he is now no longer one with the oppressed).

How—did I not give great thought to molding my career by trivial forms? Did I not vote for quietude, though procured at the price of ill humor and underlying envy? I was set for humbleness, adjusting both my mind and my economy to negative living. Here I have been working to write out the stages of my resignment—and of a sudden, I no longer need be resigned.

Are there events which one must look upon as grave intervention; are there changes which, though unforeseen, are too important for one to consider them as accidents? Already the things I move among seem foreign to me. "By what checks could you contrive to remain here?" I have asked myself, watching both wife and children unhappily, as though there were an unquestionable cause for my departure, known and accepted by us all, as though I were called away to defend

67

them. These tender fellows—I believe there is much in which I can instruct them. Am I permitted to make them of this seed, yet deny them my study of its correctives? Am I not, of all men, obliged to school them in their disease? "By what elation," I have also asked myself, "could you be brought to consider abandoning them?"—and entranced by my own thoughts, picturing my farewell even as I sat surrounded, I felt the encouragement of this woman's pitying eyes. My features, I understood, had shown pain; and I was chagrined at her kindliness, all the more poignant because misplaced. Did she assume that a headache, such as attacked me frequently in recent months, was now upon me? Unwittingly she was rebuking with her solicitations. Though fearing that I might speak in sleep or delirium to wound her, and though trying to imagine some way whereby I could be sure of not doing so, I know that I have daily offered her dismaying evidence of my unrest.

See what I had done in my manner of bargaining. How I had come here, wounded, and been restored by Genevieve. How I had married here, become the father of two children, and erected a structure of citizenship within the requirements of my neighbors— healing myself first by clandestine love, which was dismissed, and thence by some prosperity. Until persons came to me for assistance, which I found no cause for refusing them, so that a further share of good repute was engrafted upon me.

Was there not final surrender, coming with my consent to write for local purposes, a play for the students of the village? A nearby town, smaller than our own, formed the soundest butt for my shameless humor, as the audience was already pledged to laughter by the subject. And there were certain small politicians, routed in the last election, whom it was safe to ridicule. I had known a gentle-minded person who was content to do the bidding of others, but would confront a blizzard at midnight to make certain that his livestock was in comfort. I had wished him all wealth and happiness, but even prior to the growth of his deafness he was silent to the verge of ignorance. I could readily give him nobility in this play. Thus gambling with loaded dice I was assured of my dingy winnings. Thence to a partial office in the school—and thereupon, by resignment too deep for irony, my participating in the cultural improvement of my neighbors.

(May these blunt materials, in this concatenation, trace a more significant destiny. For each unimportant step led to a step equally unimportant, until the last unimportant step, with an outcome which dignified all those preceding it. Oh, vague stirrings at the embarrassed crackling of the knuckles at handshake, for her fingers had been relaxed by travel. Oh, glorious termination of a blind pilgrimage!)

If one, in fleeing, takes the piloting of his life into his own hands; if each modicum of his defense is the reward of plotting; if he digs in a secret hole and buries there at midnight the small coins of his imperfect happiness; and if in a new event, unthought of, he finds that the arrows of his life have changed their course, dare he hold that a gentler existence has sought him out? This they shall not take from me. I have considered them one by one, asking: Is he the man by whom I could be constrained through fear of disapproval—and I have seen that to a *consensus omnium*, as thus analyzed, I was almost wholly impervious.

As we stood above the valley looking down upon the trim grain fields, there was great comfort in the displaying of my acreage. "And the herd?" Florence asked me, "the herd also is yours?" "The herd also," I answered, though this was not exact, for some of the cattle had been sold recently and not yet delivered. But the herd looked smaller from our great height, and my reply was for their proper number as they would have seemed had we been closer.

Let us lie, cheat, dissemble, beg connivance of any, forestall their anger by feigned cordiality should they come to accuse us, ask them kind questions to make their indignation more difficult, praise their despicable children to disarm them; let us cajole, simper, brush hypothetical dust spots from their sleeves; let us admit all manner of compromise to avoid their forcing of an issue. But should they force an issue I will meet it. They will find such refusal to relinquish, such growling over a bone, as will recall portions of their lives long since stifled, making them go from me with a double hatred. "Do you remember, Florence . . ." I have said to her, thereupon sharing some harmless restoration of our past. Oh, Anthony, this day I confessed how I once spied upon her to learn whether in all ways she was loyal to you—and this confession was a source of amusement to us.

We recalled past acquaintances. "Hubert!" I exclaimed at her mention of him; "I had forgotten Hubert!" And were he here I could have embraced him, though he would have poisoned me for my words. For he had given more thought to making himself unforgettable than ever a Roman gave to fame. I pictured him again, racing in terror from a cow—surely a rabid beast, Anthony, for she came towards us with low-hanging udders, and mooing to be milked. The presence of the herd below doubtless suggested this incident to me. We reconstructed Hubert, who could not share a confidence without fearing that it would be abused, but despite his misgivings could not remain silent. We rehearsed his passion for the worst newspapers and the best literature. His militant fastidiousness, as he quarreled scrupulously with every servant, discharging his valets for failing to remember constantly the things which he could never once remember. His horror of noises. "Hear it, hear it!" he shrieked, as we were all walking on the beach at night. We fell silent, listening with bowed heads so that the wavelets, working among the pebbles, became intimate. And from far off came the faint, almost purring sound of a motor. "Like a trombone at your shoulder," his sister said quickly, for she knew what was expected of us. "Where shall we turn next!" and Hubert was audibly desolate. Florence recalled his helping her through puddled streets, in his politeness growing petulant when, owing to ineptitude on her part, he could not accommodate her quickly enough. "Yet there was another Hubert," I admonished her, "the Hubert who sailed his yacht in the gale, tacking at fiendish angles, panting from elation and physical strain, and howling lines from Beowulf above the storm." There were two Huberts, a land-Hubert and a sea-Hubert. And how different they both were from his crony, whom we also met here, with the sorrowing face of a hound, the victim of his gullet, sighing from the effects of his last meal, showing the reliques of some past sensitivity now reduced to appetite—gentle when not morose from his burden—and peaceably accepting his daily martyrdom of omelettes and pork as he hastened to his grave. Parts of him drooped upon other parts, as though a body's flesh were held firm by cords and all the cords of his body had been severed.

If we must have a slogan, let that slogan be the present. To move vigorously through chill water, and stretch like a snake in the sun— to do this actually, and to do the equivalent as regards the subtler pleasures of the mind—such is gratitude to Makers. If I built a house, I should want the house to stand self-assertively, at peace with its placing. Let us then be as though builded. Let man take each brilliant day as one dropped from an eternity of silence. Let him enjoy the unique organization of his hulk. Let him be rained upon, wind driven, sunned, firm-footed—living first among the elements and shaping his other experiences by this immediacy. Surely no flower protests at withering in the autumn; even subsidence can be a purpose—and days of gentle ecstasy might bring us to welcoming our decline. Henceforth I will look upon no man with envy, since he is but repeating in his terms what I have discovered in my own. Nature has become the carpet of our sportiveness. Here is a skillful seller, recommending under many guises, repeating in the sound of birds what is suggested by stirrings of the air, maintaining by sunlight what is likewise proposed by the smell of damp soil, cradling the eye by the forms of a hill to make equivalence for the rushing of water. True, there are frogs, young and incautious, which land betimes in the belly of a heron. The heron's song is not their song. There are the sacrificed—there are those for whom the world was not created, but I am not one of them. For long I have hunted—and now I am feeding. Perhaps I am content.

Those who are to drudge beneath the earth, in the mines, the sewers, the stench of tunnels—let them be bred as other than mankind, give thought to the monstrous preparing of their characters as to their sinews. Teach them that alleviation is neither possible nor to be desired, instruct them in hoglike appetites, nurture their brutality as we encourage in others affection. Do them at least this minimum of justice. Study them that their denigration may be thorough. Guide them downwards.

My exile had unmade itself. Learning that a company of actors in bad circumstances was touring the adjacent counties, I brought *The*

Merchant of Venice to this village. Upon the troupe's arrival I noted with relief that Portia was beautiful, and a second later I saw that she was Florence.

Often in recent years I had climbed the hill to which I now guided her, crossing the blunt, timbered ridge, and winding by a briary road into the next valley. Here are the ruins of an old house, among deserted meadows, the rim of hills making it a separate world. It is a lonely spot, where in summer the trout stream sinks beneath pebbles. I have gone through the littered rooms, opened musty cupboards, and rummaged among rags with the rung of a broken chair. I have examined this decrepit house, waiting—and into its dismalness I now guided Florence, that her bright curiosity might give it different echoes. Leaning in the doorway, looking down upon the rotted flooring of the porch, we talked with some gravity. "For every man," I told her, "there must be something towards which he would make his way across dead bodies." And cautiously, never without obliqueness, we discussed our feelings towards each other.

IV.

"Let this be a song"

Pæan to the excitements of love, due to Florence's reappearance. He thinks of various people whom, for one reason or another, he could include among his band.

In an age of tumult, we might best command attention by speaking in whispers. In this age of tumult note how I, gratified, raise my voice. Let this be a song, the learning-burdened lyric of one who, without hope, was relieved of illness. Like some character of legend, he fled from one country to another solely to escape danger, and in the second country became a sovereign. If, living in the city and awaking at night, one were to arise, dress himself, and go into another section of the city; if he, as though guided, were to stop at a destined house hitherto unknown to him, were to mount the stairs, and choose a door among many, knocking for admittance and saying to those that opened, "I am here"; if he should never return to his former bed, but lived another life, with other people, and greatly enjoyed this, or if he found customary places made miraculous, he would be doing in his way what I have done in mine.

In this period of respite, I feel as though I were spying upon my own alien felicity. I learn, Anthony, that I was not greatly unhappy

73

when I used to watch you with Florence—and thus the present, in becoming kindly, has placed even my past difficulties in a kindlier light. If there are processes in the body whereby the memory of sorrow is imprinted in blood, nerves, and pigment, if there is an observable parallel in my tissues so that, with the proper instruments, we could test for prior gloom by an histologist's analysis, then I believe we should find these symptoms suddenly reversed—ducts, formerly dry, must now be flowing, to fill me with biologic unction, and others must have dried which were once dangerously profuse.

I do not neglect the fact that this is error. I do not maintain that, were human living fitly managed, this exaltation would be necessary, or even possible. I say only that mankind has added sums for many centuries, that there are grave mistakes lost among the figures, and that accordingly one more mistake is needed if we are to arrive quickly at the proper total. I say that, given conditions as they are, precisely this kind of illumination was required. And I see no good reason why I should not somewhat discourage those who still are as I was—while among my former enemies I believe I could now find cronies.

Do not think, Anthony, that what you cast aside I have salvaged. These are shores previously known but to lizards. Only by the records of citizenship is Florence the woman who was once your woman. It is virgin soil that I have opened up, though you might say I have come upon a settlement. You might say I follow in your footsteps. How—is that not grossness? If one seeks new metaphors, will he not also find new women? I am not tricked when she confides that she preferred me always, though it is useful to our happiness that she should believe this slogan and feel her months with you as little more than an apprenticeship. Nor have I openly called it a deception, choosing to keep such accuracy to myself and not to stickle if present facts cause her to misread past ones. I shall permit her to invent whatever fiction she likes for bolstering up this momentous reality. In love, Anthony, I believe we were like elephants.

People may slay themselves through sheer lack of want—not in despair, but in gently letting their rich blood. We should distrust the tenacious of living, for they are unappeased. Death, if luxuriously managed, has but this one thing against it: that unlike love, it does not well up anew. Yet we must watch, under prospering conditions, lest we be without the guidance and good taste of fear. He who commands a large salary thinks little of boring his neighbors. And if we have spent the best of our years in repairing our defenses, we may find ourselves unequipped for times of peace. So I am aware that my good fortune may cancel past proclivities and leave me at zero. To this extent I am already grown shrewd, and like a pawnbroker before lending on a pledge, I hold up our affection to the light, hem, shake the head in doubt, and stroke the chin. I would not have chosen to live in a dungeon, but since I have lived in one so long, I may get a prison pallor in living elsewhere. Should such prove to be the case, we are forced to seek misery as better fitted to our talents.

What man of character has not at least two selves, one desiring to be bound and the other without encumbrances? And now that Florence is with me, the recalcitrant fellow must be heard occasionally. Must I not admit that were we living in a whole pigeonry of contentment, there would be times when it rained, and as it grew dark I should slip out to walk back and forth, along a deserted road?

But hold. In the midst of my pæan—and I sought to sing pæans cautiously—I have become disloyal to Florence. I shall return to her, with doubled attentiveness, and in apprehension, lest she has been equally subversive. Thus can one's distrust of another grow from defects in his own reliability. Yet he may be trained to such bargainings, as I am sure that she is not. And were she, during my absence, to have gone as far afield as I in speculations, then I am back with the dismalness of my damned dungeon.

To you I shall not catalogue the excellencies of Florence, since you would but misread the privilege of your priority with her. Whatever aspects of her I discovered, you would think yourself remembering. I shall only say that she is not avid of admiration, for she has not lacked it. Yet despite many hours devoted to frankness, I have retained so much of policy that I contrive to compliment her as a peer, revealing nothing of my awe. Though I have not bluntly questioned her as to her life since leaving you, she has given me to understand its profit. For reasons which she has not yet made clear to me, she is traveling with these trivial actors, whom she loves with amusement and belittlement enough to make them resentful if they knew it, though I who am outside their group need not be affected. A woman less capable might feel obliged to offer some defensive account of her presence among these moth-eaten fellows, to explain away appearances—but her delight in them, her obvious pleasure in observing their irregularities, places upon me the burden of guilt. That is, if a defense is to be offered, she leaves it for me to discover it for myself, thus making me reproach myself for having thought that any defense was needed. I recognize the steadiness of her position, her confidence maintained without effort. A well-being which I had not dared hope for, she accepts as her due.

Well, if she is among strange companions, am I not myself in a motley army? We throng the beaches, we make the noise of frogs, we greet our kind vaguely, smile partially in passing. We go about the roads at night, we are seen talking at corner tables, many of us must feel the half-neglected seasons as obscured by the metropolis, considering spring, not as it lies broadly on a remote meadow, but as seen from an office window. Let me list the group at random. There was a man of seventy who had got for himself a girl scarcely nubile. Some wag called him Goethe. And I knew an unripe druggist who, in drunkenness, would boast of his exceptional sweetheart and then of a sudden grow pale despite the flush of his liquor, fearing that he had made her seem too desirable and might tempt his listeners to follow after him, whereas in reality they were but waiting for him to finish that they might burst forth reciting glories of their own. I might further recall a couple, no more accurately described than as Walrus and Doll. They remained playful, inseparable, and enwrapped until the day of their joint death in an accident. These are among my band, as is the young woman who, though living in dissolute company and herself somewhat dissolute, persisted in chastity. Many ribald and recondite explanations were offered for her conduct, but I felt that she rightly saw in virtue her one distinction. Her closest friend was in great contrast. If a man but made some outstanding name for himself, in an exploration, a work of science, or a potato race, she could not rest until she had shared his bed with him. For the bearers of medals she had the attentive eyes of a dog lying on the hearth of his master. But the uncrowned she forgot like doormen. I should include these very dissimilar women in my band—and the wife of an ambitious lawyer, who cared for her husband assiduously, until he was prosperous enough to leave her and support her handsomely in an asylum after her collapse. And the student, joined in an irregular union with a shopgirl. Their relationship being irregular, he could not summon to his aid the old precepts of fidelity, and he could think of no new ones. I should include the young author who wrote an article in caricature of love, and confided to me that he found love generally on the wane following its publication.

Two people of my band I thought generally abhorrent, owing to the amorphousness of their bodies, the bluntness of their movements, and their sluggishness of mind. On first acquaintance I assumed that they had come together as companions in degradation, but later I understood that they had really sought each other and were delighted with what they had found. And high among this group of my fellow-thinkers were two cultured but slightly morbid men intimate since childhood. Both married, they conceived a dismal plan for testing the fidelity of wives. Each, it was agreed, should attempt the cuckolding of the other, afterwards making a frank report of his experience. One, it seems, was successful, but gave assurance of the wife's great rectitude, whereas the second, who failed, announced success with a show of reluctance.

Dare I go further among this uneven lot? No further than to mention briefly a beautiful and even picturesque woman, a Madame Durant, loved by two men. Through letters, telegrams, sudden visits, and the intervention of relatives, she carried her drama tumultuously across many states. With her arms about Joseph, she would cry out that she loved Josephus and thereupon, misled by a desire for too literal a symmetry, would cross the room to embrace Josephus and protest her love of Joseph. For to be alone with one of them seemed far greater impoverishment than to be with neither, and whichever she lived with, she thought herself conscience-stricken for leaving the other, though in reality suffering most from a drop in the liveliness of her situation. She wept in contentment, insisting that she was degraded—and friends, stopping to rebuke her for her inconstancy, would become her suitors. On one occasion I drank a toast to her elopement, using for the purpose glasses given prematurely as a present for her prospective marriage to the groom now temporarily abandoned though on hand to bid her and his rival farewell—and I left in complex cordiality, loving her, her two men, her dog, and the darkening inhospitable sky which matched my lonesomeness.

In these multifarious ways they prepare themselves for oblivion, utilizing as best they can their few clear years out of vagueness. But all, all are like the receivers of a legacy, who would keep their good fortune to themselves while sharing with others their delight in it. It were better that they were destroyed at the peak of their intensity, as boys stamp out insects in conjunction—or like the man struck down by an unanticipated bullet as he was smiling to himself, so that he passed without gradation from delight to nothingness, and was dead before the signs of pleasure died on his lips.

V.

"Despite them all, in their very faces"

*How chemicals bring solace. But love is superior to chemicals.
"Good things have been brought to me on a platter." Plans
for the future. Enjoyment of nature. Amused recollections of
the past. He caps his delight by a tirade against any that
would belittle it.*

For four purposes men have had recourse to drugs: for happiness, phantasy, intensity, and sleep. In the chemical subterfuge of morphine some have for a time found happiness, basking in the glow of an internal sunlight, sprawling upon the warm sands of subjective shores. By the drinking, or smoking, or eating of hemp, the hashisheens have contrived to make the world about them distorted and exceptional, with the burdensomeness of infinity in its proportions, and with many strange, deceptive shapes and distances. For intensity, for swiftness of movement, for a heightening of sensation almost to the point of pain, whereby the sounds of a symphony may become startling in their sharpness, the harsh alkaloid of the coca leaf has been successfully injected into the veins. And sleep is best induced by several synthetic discoveries, in particular the derivatives of coal tar, which, until their excessive use has destroyed a man, will

79

serve simply by the miracle of their toxins to quiet the nag of the most inexorable miseries, and even bring relaxation to those stone-minded who would otherwise lie for many hours of each night, staring into the darkness, their respiration an unsuspected sigh. For such purposes men have had recourse to drugs—and on many occasions in my life I have felt chemical assistance in one or another of such human blessings necessary. What, before our extinction, dare we expect as earthly glory, if not the benign cycle of these four experiences: a calm delight (morphine) in the sharpness (cocaine) and unusualness (hemp) of our day, and at the end of it (the coal tar drugs), our gently drifting into nothing? And I will tell you, Anthony, that by simply being with Florence these recent hours, I have enjoyed precisely this miraculous cycle. Like a cornucopia spilling its fruits, she has overwhelmed me with such gifts as are the reward of a ripening. I am surrounded, I am laden, with the plenty, the squanderings, the heaping-up, of a beautiful woman's affection. Not chemically, but by the fortunate outcome of life itself, I am drugged.

Why! Good things have been brought to me on a platter. The splendid weather has made us a carpet for our delight. We have studied the processes of a dawn, once by walking in a cathedral-like forest while the sun slowly turned the rheostat of day, and once by emerging at noon from a deep cavern. With Florence standing beside me, I have taunted an echo, and we have both laughed as we heard my words repeated, solemn and enlarged. We watched swans on still water, with Florence noting how the birds are weight and color, but their reflections color only (and in the sheer extravagance of our mood, we held that since the bird and its reflection could not be divorced, the reflection and not the bird is causally prior). Each place we visited did not exist until, gleaming upon it, we saw it in our own light. In particular I must remember these occasions lest, in the future, my present exhilaration has abated and my life has again come to seem rigid and unchanging. Then, recalling how the rock-like became liquid, I may realize that though one's trouble seems the logical result of many years' direction, though it be the exact consequence of one's plans and temperament, it can be wholly altered if only the unexpected enter: and recalling how Florence appeared thus unexpectedly, I shall realize that the unexpected can always enter. By the unplanned the planned will be remedied.

Yet was her appearance really unexpected? It seems (and I have told her this) that I had been drawing her towards me throughout the period of our separation, that I had been holding forth immaterial hands to her, that every day of my life I had been trying to make myself into a kind of magnet which, attracting in all directions, would bring her to me even though I were not facing her point of the compass when I knowingly or unknowingly called her name.

This poor devil has advanced, Anthony. He is genuinely lifted up. For he need seek no new thing, unless he discover that only by a new thing can he repeat such moments of pleasure as he has already had. But the apprenticeship to his present masterhood was arduous. I shall not forget the years when he would subtly beg of unknown women, and find solace in touching of them lightly. Ah, melancholy ineffectualness, retreat of snail's horns! I will say that in that era of his dismal adolescence, when he was without anchorage, he fed constantly upon such shamefaced, unavowed, and unconsummated promiscuity, and he will always harbor some vague gratitude towards those who, in their slight suffering of a gloomy and uncertain suitor, while remaining at once kindly and aloof, at once touched and intact, did serve by this ambiguousness, this oxymoron of their conduct, to keep some tenderness alive in him and to loosen somewhat the wall he was erecting between himself and mankind. There was a time when he learned Polish of a maidservant, purely that they might have something more than her doubtful treasure in common—yet when their studies had ripened to a deeper intimacy, and he was able to ask of her all that she was long prepared, I think, to accord him without this circuitous approach, he turned instead to the composition of a sonnet, poured forth his zeal and his remorse in praise of virtue, and then fell into such self-torment, such exaltation and secret abandoning, as still fills him with pain and pity when he remembers it. Gone is all this, and all akin to it. Gone forever are those days when, in the very rumblings of his stomach, he seemed to hear words spoken.

And we may number him among those who would, with great zest, leave everything as it now is, calling upon the sea to roll, the winds to howl, and the dead to lie in their graves, oh dead.

We have thought of life in a rambling place, as in the castles of mad Bavarian Ludwig—or some fanciful cluster of buildings above the Mediterranean, with rooms on many different levels, and vistas down long corridors, and angular turnings of direction—a selected existence, making for peculiar kinds of thinking, feeling, and acting; a play world for adults, pleasant with artificial insanity; a rareness of habits, caused not by grave internal canker, but simply by the inventiveness of our surroundings; distinct modes of experience whereby we might be amused at such things as people generally found depressive, and be astounded where they saw nothing. We observed the valley—and as we did so, "I understand why it appeals to you," she told me, in her breathy, teethy diction; "The droop of a horse's head, as he stands in the field at haytime, corresponds with the droop of the hay bulging from the wagon he is hitched to. The cowpaths curve, not by accident, but by law, adapting themselves with modulation to the contours of the land which they traverse, while the frequency and gentleness of their turnings suggests the leisure behind their development. The stream which runs through the valley progresses by yielding." And I repeated after her, "by yielding," since the words of a sudden seemed like a revelation to me, though I was slightly perplexed to explain how she could have come upon a thought more in keeping with myself who, in contrast with her inborn airiness, am climbing out of straits. She, rather, has always seemed as though she were dropping empty cartons in places to which she would never return—order, arrangement, husbandry being unnecessary to her privileged negligence. But I am in haste these days; I accept things in the bulk—and even if there is an apparent incorrectness in the fact that the sentences suggested themselves to her, I shall not attempt to plumb them further. Yet it is strange that she thought of them, since they go with such a man as I, indicating as they do a person who has long considered matters of comfort and defeat whereas with her, I am sure, pleasures are taken without thinking.

No, there is a certain oversatisfaction about her mood at present.

She has bewildered me too often by revealing gratifications like my own. She talks vaguely of her delight in living, and proclaims it unnecessarily. But how could I expect her to do otherwise, when I have been bubbling like a spring? I have placarded slogans of enjoyment on all sides of me, and it would be hard to understand how she could fail to be noticeably affected by reading them. I have set a pace, and the merest responsiveness on her part should cause her to follow at the same clip. There is, it is true, still some enigma about her surroundings. I do not see why she should be continuously amused by her companions, who are outstanding neither as performers on the stage nor as oddities in their private lives. A band of traveling shoemakers would be more turbulent and more productive of strange scenes. I do not hold it against her that these people are dreary, but I am puzzled to explain that she does not say so. As for her life since leaving you, there has been some embarrassment between us on this subject. I have been able simply to discover that she is amused to recall your parting, that she has married a man of money, that she has an undeniable affection for him, but on more than one occasion has seized opportunities like this acting tour as a pretext to leave him on amicable terms for a season.

We have discussed the subterfuge of the colony. "Admit to me," I insisted, "admit to me that the plans for the colony became a subterfuge. Admit that they were little more than my learning of Polish. Admit that under a terminology for improving all mankind, he conspired to magnify your relationship. Admit that this match was given importance by trickery, since he persuaded both of you that it was an incidental aspect of a plan having nothing less than the betterment of all society as its aim." I pointed out to her how neatly your general program could serve your personal ends. In your scheme that experts should live together, each pursuing his special discipline yet exchanging his knowledge with those skilled in other disciplines, you implied your own expertness; and at the same time, in holding that "the dignity of a man is not in his personal attainments, but in the dignity of his vocation," you got yourself distinction by a single sentence. In forbidding the ironical, you seemed charitable while ruling out a technique you were not good at; and in insisting that one should listen without shame to all that others might have to teach him, you were purchasing your own relaxation, as you did also when, though enshrining physical living, you proposed to ban the competitive. Your choice of the "humanistic" as opposed to the "ascetic," was a means of endorsing under a deceptive guise the life of the appetites, thus covertly setting forth the ideas by which Florence would find her union with you reasonable. At my recital of such correspondences she protested with laughter—yet I continued, showing how you both had bolstered up your courtship at the start, you by retaining your rôle as Alcæus, she by retaining her part as Mary. One loves another, I said, when that other, symbolizing beyond the self, not only is, but stands for. And here you were acting in a play, with such rôles as spread an aura about you (Mary, troubled prettily by conflicting codes of chastity and acquiescence—Alcæus the nobleman, unwavering, persistent, a poet of eager love). And as the force of this fiction dwindled, the plans for the colony came to serve in their stead. Thus you could, without boastfulness, even without your knowledge, be greater than yourselves—you were parts for the whole, particular for the general; you were glowing, amorous synecdoches. "You make me seem huge and bungling," she laughed, but I would not be put off: "Grant me all this," I insisted, and she conceded the justice of my version—and I will tell you, Anthony, that to have such accusations corroborated is very soothing, for one is not quite at rest when he has accounted for so much nobility by trivial mechanisms.

However, I did not primarily deal with you. The disclosing of your impostures was incidental. In the main, our times together have but slightly involved the explicit undoing of the past. Rather, I have found the greatest excitement in unburdening myself of my own grotesque experiences. I have reviewed the story of my flight: my reckless weeks in New York after leaving you, and my eventual conversion by an evangelist on a street corner. I recalled his group—their differing heights, their diversity of postures, their range in weight, age, and attitude (since some hung upon the speaker's lips, some were impatient, and some stood as though hired). I remembered how dissimilarly they opened their mouths when they sang, and yet how proud I was, in my drunkenness, at the man's professional rejoicing; though I did become hurt when, using me as a decoy, he pled for further converts. I had felt that I was sufficient game for one evening and that, having bagged me, he should pack up his holy weapons and go home, leaving me perhaps to the care of the one pretty member of his irregular circle. How much I have given off. I have felt like a full sack of grain, pouring its contents through a slit. And though I have listened oftener than this account would lead you to suppose, even in listening I have been unburdened.

Bah! I could continue to announce my happiness thus openly, with a free heart, did not the question of adversaries enter. But how speak out simply, when one must at every turn forestall refutation? At peace, at peace!—damn you, I say I am at peace. Should any man who also writes, see these words and choose to belittle them, I pray I have the opportunity to know of it, and to look into his own productions—for I believe that he is vulnerable enough even were one not vindictive, but with the cuttingness of vengeance added, one could surely carve him as with a knife. If you, Anthony, or any others of your competent brood, see cause to smile at my elation, I pledge myself to examine their accomplishments until I have made clear all insufficiencies in them, pursuing them with pamphlets, pasquinades, scurrilities, obtrectations from the sewers until, even though I fail to bring a corresponding disrepute upon them, and work rather to my own detriment, I shall have made them embarrassed and uneasy, and shall have given them a catalogue of their unfitness which, however they may smirk in public, they will secretly fear to be exact. In particular there are some who would give the appearance of great vigor merely by using the speech of toughs, and would make us gasp at their courage each time they brave a rain of blows on paper. Their Klondike morality is for the flabby with comfort. Justly they dislike the verbal equivalent of their intimacies—but despite them all, in their very faces, I will grow lyrical about Florence. If certain events have happened, I am required only to detail these events with accuracy.

VI.

"A weary trudging homeward in cold dawn"

Admits that he has been giving a false impression. He had not been intimate with Florence. But he now truthfully tells of their union in a dingy hotel. His subsequent disinterest and cruelty. He is named. *She tells him of her unsavory life since the time of his disappearance. His dismissal of her.*

If I gave you reason to believe that Florence had succumbed to me, and if I even took considerable pains to suggest this event as the cause of my elation, I can now admit that I partially deceived you, though adding that what I formerly misrepresented has since become the truth. Frankness is not the least important ingredient of trickery. Even while scrupulously following the facts in a confession, we lie by altering their stress, by dismissing grave details as a trifle and making trifles into a cynosure. In this instance, however, I had intended foremost to convey the nature of my happiness. And in telling you of my delight in Florence without implying my full possession of her, I should have caused you some bewilderment. My delight, that is, was precisely the delight of possession; but since it

86

flourished while we were still apart, I could best make it clear to you by inventing its motives. Such record of those days as might have gone into an affidavit would have been more misleading than the liberties I took in behalf of a profounder accuracy. I simply could not rely upon your judgment—and as an ancient master of the law courts has taught us, when a man's judgment is at fault, we bring him to correct conclusions by deception.

Take into account, however, one further difference: that the delight is all gone from me. You will not think me so naïve as to mistake mere relaxation for a permanent satiety. You will not think me so unskilled as to confuse a weary trudging homeward in cold dawn with a lasting change of outlook. For such conditions of a few hours, I can make fitting allowances. My diffidence arises from a sounder cause—and to explain it I will here give the record of an evening.

Perhaps it would have required a woman of unusual assurance, and a man much less adept than I in matters of decay, to survive the setting without disaster. For a room so dismal would necessarily bring somewhat into doubt the hostess who had invited her admirer into it. Though she were to be here but for a few days, it was hers for this period—and since the bed she had lain in, the table at which she had sat, and the walls that had enclosed her, were repellent, how could I escape the feeling that some last touch of elegance had been taken from her? The sickly lamp, unshaded, hurt the eyes when looked at, but when avoided gave forth a dirty yellow twilight. The soap dish, pitcher, and basin on the washstand, with the covered jar on the floor beside it, played too prominent a part in the haphazard furnishings. The splendid leather traveling bags, standing in one corner, reminded me of her smart arrival as she stepped from the train, yet in doing so suggested that she had not kept up to this beginning; while recalling this startling moment of a few days before, they made me think of a parade, all flowers and streamers as it advanced to band music in the sunlight, but much bedraggled after being caught in a shower.

"Your Portia is not well surrounded," she said defensively as she anticipated, rather than detected, my glance about the room—and I felt some poignancy in her being, of a sudden, *my* Portia, as though by this possessive she were trying to drag me down with her. But I was not in a mood to prize unfavorable details; I hastened to collaborate, with her, throwing all criticism from my mind and setting myself to be as elated as I could by the events of the next few hours. "When I was young," I said, "a little girl with a name I had not liked proved so delightful that she has to this day made her name seem lovely to me. So perhaps even this kind of sorry place will hereafter be appealing to me since you have passed here." But I saw that she did not enjoy the exaggerated gallantry of my tone. As I had not praised the room in spite of its appearance, she probably preferred that I had praised it—yet had I done so, I believe that she would have been equally hurt by my obvious attempt at charity. Accordingly, where both an admission and a denial would have been wrong, I believe that my answer was the better, through enabling us to bring a more minuet-like quality into the scene.

I placed a flask upon the table, and she sat on the edge of her bed, laughing as she held out one somewhat foggy glass and one thick China cup without a handle. We drank a meaningless toast together, our sentences unfinished. She spoke well of the liquor, praising "local talent" when I assured her that it came from an illicit still in this neighborhood. Thus again, in a simple remark, she showed signs of pleading; for her use of an expression originating among actors served to remind us of her vocation—a vocation whose adepts, generally throughout our history, had construed the architecture of noble verses while being themselves disgracefully housed.

We talked in low tones, partly that we might not be overheard, and partly because of the dreary light. But as the alcohol gradually kindled some warmth in us, I arose, kissed her, and asked, whispering, "May I blow out this lamp?"—to which she assented; and I will say, Anthony, that the change in our mood was astonishing. The miracle of her again overwhelmed me while I patiently, and with mumblings, undid her garments. We were for these moments blessed, as I sought to fix with my eyes her whiteness shifting hazily in the dark, contourless, infinite room. With bungling she opened my shirt at the throat—and when she laid her hand against me I was happy that, through all my doings and uncertainties, I had contrived always with conviction to maintain some bodily firmness.

Since, as we lay in the darkness, we continued to sip now and then at our liquor, the indeterminateness of the evening continued. At times, falling silent, we listened to the disparate sounds of the hotel, which were generally remote and unplaced, and then again were immediately upon us, as when a maid went down the hall to the tinkling of ice water and returned at an earnest hurried pace suggesting that she already knew of her next task. Well, I am expert enough in the sounds of darkness, Anthony, in the varying kinds of damnation and delight that go with wakefulness while others sleep. Those that lie awake are waiting—and what is waiting but a listening for sounds? Yet on this occasion it was my privilege to find a pleasurable engrossment in a state which had only too often engrossed me bitterly. It tickled me to think that the very woman who had provided the misery for my sleepless hours was now here to fill them with a compensatory comfort.

She spoke occasionally of the past, with me asking her many pointed questions in an attempt to understand the exact tenor of her life since the time I had vanished. But as she continued, I became aware that her statements, made somewhat unguarded by the liquor, were not wholly in accord with one another. To my astonishment, I found that by paying close attention I could entangle her in important aspects of her story, though I was careful to give her no hint of my suspicions. Indeed, coming more and more to believe that the discrepancies arose from an attempt to conceal misfortunes, I continually praised her brilliant and carefree existence. Even when I had become thoroughly convinced that she was not telling me the truth, I went on questioning her like a blunt student whose eagerness to learn made him meek and credulous.

Finally I decided that I should, in a devious way, call her to an accounting. She had spoken of leaving you because of her love for the man she had married—but she later disclosed that she had not met this man until many months after your separation from her. I first let her see that this important discrepancy had been noted, but immediately afterwards I acted as though I, and not she, had been at fault. "I thought you had left Anthony because of your love for this other man," I said as though bewildered; "I am afraid that some important points of your story have escaped me—for now I gather that you did not know this man until several months after you and Anthony had parted." I laughed. "Perhaps our liquor is getting the better of me, Florence. I thought I was a more expert drinker—but the things you say seem now and then to fall out of place, they will not remain where I had put them. You must speak more circumstantially, perhaps, to take my insufficiencies into account." She was chagrined, lying silent for some time; but though she seemed tense, she said nothing that would explain away this dilemma. I resumed my naïve praising of her: "Be kind to me," I whispered. "Do not be angry with me if I become befuddled. Let me share simply the miracle of you. I have always lived in awe of your good fortune, which seemed like the corollary of your character, events following a delightful and flattering order for you. You have simply flowered, simply evolved from within, assured that the surrounding world would shape itself to your best interests."

We had been lying supine, each talking into the black ceiling, but now she turned towards me. "Who am I?" she said slowly, with a bitterness that made me understand and regret the cruelty of what I had been doing. "Who am I to dispense charity to another?" And then: "Neal, Neal, John Neal," she cried to me in a voice which, raised in anguish, made me apprehensive of the other guests; "I can make this pretence no longer. See . . . I am broken." Whereupon, after sobbing, she spoke to me with pitiable frankness.

So you hurried a weeping woman, Anthony! So there came the time when Florence was not so much a person, as a stage in your life, and a stage which you had passed through? And first you became more jealous of her movements than before, and next you grew more lenient towards her, and finally you showed signs of impatience with those traits which were most definitely hers? She tried not to be too thoroughly herself, but despite the guidance of an occasional frown, she could not always be certain in what way she was reaffirming her identity. She could ferret out her own characteristic turns of phrase with some success, but the matter of her gestures and intonations was more elusive. She even changed the scent of her powder, and placed the articles on her dressing table differently, knowing that factors as slight as these could be tyrannical, but Hubert's sister was to follow—and so *punctum*. When she was certain that you had embraced this woman, "I have come to accuse you, I have come to tell you what I know," she said to you, hoping that some consternation would show on your face—but as you remained untroubled, she trumped up some trivial disclosure which she told you laughingly, to conceal her intentions and her dismay. I learn that you gave her money for her return to New York—and that she threw this money upon the floor. But you took up her purse from the table, groping about the floor for the bills, putting them into it, and snapping it shut. I understand why you yourself stooped to pick up this money, perhaps even exaggerating the business of your search and thus permitting her at least to retain some show of defiance in her defeat.

It seems that on her return to the city, a young blood, a pugilist who earned his living by preliminary bouts, ogled her crudely, with the result that she went to his apartment with him. He was at this time in rigorous training, as he was soon to enter the ring against a man whom he was not only challenging professionally, but against whom he also felt much personal spite. Accordingly he treated Florence like some strange talisman which should neither be touched nor left unguarded. He was intensely proud of her, watching his cronies with open distrust when they came to visit him at the apartment. (Such visitors were frequent, since this man was also engaged in some kind of illicit dealings, and had advanced himself from a position as bodyguard among some counterfeiters or smugglers to the point where he was managing enterprises of his own.) He would go for brisk walks in the early morning with her, and enjoyed having her watch him at the gymnasium while he trained—but if she expressed a wish to remain at home, he would lock her in her room, though hiring an old woman who sat with a key outside the door, to release her in case of some such unforeseen calamity as fire. It became a slogan with him that the night of his battle was to be the night of their nuptials. Yet as he entered the room following his victory, his face still besmeared with grime and blood, and as he tossed aside the robe he had flung about his fighting togs, a member of his gang ran in hastily to tell him that police were in the hallway. "You must not be caught here," he muttered—and then, laughing despite the occasion, he stuffed her into the dumbwaiter, piled old papers about her, and ran the car into the basement, from which she escaped to the street through a maze of dark alleys. She did not dare return to the apartment for some days, but when she did return, she found it empty and deserted, with the doors left open. An agent, on discovering her here, became suspicious, but she deceived him by making arrangements for a lease, and by giving him a few dollars of her scant funds as a deposit. She then left hurriedly, going to live in another section of the city. After some weeks she obtained a small part in a mediocre play, and has since then been bettering her position slowly. But in this revision of her former story, she made no mention of the man she previously spoke of having married.

Florence is a hunted thing, Anthony—so much in need of kindness that to gain a confidant she sacrificed a lover. I believe that towards the end of her story she fully realized her mistake, for she spoke faintly, with a mixture of illness and despair. But some vindictiveness on my part would not permit her this indulgence. I made her repeat each low-spoken sentence and fill out every innuendo, though I had understood her meaning perfectly.

"If we should meet again, Florence," I said to her, "I pray that it may be possible for us to recover the great intimacy of this evening" —thus, under the guise of a wish for our later reunion, suggesting that I took her departure without me as a matter of course. Several times I mentioned her leaving me, "I understand," I told her, "that in our advancing years the accidents of our position outweigh matters of emotion, however grave." And I even ventured to forgive her for placing such considerations uppermost, though I alone had brought this element into the conversation. I spoke cautiously, with much greater concern for her feelings than would appear from this summarized account, where I am emphasizing the purpose of what I said rather than my methods of concealing this purpose. And though I fear that my words caused her great disappointment, I am quite certain that I did not reveal any change of heart: I left her with the impression that I had assumed the transitoriness of this episode from the beginning. Indeed, I even spoke of the great gain in intensity due to its briefness—though I was aware of the fallacy in my statement and knew that, while any situation can be intense, the richest are those that grow out of long continuance. However, I felt sure that she would hold the more customary opinion in this matter and would thus assume that intensity is something caught on the wing.

Part Three

The wicked flee when no man pursueth (fugit impius,
nemine persequente).

Proverbs 28:1

I.

"Revealments that come of creation without revision"

He is prepared for the Next Phase, under the sign of a sink-ing signal. Ecstatic pilgrimage with Genevieve. The sponta-neous artist. A devouring of all experience, hectically. Stages: (1) the cult of stone (its self-violence); (2) natural places; (3) cities; (4) New York City—and vision of it sunk; (5) music in New York; (6) Bach's Passion Music in particular. How he induced Genevieve to accompany him. Rhetorical combats with those who had befriended him.

Though lives rarely have the conformity of entire plays, there are possible subdivisions corresponding to the acts of a play. A cycle or constellation of events separates itself from the general clutter—and since it can be classified, we can note its subsidence. The curtain descends upon a partial close, a converging or resolution of some factors. As I said farewell at the station, expressing my hopes of Flo-rence's return in words which formally concealed the permanence of our adieu, I felt that the fundamental concerns of several years had been rounded off and finished. It was because of Florence that I had

97

gone into this section of the country and attempted to reconstruct a new manner of living—so Florence had been primarily the force holding me here. She made me live as though there were a score I had to settle and living were a vengeance. My fear of her had been the beacon for me to steer by. But now many conditions which I had schooled myself to cope with, were reversed. I had been pushing against a great weight—and with this weight gone, I fell forward. While her train hurried down the valley, I experienced such gloom as terrified me. For even a life of bitterness was desirable as compared with a life without purpose. "You have no reason," I whispered to myself, "for doing any single thing."

Then with clownishness, I marched precisely, turning the words into a military rhythm, making a tune to fit at random, and centering my thoughts upon this arbitrarily invented conduct. For some time I engrossed myself in my mechanical attempt to ward off the growth of melancholy. But melancholy came, like the fog even then rising from the river. Slowly it gathered about me, quietly it sifted through me, and in its deliberateness it seemed as though it had settled here forever. Pausing at the trestle, I observed in the half-darkness the iron, and stone, and water. As I touched a cold rail I could still detect some vibration in it: but the arm of the nearby signal sank, showing that the track was free. "I will do only what I have to do," I said slowly into the emptiness, but I knew that this place would be henceforth unbearable. For some days I watched myself with distaste, waiting to learn the outcome of my struggle. And I could not have remained even so short a time as I did, except that my propulsion away from here was not matched by any attraction elsewhere.

Might I say, Anthony, that I put myself in other hands? For I dismissed the future. "I will stay if it is possible to stay; but if I leave, I shall leave as one obeying a decree." With this decision I became aware that a process of discovery was going on within me. I knew that I should, before long, feel definitely anchored to this spot or hear some firm, call to abandon it. The issue could be decided independently of me: there was a comfort in knowing that I should have only to wait until I was again clamoring for some specific thing. In the interim, I took an interest in chipping crude, unfinished shapes out of stone—dream-figures, obscene at times, or funny, or with various kinds of malformation which made them more detestable than pitiful. Then I would punish the grotesque things by smashing them with one blow of a mallet, though I do not know why I either made them or destroyed them. Thus imperceptibly a new certainty grew upon me. Even as I waited, it was already there, and gaining strength.

There is a serenity of stone, but I would have none of it. In the course of the hasty months that have intervened since the beginning of my new pilgrimage, I have hacked at stone with venom. Let granite be abused, I have said, until its relevant particles drop from it, and it stands forth, a statue. Here is weight for the muscles, hardness to the touch, dimensionality not suggested, but actual. Quick moods are transformed into the resistances and immobilities of gravitational mass. Men, angular, boxlike, weighted—women emergent, arched, melting back into the rock. Men striding vigorously, and motionless —women undulant, and motionless: abrupt actions, cataclysms; all violently changing things, made permanent at the point of crisis. It is astounding to see, hewn out, a movement of the muscles that would not, but for its presentation in our sound documents, ever have recurred.

The works remain uncompleted. We have vanished often, abandoning in hired rooms mute marbles of different shapes and sizes. We have gone away leaving corpseless cemeteries behind us. They are first drafts, in stone. They are the jottings of a notebook, aggregating tons. A little thing, a replica of herself, my companion brought with her from another city, but I hurled it from the window. One does not carry stone—one goes elsewhere, finding further stone to alter. During these recent months, in living and in art, I have sought the revealments that come of creation without revision. Noting how a work could be improved, I have made this improvement the subject of the work that followed.

Despite all I had labored for many years to accumulate by deliberate observation, I am now tapping some store which I had accumulated unawares. What I had watched, bewildered me; but what I had received without watching, fell of itself into a sequence. I had ceased to suffer the impress of the world and was, rather, giving out things from within me. Accordingly, I can better remember the quality of these months than their specific content. I can remember being in astounding places, but they were seen only on the fringes of my vision, as they jutted beyond the edges of my work. I can remember in a general way neat suburbs, melancholy areas where fields have become lawns and birds call among houses. I can remember that we looked down upon faintly peopled valleys, through a calm in which lie distance and death. I can remember stepping slowly into a lake, until my eyes were even with its surface, the water cutting across the eyeballs. I can remember dawns when my portion of the world turned like a sunflower to meet the day. I heard feathery things come forth, variously awakened, while furry things crept into their burrows (though I knew this rather than observed it, working as though mankind hungered for my burden, filling the room with disputes alien to the walls). And finally, I can remember cities, where we walked in the shadows of gulches, were belched upon by deleterious gases, and the very roots of our hearing were assaulted.

In the most strident of these cities, I now am. Mountains, softened with woodlands, weathered into gentleness, slowly yielding their drainage into the valleys, stand without the din of their construction—and so may this city some day stand calm and oblivious of its troublesome amassing. If it must sink to the bottom of the sea before peace descends upon it, may it sink then into deep waters, that subsequent races approach it from above and pry into dimnesses where we are now harassed by glare. Let me, to help them in imagining, here say that in the daytime this city shakes, but at night it hums and is full of secret places.

Why!—from this strident city there have risen sounds so frail, so miraculous and gently assembled, as to soften their hearers into pensive melancholians, for a time leaving them without aggression. I refer to its regiving of great music. Could we not cherish, and even encourage all harsh diseases of our living, if they can make these cautious sounds a medicament? Is it not fortunate that we need soothing, if this is how we are soothed? We are more than banqueted when the slaying of Christ is ritualized in erudite fugues and made elegant by rehearsal. A gorgeous Crucifixion, and surely attended by a greater throng than crowded upon Calvary. "It is finished: my suffering is finished," the basso mutters in his skilled mimicry of the Passion—whereupon strings and contralto linger on this fact, repeating in various ways that yes, the God-man yields, and we may yield. Note how, by eliminating their trivial moments, they have made themselves more ample—how the work, long pondered, comes upon us without the hesitancies and experiments of its inception. Adepts are employed, by threats and hagglings are instructed in duties, are assigned their places with all the clangor and vehemence of a smithy—and lo! out of fear, malice, rivalry, and ill-natured interruptions, is drawn forth the denial of all uncleanness, a broad flowing river of assertion, its parts united in one purpose as it moves steadily towards seas of the mind which lie in a vague remoteness, surging imperatively for this exceptional hour.

When I had known beyond all doubt that I could remain no longer, I went in search of Genevieve and persuaded her to come with me, not by arguments, but by answering each objection in the same words, with the same accent: "You must come." I induced her not by logic, but by corrosion. For some days we were unfamiliar to each other, which made me fear that she might still decide against me. So I talked much of the future, always assuming that she would share it with me, nor was I niggardly in picturing the pleasantnesses which I looked forward to. Finally, on our coming to a room in which there was a little organ, she played me the pieces she had learned when I was with her previously. I asked her to play me new ones, but at the sight of her disappointment I understood that this old music was a way of homecoming, and I hastened to be forgiven. It was on this evening that our strangeness fell definitely away. I surmised that often, while sitting with her husband, she had apparently sought to entertain him by her playing, but had in reality chosen such music as served to reconstruct, in his very presence, the memory of our former times together. Genevieve, how deeply I regretted at this moment the many inappropriatenesses I had forced upon you: that I should have appeared among poor rivals at a time when you were still unformed, and that I could thus by the mere accident of my priority permanently engage your faithfulness. Would that I could give you as much assurance and regularity as your attachment merits, and that I could have profited by you without bringing upon you the weight of this unwholesome paradox: for things being as they are, your fidelity must manifest itself to the eyes of others as nothing but the forsaking of an earnest and admirable man. I have heard of a beautiful woman who went about it daintily to kill her wealthy husband without detection. In this she succeeded, with the result that she was freed of an unhappy ogre and had vast sums to expend as she saw fit. Being a person of refinement, with the sorrow of this crime to prod her, she applied herself to the work of setting up a cultured way of life for many people. With each year she became gentler, more lovely, more skilled in making delightful arrangements for her friends. In the course of a long life she was able to give them such understanding of suavity as would keep them permanently lifted above their previous condition. Thus she had extracted sweetness out of a heinous act—in contrast with our Genevieve, whose virtues have led her into so much that is unpalatable. I will say in my behalf that I have imposed upon myself all possible strictures, that I have done only what I could not leave undone, and that no hungering man need defend his thefts. For we must treat as moral imperatives all acts of injustice that are unavoidable.

In Genevieve I am fortified. Genevieve, I tell myself, will take care of me. It was the thought of Genevieve that enabled me, when crooked people had befriended me, to insult them. She enabled me first to meet them, after my return to the city, and then to leave them with anathemata. Through her I could bring myself to accept the responsibilities of ingratitude—for how could I have been touched by their services without risking inclusion in their flaccid good fellowship? An attachment among them could persist only because they took indignities for granted. Or were they kept together through their secret detestation of one another, since each, in despising the rest, knew that they were his peers? There are many complexities that would, if taken into account, confound them—but being too blunt to discern these, they attributed their competence to mastery. Their luck they called talent. If they concealed advancement, it was not through modesty, but lest their friends ask too many favors of them.

One of them abused himself long after college, thus avoiding alliances until he had reputation enough to marry a person of means. Another, though puny and riddled with disease, would smooch a woman in a dark corner whenever the opportunity presented itself— and he was there upon the right occasion because he was there upon all occasions. Another, though he would turn in disgust from a juggler who dropped one of fifteen objects, would drivel in drunkenness, expecting the forbearance of every one. They helped him because he would not repay their assistance by using, to outmaneuver them, the point of vantage into which they had placed him. Not that he was kept loyal by his scruples, however, but by a general ineffectiveness. What he lacked in intelligence, he made up in temperament, and his deficiencies as an artist he covered by a splendid zeal for art. He took pride in his body, which was the caricature of itself. A fourth could be keen only by being frenzied, could be calm only by being lethargic, could show anger only by snarling and pleasure only by wagging his tail. A fifth would sit alone in his room, playing soft music and imagining excesses. A sixth had the convictions of a typewriter. Put it in Moscow, and it prophesies the dictatorship of the proletariat; put it in Washington, and it pleads for low taxes on high incomes.

There was also an expert in righteousness. He admired in his friends the qualities which, should the need arise, would enable one to fleece them, and in himself the qualities which would best equip him to do the fleecing. That is, in them he prized simplicity, gentleness, candor—and in himself a diligent using of advantages or, as he labeled it in his own mind, biologic fitness. He had learned how much one saves, and how reputably one saves it, by over-generous impulses. Through offering a bushel where a peck was lavish, he could end by parting with nothing. As for another: if his companions were walking on the right side of the street and he suggested that they walk on the left, and if they crossed to the left because they did not care which side of the street they walked on, he took their acquiescence as a concession to his authority. For when they treated him with friendliness, he preened himself upon his skill at handling them. He was proud of his clarity when he had little to be vague about —and if he made as much as three where the possible score was ten, he would give his opponent good advice. I did not resent his way with me until I saw it in a dream; for I had never really perceived it until then, when he exposed its workings in all their absurdity by displaying great distinction in the handling of a trivial matter.

They were frank when they found deception too strenuous, smiling when a smile made it awkward for an angry man to strike them, bubbling with attachment to old friends when their attempts to rise into other circles had gone amiss, and never so generous as when praise could be given in lieu of money. Find me a one of them who did not loudly champion justice, while banqueting in behalf of the starving miners—for they knew the value of goodwill, and would not so much as launch a new joke without first farming it out for one night to a Milk Fund. From them I learned that if all the loyalty, devotion, and self-sacrifice were taken out of life, there would still be greed and coxcombry to carry forward the world's best causes. They lacked enough for moderation to come easy—so they answered a loud man quietly, thereby offering a rebuke to him and to themselves a compliment. They would discuss with one another their grave concern for the good of mankind, but would grow black if a colleague, equally exalted, happened to use one of their mankind—saving sentences as his own. The one way to refute them was to cry *tu quoque*; for if you could show that their accusations against you applied to them also, you would be spared in the general amnesty by which they spared themselves.

I arose and exposed them all to one another. To each I delivered his formula, as though on a card registering his weight. To each in turn I shouted, "As for you—" and told him, with specific incidents as proof, wherein he was despicable. Whenever possible I used the words which one of his cronies had said against him—for though they were always carousing together with a show of great conviviality, they were as constantly belittling one another in whispers, with each trying to tickle the others' women unnoticed. They remained friends only because wolves run in packs. "Come, Genevieve," I said finally, and we swept from the room. What cleansing as we rushed into the street, to breathe the sharp night air—and how indebted I should feel to Genevieve, who strengthens me to live thus without compromise.

Does not this incident show, Anthony, that I had previously wronged myself? I had distrusted my own deprecation of others, suspecting always that it arose from either vindictiveness or envy. But how could I be vengeful, when these people were kind to me, helping Genevieve to support us in the city? And how could I be envious when I could not, in any important detail, select for myself a different life from the life I am now leading? If I wish for other things, I do so purely as one might wish to be here if he is there, or there if he is here—not as one might very earnestly plead, in sleeping and waking dreams and in unintentional puns, for something constantly denied him. In the past I had not done myself justice. I have been treated hospitably, I am not deprived, yet my despisals continue. Thus, since they spring forth without the provocations of a personal dilemma, since there is no canker of frustration discoverable in them, they are not a comparison, but a vocation. They occur precisely because my terminology best equips me to disclose them. So I must persevere, even at the risk of great inconvenience to myself.

Yet I could as easily have loved these people. As they stood about, half-minded to attack me, each enraged for some specific thing I had said against him though secretly in sympathy with what I had said against the others, I could not have repeated one sentence I had spoken. Even at this moment I realized that for any act, or any way of thinking, there is a tender word and a harsh word, equally applicable. Caution may be called vacillation, acquiescence may be called toadying, sturdiness may be called obstinacy. I knew there was deceit in my using the harsh words only—but unless we adopt a false position, we cannot get our truths stated. What I said was accurate because the zest with which I said it was a lie. In being more honest, I should have conveyed nothing. So, like a ventriloquist's doll, I suffered injurious remarks to rise unbidden to my lips. And I might have confessed as much to them, except that, even as I thought of it, I found myself stamping about the room in a fury and shouting for Genevieve to leave hastily with me.

II.

"Mad girl in white"

His jealousy of Genevieve. He experiments to test her fidelity. His jealousy flowers in his symbolic infidelity with a "mad girl in white." His perverse dismissal of Genevieve, and his curse upon himself.

When a casual word reminds a man of an injustice he has done the speaker two years before; or when one mentions a sect slightingly, only to realize immediately afterwards that a member of this sect is present; or when, in talking of a friend behind his back, we suddenly recall that our accusations apply likewise to the person we are addressing—such incidents are marked in an unavowed manner, by a starting up, or by a slight shifting of the eyes, or similarly. Yet, through being exceptionally alert to note when a tiny revealment of this sort has taken place, one may be more frequently misled than the sluggish. For he will feel the need of explaining a transient shade of embarrassment where the relevant information is not available to him, and thus he may fall into a false idea of motives when he could have been better guided through having observed nothing at all. It is accordingly no boast to claim for oneself skill in the uncovering of these subtleties—since one is more likely to find the right direction by striking off at random. For my own part, when I had grown uneasy about Genevieve, and felt that in some tenuous way she was turning from me, I was bewildered by a profusion of data which, though I knew they were symptomatic of something, I could not say symptomatic of what.

It disturbed me that she so often neglected to lock a door behind her, and that she left her little jewel case open. I became worried when she lay awake, for one who had lain awake as often as I, would necessarily fear that she was gnawed at—yet I was also worried when she slept, since in sleeping soundly she seemed to have gone beyond the stage of regretfulness. I was displeased at finding in her too many games and imaginings which were my own, tricks for making familiar places exceptional, jocular references to our separation, delight in the mild confusion of thinking the room turned backwards. "If she decides that my table should be repainted," I told myself, "I shall know that the arrows no longer point towards me." Yet when she did suggest that she be allowed to paint my table, her sweetness was unmistakable, and I secretly granted that if there was any centrifugality here, it could safely be dismissed. Though I knew that in all pertinent matters she would falter, I found it hard, in dealing with such secondary symptoms, to know what faltering was.

Perhaps, I feared, Genevieve does not have morbidness enough for continued loyalty. And since I have got no decorations, what can she point to when, in her thinking, she pictures herself praising me to other women? What was my right to her, when I have made no perfect thing? And how claim her with authority until I have been acclaimed? I found no valid reason why she should be attached to me —and though I might refrain from telling her as much in words, there are surely imperceptible means whereby I must convey this grim truth to her in spite of me. I had been reassured at the thought that she was used to serving me; for in being prompt to anticipate my needs, she became less likely to consider her advantages. She had taken crumbs of kindness from me so habitually that she might not know me for a beggar. "John Neal," I told myself gloomily, "if she but stamped her foot you would, deep within you, scurry away like mice." In returning to her after vicissitudes, I had proved myself subject.

How derive comfort from a woman's power to delight us when, this power coming from a reservoir of greater possibilities, she is adequate by being more than adequate, and the superfluity may take her from us? Are not women by nature kindly—and so would they not, were nothing else involved, incline to befriend each man that requires them"? And does their caution, their withholding, arise not from an abhorrence to surrender but from a desire simply to be as rare as the proprietary lover would have them? Will they, at least, transgress by the slight welcoming of anonymous and slinking suitors? The very forces that bring people together are, by continuing unchanged, also capable of taking them apart. And how if she had come upon a man who, less twisted than I, asked simply that she be wholesome and took it upon himself to supply all else that might be needed in their relationship? Knowing that I could excel in a comparison only by measurements of my own making, what guaranty did I have that Genevieve would not come to base her judgments upon codes more in keeping with other men? And was it not an unseemly state of affairs when the proof of her love for me was in the tears she had shed, and the proof of mine was in the hours I had lain awake, like living stone, endlessly what I am? I had watched, but I could accuse her of nothing. I remained silent through lack of evidence, but also as a rule of thumb: for it was my purpose to hold her, not to win in an argument—and in accusations between lovers, it is a privilege not to be victor, since one gains his point by proving that the other has mistreated him. Once, aghast at a slight disclosure which I have since forgotten, but which seemed overwhelming at the time, I boarded a train to a little outlying town, and spent the day walking swiftly along country roads. "It was a trifle, it was nothing, I could not possibly take offence," I told myself repeatedly, in all manner of ways proclaiming my lack of resentment while I pelted trees with rotten apples and stones.

I considered many aspects of the problem, devoting to it by far the keenest portions of my day. I recognized the blindness of my investigations. I knew that proofs so intangible could be interpreted only by grouping, making details indicative in the aggregate whereas none was indicative in itself—yet such grouping would require a principle of interpretation adopted in advance. And even if I did detect infractions, I warned myself, I should have little to build upon—since she might reasonably be forced into a slight margin of falsehood through trying, for my sake, to seem more demure than she was. "Does he not ask her to be shy enough for the two of them?" I taunted.

I knew a man who, suspecting his mistress of disloyalty yet unable to make certain, finally hit upon this plan: He spent an evening drinking with a somewhat hot-headed friend who was most likely to be informed. To this friend he boasted outrageously of the woman's adoration. "I have put a spell upon her," he said in drunken grandeur, and in various other ways gloried in his unusual prowess until the friend, irritated beyond endurance, leapt from his chair, hurled his glass to the floor, and shouted: "You braggart, I know it for a fact that the woman has deceived you!" I had neither the aptitude nor the opportunity to attempt this subterfuge, but I did in a dismal way experiment. In particular I touched Genevieve suggestively as she slept, calling strange names close to her ear, and cradling her gently. "He is gone now. I saw John Neal leave," I whispered to her. "Now we can be more intimate, because John Neal is gone," while I waited to see whether she would show some dream-sign of welcoming the speaker. I disguised my whispering as much as possible, though one cannot disguise a whisper greatly without absurdity, and I knew that an absurd whisper would be no test since it would not appeal to her in any case. Laying my hand against her, I increased and decreased its pressure in time with the motions of her breathing. At first she made faint efforts at resisting me; but later, to my chagrin, she acquiesced. Yet whereas I succeeded in inducing her to exhale in quick spasms, with her breath a tiny roar against the pillow, I did not know how to make her dreaming reveal itself more distinctly. I understood merely that she was agitated; but when both the sleeper and her tormentor twitched at the harsh sound of a horn in the street, I abandoned my experiments in shame and laid my head gratefully against her shoulder. If I have not been able, Anthony, to show wherein Genevieve is distinct, it is because I have applied myself to questions of motive rather than of character, and the same motive may be common to very different people, since anybody can do anything for any reason. I think that she could satisfy every need in me but the need of someone else.

I have not yet decided whether it is regrettable or fortunate, that precisely at the time of these disorders I came upon a mad girl in white. I saw her at a busy street corner, apparently engrossed in ravings of a pleasant nature, for she smiled and nodded as though answering very courteous statements. At first I had thought her speaking to some of the people that passed; but on watching more closely to see what sort she singled out, I became aware that her eyes were without focus, looking into a blur or an emptiness that had nothing to do with the irregular traffic in front of her. She was more odd than beautiful, with a litheness that was revealed in the set of her clothing. For some time she walked back and forth on the corner, never ceasing to respond graciously to the imaginary speakers that surrounded her. I happened to have with me flowers I had bought for Genevieve—and taking my cue from her manner, I presented them to the girl with exaggerated gallantry, saying: "These flowers were picked for you. I but perform my duty in bringing them to you." She accepted them without surprise, though she retained her air of pre-occupation, neither answering me nor looking at me. In a pleasant undertone, however, she thanked some cavalier of her fancy. I hastened to make other ceremonious remarks to her, suggesting above all the notion that we were conspiring together and shared important secrets. When she finally took my arm, I led her to a dingy hotel near the river, where I was not likely to be questioned, easily concealing the drabness of the place by whatever grandiloquent conceits occurred to me. The burden of our courtly conversation at last becoming too much for her, she fell silent, though walking about our room with great pomp. Henceforth no words were exchanged between us. We moved with pantomimic gestures, in deft retreatings and pursuit. I would at times turn from her, whereupon she came towards me; but as I relented, holding out my arms to her in stylized pleading, she would choreographically renounce me. My eyes becoming tactile, she should have felt them like light fingers upon her shoulders. When we left the hotel, I stepped into a bus with her, dropping back among the crowds on the street as it drove away. She took a seat by the window, and had turned her head towards the aisle in the belief that I was following, when another vehicle closed her from my sight. Thus she had vanished forever, with her flowing hair, and loose garments, and sinews correspondingly liquid. And I have asked myself: Was this incident the reverse of my uneasiness to do with Genevieve, or did the two have no bearing upon each other?

Oh, Anthony, I am bewildered by these matters, unfit as I am to distinguish between the unstable and the unchanging. I know that poets, to explain any man's excessive conduct, need but attribute to him the entanglements and proddings of jealousy. So much is undeniable, I had told myself: If a woman were long absent, and were sought by a brilliant suitor, and were befuddled by drugs, such convergence of allurements would surely overwhelm her, frailty under these conditions seeming so reasonable that my reliance upon Genevieve was basically shaken. Yet though mastery went from me, and I had been plagued with the fear of losing her, I became calm enough when I lost her in reality. "Hereafter there is no Genevieve," I repeated slowly. Far in the recesses of my mind, as a slumbering possibility, there was great anguish; but no part of me active at this moment felt disturbance. A lucky bewilderment helped me to shut away the thought of her, while I was also aided by my growing intimacy with a man I had met recently in a park. We began talking to each other after he had noted the title of a book I carried with me— and within a few minutes' conversation I had become convinced that he was exactly like me. "You are my alter ego!" I exclaimed. When it came time to leave, we arranged for other meetings here. Yet I would not let him tell me his name, insisting that I should know him as none other than Alter Ego.

Even now I understand, however, that the inconclusiveness of her departure must continue to act upon me. Finding ourselves without funds, I had sent her from our room, telling her that she could get us money from any man. And since I saw or heard no more of her, I can in no way construct her life from that moment. When she left, I regretted what I had said, and hurried to the street in search of her, but she had vanished. Yet I am sure that on leaving she had intended to return, for I cannot recall even a covert means of sealing her departure. And let me say, purely as though deposing, as though the words were being ticked by telegraph, that if I were not myself, but something that looked down upon this that was myself, I should brand it, I should in quietude put an effective curse upon it, I should corrode it with the slow acids of the mind.

III.

"Alter Ego"

Progress of the curse: concerning Alter Ego, who deserts him.
He returns to the country in darkness, but learns that he has
been erased there. Lonely return to the city.

Anthony, you the nominal recipient of these unsent letters, may I
who have so often attacked you, may I now in imaginings turn to you,
cling to you even, relying upon the simulacrum of you I carry in my
mind, wherever you may be, telling myself that one whom I have
addressed so constantly, under whose eyes in a sense I have lived, is
regardless of all insults my ally, telling myself that affection continues in the absolute, that there can be attachments underlying deep
rancor, and that my very altercations have given me some undeniable
claim upon you? Oh, I am sorry for every living thing. Could I not
go to you, show you these various items, and say, laughing: "Why,
look at all the harsh things I have been saying against you all these
years, while you have been going about the world, doubtless happily
enough. Isn't it comic, Anthony—eh, isn't it comic?" I can imagine
myself saying this to you, and imagine you considering the entire
matter without resentment; for inasmuch as you were never from
my thoughts, it is not important what I have said against you. One

generally has his profitable anchorage, his connections with ways of sustenance, his fireside moments among persons with whom he can feel easy. But those lines that go between a man and others, one by one they were severed—and we may get ourselves to that point where nothing short of genius or luck could uphold us.

I knew a dismal fellow who noted possibilities inexorably narrowing, who with the passage of each year had fewer cronies, less expectations, shorter respite, until he accepted the shelter of a companion much like himself, but moneyed. This man fed him, and said things that, because of the similarity between the two, delighted him. The first was John Neal, and the other we shall call his Alter Ego. But now Neal is quite alone, and I can tell for a certainty how Alter Ego would reassure himself. He would say that I could not suffer so much as I had in advance feared to, that accordingly his disappearance should serve as a relief in that it at least ended my apprehensions. He would say that he had but made the latent patent, the covert overt; he would feel sorry for himself that he, on this occasion, should happen to be the instrument of so natural a process. Into the silence of his room he would speak soft sentences, wishing me prosperity—and he would reproach himself only for not having left me sooner, before I had gone so far in growing dependent upon him. I turned him from me through being in too great need of him. What I should have taken offhandedly, I accepted with deep gratitude. And I had long been sure that my lack of separate strength would tell against me, for I knew that had he similarly leaned upon me I should have found him repellent. I would bring him things which I thought might please him, and sometimes they did please him—but my subservience became obvious to us both.

I cannot, in the light of my bitterness, retrace accurately the growth of our affection. I remember only that he slowly schooled me in the labyrinths of his mind, unfolding a past as desolate as my own, until I found myself looking forward with avidity to our next meeting. He told me of his fear that he would rise at a concert, during a pianissimo, face as much of the audience as sat behind him, and bow, saying: "How do you do, odd fellows." He described how, in earlier years, he had admitted vices he did not possess, and how he had made his confessions ring true by promising to renounce these vices in the future. "I can distinguish between a baby's cry and the cry of a cat," he told me, "by noting whether the sound makes me unhappy. If it makes me unhappy, it is a baby's cry; for it restores by a correspondence too deep for analysis the years of my fatherhood," though he never, at any other time, spoke to me of either his marriage or an illicit union. And he would not have it that his indulgent ways of living sapped him of any essential vigor. "With the fed and clothed and comfortably bedded," he insisted, "there arise new terms of difficulty, remote parlor equivalents to the resistances which mute forebears summoned to meet the inexorable advance of glaciers." In his study of mental maladies, he said, he realized how many valleys he had passed through, and was sometimes astonished at his survival— yet he felt that he was permanently protected through having, on two different occasions, watched a human brain rot like a carcass in summer. "Thereafter one could never permit himself that complacency with madness which is at the roots of all madness, for he could not consider such decomposition of his own gifts as in any way an effective rebuke to other men."

He was erudite in a certain kind of despair. "Some years ago," he told me, "I dreamed that while I was repulsing a woman, in twilight, two terrifying shapes appeared at a door. I commanded them to leave, but they would not—and when I attempted to plead with them, I was so filled with dread that my voice became inaudible. Then of a sudden changing my tactics, I threw my arms about the woman and laughed at them—whereupon they and the dream were gone. I awoke to find myself repeating with exceptional solemnity, as though the words were a holy text, 'Love and humor can rescue me from my specific dangers. . . . Let this be remembered as the advice of an expert.' I have since followed the advice scrupulously by observing its contrary, as befits the interpretation of a dream. I have avoided charity and humor, which enable us to shed our profounder responsibilities. In permitting ourselves the weakness of doing good for others, by the simplicity of kindnesses we are blunted to the complex. And humor shies at all fundamental risk, making our burdens tolerable by a contrivance which reduces them to trivial proportions." He had turned rather, he said, to the rigors of loneliness: "We may produce a monster merely by stressing some aspects of our nature and suppressing others—and loneliness is to be welcomed precisely because it encourages such stressings and suppressions. Accordingly, I have lived in solitude. I had so well learned to protect myself that I found it necessary to invent ways of placing myself in jeopardy, lest the best muscles of my mind grow flabby." At one period, however, when his tests had become unbearable, he answered many advertisements, that he might receive mail daily.

"I have no memory of my parents," he told me one mild evening after we had walked through the busier sections of the city, and were seated on a deserted stretch of green overlooking the river. "I was raised by a guardian who at times was very brutal to me, and at other times would come to me in tears, asking my forgiveness. Shortly before I was of age, this silent and unstable man became dangerously ill. Thinking he was on his deathbed, he called me to him and confessed to squandering most of the fortune which he had held in trust for me. He recovered, but I made no mention of the matter to him. I took over the remainder of the estate soon afterwards, and was relieved to find that at least there was still enough for me to live on. Except for brief conversations on very unimportant subjects, there was henceforth a complete silence between us. I never reproached him— and through not accusing him, I robbed him of a defense. It was the one form of retaliation left me." After a pause, he continued: "If you do not accuse a man for an unfairness he has done you, he will accuse himself—and since self-reproaches will go much deeper and be more accurately aimed than any attack from without, he will never forgive you. I was gratified to see this man, who now had no authority whatsoever over my resources, consume himself with an ineffectual vindictiveness. I believe that he practically withered away through hating me." And he went on to discuss the corrosiveness of the unavowed, telling me among other things an anecdote of an unbeliever he had known, with a pious wife. "He feared that she was praying for him— and indeed, at certain times of the day or night he seemed to feel the processes of her prayer. When she repeatedly denied that she prayed for him, and he had convinced himself that her piety would not permit her to misstate the matter, he became certain that she was praying for him without herself knowing it. In the end, the intangibility of the situation drove him to such lengths of brooding that he struck the poor woman as she knelt beside her bed, and he then went mad fearing the wrath of a deity whose existence he denied."

"But you have suffered times wherein the thought of you was nauseous?" I pled with him, for it was exceptional solace, when his thinking touched my own at so many points, to find still further likenesses in our experience. "I believe I have spent my life in the realm of detestations," he answered me. "And occasionally, that the rules of conduct might grow simple and decisions come easy, I have deliberately sought the approval of people I despise. One cannot take such measures until he has been thoroughly disgruntled with his own limits. I understand now, that when undergoing strains upon my self-respect, I was greatly assisted by the prevalence of Hebrews, who unknowingly bore the brunt of my difficulties. Regardless of how humiliated I might feel, in my belittling of this race I took on dignity. In calling a man a Jew, with fury, I was assuaged—for here was a dishonor from which I was forever saved. To denigrate him was to lift myself above him, not by the uneasy method of going off alone, but by the comforting inclusion of myself in a vast opposing band. So I should judge the presence of a discredited people very helpful to the thwarted and to those stung with a general rancor." Then taking up a stick, he began making figures in the dust. "Why, I was so thoroughly enmeshed that I would everywhere make the same representation of my dilemma, first an angle opening to the left ($\rfloor$), then an angle opening to the right ($\llcorner$), and then a line ($\_$) beneath the two, serving to join them; thus: $\underline{\rfloor\llcorner}$. On noting that I had for weeks been drawing this form on the margins of newspapers, in the air, and even by running my eyes along the edges of buildings to translate other designs into this one, I realized how deep-seated was the conflict I had expressed thus graphically, and how constant my need to resolve it." As I said nothing, he added: "Yet through dividing oneself into parts, one will be exalted in moments of their sudden reunion. Distrust is but the preparation for certainty—and when doubters have ceased to doubt, in certainty they give no quarter."

He was competent at the piano, often devoting many consecutive hours to moody pieces, at other times preferring music in which there was much ingenuity. One evening when we were in his apartment, and he had interpreted an operatic score for me with unusual zest, after we had drunk somewhat, seeing that we were alone, and not liable to be interrupted, like youngsters we toyed with each other. A few days later, he invited me to live with him, which I did until the time when he proposed that we take a short trip together. On returning to the city, he suggested that I go straight to the apartment and that he would follow me shortly. But when I arrived there, I found that all his furniture had been removed during our absence. And on a windowsill was a brief note from him containing money and explaining that he had vanished. Standing in the midst of this desolation, I recalled words he had said to me when we were last together in this room. "If there were some act," he had said slowly, "if there were some act, greatly degrading, I should go and commit this act, for the immoral alone have the true keenness of moral strivings. A thief is nearer to God than is any man of honor, because he is nearer to fear and nearer to the yearning not to steal. It is among the untroubled that virtue and religion perish." I understood now that when saying this to me, he had already decided to abandon me.

One tells himself: You are a clever fellow; you have talents; some women have liked to kiss you; you can, in various manners, battle. One tells himself: You are not fat, not generally abhorrent; you have had friends with whom there was satisfactory interchange. Not yet starving, not yet living in a hovel, not subject to the oppression of an alien conqueror, not greatly weakened by illness. One considers his assets, thus negatively, seeking to arrive at assurance by elimination. But there is good cause for uneasiness when one finds so late that he has accumulated nothing, that no material possession is his by the inertia of the law, and no person is bound to him by the habits born of long affection. Through being apprenticed to a shoemaker one ultimately becomes a master, but there are no outward signs to mark the degrees of our particular discipline. If we, in periods of respite, had trained ourselves to deny God calmly, and even reverently, perhaps we could be assured of our continued stalwartness when under stress. That one should live in such a way that he had with him these three considerations daily: madness, the Faith, and death by his own hand! Still, on seeing the moon rise over the city, I do not think of death primarily, but of that Chinese poet, long dead, who wrote of drinking alone in the moonlight. Many pleasant schemes of existence have vanished, as such well-written documents from the past can testify. Henceforth, Genevieve, I will deserve you (he will deserve you, that is, if you will not hold against him the negligible shred of comfort he had got for himself recently by talking in two voices).

Purifyings by ritual, relief by the utterance of a formula, contrivances whereby, after so many sentences, the supplicant becomes a new man, denying such untoward yesterdays as are still recorded in the upbuilding of his tissues—I will not allow that things can be so erased. I will consider all past happenings as preserved in the present; and what is to be undone, will be undone only by our heaping a vast future upon it. I will permit myself no subterfuges of silence. I will not yield to the irresponsibilities of the Faith, which comforts by dismissing all variety of problems in the lump. For each particular difficulty, let there be a new statement. Let us not allow the evasiveness of one reply, worded in advance, for everything. I will not put myself among those blunt praisers of God who say "Glory to Allah" when there is an earthquake, "Glory to Allah" when there is a rose, "Glory to Allah" when they are fed, and "Glory to Allah" when Allah's glory itself is brought into question.

Does this bold man terrify you, Anthony? Then know that he went on a secret journey recently, arriving at nightfall, making his way unseen beyond a rainy town, creeping across a lawn, and peering into the windows of his former house, where he saw his former wife quite clearly. Then he stepped along a wall, among wet flowers, to the front door—and though he did not dare strike a match, he felt in the darkness where an embossed nameplate with his name upon it had once been fastened. There was a nameplate here, which he could not decipher, but as he counted the letters by touch he could tell for a certainty that neither his name, nor the name of his wife, was printed there. He returned to the town, and that he might leave as stealthily as he arrived, he boarded the next train from the dark side of the station.

IV.

A story by John Neal

Progress of curse. It is told indirectly by a story that he writes about a lonely man and a dummy policeman. Written around quotations from Blake. Particularly towards the end, we see a close interweaving of the story and the narrator's personal situation.

Sept. 25

My dear,

All day I have been walking the streets in mild despair. In the late afternoon I sat on a bench in one of the small parks, and watched the sun sink. He too, in this mid-September weather, is mild and a little weary. His long debauch of summer has weakened him but I, except for a few miraculous hours not many months past, have known no strong passions to be weak from. Oh, half of my soul, *animæ dimidium meæ* as our bleary-eyed old Horace put it, let your affection for me do what my affection for myself could never do: let it lead you to forgive this indiscreet wailing. Without you to hear me, I have no one. Of all these millions of people, the single one who has shown me a spark of recognition is a wooden policeman in front of a cigar store nearby, a dummy if there ever was one. He and I are akin, for his waxen dignity, his benign officialdom, is as eternal, as hopelessly inalterable, as my mild despair.

But you see what unhealthy preoccupations I have fallen into. Lampposts, streetcars, gutters have characters for me, when people do not. And as a consequence, I cannot continue my work. I am subdued, and a little dazed. My uprooting has not given me the assistance we thought it would. So you must not delay much longer. For if an occasional quick breath of hope raises this burden of dismalness that is upon me, it is because I dare expect you. Yet I can promise you nothing, nothing but the abject tributes of one who loves you "like the little bird that picks up crumbs around the door," if I may quote again a passage from Blake which you have heard me quote so often. I have stood before the glass and told myself, "What claims do you have upon her? By what right could you ask her to come here?" If one must expect much to get a little, how can I encourage you to join me? For if attainments fall short of ambitions, and I dare look forward to nothing, what a ghastly result we have after the subtraction!

Yesterday, in spite of my loathing, I forced myself to work at the twelfth chapter, where my hero clearly sees the implications of his character converging upon him. The sort of life he has constructed is becoming inexorably apparent to him. He is lonely, my dear, even as lonely as I—and his loneliness will undo him. He has made himself a Mole, to learn what Eagles cannot imagine. A writer can, out of the depths of himself, invent but one new aspect of vice; no wonder that he prizes it greatly and dignifies it by having it cause the destruction of his hero. So in my behalf, the poor devil must suffer. We have allowed him to retain a kind of sullen optimism, an ill-natured praise of God, but I would not put any faith in the chances of either himself or his author.

Oct. 12

My dear,

If you have not received any letters from me for a couple of weeks, it is not because I have not written to you. No day has passed in which I have not devoted many hours to you. But I have always become ashamed of my complainings, and have destroyed them. Will she ever have us, I have warned myself, if we go on discouraging her with our self-doubts? I thank you that you have not scolded me for my silence. I worked doggedly all day today, despite the repugnance of the task, and succeeded in piling up eight thousand more sluggish words. (Eight thousand more, by count. Remember our Blake: "Bring out number weight & measure in a year of dearth." He knew this curse, through knowing so well the corresponding privilege:

"Every time less than a pulsation of the artery
Is equal in its period & value to Six Thousand Years,
For in this Period the Poet's Work is Done, and all the Great
Events of Time start forth & are conceiv'd in such a Period
Within a Moment, a Pulsation of the Artery."

I read him often now, our Blake. I marvel that he could invent such "Giant forms" as never were, yet could know beyond hesitancy how each one looked and how each one would have spoken. It is only in my letters to you that I am fluent—but these, in sheer self-protection, I must repeatedly destroy. My genius resides in loving you abjectly.)

Still, there are compensations. For I was exhausted, and I swear that I should never touch this desolate work again were it not that I must earn you, that I must make some visible thing which entitles me to you. I was exhausted, until my very tissues drooped with nausea. I fled from my room into the crisp fall air, hoping only for a physical recovery. But the wind attacked me, and I walked furiously, tingling. And of a sudden I understood that something more than mere bodily exaltation was upon me. "What does the damned book matter," I cried, "when she will soon be here to comfort me!" I felt again the prodigal ambitions of those days when you talked with me and pictured for me the future of both of us. You, I understood, would make my work prosper. And I felt so very good that on the way back to my room I could not resist one happy wink at my friend, the dummy policeman. Indeed, I did more than that. I noticed that on his pedestal he bore a message recommending a certain brand of cigar. I immediately entered his store and bought one. It was a wretched cigar, and as you know I don't care much for even good cigars, but I played fair, and smoked that cigar to the dregs.

> "Dear Mother, dear Mother, the Church is cold,
>   But the Ale-house is healthy & pleasant & warm,"

I sang to myself, the little vagabond did sing—for at the thought of you he had left the gloomy Church of his recalcitrant novel, to sit in the cozy Ale-house of his love. I did not mind my previous miserableness, since its cure was so thorough. And I was shamelessly indebted to you. If one has great distinctness, he will search long before he finds in another that sweet combination of traits which forms his precise complement—and if he finds her, is it not reasonable that he should think of her unceasingly? Oh, do not mistake me. In speaking of my distinctness, I do not hint at exceptional abilities. A man would be distinct with noses for ears. I mean simply that for each lack in me, you brought the corresponding fullness; that wherever I was in need, you had the fitting kind of charity. Thirst is a delight where there is water; where food is plentiful, hunger is a luxury. I did not now regret my particular ills, since they turned me with such avidity to you as the cure for them. You recall, in *Jerusalem*, the passage on Mary's love which we enjoyed so greatly, and how you would laugh when I insisted that with us the sexes should be reversed—me Mary, and you Joseph:

> "Then Mary burst forth into a Song: she flowed like a River of
>   Many Streams in the arms of Joseph & gave forth her tears of joy
>   Like many waters, and Emanating into gardens and palaces upon
>   Euphrates, & to forests & floods & animals wild & tame from
>   Gihon to Hiddekel, & to corn fields & villages inhabitants
>   Upon Pison & Arnon & Jordan . . ."

I felt this expansiveness of Mary. I felt as though I were pouring forth bounty—is that not funny, when I was silent even, had not even one sentence to offer, could show nothing more ambitious than my gratitude to you?

Nov. 7

My dear,

It would be a relief for me to think that for once I can write you about something other than myself; and I should be thankful for this respite were it not caused by the pressure of a topic equally repellent. How, *animæ dimidium meæ*, could you have confessed to me so casually that you found your interest in Blake waning? You still *perceive* his excellence, you tell me, but it no longer matters whether he is excellent or not. Has he himself not obliquely refuted you when, in his *Marriage of Heaven and Hell*, he reminds us: "Truth can never be told so as to be understood, and not be believ'd"? If his excellence has ceased to matter, then you have ceased to perceive it—and where am I to turn, who realize only too well that the very foundations of our union rest upon Blake? If there was one event of great import in my life, it was the day in Altmann's meadow when we read *The Everlasting Gospel*, with its sublime doggerel so helpful to us in our uncertainties at that time. For it enwrapped our humble desires in a gorgeous vocabulary, making us feel that not merely you and I, but all Mankind and Womanhood, were on that day approaching each other. We were encouraged to scorn a law "writ with Curses from Pole to Pole," were told that God himself is no more than man, and that "Mary was found in Adulterous bed."

"But this, O Lord, this was my Sin
When first I let these devils in:
In dark pretence to Chastity
Blaspheming Love, blaspheming thee."

You, to my astonishment, paused to repeat these lines. I was terrified at your sudden lewd promise, stated thus with the authority of a great poet, and I myself begged you to put me away until I should make myself more worthy of you.

So consider, my dear, how much you would take from us by this moody heresy. Let us admit no "idiot Questioner" in matters of such great moment to our relationship. And you should not protest at my homage. How could you in any way feel yourself "absurd" when I write you as I do? You should find it only natural that I praise you diligently; you should receive me amply, and think no further.

Yet I have been more disciplined than you would suspect. I have spared you all the letters I wrote you following the announcement of your delay. I had bought tickets for the opera, which I could ill afford; but that I might not be there wholly without you, I did not turn back the ticket to the seat which you would have occupied. Thus by my subterfuge, in your very absence you were somehow with me. "The weak in courage is strong in cunning"—and I have contrived many tricks of thinking to help bear me up.

How pleasant, after the strained hours I had spent recently in the coercing of my story, to place myself at the disposal of a master, to let him dictate when there should be risings and when subsidences. I assisted him—and together we mounted to assertion, capped by kettledrums. And as another evidence of my cunning, I left the theater before the close of the performance, I went away while the violins were repeating a design in unison, ever more softly, and the stage gradually darkened, suggesting the submerged castle of a fish bowl and the mighty distances discoverable there by peering. I left before the end that I might carry away the sense of the opera's continuing— and for several hours afterwards it seemed as though that vast battle were still in progress. I went from opera sounds to street sounds, but the imperiousness of the music was still strong in me, and every casual noise was translated into the perfect note most like it. Thus the discordant city sang melodically and contrapuntally. Were I a charitable deity, looking down upon what was there myself, if I were such a deity, observing that hollow replica, and concerned with nothing but his particular respite, I should have said: "Strike him down—let him at this moment cease." And if there is disloyalty to you in such a thought, take it as the one sign I will give you of my discouragement at your delay. Oh, I am tired—tired of trying to deserve you, tired of writing you so constantly and so unmanfully. May you come soon, to repair, all this—may you come, that I may nestle against you, and repeat then with comfort:

"Ah! gentle may I lay me down and gentle rest my head,
And gentle sleep the sleep of death, and gentle hear the voice
Of him that walketh in the garden in the evening time."

Jan. 19

Please do not hold it against me that I was so long in answering you.
You will understand me when I say that I had to wait for a little competence. I had to find such a way of writing you that I should not
pain you either by vindictiveness or by too greatly appealing to your
pity. I could not write to wish you well until not only my words, but
the man writing these words in his empty room, could wish you well.
And in all fairness, I must agree with you as to the wisdom of your
choice. I did not hold out a very encouraging future to you.

"Damn braces. Bless relaxes." Yet I will not equip myself against
you by venom. I will tell myself always that you were sweet, and thus
I shall remain unfortified. For if I hated you now, how could I continue to love you in the past—and for me not to love you in the past
would be an impoverishment beyond endurance. Oh yes, I will not
deny that for some weeks the Undersigned has been a "Male Form
howling in Jealousy," his Emanation torn from him. He "furious
refuses to repose." He has the disconcerting documents at his finger-
tips, recalls that "the nakedness of woman is the work of God," that
"Women, the comforters of Men, become their Tormentors & Pun-
ishers," nor can he dismiss the recollection of a lovely twilight when,
after the two of them had walked for many miles, and had eaten the
supper he carried in his knapsack, they nestled together under birch
trees. He needs but imagine another in his place, and the picture is
circumstantial enough. "Dip him in the river who loves water." Yet
not Blake, but you, have taught me not to invite disaster.

"The Hermaphroditic Condensations are divided by the Knife,
The obdurate Forms are cut asunder by Jealousy and Pity."

Of jealousy I have spoken. I know that in jealousy the world is lost.

Yet jealousy is but incidental to deep single love; it is the risk, not the essence; and if the world is lost in jealousy, in deep single love the world may be well lost. The possibilities of delight were worth the eventualities of torture. As for pity, though there is a division in pity, and though I had sworn not to ask for pity, I shall be content with pity. I shall tell myself that you have not ceased to worry for me. Thus I shall relinquish a great deal that I may salvage a little, for one should not try to save too much in a fire. Oh, I am caught in the "mind-forg'd manacles," though in this case they are not the manacles of reason, but the manacles of a relentless, unreasoning memory.

I know of a man who, in a moment of blind self-interest that undid its own purposes, had sent away a lovely woman. Needing money, he had suggested sullenly that she procure some as best she was able, yet there had been much delicacy in his possession of her. She left the room without reproaching him, but he never saw her again thereafter—and with each succeeding month he understood more bitterly the destitution he had brought upon himself. He found that she alone had upheld him, for there was no pliancy in him that had not come from sources within this woman. He remembered how they had crept together, with the city roaring about them like a monster; how he had felt the warmth of her while she slept, as though they alone were spared from a cataclysm, as though all mankind, torn by madness, were fleeing from danger, while they lay safely in sweet segregation, enclosed in the Ark of their four walls, and the torrents of the metropolis pounded outside their windows. But the room had since become barren of her—so he grew humble, he grew really pitiable, and I was very sorry for him, particularly as I saw a feeling of strangeness and loneliness come over him, and I knew that by his very need of companionship he drove people from him. There seemed no way of rescuing him, for if someone spoke to him easily, he would promptly whisper to himself, "See, the man felt no strain in addressing me," and in thinking such thoughts he would betray them to the speaker, who then felt uneasy, and shied away at an excessive leaping-up of gladness. Let us hope, my dear, that I do not, in my own way, gradually lapse into this man's strangeness—but I fear lest all that smiled readily in me has been taken from me.

I enclose, along with my felicitations, my unfinished manuscript. What cause could I have to plague myself with it further? It was meant purely to earn me certain privileges which are no longer available. With this I say good-bye. And that you may not think me wholly alone, I say good-bye also in behalf of the wooden policeman, who must know something about you since he has stared his paint-stare directly into my eyes. I shall write you no further. I have not the slightest notion what I shall do next. I shall vaguely advance—and perhaps, by the subterfuges of the cowardly cunning, I shall have nothing more real than the wooden man for my grotesque crony, as I go towards the tangled and uncharted, into

"Realms
Of terror & mild moony lustre, in soft sexual delusions
Of varied beauty to delight the wanderer and repose
His burning thirst and freezing hunger!"

Henceforth I shall at best be one of those "that live a pestilence and die a meteor and are no more."

March 8

To my dear dead Mistress,

I did, it is true, promise never to write you again. But surely you will allow me the harmless pleasure of a make-believe correspondence, writing letters you never receive, and answering letters you never sent.

Well, it has not been so painful as I had feared, this being deprived of Emanation, and cursed by Selfhood. With the unfinished manuscript I sent you, the bafflements of fiction have ceased, and now I roam about devoid of any such grave responsibilities. One tramps streets of dirty, half-melted snow, observing the minor incidents of traffic. In sitting among audiences, and looking in the same direction with them, one feels not wholly outcast. I read but seldom, even Blake I read but seldom. The Ariel-like songs run through my head occasionally, but I am not, at this time, so greatly attracted to his mythological pieces, with their clangorous forge-music, "uttered with Hammer & Anvil," their cosmic lamentations, their accounts of vast Beings' wombs raped vastly, their torrents, violent awakings, earthquakes, rebirths. Such fountainheads of poetry are not wholly germane to my chief problems at present. I have heard of people who found it impossible to prevent themselves from counting numbers, and continued long into the night, in anguish, piling up their involuntary sums. Similarly with me, the idea of the dummy policeman has come to be troublesome. Perhaps I should take a room in some other section of the city. For this absurd figure stands too prominently in my path. With a life so uneventful as mine, it becomes too much of an event for me to pass him. And even while sitting in my room, as let us say on some snowy night when I have no intention of going out, I keep thinking of him on the street below, with stolidly upraised hand, the sleet curving about his pedestal. There is nothing particularly unpleasant in the thought of him except its constancy. And I can assure you: he is so unchanging, that to think of him repeatedly is to feel the mind inexorably rigid. To consider him against one's wishes is like maintaining a constant muscular tension. So you may, before long, find me in retreat from this grotesque danger. If he continues to claim more of my attention, I shall certainly take a room in another section of the city.

March 28

My dear dead Mistress,

One reason the figure has taken such a hold upon me is that I have had little opportunity to bury its effects beneath more natural kinds of relationship. Seeing a child in a carriage, I took advantage of its ignorance to wheedle a smile from it—and the mother came near me hurriedly, meaning no insult, but clearly nervous at finding me so close to something she thought precious. A sweet woman once took delight in the touch of me, and I sat in many ordinary places conversing with strangers readily enough, and people did not think it odd—but now I can approach no human thing without remarkableness.

Two young men recently sat on the same bench with me in the park. They seemed like students, and from their conversation I knew that their studies were of great import to them. Thus I felt I could tell them things which might somewhat engross them; but when I spoke, though I quoted good authors in order to make my equipment apparent to them in my opening sentences, they showed clearly that they resented my intrusion. The far one uncrossed his legs, so I knew that the boys would leave me as soon as possible. I talked hastily to them about the vicious circle, calling it both "vicious circle" and *circulus vitiosus*, using the Latin that they might know me for no ordinary man on a park bench, and the English lest they might not understand the Latin. "I am in a vicious circle," I said in haste, for they were growing shifty. There are accounts of such vicious circles in folklore, I explained to them, as stories of a once handsome prince locked up in a repellent form. "These are stories of the vicious circle," I told them, "for the Prince will not be freed until the love of a beautiful woman has freed him—and how, short of magic, can a beautiful woman love him until his true form is revealed?" But I had made them very uncomfortable, so I turned abruptly and went away from them. Surely they smiled to each other behind my back; yet had they made friends with me simply as an oddity, and admitted me into their lives on any terms, if only as a king might keep a dwarf or a parrot, I should gradually have been reclaimed. Of this I am certain.

April 3

My dear dead Mistress,

I am a little frightened today, for the rigidity of my existence is unquestionably beginning to tell against me. If one were to make his hand into a fist so tightly clenched that the whole arm trembled, and were to translate this feeling to mental things, he could imagine somewhat how my mind is. It is as though my mind had muscles, and these muscles would not relax. The steadiness of my preoccupation causes this feeling of muscles under tension. It is as though the pulpy substance of the brain were turning into muscle, and these muscles were straining to tear apart their own tissues. This feeling is clearly the result of a tension caused by a changeless image which I cannot dismiss. But just as the eye accommodates itself to blinding lights, or the skin gradually learns to withstand heat of great intensity, I could probably make myself sufficiently at home under this discipline, did I not have a fear that its severity is growing. I had become competent enough—but today, when I passed my policeman, a quick impulse seized me, and before I knew what I was doing, I had spoken to the policeman. I wish I had not done this—and I should not have done it had I been aware of the temptation in advance. Just as though he were alive, I smiled at him and spoke. I was passing directly in front of him when, to my astonishment, I heard myself saying, "Hello, Joe." I could have done the same under happier circumstances, but the meaning would not have been the same. It is quite natural to address inanimate things—it is no more foolish than confiding secrets to a dog. But as I looked about apprehensively, I saw that a woman had observed me. She was pretty, and insolent, and was watching me intently. There was no kindness in her eyes, nothing but cold curiosity. Her eyes, my dear, passed a terrible judgment upon me. And to escape her judgment, I repeated my greeting, this time leaning back, squinting, and waving my hand, as though I had been speaking to some one in the recesses of the store—but now I noticed that the clerk inside, with a bewildered moonface, was staring at me glumly. I am now bending beneath eyes, the wooden eyes of the policeman, the cold curious eyes of the woman, and the glum eyes of the clerk inside the store.

April 7

To my dear, dead Mistress,

My life is a funnel—and with each day I am squeezed farther into its narrow end. This morning, with a strange assurance, I leapt from my bed, dressed, and hurried down to the street, just that I might pass the policeman and show myself that I could pass him without speaking. I did pass him without speaking, without even a desire to speak to him. But when I had returned to my room, a voice said to me, "Could you pass him again without speaking?" So I went down and passed him again. Five times today I have passed the policeman, to convince myself that I need not speak to him as I pass him; but each time, as I go back to my room, the doubt returns.

Now, it has occurred to me, why should I not speak to the policeman? I have been plagued by the conviction that I should not speak to him—and the obvious way of overcoming that is to let oneself speak to him. I had made a new temptation by making a new crime—and I shall remove them both at once. Hereafter, if I happen to desire to address the dummy, I shall do so. I shall speak to him as often as I please. And as a precaution against cold curious stares of unsympathetic women, I shall speak to him covertly, from the corner of my mouth, behind my handkerchief, or by hiding my mouth with my hand as though I were scratching my nose.

MEMORANDUM: Rules to Self: If a person whistles or calls, give no evidence of hearing. The signal was not intended for you. If children begin shouting, do not quicken your pace. The shouting has to do with some game of theirs. You are dressed like every other man that passes along these streets. If strangers in the city stop to ask you directions, act as though you spoke another language and did not understand them. You know by now that when they ask you questions, your knowledge of the commonest streets will vanish from your memory. So avoid embarrassment by acting as though you could not understand them. Never stop beside someone who is looking in a shop window, if he is alone. For you know how it irritates you when you are standing alone looking in a shop window and some one stops beside you and begins looking at the same things. If you decide to go the other way, try to remember not to turn suddenly—for likely as not there will be some one behind you, and his face will be thrust directly into yours.

April 8

My dear Mistress,

No, you are not dead. Praise God, you are not dead. When I finally need to do so, I can really write to you, can actually mail one of these letters to you. So you may soon be hearing from me in reality, for I may need your help, I may have to call upon you to end a certain process. Today it seemed that the policeman actually acknowledged me in passing. I know that the policeman did not speak to me. It was probably some chance street-sound that was interpreted, by my tired body, as a voice coming from him. And it was probably a mere quiver of my eyelids which made me imagine for a moment that his lips moved. Besides, any rigid thing, if watched intently, will seem to stir. Who has not, on observing a statue or a corpse, seen the breast heave in respiration? When the dummy seemed to stir for a moment I was not frightened. But a second later, apprehension came over me. I looked about—and as I had feared, the cold curious woman was eyeing me, and passing the same judgment upon me. Oh, I am very tired. I should like to fall into a deep sleep, and on awaking, find every single thing around me altogether different.

I said that I could write you? On the contrary, I must not think of writing you. Probably it was the weakness of these make-believe letters that first started me on my course into the funnel. I must put myself under severer rules. I must deny myself all these little subterfuges which pamper me. This is the last word that passes between us.

V.

"In partial recapitulation"

A selective, and amplified, review of his life.

There are, underlying the Church, many ingenious heresies so thoroughly silenced by the sword that they survive only in the refutations of the faithful. There are subtle schemes deriving the best of human insight from Cain, or centering salvation upon the snake, or lauding the act of Judas Iscariot which procured for uneasy mankind a God as scapegoat. To look back upon them is to consider a wealth of antinomian enterprise expended in ways which seem excessive, troublesome, and unnecessary, their gratuity being surpassed only by the same qualities among the orthodox. But let one not be misled into thinking that the heresies have perished. They rise anew, changing their terms each time, to stand against the new terms of the Faith, squarely. Their doctrines need not be handed down jealously from generation to generation, but may be neglected without risk of loss. Our Bulgars require but the spirit of their cause, a spirit which takes form by the form of the current dogmas, knowing what not to accept by noting what is accepted. Oh, lepers of mankind; gutter-rats; printers in the sewers; you the pale with prison pallor; the discredited, the unprosperous, you who can make no answer, for your voices

134

are drowned by the roar of the believers (they need not refute you, they need but restate to one another all that they had already said, humiliating you by thinking of their own plans and singing among themselves); you the worthless, the salt-smugglers, the bringers of illicit drugs to comfort the unhappy to whom the moneyed would permit not even chemical relief; you the thieves, who outrageously disturb the security of the privileged; you the insidious promoters of subversive doctrines which would allow the starved to nibble some- what at the world's plethoric stores; you who are gnawed by misgiv- ings, who would gladly renounce your own bitter birthright, gladly take your place among the exclusive, scorning your old companions, turning from oppressed to oppressors (and thus, precisely in your state of rebellion you uphold their systems, considering your insight wickedness, yourself admitting your degradation, yearning for acceptance by those very persons against whom you are pitted)—oh, you in every manner unequipped, you the deprived of logic, the improvident, the indolent who cannot strive for such crooked kinds of happiness as those in authority would force upon you—all you disheartened, discountenanced, disorganized—I salute you, for if there is to be a remedy, this remedy will come because you have made it imperative.

Some years ago, in this very city, I stepped lightly through a door leading to the street—and as I walked vigorously away, triply elated with liquor, a sense of futurity, and the briskness of the autumn weather, I felt no quarrel with anything this city stands for. Why should I complain at the rules of a contest in which I seemed likely to do well? True, I had doubts about the standards by which achieve- ment would be rated, but I felt that one should first be successful by the criteria of other men before setting up criteria of his own. Let him make money, that is, before railing against wealth; let him get reputation before calling all reputation worthless; whatever he would renounce, let him first acquire it in ample quantities, that he become immune to hecklers. The weather, as I have said, was crisp, and I was young and slightly drunken, and still buoyed up by the good out- come of some financial dealing, and I smiled negligently at a woman, not needing her since a woman even then was awaiting me. I could regret a plague in India, or sigh that some men went hungry, but I was prepared to take all this with resignation, feeling that our fate is but the tossing of a coin, and relieved that I happened to be on the favorable side of the toss. Entering another building, I rode to a high floor—for one must go up into high places to be tempted—and from here I surveyed the jumble of the city. Ah, Anthony, perhaps I have since been better than I thought. For did I not put every action beneath questioning? Though I may too often have ended in a sanction, I can assure you that the question was what mattered. I devoted my best efforts, not to making myself more effective in some given purpose, but to a weighing of this purpose. If I spoke much of fitness, and seemed at times too shrewd in profiting by the simplicity of Genevieve, I swear that this was but a flare-up before extinction, as men do not study folkways until these folkways are passing. At great inconvenience I maintained the integrity of my character, often choosing to grow sullen where I might have dismissed a dilemma by laughter—laughter, which leaves us untried, which is a stifler in the interests of comfort, surrendering in advance, renouncing prior to excess, enabling a man to avoid the ultimate implications of his wishes. I put Genevieve from me, not because our relationship was faulty, but because I had to put some dear thing from me. And if I showed great adulation of prosperity, be it prosperity in matters of health, money, or affection, I did so because I felt great prosperity necessary to equip the body for the strain of investigation and possible insight.

I did things. At the time of doing them I told you why I did them. And now, if I assert that I did them for other reasons, by what authority can you say that I was then correct in my analysis and am wrong now? You must hear me out, when I can observe my course through a considerable stretch of time, can verify and correct earlier tentative calculations, can better know what I was making for, by seeing what I have come to. Consider with what difficulty one would go about it to attain something he very much desired. Add to these obstacles the exceptional burdens of my particular character. Add further that I could think of no specific end towards which I would undividedly strive or the attainment of which would give me sound satisfaction. And thus you see how I was buried, three layers deep. If one questions the beliefs of other men without having well-grounded beliefs of his own, he will find himself deficient by any scale of measurements.

Though no one would choose failure, we may yet maintain that failure is a choice, since one may persist in attitudes which make his failure inevitable. Yet, I have fondly pictured groups of citizens coming to reward me, entering my room while a band plays in the street below, and announcing, "The time is over," thereupon presenting me with testimonials of their respect and explaining that they have picked me for some minor office. I should work hard, I should justify their confidence fully, I have told myself—yet I have never made the appropriate efforts which would prepare me for distinctions of the sort. Place a man among these streets, instruct him to choose some act which puts a strain upon his temper. What work will he perform here, if it is work in the absolute, and not the accidental matter of flunkeying to an employer? If he does not mean by work the earning of a little money through assisting in a superior's blind purposes, but the straining of his resources, what manner of living must he choose? What indeed but risk, risk of imprisonment, of disease, of ridicule? How be called muscular if you did not prefer the sewers and rat holes of the metropolis? If you are able in ways that bring you no advantage, would you admit yourself unable? Choose rather the dignity of a savage chieftain, which coexists with vermin. What did Alter Ego say? "There are many kinds of effort," he said, "which people without spirit and without physical enterprise are best equipped for, just as cockroaches are more likely than tigers to flourish in sinks." While I hesitated, buyers and sellers had faith—and though their faith is such that it ultimately brings the world to hell, it will have brought them privilege and power in the interim. Die as a mangled wasp dies —its body hunched, its wings futile, but its sting groping viciously for its tormentor. Prowling about the wharves, I have ministered to unclean men, for in this there was some ghastly decency, something beyond mere safety.

Oh, there is a revolutionary unction. There are the blasts of the well fed and well entrenched, comfortably summoning the people to rebel, calling for the destruction of a system built for bankers, and all the while they are bolstered up with stipends from the bankers. They are the bankers' conscience—and in proportion as the bankers gain further questionable wealth, so will these consciences of bankers be generously treated. But note that they make their protests more picturesque than malicious, and can be kept about the house like castrated lion whelps, providing a certain edge of excitement but no serious danger. Are they fostering defiance, or milking a cow?

Let me, in partial recapitulation, recall that, all my life, I chose unerringly. How, at the farmhouse, I went alone to the stables, that you might walk with the girl by the river; how I procured for you the part as Alcæus and for Florence the part of Mary, thus enabling you to transfer these flattering rôles into your relations with each other; how I schemed to my detriment in the matter of keys; how, on the island, I industriously made myself repugnant; how, when I had fled and had earned modest distinctions, I refused to please myself with them, but still lamented and imprecated as though I were generally looked down upon; how I was careful to eschew any permanent elation at Florence's return; how I vilified a group that had befriended me; how I saw to it that Genevieve, who could comfort me, was driven from me; and how, though I anticipated the results, I permitted Alter Ego to understand my dependence upon him, until he vanished. Know me, Anthony, as a man whose purpose never wavered. Through living under difficulty, one learns the mode of thinking, feeling, and acting best suited to cope with difficulty. No wonder he prizes a discovery which he has made at so great inconvenience to himself, and will not relinquish it but calls upon it to maintain precisely those adversities which it was at first designed to remedy.

Let us consider the matter in this wise: Take as a hypothetical case John Neal, a somewhat quarrelsome fellow who was ingenious in the cultivation of an illness not yet completely catalogued. I, had I met him, could have made proper allowances for him; but others had no cause to do so, especially as he was without authority, and kowtowings on their part would have gone unrewarded. Where they might have felt nothing, he forced them to resent him a little; and when he had made them resent him a little, he lay awake calling for their forgiveness, calling so frankly, so unstintingly, that by morning the cycle of contrition had run its course, and on next seeing them and finding them still resentful despite his unavowed beseechments, he was annoyed, and sought to punish them for their uncharitableness, thereby adding to their resentment. Subsequently, as the result of this process, our John Neal was without cronies. And at this point he prayed, calling upon that Name which heretofore had been for him an oath.

He prayed under no mean circumstances. For he had left the city, had gone to a little hut on a hilltop, and was living there alone, feared by the children of the nearby village though I can assure you that he would not have harmed them. A stifling August twilight had been converted, by sudden clouds, into a blackness without direction. A storm of vast proportions had let loose against the hut, which shook, for it was a little Ark, and outside was such a chaos as beat upon the Ark. That night a battle was waged. There were two storms that night, one at the roof, the other in a lone man's brain. I believe he knew the fertility of madness, the estimable range of madness. Alone in his Ark he cried out, calling for his former friends as though they could ride upon the storm. Suddenly the door was wrenched open—he leapt forward, "I greet you, damned demons!" he shouted, then closed the door hastily, shutting out the rain-laden wind, and leaving nothingness within. Mountains of thunder were piled up and toppled. The lightning, which made a licking sound, was crowded by new flashes. And all the while he called down violence upon him, demanding greater and greater extravagance of the elements. In the morning, when this intense effort had subsided, and the sun, as seen from the hilltop, rolled above a sea of mist, he walked beneath dripping trees, across a field mowed recently, down to a little lake which lay like glass beneath pink mist. Here he found nine cranes, pure white, their great whiteness making their silence deeper silence. He approached them with caution, with no abruptness of movement, for their timidity was multiplied by their number, all being sensitive to the misgivings of each. Eventually they arose, and with adjustments of the group they disappeared above the trees. Thus, after fury came white gentleness, and he understood that a sign had been vouchsafed him. He knelt, while love poured from him, or poured into him from all outward things—and to his vast astonishment, he heard words of

139

prayer issuing like missiles from his lips. For a manner of under-standing, unsought for, had blossomed within him.

With each moment the universe is new created, each succeeding tick of time presenting the same alternatives: Will all life vanish in oblivion or will it be divinely prodded to continue into one further modicum of future? The following moment of existence comes; the universe still flourishes, not revealing in its magnificence that it has been spared by a mere choice between God's acquiescence and His refusal—whereat again there is the risk: Will all life be sustained, or will it lapse? God the Creator as God the Eternal Re-creator, with the universe suspended by a thread of prayer rising from human lips. If that day comes when all humanity is busied with its prosperity in human terms, and the miraculous thread of prayer is broken, then will our ingratitude have snapped the continuity of existence. In ages of dwindling piety, let adept worshippers keep long vigil, lest there arise a fatal moment of lapse when no thread of prayer joins us to our vital sources and the props and underpinnings of the universe are thus removed. Of those few earnest men scattered across the world, when all but one have fallen in exhaustion and are sleeping, upon the shoulders of this one alone is born the full weight of universal life. So it is good that some men are scorned by their fellows and made to feel homeless among them, since these outcasts are, through their sheer worldly disabilities, vowed to graver matters and could not, even if they would, prevent themselves from pouring forth their neglected love upon a formidable Father. By their very inadequacy they are shielded, being led back to God if only through their incom-petence at betraying Him. So we may say that a man's sufferings are not unused if they but bring him to extremities—and by lone anguish on a hilltop, while storms tear at the walls of a house and the walls of a human mind, snug homes in valleys are kept secure. Those who were crucified were but erecting mountains of prayer, masses to carry beyond the subsequent moment and serve perhaps through centuries of silence.

Then John Neal, in choosing difficulty, was not acting without purpose? In his lying awake there was a preparation, in his selecting of misfortune an apprenticeship? Only those persons of pale desire are balked, and if they tell you how earnest and continuous are their hopes, talk with them a little further, until you see how soundly they sleep, how without discipline they glut themselves, how they do not compel themselves to walk at night in a bitter wind, how they do not take lighted matches and burn themselves for having made a faulty rejoinder, how they do not grow thin with study and admonitions. Thus they will reveal the falsity of their assertions by the flaccidness of their living. So I will not agree that this John Neal was denied what he desired. Throughout the tight continuum of the universe, what uncomplemented thing is possible? Need and fulfillment are one, as bursting cotyledons and laden stock are one, germination and fruition being aspects of a single happening. That which causes cannot act without that which is caused, whereby the prior is evoked by its consequences. The doing, the need of doing, and the done are indistinguishable. If some fulfillment of importance is to be granted us, this fulfillment is foreshadowed as a need. A yearning is but the premonition of an end. Seeing the ground thirsty, the leaves parched, dust-covered, drooping, the brooks sunk beneath their pebbles, we see the origins of a downpour. There is no cry for rain in a desert; there is a cry for rain where storms are brewing. Our complaints are the adumbration of a coming proficiency; in greatly suffering a need we but sense the earliest evidences of a fulfillment; I would not say that those who call out are answered—I would say, rather, that those destined to be answered must call out.

Thus documented, John Neal loved all mankind and prayed? On the contrary, he went to no hilltop, he shouted against no storm, he invited neither friends nor demons to ride Valkyrie-like. But sitting in his room, in this inexorable city, he said, rather: "Watch the mind, as you would eye a mean dog. Wait. Die as a mangled wasp dies." He constructed for himself a story, picturing himself as gentle, and imagining Genevieve as a woman who had deserted him (which was not difficult to imagine, for he had called her so often in his thoughts, that she seemed cruel in refusing to answer). But the sanction of no vast mythology was permitted him.

VI.

"Testamentum meum"

Jottings.

would liken God to a little mouse, since the differences are obvious
—whereas in likening God to the day, we obscure his splendor by
suggesting the splendor of sunlight.

if one must seek solace, let it be in the cultivation of some power.

there were marked aspects of himself which Alter Ego would have
greatly preferred to abandon—and on finding the same aspects in
me, he quasi-abandoned them by abandoning me.

the liver gnawed by vultures, though you brought fire to no one.

madness, travel, drugs, the Faith, death by one's own hand.

to guard against prayer, particularly that secular form of prayer
which is ambition. An act is but the simulacrum of a deeper act, a
disguised way of coming into port, of feasting after hunger, which is
the essential process of the universe. And in too greatly desiring

some specific thing, either in prayer or in the strivings of the ambitious, we forget the metaphorical quality of all desires. The universe is Cause and Effect in one, Command and Obedience in one, Need and Fulfillment in one. Throughout eternity there is hunger in the fact that the universe *needs to be*, and appeasement in the fact that the universe *is*.

there is an eye, firm as the eye of the newly dead. When I am alone, this eye inspects me.

you cannot renounce, for none but the rich dare speak in praise of poverty.

have said: This is the day. There will be some sign, or more than a sign, a clear alteration. Today some thing has been changed to meet my needs. And if night falls without this new thing's becoming apparent, then the event was a letter written at a distance and started on its way but not yet delivered; or a decision reached by someone who has still to act upon it; or if the relief is to come wholly from within me, the process is even now at work, but has revealed its presence before revealing its nature.

if they cannot have religion, they should have lotteries.

speech being a mode of conduct, he converted his faulty living into eloquence. Then should any like his diction, they would indirectly have sanctioned his habits.

can conceive of two men, one rebellious, without compromise—the other given to half-measures. This second man, by his yieldings and flunkeyings, gets himself some modicum of independence—but the more thoroughgoing man has been too often routed in the interim: it is he who, to exist, must court favor.

not his worst qualities that got him into the worst trouble.

a sire, a bull for breeding, kept stabled, his eyes hooded, the movements of his legs hampered by thongs. He tramps restlessly, in darkness and confinement, no muscle permitted a sufficient range of movement in which to vent its powers. Held in abeyance, to be given freedom at the requisite moment, and burst forth in fury, a monster, bent upon rage, upon pleasure, upon assertion. To lie unused, to be fettered by lack of purpose, to champ, to rub weighty buttocks against the sides of the stall . . . to be called forth, bound upon some task . . .

a groveler, in boasting, must say that he would not be otherwise than he is.

do not watch him so uneasily, Woman. He will not approach your child. He is already disciplined in these matters.

stopped a stranger in the street and told him of my misfortunes, though he kept glancing in the direction of his appointment.

testamentum meum.

he might sally forth, try things as he chose—and if the situation became unbearable, he could announce that he was returning to his refuge. In this refuge all the old voices would be silenced—one could detect only such sounds as he had never heard before. The new sounds would be like gifts—he could hold them in his hands, or even lay his head against them.

had grammar, dialectic, and rhetoric as their trivium, yet knew so little about the deceptions of speech.

I went to her and turned her face to the light, but it was not Genevieve.

would not insist that we are, or are not, free to choose. But do insist that, when choosing, we cannot foresee all the factors involved in our

choice—and how could a choice be called free when its consequences are unknown at the time of our choosing?

The man did good for the oppressed? Then he made them oppressors.

A dream of Anthony. He referred on several occasions to his "exile,"
though it is I that was in exile. And without playfulness, he addressed
me by his own name, nor did I find this unusual.

humbled that all negatives must be affirmed—for how advocate
silence silently?

lapsing into the unformed.

if enough men could be brought to realize their plight, then we
could at their instigation have a reshuffling.

this pledge of fidelity: Were you, Genevieve, to return and by your
sweetness to lift me from the entanglement into which I have got
myself, were you to be the woman of a new era for me, in this new
era I pledge fidelity. I should seek no further turmoil, not even were
my life to lack freshness.

had he found the matter ludicrous, he could have spared himself
much indignation.

now that she is gone, you cry out for her. But if she were with you,
might you in some new way dismiss her?

could I, by a ritual, like the old Jews, load my sins upon a goat, I
would beat it mercilessly and drive it into the wilderness to die.

each time I insulted them, they toasted me vociferously. They clamored, huzzaed, pounded the table in delight. And finally, tiring of
me, they pummeled me and pitched me from the room, though their

good nature continued—and when I called for money they threw a few coins after me.

the practice, among conquering tyrants, of putting to death every twentieth man. Am I the victim of my attitudes, or a victim of vigesimation?

a few hours of abundance, to prepare for a lifetime of famine.

if decisions were a choice between alternatives, decisions would come easy. Decision is in the selection and formulation of alternatives.

I was but a harmless moth, made by its markings to look ferocious. I was a pumpkin to frighten children. Yet for this they have punished me.

have dreamed of Genevieve's return, but the nature of the dream confirms me in my fear that she is dead. Dreaming, I saw her in a mirror, where she spoke mirror words—and the flowers on her breast had mirror fragrance.

sitting on the same bench with me in the park . . . they seemed like students . . . while listening to their conversation I felt that. I had things of importance to tell them . . . "*circulus vitiosus*" . . . yet they resented my intrusion . . . otherwise I should not have asked them for money.

if I could contrive some toy, such as a doll which, by an inexpensive mechanism, could be made to act insolently. Then I could take it to a man of enterprise—and if I were careful as to how the contract was worded, I might get substantial returns from he foolish thing.

they must train themselves in ingratitude, since they can live only by taking alms from the enemy—and how is the enemy to be vanquished unless they are prepared to bite the hand that feeds them?

there comes a time when one must abandon his vocabulary. For the rigidness of words, by discovering a little, prevents us from discovering more. There is a time for silence—not only outward silence, but even the silencing of one's own thoughts. Soon I shall open a door and pass through it, closing it softly behind me—and thereupon I shall be sitting in a chamber of silence.

I vilified them, but they enjoyed me as a king enjoys his parrot or his dwarf. The more I attacked them, the noisier grew their delight.

if I became well known, and she were still alive, the newspapers would assist me by printing throughout the country the story of my search for her. But recall the Prince locked up in the Beast. She must find you before you are released to go in search of her.

became bat-blind, that he might have bat-vision.

resurgam! resurgam! I shall rise again! Hail, all hail! Here is a promise: *resurgam!*

stop and examine dark alleys, as Genevieve may be there.

though you, in learning, brought trouble upon yourself, let no man discredit your discoveries by pointing to your troubles. Nor must you turn against your bitterness. The sword of discovery goes before the couch of laughter. One sneers by the modifying of a snarl; one smiles by the modifying of a sneer. You should have lived twice, and smiled the second time.

could not escape misfortune unless they all did as I did.

what voices would one hear were the mind to be plunged into total silence? Were he to say nothing, not even in his thoughts—were he to live in the stillness of a void—could he hear the cells of his body speaking? Might he distinguish the songs of the myriad little tenants in his blood, as we can contemplate the pulsing sound of frogs rising above a marsh?

if they would let me stay about to amuse them, as the old kings kept dwarfs, I could say all kinds of scathing things to them that made them laugh—and each of them could tickle himself by prodding me to attack the others.

all I have pondered in malice, some one, coming after me, will consider comfortably. What I have learned through being in grave extremities, he will handle with ease.

not only not responding, but even refraining from soliloquy—for if we tell no one, the grave burden accumulates within us. Henceforth silence, that the torrent may be heard descending in all its fullness.

THE END

TWENTY STORIES

Lascivam verborum licentiam . . . excusarem, si meum esset exemplum: sic scribit Catullus, sic Marsus, sic Pedo, sic Getulicus, sic quicunque perlegitur.

Martial

The White Oxen

Part One

1

It is doubtful just what might have happened. But as it was, the inheritance came opportunely—almost immediately after his graduation from a middle-western university, in fact. Marcel Carr was enabled to marry and settle down without ever having come to grips with life. Immensely relieved, he gathered up his minerals—including a valuable agate from Sicily—and placed them down in the house that was to be his home until death. Every fair day he would take his notebook, a small pick, and a little black box which carried five graham crackers and two apples, kiss his wife a meaningless good-bye, and start off with a final assurance that he would be back by six. The day was spent in serious research along the river and among the adjoining hills, for Marcel Carr was preparing a document, a "Mineralogical Analysis of the Upper Ohio."

In the evening he heard Dorothy, his daughter, and little Matthew go over bits of their lessons chosen by him at random, lessons which Dorothy, the mother, had taught them during the day. It was a quiet household, the only disturbances being of little import, as when Matthew cried over his bewilderment in trying to explain Caesar's bridge, or Dorothy, the daughter, answered when her father had called Dorothy, the mother. This misunderstanding, however, was of slight consequence, even though it had gone on for years, since Marcel was not of an irascible nature, and each time the mistake was made he corrected it as though it had never been made before; furthermore, it was all finally settled by Dorothy, the mother, getting up from her Grieg one evening, turning a white, frightened face towards her dozing husband, and sinking dead to the floor.

In their subdued way, there was grief in the Carr household. Old Marcel walked about his wife's bedroom with a steady pace, mechanical even in his sorrow. Matthew moved on tiptoe, a little more embarrassed than sad, and crying only when he saw the forlorn little form of his sister, who kept sobbing as softly as the fall of fine rain.

But in time even quiet grief diminishes. The coming of spring found old Marcel leaving in the morning with his little black box, kissing his daughter as he had kissed his wife, and making the same promise to be home by six. The two children started to public school, where they got along well enough, although they had already become too accustomed to being alone to mix with the other students.

A kindly Mrs. Huntington—the same Mrs. Huntington who was president of the Wilkinsburg Women's Euchre Club before certain things which she found out prompted her to resign—a large woman with a wart on her nose, and nine children, spared the time to mother Matthew and Dorothy for a while, but finding it a thankless task she soon gave them up. From now on the Carr children slowly acquired the reputation of being "nasty." They were left now entirely to themselves; their isolation was made more complete by the widespread report among their classmates that white shapes had been seen at night to dance about the Carr chimneys. Grownups explained this by the fact that Carr was one of the few people in the neighborhood who still used coal, but the tale persisted.

Quietly, steadily, as regularly as the beat of a pendulum, old Carr's incompetence lost for him the money he had inherited, until at last he rounded out an uneventful life by slipping from a rock and breaking his neck, probably the only vigorous action of his career. Fortunately for the old man's peace of mind, his death occurred one week before the arrival of a large envelope announcing his complete ruin. And when, within two years, Matthew's sister was also dead,

Matthew was left alone, except for the aunt and uncle he and Dorothy had gone to stay with in Pittsburgh.

2

There was something so subdued, so placid about his sorrow, that it was almost a kind of dull contentment. He spent his evenings—the hushed cool evenings of early summer—in walking about the better districts of the city; over Squirrel Hill, where the houses were surrounded by wide lawns and little clumps of timber, and where the smell of moist green spread out from the automatic sprinklers; or out Highland Avenue to the park. Here the roads squirmed in and out among the slopes; and when he had attained the northern limits of the park, he could look out at the Allegheny bounded by the lights of the towns on the opposite shore. They were dirty little towns, but at night, when only the lights were visible, thinning out as the eye went east until the river was lost in black, Matthew was happy to rest on them. Then he would lie on his back and look straight up at the tangle of stars. They would leap to within a foot of him, and then of a sudden be gone again, billions and trillions of miles away. A languor of melancholy sifted through his body, until he felt as though he were softly dripping away. At such times his respiration became faint, almost imperceptible; his eyes glazed; his emotions were so nearly extinct, his desires in life so uncertain, that he might even have been happy over the loss of the three people whom he had loved.

His days were spent in running little errands for his aunt, in helping her with the housework, or in walking about the city. He loved hot days, with a sun that fell like blows. He would go out through the park, past the zoological gardens to the river, get himself wet and then stretch out on the bank. He said this proved that he was descended from a snake, since he was sure that a snake asked nothing more than to doze in the hot sun; it was the one witticism he ever attempted. He never read, perhaps because his father had allowed him only the best of books, and they did not interest him.

3

One afternoon on his way back from the river he stopped in the zoo-logical gardens, an immense square edifice in the center of the park, approached by a long series of broad stone steps. It had always pleased him so that he was glad it was there, but until now it had never tempted him to enter. Now he was attracted by heavy roars. Two or three people who had been sauntering in front of the outside cages ran into the building. Matthew began taking the steps by twos.

Inside, he looked about him until he caught sight of a group of people standing before a cage at the far end of the hall. It was from that cage that the roars were coming. As he came up with the others, he saw a lion raging five feet in front of him. The animal was pacing in his den, so near the bars that when he turned, his nose scraped against the iron. With each exhalation of breath thick guttural quak-ings leaped from his jaws, and his loose chops trembled with the vibrations of his throat. The end of his tail twisted spasmodically; his muscles rippled with the advance of each paw. After one louder burst, the roars gradually subsided, until the final two or three were lost in his massive mouth, hardly more than a raucous natural respi-ration. He ceased prowling, and stood motionless, looking through the corner of his cage at a door far up the hall.

"It's nearly feeding time," somebody said; "the animals are getting hungry." A slight roar at the other end of the hall began. Slowly, mechanically, it increased in force. Most of the crowd bundled off to see the spectacle repeated, but Matthew remained behind, fasci-nated by this yellow mass of energy in front of him. Suddenly he caught a glance of eagerness; an attendant had appeared, carrying large buckets full of raw meat. The attendant worked down the hall slowly, shoving food into each cage in turn, and followed by a little knot of sightseers. Now he was at the adjoining cage; a tremor of im-patience flowed down the lion's back. Then the attendant was before him. Disdainful to the last, the lion retained his superiority even while being fed. He greeted the attendant with a baring of yellow fangs which gave the impression of sneering; and he snatched the meat from the iron prong with a growl, as though he were stealing it. He kept his eyes on his feeder until he had disappeared, and then began tearing the flesh from the bone by licking it with his rough, scaly tongue.

Matthew watched him until there was nothing left but two white bones. The lion mouthed at these a while, looked out at the world in general, lapped up some water splashily, took a few turns about his cage, and crawled into his little stone house for a nap—leaving, as one parting intimation of his attitudes, a tail and rump protrude for the curious to feast their eyes upon.

Matthew walked away, observing the other animals as he went. There were tigers, hyenas, leopards in the same hall. Each animal recalled in him the feeling he had experienced when looking at the lion: a discomfiture at the thought that these living things were unhappy, and a yearning to inculcate into them an understanding of friendliness.

"They are all treacherous," he murmured to himself. These animals could not be petted; they would misunderstand. Or worse, even though they understood they would not care, and would treat an arm stretched to them in sympathy merely as a piece of raw meat. They would snatch at it, and devour it.

Outside, he paused before the polar bear. The poor fellow was lumbering about in his prison dejectedly, incorporating into every movement a complication of motions, as though each part of his body wanted to go in a different direction and had its own peculiar ideas of locomotion. He felt more at home before this polar bear; there was less suggestion of ferocity here. But this animal, too, was restless, nervous, like the ill-tempered lion, or the slinking hyenas. Matthew turned away.

To the right of the zoological building proper there is an abrupt hill, and at the top of this hill the smaller things are kept: peafowls, pigeons, ducks, vultures, coyotes, skunks, foxes, mountain goats, antelopes and the like. Here also, like one calm persistent note in a hurricane, a group of large white oxen added a peculiarly sweet smell to the assembled cloud of pungent stenches that rose from the cages of the other animals.

The birds were in a state of continued agitation, hopping about, trying their wings, jerking their heads, dipping for a grain of corn, peeping. The vultures and the owls, it is true, were quiet, perched stolidly with dull eyes looking out into nothing, as lonesome as dead oaks. But the ugly curve of the vultures' beaks made them more unpleasant to Matthew than even the lion had been, while the sulking owls simply left him disinterested. The coyotes, foxes, and skunks were repugnant; they were as lawless as the big animals, but with none of their dignity. The antelopes and the mountain goats he liked. He laughed outright at the self-conscious buck who stood posing on his hillock, scenting the four breezes; the slope of his hillock was quite steep, and gave him much the position of a rearing horse. Head up, nostrils dilating, he held the attitude while some visitors took a snapshot, then descended immediately, as though quite aware of what they had wanted. Matthew moved on to the white oxen.

They were chewing in deliberate contentment. At times they would move their heads to look in another direction; at such times they ceased their chewing, as though disapproving of too many simultaneous motions. But once their head was firmly established in this new direction, their chewing would be resumed. Calm, harmless, sleepy, they lolled about their cage. Each movement of their body went through a graded progression: it was prepared for by an unhurried tautening of the flesh, executed with absolute assurance of the result, after which the oxen easily and imperceptibly settled down again into a state of relaxation. A bit puzzled, perhaps, by man's interest in them, they had nevertheless come to take it for granted, and dozed on secure in their knowledge that food and drink would be given to them at the right time, and that their stalls were ample protection against bad weather. Except for an occasional spring, when an unruly and unmannerly bull was let in for a time, there was nothing in the world that could trouble them; and perhaps even the bull was for the best, since there were certain vague yearnings in the spring which were strangely stilled after he had departed.

Matthew watched them for nearly an hour. Their tranquility found a response in him. Unknown to himself he was smiling, and trying by means of his eyes to make them appreciate that he was going to love them, trying to pass over to them through the shaft of his vision some intimation of sympathy. He wanted to feed them, but was detained by the memory of the signs scattered about requesting that visitors please do not feed the animals.

But it was late; he began hurrying home. Nevertheless, he found himself taking the roundabout way past the upper reservoir, as though his new attachment demanded a more auspicious exit from the park than Negley Avenue. He came down Highland, broad and sloping, lined with the houses of the rich, and stained an aristo-cratic black with the drippings of automobiles. The houses allowed only glimpses of themselves through the surrounding foliage. Sober, composed, they atoned for their shallow ancestry by this willingness to remain unnoticed.

Matthew was so contented with them, that he had often been struck by a daring inspiration in passing them, a feeling that it would be quite proper for him to walk up one of those winding gravel paths, ring the bell, and ask for the master of the house. When he was ushered into the presence of that personage, he would announce modestly and quietly that his name was Matthew Carr, and that he approved of—no, not "approved of," "liked," rather, or "admired" —that he admired this house, and forthwith depart. He was sure that the personage would understand, would look at him with a mild and merry twinkle in his eye, perhaps, and say something generous in return. But such wild transgressions were only for reveries.

As he went hurrying by these houses now, their effect on him was a totally unconscious one, and contributed to his elation only in so far as they did not disturb him. He went on down Highland until the big houses were left behind, and he nearly reached the little cluster of churches north of Penn Avenue. He turned to his right into a suf-ficiently mediocre side street, where an occasional but dutiful poplar gasped in its struggle with city dust. Another turn to the left, and he was home. He entered the kitchen to a sizzle of frying lamb chops. Thank heavens! he was home on time. His aunt was moving about the kitchen.

4

There are only two kinds of women: those who get fat with age until they are convinced that no corset can hold them any longer, and give up the fight against nature and good eating to carry the shape of a stuffed potato sack to the grave; the other is the withering leaf kind, whose skin tightens on their bones, who eat little and sleep lightly, and whose temper with time threatens to become as sharp as their nose. Already the edges of Aunt Maggie's corsets showed across her back and below her hips, protruding like misshapen bones.

"Am I in time, Auntie?" Matthew asked, it never occurring to him that at the sound of the frying meat he had already settled that question for himself.

"Oh, here's Matthew now," she called into the dining room, where her husband was reading. "We were worried about you, Matthew. You must always be careful when you go to the river."

"I am always careful, Auntie. But I stopped at the zoo; that's what made me late." He passed on to the bathroom to wash, calling out a hello to his Uncle Charles.

Uncle Charles, as if it had been decreed that the average weight of this childless family was to remain stationary, was already displaying as many symptoms of corpulence as his wife of leanness. Although the paunch of his stomach was still small, he had acquired the fat man's way of sitting: feet close together, knees spread far apart. He sat now fingering a cigar as he read his newspaper, nervously impatient to be pulling at it; but as it dare not be lighted until after the meal, he tried to quiet himself by toying with it absent-mindedly, much the way a gluttonous baby is pacified with a blind nipple. Good-natured, interested half-heartedly in his business and passionately in the solving of rebuses, he was the kind of man who knew how to throw back his head, open his gullet, and let his stomach agitate up and down with mighty mirth. Nor was his mirth of an exacting nature, so that a good part of his waking hours was spent in pleasant upheavals of the flesh.

That evening at the supper table Matthew's noctambulism came up for discussion. He had asked permission to go to the park again.

Uncle Charles looked as mysteriously wise as his pudgy cheeks would allow him, inspected his nephew steadily through two wee eyes squeezed into mere slits by the physical tyrannies of his merriment, and suggested slyly in a voice fraught with imminent laughter, "Starting early, young man, eh?"

Matthew looked bewildered; he never could keep pace with the vagaries of his uncle's willing wit. "Let's see," he went on; "how old are you, Matthew?"

"Nearly fifteen," Matthew answered with something like relief; here was a straight question which could be straightly answered.

"Nearly fifteen, eh?" the examiner continued, as though he had trapped the unsuspecting defendant into another compromising confession, and was on the very verge, after one last clinching inter-rogation or two, of hurling his tremendous accumulation of damn-ing testimony upon the shoulders of his victim, an impetuous and overwhelming blow. "When I was fifteen, I didn't go around—please pass me another chop, Madge darling." The break was deliberate; and those who knew Uncle Charles knew also that when he called his Maggie "Madge darling" there was deviltry in the air. "Matthew," he went on inexorably, unaware that his pause, instead of producing in Matthew the desired sweat of suspense, had merely given him an opportunity to slip back into his own channel of meditation, "do you prefer light hair, or brown?"

"I don't know, Uncle Charles. Dorothy's hair was dark, like mine."

"Then she has light hair, eh, Madge darling?"

Madge darling looked at him with disapproval. Sitting up more erectly, she placed her hands on her hips and stretched her body upwards to readjust the set of her corsets. "Matthew doesn't think of things like that, Charles."

"Things like what, Auntie?" Matthew had failed to follow the conversation as much through lack of interest as through inability. He had already become convinced that his uncle was too deep for him, and once he had come to this conclusion he made no further attempts to penetrate into this cavern of forbidding profundity.

"Matthew," and now Uncle Charles employed mock thunder, making it a little less realistic than usual, however, since he allowed for the exceptional dullness of his present audience; "Matthew, I believe you are in love. Boys don't want to go to the park every morning except for one thing, to moon and coo and cuddle up. And I warn you, Matthew, I warn you. . . . If you have to marry her—"

"Charles Bowman!" a curt thrust of shrewish eyes, a glance of all-withering scorn from Aunt Maggie. "Matthew doesn't think of things like that." Matthew, now really troubled, wanted to cry, but the obligations of his fifteen years held him in check.

"I don't know any girls, Uncle Charles."

"It is awful the things you say, Charles. Matthew is a good boy. And you shouldn't say things like that; they're not funny. Let Matthew alone. He never thinks of girls."

Uncle Charles was thoroughly routed. The edge was taken off his enjoyment. But now, although the heart and soul of his little joke had vanished, it devolved upon his dignity to see the thing through. He plunged doggedly on, keeping preserved amid a woeful twitching of his facial muscles a valiant simulation of his former genuine radiancy. "If you have to marry her, Matthew, I . . . I . . ." He stopped because of a sudden terrifying discovery that the conclusion to this hypothesis had been forgotten. "Matthew," he continued the struggle, desperate but smiling, "be good to her. Do not wrong her, Matthew. It is—"

"Matthew, your uncle is making a spectacle of himself. You must not mind what he says. He means to be funny. I hope that hereafter he will succeed better. He knows as well as I that you are a good boy, Matthew, that you would never do anything wrong. And that's right, Matthew, never do anything wrong, and you'll have nothing to repent of. Always be a good boy, and above all, be good to women. Remember that your mother was a woman, and that your sister would have been a woman had our Lord so willed it, and that your aunt is a woman. Your best friend on earth was a woman, Matthew. Please, please, for your poor old aunt's sake, never do wrong. And I know you won't; I know you're a good boy. Only the other day Mrs. next-door said to me, 'Mrs. Bowman, that's a fine nephew you have.' And I know you won't, Matthew; it would be the death of me." And as she felt the big tears detach themselves from her cheeks and plunge off into space, she added, "Don't cry, Matthew, there, there, don't cry." Whereupon Matthew, who up until now had acted like a little man, unloosed the flood gates, wept bitterly and long, while Uncle Charles suspended all psychological operations, resolutely centered his whole life about the distributing of salt over his potatoes by heaping it on the end of a knife blade and gently tapping the blade. . . . After a time order was resumed, Matthew went over to his uncle, the two men shook hands and then fussed over a mechanical trick toy while Aunt Maggie brought in the dessert.

That evening when Matthew started out for the park he went a redeemed man, free of all incrimination, it being explained to his aunt and uncle exactly why he was going, and his uncle admitting frankly and openly that he believed Matthew was going for that reason. But a storm blew up, and it was two evenings later before Matthew saw his white oxen again.

5

It was a calm, moonless night when he returned to them, but the light from the stars and the boulevard lamps a few hundred feet away made it easy for him to see them. They were still out in the open, awake and ruminating, five grouped socially together, one loitering a slight distance apart from the rest. As Matthew stepped softly along the gravel path in the darkness and stopped to lean on the railing before their cage, they adjusted their heads to observe him, found him unalarming, and forthwith forgot him. For a time he was content with merely peering at the half-vanishing forms. Then he began talking to them; his voice was rich with persuasion, and though subdued it carried through the darkness by force of the eagerness that propelled it. But this, too, after a time, was not sufficient. There was no bond of friendship yet established between him and them.

He knew the one sure method of proclaiming his concern for them. He must feed them, regardless of the warnings. He remembered a clump of tall grass behind the coyote shed, a patch that the lawnmower had failed to reach. He got this grass and shook it against the wire—for with the white oxen a cage was a mere formality, a few feet of light wire stretched about them. After shaking the grass a second time, Matthew drew the attention of the lone ox, since it happened to be nearest. It approached without haste, but began eating as soon as it arrived. The other oxen looked up inquisitively while it ate; finally another came over to where Matthew was holding the grass. Then one by one they got up regretfully, and pulled gravely at the grass held out to them. They pressed their big blunt noses against the wire, were unostentatiously pleased with the fresh green food that was given them, but when it was finished, after lingering a while like polite guests after a dinner, they went back to the place where they had been lying, rearranged themselves, and were as unambitious as the dead.

Very often after this Matthew would come to their cage in the evenings; they began to recognize him, and would stumble up at his approach.

Once while he was feeding them, he became careless in the handling of the grass, with the result that one of the oxen bit his finger. He jumped away with a little cry; the oxen were frightened, started back, and then resumed their chewing. Matthew was not bothered by the incident, however. He knew the ox had bitten him unintentionally.

Part Two

1

As the summer went on, Matthew continued his trips to the white oxen. The first eagerness of his attachment had worn off, of course, but he continued his visits largely through an obligation of loyalty which he took for granted. Took for granted, since it never occurred to him that he could simply dismiss the white oxen from his life. They had entered within his horizon, and would remain there until something removed them.

This something came with the opening of high school. When one is not a ready student, it is necessary to devote much extra time to dull and mysterious books. The discovery of this was Matthew's initial realization of the ways of life. He had chanced upon it quite casually one evening when he had risen from his books, turned for his hat, and in searching for it let his eyes drop on a physics book. He had forgotten to study his physics! He suggested to his aunt with mild cynicism that dull people like himself must have a very hard time of it in life. She agreed, and called to witness a boy whom Uncle Charles had in his office. But that poor chap had only a public school education. It would be different with Matthew, if he stuck to his studies, since Matthew would always have a high school diploma to strengthen him in his struggle with the world. And perhaps Uncle Charles would even be able to send him to college, a small college, of course, but a good one . . . a good one. Matthew thanked his Uncle Charles, who admitted his good-heartedness with an embarrassed and preoccupied grunt, a grunt tempered both by his manly pudency at being anticipated in a generous act, and his resolute effort to get his prisoner out of thirty-six cells by taking him through every one once and only once.

Matthew was in his fourth year at high school before making any serious acquaintances; and his first serious acquaintance was Waldemar Jones. Jones was a tall, skinny fellow, of an ethereal build, but in retaliation he could launch forth the voice of a bull, a shout that had come to his rescue in many an argument, a grinding of heavy wheels that made the halls tremble at noontime with the decided opinions of Lowell Waldemar Jones. Universally disliked, he had already learned to carry his unpopularity masterfully by universally disliking; he wafted about him an aura of contempt in general, aided by a massive nose to sneer with and an unusually wide mouth. There might have been germs of promise in Waldemar, but at present certain features were precociously developed while others had hardly begun to exist, so that all in all he was as picturesque as a colt, and just about as established. The consequence was that Lowell Waldemar had set out at this early date to be the sunflower of erudition. An omnivorous reader, he applied his reading inexorably; he wore his learning as his archididascalus, his Lord and Savior, Oscar Wilde, had worn his green carnation. In Ibsen he saw the protest, in Shaw the flippancy, in Chesterton the machinery of brilliance, in Wilde the perversity, in

Meredith the high disdain of ordinary people, in Baudelaire the hashish—in every writer he ascertained with fine eclecticism some superficial and inconsequential fault to incorporate into the great circus tent he had stretched to draw the gaping world. It mattered little that the world did not come; he snubbed the snubbers, excluded the exclusive, and went merrily on hurling his bolts against society, a misogynist, a stormer and stresser, a belcher forth, a striker in the face, and above all—noisy, noisy. It was Lowell Waldemar Jones of all men that had been picked out for Matthew.

The meeting came about one afternoon after school hours. Matthew's Latin instructor, a Mr. Norman E. Wilsey, had detained him to help him with his Virgil. Wilsey had noticed Matthew's earnestness with his lessons, and being one of those wormy individuals who teach high school not because they have failed in something else but because the good God made them to be high school teachers, he had taken an interest in Matthew—which in Mr. Wilsey meant a sympathetic desire to help. But he was a busy man, as restless as the whiskers of a mouse, and had any number of things to attend to before he could give Matthew his attention. Just now he was discussing with another instructor his plan for some charts defending the study of Latin, while he ate the apple that pressing affairs had forced him to forgo at lunchtime. Matthew was glancing at a Sallust he had picked up from the desk. Of a sudden he became aware of a disturbance; Jones was entering the room in a frenzy of haste, as violent in his movements as though struggling with some invisible adversary. Seeing that Mr. Wilsey was occupied, he walked straight on across the room, approached a window, continued his ferocious stride until he was within a step of it, and brought his elbows down on the sill with an emphatic thud. For a few seconds he stood motionless; then he moved to another section of the room, where he toyed for a while with a model of a ballista; next he examined a little case of Roman coins; from here he moved to the desk beside Matthew and could at last accomplish his object—he could see what book Matthew was fingering.

"You read Sallust?" he asked.

Matthew answered, "No, I was just looking through it."

"I wondered. It would have been most unusual to find a pupil here reading Sallust, since he is not in any of the courses. Naturally," he added, "I have read him." He went on, "Remarkably easy Latin, I find. What do you think of him?"

Matthew began patiently to repeat that he had not read Sa—but Jones interrupted: "Oh yes, beg pardon. You see, it is so hard to believe. I thought everybody had read Sallust, just as everybody must have read Tibullus and Athenæus. Of course, Sallust is not an important writer, but one has to have read him, before he can hold his head up. He is like some of the minor Elizabethans in that respect, don't you find?"

At this point Wilsey came over to offer his apologies; he would not be able to keep his appointments with them this afternoon, as a matter of moment had turned up unexpectedly. Matthew began preparing to leave.

"Which way do you go?" Jones asked, and when Matthew answered, he exclaimed with fine irony, "Excellent! I go that way myself; we can continue our discussion of Sallust." The two boys left the building together. Jones now set about to lead the conversation before the mouth of his mightiest cannon, religion. It was a favorite satanism of his to ask his victim what faith he professed. When the victim had answered, he would ask about the tenets. The victim would give two or three readily enough, stumble through a couple more if he was especially intelligent, and then, while the flame of his memory was guttering, Jones repeated every tenet of the victim's faith. But this was only the forerunner to the death blow, the "No, I do not belong to your church. I am an atheist. An atheist, you see, is a man who knows all the religions." He was not exactly proud of this performance, but he accepted it as an inevitable martyrdom, since he was doomed to find only stupid people for his enemies.

But Matthew, out of the citadel of his simplicity, hurled down at Jones a most annoying disappointment. When asked his religion, he made an honest effort to remember, and then admitted that he had forgotten. "I am not sure that I had a religion. My mother used to read the Bible to my sister and me, but my father didn't believe in churches."

"Immense, immense!" Waldemar raised an approving voice to the universe, although secretly disappointed. Further, he saw that his atheist bolt would glance off without effect, and let it lie back untried. "And so you don't believe in a God?"

"I never really thought of it," Matthew answered earnestly, a bit worried. What was Waldemar to do? Here was a quiet Philistine who tore speeches from his tongue as innocently, with the same sweet well-meaning, as a child pulling apart the wings of a butterfly. He soon found himself defending Catholicism with all the passion of an early father, glorifying the confessional, emphasizing the beauty of the ceremonies, and adding—a remark which meant nothing to Matthew—that any religion was justified which caused the building of a cathedral.

He made a deep impression on Matthew, who surprised him at parting by thanking him very gravely, and expressing a strong desire to become a Catholic. That day Lowell Waldemar received from slow-moving Matthew the first sobering influence of his life. His technique had failed him. He was somewhat upset, filled with a sense of responsibility even. For here was a man—he liked to think so at least—whose future existence might be radically affected by things said in a moment of idle irritation. He decided to deliver Matthew over into the hands of a good Catholic, and wash his own hands of him forever.

2

The next day he introduced Matthew to Edward Carroll, a studious, slightly myopic little fellow who went on steadily maintaining his reputation as the best student in the school.

"I have brought you a neophyte, Edward. *Ecce discipulus tuus.* He wants to become a Catholic, and I brought him to you as the most frightfully thorough Catholic I know."

Edward smiled at Matthew, and shook hands. "I don't know, Carr, but that Jones here knows more about the religion than I do. He would make a very good Catholic in——"

"In a world of Protestants," Jones interrupted complacently. But he had made a good curtain remark, and left immediately, grateful for the slight laugh Edward sent after him.

Matthew liked Edward, and felt very comfortable in his presence. "Do you play checkers?" Edward asked him.

"A little, but not very well. My uncle and I play once in a while; he always beats me."

"I am not very good at it myself. But maybe you would be willing to come home with me this afternoon; we could play a few games together." Matthew agreed eagerly, although he had very little interest in checkers. And he made something like a show of spirit when the physics instructor threatened to retain him.

"I can't stay in this afternoon. Wouldn't tomorrow do as well?" For a time it looked as though tomorrow would not do; at last he was told that he could go home at the regular hour.

Edward met him in front of the principal's office, and the two boys started on their way to his home. Without knowing it, Matthew was being lulled in a cradle of quiet satisfaction, as when he had seen the white oxen for the first time. The oxen crossed his brain now; he imagined them chewing dreamily at their cuds. In another instant they were forgotten, and he had not suspected the association which had brought them to his mind.

When they had reached his home, Edward introduced Matthew to his mother, a large, stout woman, as homelike as the smell of the bread baking in her kitchen. He also met one of the older sisters, and a brother. The two boys sat down before the fire in the parlor and played five games, amid a desultory conversation and the interruptions of Edward's mother, who kept him moving about for this and that. Edward won three straight games, after which he thought it best to lose the next two.

At the end of the fifth game, Matthew got up to leave, as his aunt would be expecting him by now. Edward volunteered to walk a few blocks with him, but Matthew would not hear to it. He was glad, however, when Edward insisted on accompanying him.

3

This was the beginning of a strong mutual absorption. At times, with apparently an illogical impulse, one of them would take the other's arm; although there had been nothing in their conversation to occasion such a move, it was accepted as perfectly natural. Then their interest in Elsie Williams, a light-haired, chatty little girl who gave a second glance to neither of them, added a touch of earnestness to their talk, and gave them many a delicious spell of embarrassed half-confessions. When one of them would have a little triumph to boast of, as the way Elsie had said "Thank you" when she had returned an eraser to Edward, it was the time for magnanimous rejoicing on the part of the other, of a resolute struggle against envy, an opportunity to be noble.

Although Edward was in the parish of Sacred Heart, he would often go to the big cathedral on Craig Street with his friend, or to the dingy old church downtown, since these were the only places, according to Matthew, where he could comprehend religion. And by comprehending religion he meant letting his eyes wander in the vaulted ceiling while the Mass drummed mechanically in his ears. He liked the conflict of wood and stone, of lighted altar and shadowy pillars, of Edward kneeling here beside him and the words of the priest floating in from a distance. He was pleased that at a signal, everyone bowed simultaneously. At times he caught the far-off tinkle of a streetcar bell, and he listened for the little stifled coughs that started from different corners of the congregation. But the comfortable numbness of the brain which was the characteristic of his happiest moments was gradually becoming dependent upon Edward's proximity; for Matthew there could be no greater meaning to friendship than this.

With the coming of warm days, when the snow was nearly melted, and what little remained was mixed with dirt, there was something of the quality of last autumn in the air. As Matthew's impressions of such weather were linked with the memory of his last struggling visits to the white oxen, he had a strong desire now to see them again. A series of pilgrimages began which increased with the coming of good weather. Moved by a somewhat arbitrary sense of things as they ought to be, he did not invite Edward to come with him; furthermore, there was a secret fear he would not be interested, and Matthew preferred to avoid such an issue.

One afternoon he was hurrying off to them after a miserable

showing in his classes, when Edward happened to see him. "Ho, Matthew, come along with me, will you?" he called out, and Matthew went off with his friend.

But the efficacy of the substitute took hold of him. He understood now with perfect clarity the nature of Edward's appeal. Edward was one of his white oxen! Like them Edward was peaceful, and in repose. Like them, he asked little of life. When taking his arm Matthew had experienced the same warm confidence as when the white oxen shoved their big blunt noses against the wire to eat grass from his hand. He took Edward's arm now, and gave it a little squeeze, happy with his discovery; he had found now that he loved white oxen.

Part Three

1

After graduating from high school, the two boys went in different directions. Edward started to college in another city. Matthew fought against the kindness of his uncle, who wanted to send him along with Edward; no, he was grateful for the offer, but he felt it his duty to begin supporting himself. His uncle finally agreed to get him a position in the office of a friend of his, with the result that Matthew continued on in Pittsburgh, spending his days in business and his evenings either alone or with his Aunt Maggie and Uncle Charles. He saw Edward only during vacations, and once when he had come home for a week on account of the death of a sister.

But they corresponded very regularly. Edward's letters were filled with accounts of college activities, while Matthew was content to atone for a lack of variety by repeating how much he missed his friend. Although Matthew saw in spite of himself that Edward showed little real need of him now, Matthew watched his friend's letters becoming more and more impersonal, and the protests of friendship becoming scarcer and more mechanical. Still, he could not help clinging to this first of his white oxen, and accused himself of petty jealousy for the way he watched his friend's letters.

Gradually, however, Matthew's letters became more guarded. Now that Edward needed him less, he began to feel less need of Edward. But just as the intimacy of Matthew's letters had very nearly dribbled away, at the very time when he was ready to accept it that he was alone again, something dreadful happened to him, something that seemed to him so hideous, that he was thrown back into treating Edward as being all that he had once been. For Matthew needed a confidant badly.

2

"Perhaps, Edward," he wrote, "you will wonder what right I had to be in that quarter. And I confess it, I was there for exactly the reasons your suspicions may lead you to think. It is hard, Edward—and I know you will forgive me if the words sound vulgar—it is very hard to fight down the taste of sin when you are twenty. I hope you are different. Indeed, I know you are. You would not be of so flabby a character. I can tell by the jolly tone of your letters that the filthy needs which have been coaxing me have not sullied you. It may be that I am a monster. If only I had a religion like you to protect me! But no, I am simply exposed to all temptation, with nothing but my shame—and even that has not been very strong!—to keep me right. There is another man like you at the office, Gabriel Harding. Sometimes I look at his kindly, carefree face and feel humbled. Why can't I be like that?" A long passage about this Gabriel Harding followed, a passage of sour comparison.

"For some time," the letter went on, "I have been walking in that quarter, just roaming about with thoughts, more mean in my yearnings than the rottenest of debauchers. It is tenderness I want, it is to cry on a woman's breast, and yet why is it that I walk here of all places, regardless of my desire for these beautiful things! Is it my ugliness, so that I feel that what little I touch of woman must be bought? But I can't buy what I want. Realize it, Edward, please understand me, I am not vulgar. I have walked here, I have dreamed harsh dreams about the most brutal of things, but it is something else that I want. Perhaps if I knew that a woman loved me, that would be enough; but with no woman to love me, I have nothing to lift me above horrible things. I pass men on the street, and immediately I think—what? That they are well dressed? That they are going to the theater? That they are pleasant? No, I wonder whether they have been in those unspeakable places.

"After such nights of roaming I would return to the office the next morning to face the clean, innocent eyes of Gabriel Harding. He would look at me and smile; oh, God, would he smile if he knew what was at the bottom of me! I almost feel at times as though I were corrupting him merely by letting him smile at me in so friendly a fashion." Another passage about Gabriel Harding followed a passage of high praise for the happy and the chaste.

"But my self-respect returned in the most miserable of ways. I was walking on one of those nightly journeys, wishing, wishing, and daring nothing, when I heard a rustle, and something like a groan. I looked, and saw a black shape moving, huddled in a dark corner, the entrance to an unoccupied store. The street was a dismal one, with the lampposts very far apart. I went over to the dark, moving bundle, and touched it. It was a woman! I do not want to tell you the unpleasant details, Edward, of what followed. Perhaps I might have gone on, but the night was chilly, and I pitied this poor woman. When I asked her where she lived, she was unable to tell me. I picked her up and found her garments filthy with the spew of her stomach. I would not tell you this, but the bitterness of what happened later is in me, and I want to say it, cruelly and brutally, how impure she was.

"Finding no evidence of an address on her, I led her staggering and bawling to one of the 'hotels.' Yes, though I had never been in any of them, I knew where they all were had often stood hungrily in front of them. I remember now that I felt proud of the look the proprietor gave me, an understanding look; he thought I was experienced at all this. Oh, God, to think of being proud of so low an accomplishment! That any one should want to appear competent in such matters as these! Now I suffer for whatever squalid conceit I felt then. And I am glad to suffer; it is a relief to call up every vile act that I have done, a fierce retribution.

"Forgive me, Edward, and you, my unsuspecting Gabriel Harding, for what happened during the next few weeks. For we became friends; this woman of the streets and I became *companions*! She became to me what you had been when we sat in the cathedral on Craig Street. She made me forget poor little Dorothy. And I was indifferent to Gabriel Harding, whom I had wanted before as a friend. I treated her as one of you. 'She is one of my white oxen,' I told myself. That is what I said of a woman of the streets, that is what I said—yes, I will be as inconsiderate of myself as possible—that is what I said of a whore.

"But wasn't there some justification, even so? For you must understand, Edward, that there was a great deal in our relationship to promise well. The vulgar needs of the flesh were gone from me, even without having given in to them. There was nothing impure between us. Oh, why couldn't things stay as they were then! It was a peculiar pleasure, a feeling of being more than chaste, to speak to this woman as I might have done to my mother or to one of your sisters. I loved to think of her as pure, and that thought persisted even though I knew how she was still earning her living. She was very tender to me, and cried once when I brought her some carnations; it had been many a year, she said, since any one had done that for her. How comforting it was to hear her cry, and to soothe her. 'There, there, you are one of my white oxen,' I told her. She listened very quietly while I told her of the white oxen, and kissed my poor ugly face when I had finished.

"As I look back on this time of sweetness, my remorse is almost gone. For there is nothing here to repent of, Edward. To love this woman who had been kind enough to kiss me, to seek something noble here where other men sought a moment's lust—is there anything in that to be ashamed of?

"But even then the dreadful thing was coming. Why should she have done so monstrous a thing! Why should it have fallen to *her*, who was continually possessed of other men, to shatter a relationship which I could have preserved forever, although I looked at no other woman besides herself. Or if the laxity of a lifetime had told against her, so that she knew nothing of self-restraint, why should she make so hideous an advance to me? For it was so dreadful that I shall never breathe word of it, let alone place it here on the page before you. Enough to admit that it is unspeakable, that she approached me in a way that neither god nor devil had ever meant for man. And I yielded, sinking back sick with anguish, faint with voluptuosity and horror.

"I know I should never send you this letter, Edward. The vision of my depravity may turn you from me forever. But the feeling of disgust is still strong upon me. I shall never see her again, I swear. The first of my white oxen has failed me, Edward. Don't you flee from me in repugnance now as I have done from her. I need you, Edward, very much."

3

The letter was sent, and for the next few days Matthew was wretched. Would Edward answer him! He hoped at least that his old friend would think enough of their former companionship to overcome what disgust he might feel at the letter, at least to send one last note expressing that disgust. He was sorry now that he had sent the letter.

Edward, however, had dropped into the mailbox a greater bomb than Matthew had feared at the height of his anxiety. When Matthew had gone with this boy of sixteen, Edward passed as one of his white oxen mainly because he was undeveloped. His future possibilities were still vague and subdued, probably owing to the awkwardness of expression that is common to adolescence. By now, however, all these possibilities were blossoming gloriously, as Edward's letter testified.

"And so, old boy, you have at last wakened up. Be cheerful; I give you my word that everybody has some such regrets the first time. You were a bit unfortunate—or a bit fortunate, whichever way you take it —in running up against a perversion the first time. It is better to evolve gradually into that, you know. I showed your letter to a friend of mine"—the hot blood pumped into Matthew's face at this—"and he suggested that you read some of the sex psychologists. You will get a new idea of these things. He will send you a list of books, if you want it.

"And don't be too hard on the girl, Matthew. Her steady experience in the usual way of expressing love had deadened her to it. She must naturally, therefore, go a step or two farther. Go back to her, and—if you won't get jealous—I'll pay her a visit myself when I return for the Easter holidays."

There was more, but Matthew did not read it. The letter went unanswered. Matthew had lost two of his white oxen now, since Edward's congenial apostasy had wounded him more than his affair with the harlot could ever have done. He settled down into himself, almost resigned to expect nothing more.

But there was still Gabriel Harding.

Part Four

1

The two weeks after the loss of his first white oxen had been a graded descent into despair. He had never needed so much as now the caress of his harlot, or the relief of writing long letters to Edward; yet the people from whom he should expect consolation were the very ones who had brought on his need for it. His Uncle Charles and Aunt Maggie realized that something had happened to their nephew, but they both felt themselves awkward in dealing with so mysterious an emotion as this seemed to be, and said nothing. Aunt Maggie did, however, suggest a few general propositions of comfort while they were at table; we should thank God that we are alive; everything is in the hands of a Loving Father and will turn out for the best; we are fortunate that we have our health. Uncle Charles fairly exploded with brave witticisms. But it was Matthew's strained efforts to reply to each of them which finally silenced them both.

As always had been the case with him, his unhappiness had nothing of triumphant woe about it; there were no wild fits of dejection. But in retaliation, it stayed with him longer. When he awoke in the morning he had the impression that he must have been unhappy even in his sleep. He tried to keep himself busy, since it was no longer pleasant to let his thoughts wander. . . . This sky could never be cleared by a magnificent downpouring of rain; rather, the clouds would hover about until some gentle, insistent wind, neither too warm nor too cold, came to blow them away. Gabriel Harding, then, was to be this gentle, insistent wind, neither too cold nor too warm.

Harding was a neat, middle-sized fellow, well up in his twenties, with the colorless but beautifully smooth skin which comes of a good digestion without much exercise in the open. His forehead passed unnoticed, but his rich blue eyes were the kindly eyes of a man of sympathies, while his mouth bore out the impression by means of a peculiarly soft smile. A smile too soft, in fact; when he smiled to himself while leaning over his ledger, the expression on the lower part of his face had a touch of weakness about it. An enemy might have called it a touch of imbecility, if by any stretch of the imagination Gabriel Harding could be thought of as having an enemy.

With his soft smile, he approached Matthew one evening as the two were leaving the office. "Carr, you look unhappy lately." Matthew turned questioning, unmeaning eyes upon him, and he continued, "Perhaps I am being too bold, but really, I—I can't stand seeing people unhappy."

Matthew struggled for something to say. He saw that Harding thought his remarks were resented, and was about to hurry away. He said hastily, "Thank you—thank you very much." That was all. Harding increased the degree of his soft smile—it had never ceased flickering about the corners of his mouth—and went on his way without another word.

But he had given Matthew something to think about. For some reason or other, these few words kept returning to him. And they served to preoccupy him in a measure, so that his aunt and uncle agreed in whispers after he left the table that Matthew looked like himself again.

He was no longer the incautious yearner after sympathy that he had been. He looked back on Harding's approach with something almost like shrewd distrust. "Thank you—thank you very much," had been too concessional, he felt. It was the first step towards placing his happiness again in another's keeping. He decided to think no more of this man. The smile had been given in all good faith—Matthew's scent for the traces of human sympathy were too acute to deceive him there—but so had Edward's letter been in all good faith, and her . . . but faugh! he dismissed her. No, he would remain alone. He would learn to be sufficient unto himself. And he would repel Harding before the man took a lasting hold on him. With this, he started off the next morning to face the soft, welcoming smile.

He met the smile, and . . . and answered it.

2

It had been his last protest. Matthew recognized too well in Gabriel's smile the appeal of his white oxen. Gabriel began taking his Sunday dinner at Matthew's home. Then an Italian opera company stopped at the Alvin for two weeks, and Gabriel took his friend to hear *Lucia di Lammermoor*. It was an epochal evening for Matthew; when the famous sextet was sung, he closed his eyes, to let the weaving, inter-mixing voices reach him out of the darkness. They also went to *Carmen*, where Matthew was vaguely happy over the clean bravuras of the tenor, and the agile, full-throated contralto.

Although Gabriel was perfectly sincere in trying to become inti-mate with this "quiet, rather sentimental fellow," as he thought of him, it remained for an error to tie the final knot in their friendship. This error was due partly to Gabriel's landlady, partly to Gabriel himself. He had a couple of books which he wanted to send to a friend in another city, but he had hardly begun packing them when he noticed that he was going to be late for work. His first thought was to rush off and let the books lie there; then it occurred to him that the landlady might pack them for him if he asked her. He wrote the address on a piece of paper, laid it on his table, and stopped in the kitchen to see the landlady. She was willing enough to send the books; he told her the address was lying on the table, and rushed out. But there was also a paper on the desk containing Matthew's address, the paper which Matthew had given him the first time Gabriel was invited to Sunday dinner. The landlady saw this paper, looked no further, and sent the books to Matthew.

Although Matthew cared very little for books, he was more touched perhaps, by this useless gift than if he had received something he actually wanted. The receiving of a useless gift is tinged with gratitude that is very near to pathos. Yes, mistaken kindness is a bit pathetic, and as such often earns more gratitude than kindness well placed. As Matthew was always a prey to such naïve reactions as these, he was overwhelmed with Gabriel's kindness, so overwhelmed, in fact, that Gabriel could not bring himself to explain the mistake. There was an inkling of guilt in the soft smile which Matthew did not notice; but Gabriel soon effaced this with the consideration that it is good to make someone happy, even if by mistake.

It was soon after this that Aunt Maggie began ailing. Matthew talked it over with Uncle Charles, and finally decided that if he left them it would save her a good deal of work about the house. It was decided that he take a room alone, but when Gabriel heard of this he suggested that they room together. Matthew accepted with readiness; and not long after this the two friends were snugly installed in a three-room suite, two bedrooms and a room to lounge in.

For the first weeks they were both enchanted with the arrangement. They went to work together, ate together, came home together, and spent their evenings together. Then a beautiful-smelling letter came for Gabriel, and he explained that he could not be with Matthew that night. Matthew paid a visit to his aunt and uncle. Gabriel did not get home until the next morning, but as it was Sunday, he spent the day sleeping. Matthew felt grieved at this, but as he could find no legitimate objection to make, he said nothing. Unknown to himself, he had been a tyrant in his unpretentious way, a man who demanded that things be absolutely as he wanted them. What he found disagreeable, he avoided—even if that were his last attachment in the world. But he decided that he had no right to interfere with Gabriel's comings and goings, and that he would refuse to admit any resentment. After all, it was his own fault if he could not offer Gabriel enough to keep them continually together.

Another point was Gabriel's love of reading. Although Matthew had very little to say, he loved to have someone near him to whom he *could* say something if he wanted. But when Gabriel was reading— and he read so much!—Matthew felt singularly left out. Once or twice he had tried to start a conversation. At first he received polite responses, and later responses that were plainly impatient. This again Matthew accepted.

There were other things, more difficult to deal with, as the time when Gabriel had suddenly looked up from his book at Matthew, who was lying vacant on the lounge, and said, "I say, Matthew, you *are* a simple soul, aren't you?" What had he meant? And why had he said it on such an occasion, for no apparent reason? Matthew felt there must be something almost mysterious about his friend, some side of him which he had never seen, and never would see. Those fits of petulance, when Gabriel would hurl something across the room! —Matthew felt somehow that he was the cause of them. After such outbursts, however, there was always a period of renewed warmth, so that Matthew was almost glad of these outbursts. His friend excused himself on the ground of nervous headaches; Matthew was grateful for the excuse, although he suspected that it was not true.

The fact was that Gabriel had begun to be irritated by Matthew. He sensed the dog-like fidelity behind his friend, and it irritated him. But he was ashamed of his own irritation. It seemed to him that he owed Matthew kindly treatment, so that he always felt humiliated after an outburst. But this humiliation, which made things lovely for a few days, was only the germ of another outburst. In order to be on better terms with Matthew, he contrived to see him less often.

The trouble with Gabriel was that he had a refined sensitive equipment, but that he was thoroughly shallow. Such people are given to short-lived enthusiasms, with an acute need of variety. And Matthew of all men was incapable of giving variety. He was a lover of established order, asking nothing more of life than that things remain as they were.

Nevertheless, there were times when the interest that had brought them together originally became operative again, and Gabriel smiled his soft smile. Matthew would forget all the past difficulties between them in the sudden rediscovery that here was one of his white oxen, harmless and kindly. The two would spend glorious evenings together.

After about two months, something happened which finally brought the soft smile into its own. Gabriel had been looking troubled for the last few days, and often seemed on the verge of confessing something to his roommate. Although Matthew had tried to make it as easy as possible for him to speak, he had said nothing. The culmination came when he was seen walking into the manager's private office, with the soft smile struggling weakly; he came out again with the smile completely gone. While eating with Matthew that evening he said very little. But after they were back in their rooms he began to stammer out his predicament.

He wanted to tell Matthew the absolute truth, and yet, in spite of himself, with an illogical shame in explaining to him things which he was not ashamed of, he changed some of the details. The start was sincere enough: he needed money, and had made an unsuccessful attempt to get an advance on his salary; he had asked for thirty dollars of the amount that was not due him for ten days. When he intended to go on and explain just how the receiving of beautiful-smelling envelopes can cost money, he suddenly felt disinclined. Another excuse was just as good, and the important thing was *that* he needed money, not *why* he needed it. He found himself inventing against his will the tale of a needy friend. But he was right in his conjectures: Matthew stopped him in the middle of his lying with a cry that he would get him the money. Gabriel was a bit humbled by this; he opened his mouth to tell everything as it really was, but no words came. Matthew went into his own room, returning with a number of bills in his hand.

"I can give it to you immediately," he said, and threw on the floor with a mock-millionaire gesture a sum of ten times the amount asked for.

"What are you doing with all that here, man?" Gabriel seemed almost savage at his friend's stupidity. "Why don't you take it to a bank? Great heavens, who ever heard of a person having so much money in his room!"

Matthew explained that he had been saving ever since he began to work, and had kept the money in his Uncle Charles's safe. Uncle Charles himself had suggested that he take it to a bank. He had brought back the money with this intention, but he simply hadn't deposited it yet. Gabriel snapped out the advice that Matthew get the money safely behind steel doors as quickly as possible. But Matthew was incorrigible; he went on to defend himself, and before Gabriel could stop him had told him where he kept it, appealing to him whether a thief would ever think of a place like that. He was a bit bewildered by Gabriel's anger, but secretly pleased that his friend should be so concerned about him. For the rest of the evening, Gabriel was weak and nervous. He had taken his thirty dollars with hardly more than a dutiful "Thanks."

The soft smile had come into its own; that night he stole the money. For hours he had lain awake, fighting resolutely to fall asleep. Then he caught himself listening to the rise and fall of Matthew's breathing. He knew what that meant! But even as he crept into Matthew's room, he did it with a feeling of faith in himself, a consolation that he might be able to go so far as to touch the money and yet return without taking it. He touched the tin box, and his fingers closed about it through mere reflex action. As he sneaked back with it out of the room, the hope that he would not take it was stronger than ever. He trusted that in some stage of the theft a new emotion would come over him, some totally different current which would enable him to return the box to its hiding place with every dollar still in it. The key was in the lock. He turned it softly and raised the lid. The money was darkly visible, illuminated indirectly by the faint reflection from his white nightshirt of an arc-lamp out on the street. As he caught sight of the bills nestling there in the shadows, a sudden resentment came over him. Why had this man been so stupidly incautious! He began to dress himself, trembling not so much through fear as through the excitement of the unusual situation. This was no time to pack his things; he would take only the clothes he wore. Softly, he took out the money, and tiptoed back into Matthew's room to put the box where he had found it. This might delay the discovery of the theft. How deeply the man slept! He felt there was something brutish about such solid slumber. . . . Perhaps he might not leave at all, but simply throw the box out the window, and set up a clamor; Matthew would never accuse him. But no, he couldn't face Matthew after this. He came back into their common room, picked up the money, and started for the door. Then he returned to Matthew's room, got the box again, and left it lying open on the table. He wanted Matthew to understand immediately. He could not bear the thought that his friend would get up the next morning, find him gone, and begin a faithful worrying as to his whereabouts, without suspecting that he was a thief. For Matthew would never think of the money. The thought hurt, and filled him with admiration for Matthew. He wanted to press his friend's hand, to throw his arms about his neck and hug him. He pitied Matthew, since he realized how much the loss of a friend would mean to him. As for the money, Gabriel knew that if he had asked for it all it would have been handed over to him. He could have had it for the asking, and yet he was stealing it! . . . As he closed the door, he was resentful again. His actions would be misunderstood; they would be taken merely as actions, with no appreciation of the generous emotions he had experienced in doing them. He, Gabriel Harding, was to be the wronged party. Matthew slept on, unaware that the last of his white oxen had failed him. But he still had the white oxen themselves.

Part Five

1

Decidedly, Matthew Carr was a reliable man. Of good health, he came to the office regularly, and discharged his duties with a gratifying rigidity of scruple. The important thing was that he was steady, a quality which was much more valuable in routine work than wide-awake business acumen. Given something to do, and told how to do it, Matthew was sure to do it satisfactorily.

The other clerks in the office wondered a bit that Matthew said nothing about Harding's disappearance, since the two men had been noticeably intimate. But in the last analysis they accepted it as one more evidence of his quiet nature, and thought no more about it. As a consequence, Matthew never had any explanations to invent, and the secret of the theft remained undisturbed. He came to the office and returned to his room, evidently too wearied to be called sullen, and too meek to be called cynical.

He was now twenty-five, and was under no other obligations than those of eating and sleeping. He expected nothing, and received nothing. When he looked about him, he saw jackals and coyotes where he had once seen white oxen. But he looked about him very seldom. People had no more meaning to him than the pavements he walked on. Matthew was paying now for his lack of clear vision, the inability to learn, by looking at people, what he must not ask for in life. His only way of learning what he must not ask for had been to ask for it, and ask for it with complete assurance that it would be granted him. The result was that his lesson had become an organic part of him, as much an instrument in the conducting of his life as his heart or his lungs. What most people learn of humanity in a good-natured glance of the eye, he had to acquire laboriously by the cudgelings of experience itself. His life had been the gradual closing up of a shell which was never quite open.

But there was one attachment left; there were the white oxen. They, at least, had remained stationary.

2

How good it felt to walk up the long stone steps to the zoological building, to go around it to the right, past the cages of the squirrels, up the wooden steps, and out among quackings, peepings, and flutterings of the birds. They would be there, down to the left now, in that cage next to the self-conscious old buck who had posed for the camera the first day he had been there. Already he could see the mound where the buck had stood. He became impatient. He wanted to run down the gravel path. But no; he would tease himself. He continued his slow gait, almost exaggerated it, in fact, He caught the smell of the smaller animals off to the right. It seemed like a very short time since he had been here, although it was nearly ten years. Everything was the same. He peered ahead through the haze of wires to catch sight of his oxen, but they were not visible. Lying down, perhaps, for the thought never occurred to him that they might not be there.

A few more steps, and he was in front of the cage. He glanced about him, recaptured all the past memories at one switch of the eye. And sure enough, his old friends, the white oxen, were lying negligently about their cage, so oblivious to the passage of ten years that they were even chewing the same cuds.

Of course, they had forgotten him. Two of them looked at him without concern, and then let their eyes roam on past to wires, posts, and cages. He meant nothing to them. But that didn't matter; tonight he would return and feed them.

He did return, and in a short time the old commerce was restored. They came to recognize him, and rubbed their blunt noses against the wire. He talked to them; they were the one thing on earth that loved tranquility as he did. They looked upon life without question, accepted it with a liquid mind, the way he himself would have done had he been permitted.

One evening as he was feeding the oxen, another human form approached him. As it came nearer, Matthew saw it was a guard. And he expected trouble, since he knew that it was not permitted to feed the animals. But the guard was remarkably considerate, with none of the gruffness usual to petty officials. He struck up a conversation about ordinary things; it was fully five minutes before he came to the matter of the feeding.

"You see, young man," he explained, "it isn't allowed. I've watched you here, and I know you mean all right, but you're liable to be hurting the oxen. All feed is given here scientifically, at certain times of the day, and in certain quantities. So you may be actually harming the oxen by doing this." Matthew agreed to quit. He had never thought of it that way. Perhaps he was killing his old friends!

That was the last time the oxen received grass from his hands. Thereafter, he simply stood before their cage and watched them. It hurt him to see the animals come to greet him at his approach, shove up their noses in expectancy, and finally tired of waiting, return to their favorite lying places, noticing him only now and then with a look of silent rebuke. But it hurt worse the night he returned and only two of them came up to meet him. The next evening not a single one arose; they simply turned their heads in his direction, let their eyes rest on him a moment, and then shifted them stolidly away. He was deserted. Half in earnest, he puckered up his lips, and explained to them in human speech just what was the trouble. But to them, grass was the only way of settling the matter. He determined to feed them just once more, went for the grass, and returned without it. He stood for a long time, looking from one dimly outlined form to another. He rustled the wire, and as they looked up hopefully he was humbled by the cheapness of his ruse. He turned away, and walked slowly down the path. Without consciously guiding himself he continued straight ahead after the path had stopped, crossed a slight grassy slope to the boulevard, crossed the boulevard, and found himself looking down over the bluff into the valley below. It was all like ten years ago. The lights lined the shores of the river, and thinned away as the river serpented off into the blackness of the hills. To the left he saw the steel mills of Millvale and Etna, with their quick flames licking at the sky. Hundreds of feet below him, a cluster of lights was moving regularly with the current. He stood motionless, letting his eyes roam over these miles and miles stretched out beneath him. . . . And of a sudden a feeling of promise came over him, the hope of a boy of sixteen who sees a vision of futurity, of the world before him. He felt an acute interest in what life might have in store yet, a trust that there was going to be a great change, a faith in the proximity of some new vista. For a few moments he was rich with this unreasoning foretaste of conquest.

Then it was gone, leaving him almost physically weakened. He thought again of his white oxen there behind him. They had none of these painful tilts with life; to them the supreme gift of God was to sleep and know that one is sleeping. He yearned to see things with their dull, slow-blinking eyes, to retire into their blissful sloth of semi-sensation. He yearned to be one of these white oxen—he, the purest of his white oxen.

Parabolic Tale, with Invocation

And the old man, being an old man, and therefore a *senex*, and entitled to give counsel, asked the young man:

"Young man, what do you know?"

And the young man, who had felled trees, had girded mountains and swum rivers, done many things, and who never took counsel, immediately answered:

"I know everything, father."

And the old man rather smiled and said:

"I know nothing."

And the old man, being old, then gave the young man counsel, which the young man tossed aside with anger. And the young man continued to do many things, while the venerable *senex* meditated in silence and was mildly discomforted by the young man's stubbornness. And the old man's mind became quiet, and magnificent, and awesome, like a deserted Cathedral full of vanished echoes. And his soul became tall, and calm, and Gothic, like the Cathedral. But he was still vexed at the sacred stubbornness of the young man, and still gave counsel.

Until finally the young man hearkened a little, and found that what the ancient *senex* said was wise. And the more he obeyed, the less often he swam a stream too swift.

And the old man wrote his counsel, that other young men might read of it, and died. And the young man became old, and counseled the young. And these young men hearkened to him, at first not at all, then more, and more, until they, too, were *senexes*, fit to give counsel. And having spoken, they died.

And as time went on the young men were led more and more by the accumulated wisdom of the old men, and their mistakes became fewer and fewer.

They are trying to guide me; O God, be merciful, and spare me, who should be young yet, from the wisdom of death.

The Excursion

Having nothing to do, and having searched in vain among the notes of a piano for something to think on, I started off on a walk, trusting that I might scent a scandal on the breeze, or see God's toe peep through the sky. I passed a barbershop, a grocery store, a little Italian girl, a chicken coop, a roadhouse, an abandoned quarry, a field of nervous wheat. All this distance I had walked under God's blue sky, and still without a thought. But at last, after trudging on for hours, I came upon a thought. Miles upon miles I had walked for a thought, and at last I came upon an anthill.

Idly curious, I stopped to look at the ants. They would go from one place to another and return to that first place again, and for no reason that I could see. Little ants with big burdens, big ants with bigger burdens, and ants with no burdens, the most frightened and panicky of them all. As I watched them they seemed so human to me that my heart went out to them. "Poor little devils," I said.

But I grew tired of watching the swarming mass of them. "I shall watch just one of them," I said to myself after much deliberation. And I picked out one frightened little ant to watch. He went running about unaware of my presence, not knowing that a great god was looking down on him, just as I did not know but that a great god might be looking down on me. And with the toe of my shoe I marked out a rut in his path, so that he had to climb over it. And then I began dropping little bits of sand on him, and turning him over with a blade of grass. "I am his destiny," I whispered; the conception thrilled me.

187

As the poor little fellow rushed about in terror, I realized how massive his belief in life must be at this moment, how all-consuming his tragedy; my pity went out to him. But my blade of grass was too limber; I picked up a little stone to push him with. I drew a circle. "May God strike me dead, little ant, if you get out of that circle." I took that oath, and the battle was on. It was long and uncertain, with victory now on his side, and now on mine.

The little ant, in a last despairing burst, made for the edge of the circle, and crossed it. I was aroused. "I'll kill the ant," I shouted, and brought the stone down on his body, his passions, his dreams. Destiny had spoken. For an instant I was ashamed, for I had been unfair. He had beaten me under the terms I had made myself. I should have let him go free.

I began watching other ants. They irritated me—they were so earnest, so faithful. Two ants came up and touched. I wondered what that could mean. Do ants talk? Then I watched one of the ants which had touched the other to see if it touched still other ants. For it might be a herald of some sort; perhaps ants do talk.

One little ant was tugging and pulling at a dead bug. Slowly, carefully, I took my stone and drew it over two of his legs, so that he was wounded grievously, and began writhing in agony. My face was distorted with compassion; how my heart bled for him!

I ran the stone across his other legs, and the motion was like a thrust into my own flesh. I was almost sick with pity for the poor little ant, and to end his suffering I killed him. Wide regret came on me. "Perhaps," I thought, "perhaps, he was a poet. Perhaps I have killed a genius."

And I began stepping on the other ants, digging up the anthill, scattering destruction broadcast about me. When my work was finished, and only a few mangled ants remained alive, my sorrow for the poor little ants had grown until it weighed on me, and crushed the vitality out of me. "The poor little ants," I kept murmuring, "the poor, miserable little ants." And I was bitter with the thought of how cruel the universe is, and how needlessly things must suffer. I stood gazing at the death and slaughter about me, stupefied with calm horror at what I had done. I prayed to God.

"O Great God," I prayed, throwing back my head towards Heaven and stretching out my hands like Christ on the Cross, "O Great God" —but I didn't really throw back my head, for I still kept looking at the ants, and I did not address God, for at times I even wonder if there be no God. I didn't do these things, I say, since I was too intently watching the ants. "O Almighty God," I thundered out in mighty prayer, throwing back my head towards Heaven and stretching out my hands like Christ on the Crucifix, "Thou who art Ruler of us all. Now I know why we suffer, and ache, and I pity Thee, God."

A Man of Forethought

1

Carter admitted it to himself: his hand was trembling. For after all, there was no reason why he shouldn't admit it; and there was no reason why his hand shouldn't tremble. He was to decide a woman's destiny today, and the woman was atrociously good-looking.

As he stood with his eyes fastened on the dull little penny that lay in his quivering palm, Carter mused poetically on the idea that a mere penny would decide his fate. Any number of people had thrown caution to the various winds when tempted by an obese wallet; he even remembered having read a touching tale of a girl's having gone astray for a pair of shoes; but here he was, the prince of all lost souls, following the dictates of a penny.

Perhaps he had better make it the best out of three tosses. After all, one lone final toss was too sudden, too brutal almost. It was like having the electric light switched on when one had been dozing in the dark. It was like trying to step up one more step than there was, and getting oneself disturbingly jolted. The little penny, as it lay head upright before him, shouted its commands at him, and he resented it. By heavens, he would make it the best out of three tosses!

Still, that was unfair, both to himself and the penny. He had sworn on the Blue Book that it would be one toss, and only one. Very well, he would compromise.

He opened the second drawer of his desk and took out a pack of cards. If an ace turned up within the first eleven cards he would take three tosses instead of one.

He shuffled the cards nervously; in his excitement he dropped a couple. They fell face up on the floor, and he saw that one was an ace. He had a sneaking temptation to put it on the top of the deck and begin dealing, but one last spark of manhood held out, and he shuffled the ace out of knowledge into the pack. Then he began dealing.

The fifth card was an ace. He breathed easier. Now he was entitled to two more tosses of the coin.

He took a glance at himself in the mirror and decided that the pallor caused by this excitement made him very handsome. He gave his hair an unnecessary stroke or two. Then he steeled himself for the second toss.

"As before, heads—yes, tails—no; get ready, get set, one, two, three, go!"

The penny sailed high into the air, clinked against the ceiling, fell promptly and rolled under the piano. Carter strained himself to get it out without bagging his trousers. Good—it was tails.

He had earned an intermission. He poured himself a generous drink of his favorite cognac. He paused a bit. Then, made more courageous by the alcohol, he picked up the coin and threw it on his little mahogany gueridon with a magnificent carelessness.

Done!

"In God we trust . . . Liberty . . . 1916 . . ." and the serene profile of Abraham Lincoln with his eyes seeking the decanter of cognac.

John Carter cursed *pianissimo*. But his fate was decided—absolutely. Destiny had spoken; and poor dear Clarisse must pay the penalty. For it is the woman who pays; it is not the tempting man but the tempted woman who must suffer. Carter was decidedly comforted by repeating to himself this beautiful commonplace.

But he must act immediately. He knew only too well his deucedly cautious nature. He rushed to the phone and told the operator in the corridor of the apartment hotel to call a taxi. Then he added a few feverish touches to his toilet.

He reflected with a certain relief that this half-affair between him-self and Clarisse was to be settled at last. It had hung on for years now, ever since long before her marriage. Of course, it was a miser-able thing to do to Dick. But he had had too much consideration for Dick already. Beginning with the days he had pulled Dick through his Latin at prep school, and ending with his noble stupidity of com-ing all the way from Italy to be best man at their wedding, Carter's life had been one long list of self-sacrifices for Dick.

Bosom friend or no bosom friend, Carter had at last decided to obey the commands of the tossed penny. He was desperately in love with Clarisse, so much so that he had taken all his other women off the mantelpiece. And such an absorbing love, that might some day spoil his appetite, deserved expression.

The phone rang. Carter swung around with a frightened jerk, and overturned a pile of music. He snatched the receiver.

"Taxi? Yes, be right down. What? No? Oh, pshaw! Tell him I'm not at home." He slapped down the receiver and began picking up the music. He was shaking all over.

"Damn it, I'm too nervous," he muttered. "I'll force myself to be quiet. I'll play something, something of my own, something very gentle. But I have nothing very gentle. I don't turn out things like that. Let's see, there is a soft little thing of Debussy's. But all the little girls play that now after they're through with the 'Dance of the Witches' and 'Snowy Dewdrops.' Grade 3 A. The devil. There is a lovely little minuet in one of Beethoven's sonatas. The old masters, something with good solid harmonies . . . that's what I want. Perhaps a good-humored bit of Haydn. Perhaps . . ."

The phone rang. It was the taxi. He rushed out of the room. What luck, what divinely auspicious luck . . . he just caught the elevator. Evidently everything was going to go well. He tumbled hastily into the cab and almost whispered the address to the driver. The man looked at him sharply, as though he understood. The insolence! Carter felt himself getting angry. What was the ass waiting for?

"Hurry. I am in a dreadful hurry. I will make it worth your while."

"East or West?" the driver asked.

Oh, so that was the trouble? In his precipitancy he had merely neglected to say which side of Fifth Avenue. How ridiculous of him to get angry when it was all his fault.

"East," and the taxi was off.

As he was jolted about in the capricious taxi, he tried to form some definite plan of action. For decidedly he was a man of forethought. It wouldn't do to stumble in abruptly, drop on his knees, and blubber out "I love you." Yet, on the other hand, this very suddenness might be effective; women are often highly susceptible to that sort of technique. Still, if he began immediately with these sudden tactics, it might lead to something embarrassing. He had better delay until he had made sure no one was there besides Clarisse. It would be just as well, after a mysterious silence, after five minutes of vague and absent-minded conversation, to be then transformed into a passionate whirlwind.

But about this "I love you." Here was a problem that always kept turning up, and for which he had never found a solution. Does a phrase, when applied to these ultimate issues, gain by being so hopelessly banal, or does it lose? Women aren't so particular about the brandnewness of a sentence as men are. They are more taken with the impetus of it, and an "I love you," said quiveringly enough, was probably the best one could do. They like to think one is speaking the eternal sentence; it lends a certain cosmic air to their love. Just as the little birdies and grasshoppers have chirped the same love-chirp for centuries and centuries, so this poor man, prostrate before them under the heavy burden of this ultimate issue, must make the same noise as his ancestors, the same meager succession of syllables must trill from his love-thick tongue.

2

The taxi, getting suddenly clear of all traffic impediments, took a short spurt, and the realization that he was nearing Clarisse so swiftly stirred up a little panic in Carter. When he had calmed down a bit, he resolved to be less practical in his meditations; he grew ashamed of their cold-bloodedness. He huddled himself into an amorphous jostled mass, and let his mind wander back to the more idyllic phases of their attachment.

The various attitudes he had gone through had purified him, he decided. For the first few months after their marriage he had refused loyally even to lift his eyes to her; he had tried to get her out of his thoughts. What a noble time that had been!

First, in the vain effort to forget her, he had written, and published at his own expense, a book of essays on his travels in Italy, but only to spoil it all by the pregnant dedication, "To C."

Then he had become more desperate, and more noble, and sought distraction among the vulgar beauties of the stage. He was nearly succeeding when his funds threatened to give out, and he was thrown more inexorably than ever into the clutches of his dolorous love for Clarisse.

Then Dick had got it into his good-natured stupid old head that Clarisse and Carter should see more of each other. Carter told him outright that Clarisse troubled him—*intrigued* him, as the Café de la Paix would put it—but the man had simply laughed, and felt a little flattered. Carter thought him a charming ass, but he said no more about it.

Then came the day when Carter saw her with a headache, a neat little white cloth tied about her temples. He had tightened his jaw with the sudden realization of how inevitable she was to him. He was proud of the feelings he had had towards her then, for there had been a note of decided Christian cleanness. He had simply wanted to kiss her on the forehead, to advise her, to smoke big cigars and tell her things. It was a period of uprightness, during which he had maintained the most loyal of attitudes towards her and Dick. And most important, it was an excuse for everything that might follow.

But alas, it had only been a period of transition. Slight touches of her skirt as she whisked by him, her smile, the way she said "no," the night she hurt her ankle and leaned against him—these things had contrived to change him. He wished he could have remained the big brother he had once felt himself to be. But things had turned otherwise, until now . . . he noticed with a shock that the taxi had turned into her street.

Another three minutes! Why did he breathe so? There was no danger. Dick was sure to be away, and even if he were at home there were excuses enough. Another two minutes!

The vividness of the prospective scene renewed his zeal. He saw himself drop down before her, and take her hands, and kiss them . . . kiss them. For once in his life he would be wild, incautious. Perhaps it would stir him into a different sort of life, a careless, vicious existence with a maximum of dash, far from his neat apartment with its cut glass, its quiet rugs and mahogany. Perhaps he could write a novel about it. Perhaps . . . another minute!

He saw himself there on his knees, pleading. It was a delightful morsel to dwell upon. But had she been prepared to love him? Had she gone through a period of resolute indifference, then brave sisterhood, then metamorphosed gently into a woman ripe for the love of him? Perhaps she would feel a monstrous disgust at his advances, and turn away from him with scorn, as from something evil and filthy. Or perhaps she would be wounded, deeply wounded, at the insult he offered her, and would run away from him, frightened and whimpering. She was a good girl, and faithful to her husband. He had no right to expect such unworthy things of her . . .

There was the house now, the one with the colonial portico. What he had been thinking of was impossible. She was not the sort of woman who yields to other men. The calm, smooth life she led permitted of nothing irregular, nothing out of the way. . . . The taxi stopped.

"Drive through Central Park."

"Yes, sir." The driver's voice was puzzling, as though he took a personal interest in all these numerous scandals which he drove people up to and away from. The taxi leapt ahead.

Crushed! Eternally a man of forethought! Carter was thoroughly sick of himself, as if he were a disagreeable food in his own stomach. He would get drunk. Drunk, faugh! What right did he have to get drunk? Drink is for those whose lives are of sharp edges and deafening crashes. The souls that are impelled to drink climb craggy mountains and topple into abysses that are dizzy, very dizzy. For Carter there was nothing; he was ever a man of careful, deliberate, painstaking forethought. He had had the forethought to see that Clarisse was unattainable; he must pay the penalty with his endless mediocrity of action. . . .

Two days afterwards Dick came rushing into Carter's room, savagely drunk.

"She's gone!" he screamed. "The harlot! She deserted me; she's run off with a movie actor!"

Carter promptly left his room, bought a revolver and some cartridges, loaded the revolver, put it to his head and, being a man of forethought, didn't shoot himself.

Mrs. Maecenas

1

Ego vox clamantis in deserto.
WORDS OF ST. JOHN

After many years of faithful service, the professor had become president of the university, taken him a somewhat scandalously younger wife, and died, leaving a string of pompous titles to the wind, and a flourishing widow over thirty to the world. The wife of the head of the physics department, who was usually well up on such things, had prophesied that the president's widow would soon quit the little town for ever, but contrary to expert opinion, she continued living in the same house, nay, even maintained her former connections with the university. The unexpressed consensus of opinion was that this woman was too charming to be beyond suspicion, but yet her scutcheon was radiant with blotlessness. Propriety had been observed with a rigidity that was perhaps even a bit dogmatic, as in the case of her dismissing the chauffeur. And besides, she was left with a little girl, which was even more reassuring.

After the fitting period of black, and another fitting period of subdued colors, she gradually drifted into a superbness of attire that was perhaps not quite so fitting, but was still within the code. For she never appeared again in smart clothes; in fact, even the most unfriendly had to admit that she was almost matronly. A big-busted woman, she carried herself with firm dignity, and talked with a Southern accent in a voice that was rich and deep, and might even indicate that she had once been an instructress in elocution.

Within two years after her husband's death, she had acquired a unique position in the life of the university. There were fussy young girls who, as the expression goes, just idolized her. She was the unfailing chaperon at all school functions, since she had succeeded in the difficult task of both entering in with the feelings of the students and yet making them remember that she was not one of them. If she appeared at any of the games, the students, at a sign from their cheerleader, would doff their caps, and cheer for her. There is no greater tribute to her tact than the fact that she was honorary head of both the Athenian Literary Society and the Society of Fine Arts, two organizations which were always facing each other with backs hunched and teeth bared. It was as patroness of these two organizations that she acquired the flattering nickname of "Mrs. Maecenas." For of all her interests in student activities, her guidance of "the arts" had been most faithful.

In the course of her five years at the university Mrs. Maecenas had judged twelve debates on the single tax, fifteen on the inferiority of women to men, and nine on various phases of prohibition, state, national, and locally optional; and to her credit be it said that her verdicts were not always the same on the same subjects. Mrs. Maecenas had read a gross of horror stories that had received good grades in English Composition 22, and were written after the manner of Edgar Allan Poe; and another gross or two that had been cribbed from O. Henry. Mrs. Maecenas had gone through thousands of rhymed documents on pubescent and adolescent affections, still in her capacity as a protectrice of the arts. And when the war started, and a big man in the German department had called the French a degenerate nation, Mrs. Maecenas had written a charming letter to the school paper in which she denounced the Huns and spoke very beautifully of modern French poetry.

But the truth is that Mrs. Maecenas was getting weary. She had seen ten semesters of the university, and her hopes of mothering a little renaissance out here in the wilderness had gradually pined away as the engineering and agricultural schools grew steadily more vigorous. Everywhere, everywhere, typical young Americans were springing up, sturdy tough daisy-minds that were cheerful, healthy, and banal. How could art thrive here, she asked herself, in a land so unfavorable to the artist's temper! These lusty young throats that cheered her at the football games, they were miserably sane and normal. And Mrs. Maecenas found herself entertaining uncharitable feelings towards these fine young men and women who thought so much of her.

Under the plea of ill health, she began to appear less at school festivities. Also, her child was getting older now, and the need of giving it more attention added motivation to her retirement. She became less kindly in her opinions of the stories and verses she was given to criticize, until this burden had decreased almost to a total nullity. As a consequence, within another year Mrs. Maecenas was hardly more than a widow with a little daughter. An occasional attack of her old weakness for genius-hunting would lure her now and then to one of the literary clubs, but she usually returned from them with such a feeling of exhaustion and disgust that she wondered how she ever could have stood it.

Mrs. Maecenas settled down to be the voice of one whispering very quietly in the wilderness. The great machine of the university could dump its annual output of standardized "leaders of America," could ship them off every commencement day labeled "with all the advantages of a college education"; the alumni could put up a sundial or a gate, or an iron railing, every year in sacred memory of their dear Alma Mater; the great auditorium could tremble with cheering and shouting when big Dick Halloway, handsome blond-haired Dick, the hero of the university, shot the winning goal; all this could go on if it would—but Mrs. Maecenas got farther away from it all, and nearer to her books and her piano. The university became healthier, and she quietly blushed for the future of America. . . .

And then it was that her genius came. By the purest chance she had gone to the Athenian meeting. She found the room peculiarly astir. Little groups were talking quite low together, glancing now and then towards one corner of the room. In this corner, with his back turned towards the members of the Athenian, a rather gawkily formed young man was reading a yellow paper-covered volume which Mrs. Maecenas recognized to be a French novel. There was a slight smell of whiskey in the room.

Mrs. Maecenas knew she had found her genius. Yet at this time Siegfried was barely seventeen.

2

Ecce quam bonum et quam jucundum habitare fratres in unum!   PSALM 132

Siegfried presented himself at the home of Mrs. Maecenas late the following afternoon. He was just as gawkily formed as the night before, and another yellow-covered book was in his hand, but his breath this time smelled strongly of coffee beans. In spite of the coffee beans, however, Siegfried had had no more whiskey; with peculiar astuteness in these matters, he had realized that it would probably be a false step to exhale the same shocking odor of the previous night; but on the other hand, to exhale the standard destroyer of this odor might give the precisely proper variation. Siegfried selected his breath with as much care as less imaginative souls give to their neckties. The door was opened by the widow herself.

"Mrs. Maecenas, I believe?"

"Oh, Siegfried, won't you come in?" She had always insisted on calling the students by their first names.

He stepped into a dark reception hall, and then followed her to the left into her library, Mrs. Maecenas having dispensed with the small-town parlor. "I am very glad you came to see me, although . . ." and here she laughed with her widow roguishness, "although I'm not so sure that I ought to be."

Siegfried was startled. He had not hoped to be taken so freely. But he skimmed the cream of the occasion, and cast away the yoke of his youth in the quality of his equals-to-equals answer, "Throw all caution, etc., I implore you, Mrs. Maecenas, and be less churchly and more Christian. I have come to you as a last hope; deliver me from this American captivity." He began looking over her books without further formality. Mrs. Maecenas sat down tentatively on the piano stool, facing away from the piano, and her two arms stretched back on the keyboard.

"Your remarks might lead me to conclude that you are not an American yourself, my dear boy, but nevertheless I'll risk my life that you, like me, were raised under the tutelage of the chopped-down cherry tree." At this Siegfried turned suddenly, like an ill-tempered dog.

"Ugh! My father was an alumnus of this university. Is that credentials enough?" And then just as suddenly cherubic again: "But you have them all, every one! I might think I was by the Pont Neuf."

"The books? Yes, and I should be pleased to lend them to you, if you should ever want any of them."

"And no George Sand! And no Sandeau! And no Bourget! Why, Mrs. Maecenas, I am in the library that *I* shall own some day. Oh, please let me come here, in this modern *thébaïde*, in this elevation above the chewing gum and sarsaparilla of our beloved countrymen. God bless them, they have carried their Monroe Doctrine into culture. And what a beautiful set of Flaubert!"

"*Shhh! Et les bouquins! Viens!*" With mock caution she led him by the hand to a corner where something square was standing, covered with a drapery of dark purple. She lifted this slowly, disclosing another bookcase. "Popery!" And she slipped out two heavy breviaries, with black leather bindings, and rich gilt edges. She opened one of them at random, and displayed a beautiful front of red and black, with illuminated capitals. Then she pointed to a Dutch edition of Boethius's *De Consolatione Philosophiæ*, in the russet-leather of the seventeenth century. There was the Vulgate in five volumes, the *Peristephanon* and *Psychomachia* of Prudentius; Siegfried's eyes followed her hand as it brushed along the books. "I must admit," she said, "I did not collect these. They were my husband's. We spoke of them in secret, as though they were the limbs of a child we had pulled apart and stuffed up the chimney." There was also a copy of Huysmans' *Sainte Lydwine de Schiedam* in Gothic type, Rémy de Gourmont's critical anthology of mystic Latin verse, and Saint

François de Sales' *Introduction à la vie dévote* in a paper cover of ludicrously innocent blue.

"Popery, bah!" Siegfried exclaimed. "The de Gourmont gives you away. And that, down in the corner, that Petronius! Madam, you are a pagan, for who but a pagan would own such lovely tomes? Nay, you are worse than a pagan; you are a lover of art. I am scandalized. I shall expose you before the world!"

Mrs. Maecenas laughed. "Art was once loved; then it was tolerated; and now it will soon be prohibited, so that we must express our devotion to it in secret, deep in the catacombs. Those are, more or less, the words of de Gourmont. And so you must come here often, Siegfried, and we shall kneel together before the clandestine altar."

After this, they knelt together no less than twice a week. Although Siegfried was more cautious, Mrs. Maecenas plunged headlong into her epithets, and described their evenings as "something rare and wonderful." Love, art, death, renunciation, the beautiful—the two of them drank long draughts of these deep red vintages, for they each loved art eloquently. Huddled darkly in the crypt, they would discuss all eternal and universal things, and he would read his prose and verses. She didn't write herself, but what a warm critic!

Perhaps no evening was more wonderful than that sleety night before the holidays. Siegfried had struggled against a persistently vindictive slashing of hail, and arrived with his overcoat feeling like a hulk of iron. As he turned from the street towards the widow's home, he saw the subdued red of the drop-light, "their light," glowing in the window. He felt so deliriously conscious of his health, of his strength, as he stamped on to the porch. Mrs. Maecenas opened the door before he could ring.

"Whew!" he exclaimed, "how many enemies I have out in this night!" He knocked the drippings from his hat, and shook his coat, then stepped into the warm hallway. "I was hardly more than a primitive out in that storm, battling savagely with all the little gods."

She took his coat. "Ah, you have noticed that? It is so easy to understand when one is fighting a storm, just how the original man had to imagine the world peopled with demons. A cutting wind in your face soon seems like a challenge aimed at you personally, just as a fist in the face might. And you can't walk against it five minutes without squaring your jaw, or even shouting as though you were a fiend yourself."

Thus was the platter handed to Siegfried. He returned it graciously as they stepped into the library: "And then, to continue the same viewpoint, think how extraordinarily secure this original man must have felt when he had gained his cave, where there was fire, and light, and warmth to reassure him that he had outstridden the demon. . . . Perhaps that is why I feel so peculiarly comfortable now as I see those logs where I can warm my hands." He laughed. "Congratulate me; I feel that I unwound a pretty statement there. . . . But as to the warming of hands, it is a pleasure to warm them before a log fire even when they are not cold."

"Once the hands are warmed before the fire of logs, we can then warm them before the fire of life," and the widow had acquitted herself.

"Ah!" After which, for no defined reason, he thought this a time to summon all his boyishness in a toss of the head, and a patent carefree laugh. "How fortunate it is that Landor is not popular."

"Yes, if I were deprived of that lovely quatrain! How *right* a thing to compose on one's seventy-fifth birthday!"

"Isn't it? It must gratify a man to evolve so perfectly concomitantly with his years, to write patriarchally when he is old, to be so complete an entelechy."

"The entelechy, I always felt, was one of Aristotle's most valuable conceptions," Mrs. Maecenas fell in, thereby advancing the conversation another stage. They were gratified with the way they were talking this evening; already they had, by logical steps, moved from the storm to Aristotelianism, and Siegfried's feet were hardly warm yet. And this in the light of the fact that they had begun with the most deadly of conversations, the weather. Nor had either of them failed to note that the weather itself had been done satisfactorily.

Siegfried was worthy of his task. "Aristotle came centuries too soon. If the divine chronology were in perfect ordination he should have come now, after man had flopped and floundered for so long and so distractedly. For if he came now, and offered his massive sanity to the world, men would open their eyes with wonder. But as it is, this astonishing cure for dark thinking was propounded before we began to think darkly, so that we are still waiting for someone. If the world should—"

"Pardon me for interrupting you, Siegfried, but I have been watching you. I have been watching your eyes. Siegfried, do you suffer from headaches?"

Siegfried was content; the interruption was significant. Remarks like this had been an ever-swelling note in their song of late. But one must be cautious. "My eyes—yes—Aristotle . . . oh! Do I suffer from headaches? Why, I suppose they are headaches. I had an aunt who went mad, but I don't suppose . . ."

"No, no, no—nothing like that. Don't say it, Siegfried!" And Mrs. Maecenas stopped her ears, so that Siegfried noticed her full white arms. . . . There was a lull in the conversation, as was fitting. The big clock in the hall suddenly became important, and flooded the library with its ticking. Siegfried looked lugubriously into the fire, religiously observing the ceremonies of the situation. After a time, the widow ventured a timid triad. It was delicious to be pampered this way! Siegfried was basking in the warm sun of sentiment. Then, as if putting aside a great burden, she broke the silence: "Did you bring anything to read to me this evening, my boy?"

"Some more of my Bible. I did good work on Chapter 37 of the Second Epistle of Josephat. And I have the Forty-first and Forty-third Psalms of Obad. But the latter are too rough yet. You would accuse me of excessive youth. I brought only the Josephat."

"You have been working hard, Siegfried." And she closed her eyes in voluptuous expectation as Siegfried opened his briefcase.

Siegfried returned and sat down by the fire. He prepared to read, then put down the paper again to clear his throat. He cast a quick glance in the direction of the widow; she was ready:

"Second Epistle of Josephat.
Chapter 37, Verses 9–17.

9 And the prophet Mehovah, when he was come

out of the dry places of Arabia, lifted his voice before the multitude assembled, saying:

10 Many are the sorrows that beset the ways of sinners and those that trespass against the Lord, for His eyes of vengeance are manifold, and His wrath endureth for ever.

11 He shall slake their thirst with salt, and feed their hunger with the dry bones of His laughter; their bellies shall be empty, and the tongues parched of those that have sinned against Him.

12 He shall smite them until they cry out with madness, and gape and blubber at the sight of seven moons.

13 And they shall be made to run naked in fields of thistle, where the thistle barbs shall prick them, and strike out at them like hissing snakes.

14 And they shall wander in night as black as their iniquity; in the blackness of night, beasts shall brush against them, and unknown things, and voices shall whine out of the funnel of darkness.

15 And they shall wend from the valleys up into the mountains, and from the tops of the mountains back into the valleys, and find not what they seek; no, not even shall they know the things they are seeking.

16 All these evils and many others shall visit the sons of Belial, and Belial's daughters, but for those blessed with righteousness there shall be playing of harps and dulcimers, and an abundance of honey.

17 And when Mehovah had said these things, he turned again into the desert."

"Excellong!" the widow cried out immediately. "Let me have them. And you recited so beautifully!" Siegfried handed her the manuscript. Glancing through it, she made her criticisms. "The delicate irony of the prophet coming up out of the desert just to deliver a speech of about a hundred words, and then going back again, is the kind of thing we love to find out for ourselves. France would have loved to do it. And how much more capable your prophet was of imagining tortures than bliss; the point is ferociously well made. But, Siegfried, I am afraid of you, with your eager *sadisme littéraire*. Your mind is so gloriously unhealthy, so à la Baudelaire. If *Le Mauvais Vitrier* were not already written, I am sure you would do it sooner or later. Or some of de Gourmont's *Oraisons mauvaises*. You are an incipient Giles de Retz. And—pardon me—so young! But why aren't you younger still, Siegfried, so young that I could throw my arms around you and kiss you for this magnificent performance? Siegfried, you are going to redeem America in the eyes of the world."

Siegfried nursed the moment in silence. Mrs. Maecenas went on. "But there are things lacking yet, Siegfried, *big* things." Thoughtfully: "If you can do this much without experience, on air, as it were, great Heavens, what will you come to when you have lived! Sometimes I feel it is my duty to—to—*aid* you, Siegfried, to be a—a *real* Maecenas, or a real *Mrs.* Maecenas rather." Then explosively: "Oh, Siegfried, my poor, dear boy, the wonderful things you are still to learn." Abruptly: "Think, Siegfried, you haven't even been in love yet!" He said nothing. "Have you?"

"I'm not sure, but there's a charming little prissy in one of my classes whose delicate-pink cheeks I should love to slap."

"Faugh! How young you can be at times! Not to know more about oneself than that! You will begin by loving an older woman." With a laugh: "But we both know that you must find out all these things for yourself." And with the echo of this interlude still rumbling in the far valleys, the conversation again turned to art.

As he ploughed back through the slush that night Siegfried attempted to place his relationship with Mrs. Maecenas, and finally contented himself with the conclusion that the general was leading to the specific. Or there might be room for some sort of a syllogism somewhere: he needed *Experience*; Mrs. Maecenas wanted him to have *Experience*; ergo . . . but that didn't quite fit together. In any case, on the whole the thing had a slight *savour* of the Aphrodite-and-Adonis, with him playing Adonis merely because he didn't know how to play anyone else. He hated to be so frank about the thing, but it *did* look as though the day was approaching when he could face the sun stolidly, and proclaim with firmness, "I have become a man." But the important thing was that these evenings were excellent, and it was delightful to be so worried over.

3

Nemo mundus a sorde, nec si unius diei vita ejus sit in terra.
BOOK OF JOB

A week later. The dim red drop-light was burning in the window, which might have told the world that this was one of Siegfried's nights. Outside, a soft snow was sifting quietly, making a mystic haze about the streetlamps. Siegfried had just finished playing the *Moonlight.*

For a moment he sat motionless, still facing the piano. The big clock in the hall, ever on the alert for such times, promptly loomed up again. The flames of the gas-fire climbed noisily over the asbestos. He turned slowly towards the widow. "And just think, Mrs. Maecenas, one isn't allowed to like the *Sonata Quasi una Fantasia* anymore! ... But who knows? Perhaps I shouldn't either if it were literature and not music. ..." She was looking out the window, and made no answer. He let a few moments go by, then instinctively, he plunged into another direction. "You are looking out into the night? ... It meant a lot to me to come to you through a night like that. It felt as though I were stealing to you. Or as though I were here by the special dispensation of a good fairy who had warned me that I must be home again by the stroke of twelve. ... The night is full of whisperings about Cinderella. ... I had to play the *Moonlight*, you see. But I am silly? Yes?"

"A little, Siegfried—but pleasantly so." They both thought her answer had a sweetly Shakespearean flavor.

"But you should forgive me. We who have not had the big things of life yet, you will find that at bottom we have a horrible amount of silliness; silly little dreams, silly little expectations, silly little long-ings. Perhaps we are not so pure as the little girls in a convent, but we are every bit as silly.

> 'Little Doris of twelve, what is sillier, Dorrie?
> Is it you, or is it I,
> Or the silly little morning-glory?'

Yes, they are mine; but I never brought them around. I never dared to."

She turned and faced him, having contrived dexterously to keep the divan from creaking. "You should have, Siegfried. I was coming to think of you as a monster. And after all, are we not peculiarly close in our present predicaments? You have not had the things of life, and I . . ." with an uncertain sigh, then explosively, "I have passed them by, I suppose."

Siegfried was sure the flower was in full bloom, but in spite of him, Adonis answered: "Yet we always hold back. There is some sickly longing in man to deprive himself of those things which mean most to him. We are proud, not when we have been happy, but when we have wallowed in misery. *If anyone have anything of which he is especially fond, let it be taken from him.* That was, I believe, one of the rules of the Benedictines. It is a sentence that is very beautiful to me, and yet there is no sweeping simile, no brilliance of epithet, nothing but bare bleached bones. It is its sheer austerity which makes it allur-ing, the mere conception of these self-flagellating temperaments so eager in harvesting their tortures. . . . We no longer have religion, if by religion one means the hierarchy of the angels, and a *Janitor Cœli*, and a God to sit massively on his throne, but ah! . . . how appealing the *instincts* of religion still are to us! I could take the vows of an anchorite, not to attain some ultimate Kingdom of the Blessed there-by, but merely through a vague urge towards asceticism, even though I have nothing for which to be ascetic. For we are all tinged a bit by the stench of holiness, *sanctitatis odore.* . . . Perhaps I might be asce-tic for my art, but you tell me that the artist must *live*, not *flee from life*. Blind mouths, as Milton has put it. Blind mouths! We are like frail little kittens hardly a day old, nosing around for the mother's teat." Siegfried was dissatisfied for once, even though his rhetoric had been faultless. Still, he had ended the flight happily enough, it might prove.

There was a long silence. Then the widow began speaking very slowly. "My eloquent child, my baby Nestor, have you ever seen Thackeray's cartoon of Louis XIV? You remember the one drawing of the silly runt of a king, old, sallow, dried, hideously devoid of kingliness. Then steps forth Louis the Great, the official Louis, Louis the Emperor Augustus of France, Louis the State, the King of Corneille, of Racine, of Molière. He is stilted, and bejeweled, and sumptuously robed. He is draped and decorated. He is magnified with scaffolds. And behold, he is Regal! In the same way, Siegfried, I should love to make a cartoon of what you have just said. For you have done nothing other than Thackeray says was done to Louis. You have taken a condition that is devoid of interest and value, and you have decked it with royal purples. . . . No, Siegfried, you can say what you like about the beauty of asceticism; but after you have perverted and twisted and beautified to your heart's content, at bottom the original thing remains. . . . For your art's sake, for *America's* sake, you must get up and move. . . . The Muse is a woman, Siegfried, and the formula is that the worse you treat a woman the more she loves you. You may find that if you forget art long enough to live, your art may be all the stronger for it afterwards."

Siegfried was content. He found it pleasant to be exhorted, and pled with. But he wished for a way to get off this Adonis strain. He cursed himself for his praise of asceticism; it might have been too discouraging. But while she was making cartoons, why didn't she make another, showing his true attitude towards Experience? Taking the royal purple off his "urge to asceticism" might reveal an urge of an entirely different sort. Siegfried had no essential objection to being Experienced. But, hell . . . there was plenty of time. Yet it was disagreeable to think so practically about these things.

"But the play, Siegfried! We have wasted all this time, and I am determined to hear the entire play this evening. The little snatches you have told me of it . . . I am mad to hear it all. Begin it immediately."

Siegfried rose from the piano, and went out into the hallway for his briefcase. Mrs. Maecenas pulled a chair up to the light for him, and fixed herself on the sofa, with eyes closed. Siegfried returned and took his seat by the light. He paused. Mrs. Maecenas readjusted her pillow, glanced down at the white of her exposed neck, and then over at Siegfried.

"But, Siegfried," she cried out in sudden horror, "what is the matter with your face?"

He looked up in astonishment. Then he thought he understood: she was pampering him, no doubt. "The paleness? Am I unusually pale tonight? I was smoking a lot today."

"Uh . . . y—yes. Why, yes, the pallor." Then she seemed to recover. "But that is not unusual, I suppose. The artist's temper . . . nervosity . . . pallor would be natural."

Siegfried understood now. It was not the *pallor*, then, but the *redness*. *Nemo mundus a sorde*; nature is such a tyrant. Yesterday they had broken out, and today they were all over his chin. But how annoying that she should react so to pimples!

A few more sentences were offered. She seemed very tired. Siegfried decided tentatively to remember an engagement. "Oh, I am awfully sorry, Siegfried." She would let him go so easily, then? . . .

A few months later they passed on the street, and she nodded to him very sweetly. They even exchanged a couple of words.

She hoped he was getting on well, she said.

The Soul of Kajn Tafha

Nobody knew when Kajn Tafha had been young. Old Kajn was like the great trees, which in their turn are like the great angry rocks. The point of his beard extended down to his navel, and the hair of his brows grew over his eye-sockets like shrubbery about the Poison Cave. Nobody knew anything about Kajn save that he was as wise as the little animals and that he ate no meat. The lobes of his ears had been torn off; some say it had been done by a passing demon who tried to whisper false counsel, and bit at him when angered by his indifference; others say the priests had done it as a punishment when Kajn called it a sin to throw she-babies into the Ganges; but no one knew. Mothers frightened bad children by telling them Kajn would get them, and yet when people were sick unto death they called for Kajn. Kajn was very wise, so wise that it is horrible to think about.

Then one day, just before the last bleeding agony of the sun, when the dirty brats were gathered in front of their own homes, and every one was tired, Kajn appeared in the midst of the village, and lifted up his voice in prayer to his own gods.

"O ye miserable gods, you have made me wise, until I can foretell the darkening of the moon, and know to fear not the quaking of the earth; nor do I fear the heavens spewing fire and turmoil. For years I have walked upright with the awareness of my wisdom, and now that I am wise, what has it gotten me? The ignorant children about me pull back their lips from their teeth, and I know that is a sign of laughter, which is a sign of happiness. I would give my soul to be one of them. The weary toiler of the field comes home and looks at his woman, and the look is one which, with all my wisdom, I cannot understand, but which I would give my soul to be able to practice for a day. Last night, while I read of imminent spirits, and told myself how wise I was to know of them, I heard the voice of a young girl swell above the noise of the little animals, and I was made uncomfortable, and wanted things. And for those things I would sell my soul. Like a seed fallen on the rocks, I am withering away; I am dry and useless, like that seed. I turn against you; I will sell my soul."

And thereupon Kajn spat, and walked out of the village.

And the story went through the village like a wind of sudden death. And when Adab Teegal heard it, he said:

"I am only an ignorant pariah; I know nothing of the things that Kajn knows, but I have made two stocks of wheat sprout where my father had made but one, and I have seen the ocean. I must find Kajn Tafha." And he walked out of the village in the direction Kajn had walked.

Outside the village, Kajn came upon a rich merchant who was riding on the howdah of a white elephant, with tusks that were carved with sacred inscriptions. His servants carried caskets of rugs and far ivory, and opium brought from a great distance. Occasionally one of the servants would stumble under his excessive burden, and the merchant would order him beaten. At such times his cries of delight were louder than the servant's cries of anguish.

"I would sell my soul," Kajn called up to the merchant as he lay back on this rolling mountain of flesh.

"I will barter with you ivory taken from male elephants that live beneath the earth, and which breathe out fire and pestilence. I have rugs that were woven by monstrous spiders bigger than oaths, and opium which will make you dream of nine evil women. Here is the crystal of Confucius; if you gaze into it you will know all things but one. And here is a potion made of the eyes of live virgins which will teach you that one thing. The man who rubs this stone will live though vast throngs wail and die about him. And here is a magic fruit, which you can eat for ever."

"I would sell my soul," Kajn answered, "and I will sell it for one thing—youth."

Whereupon the merchant became angry, and jabbed a goad into the elephant's ear, until the animal roared with pain. Then he began laughing disagreeably. "Listen, old man. When I have passed out of sight, move the first finger of the hand on the side of your heart, move it so fast that it drops off. And when it drops in the dust, you will be young again." But Kajn, who was wise, knew that the merchant was toying with him; he continued on down the road without moving his finger.

Then Adab Teegal came upon the merchant, and addressed him, saying:

"I am only an ignorant pariah, but I own two houses where my father owned one, and I have seen the ocean. And now I am looking for an old man, Kajn Tafha, who is very wise, and passed down this road, and wants to sell his soul. And I wonder if the magnificent stranger has seen him." But since he was a pariah, the merchant did not answer him; one of the servants, however, furtively pointed down the road, and Adab knew that Kajn had passed.

In the meanwhile Kajn had come upon a very golden pathway leading from the main road. It was the pathway to the Beautiful Woman. He entered, and found her watching two naked servants at play. Their game was to wrestle before a table of gorgeous foods, and each was to prevent the other from eating. The Beautiful Woman lay watching the snake-jewels the merchant has just left her. They writhed in her hand, and tried to crawl between her fingers. When Kajn appeared, she laughed, and sang, "What do you want here, old man?"

"I would sell my soul," Kajn answered; "I would sell my soul for youth."

"I don't buy souls, old man. I sell my own."

And Kajn went on down the road.

Then Adab Teegal came upon the very golden pathway. He first prayed for protection, and then entered. The Beautiful Woman was teasing her flowers. She would dart a glance at them, and they would blossom and give forth delicate odors, for they loved her. And when she looked away, they would close up again, and lose their fragrance.

"I am only an ignorant pariah," Adab Teegal said to her, "but I have had two wives where my father had but one, and I have seen the ocean. And now I am looking for an old man, Kajn Tafha, who is very wise, and passed down this road, and wants to sell his soul, and I wonder if the Beautiful Woman has seen him."

"It is late, and will soon be dark. The night will be restless with prowling things, and spirits that whine. Perhaps the stranger may care to lodge here until sunrise. For I have seen no old man pass here." But her jealous flowers cried out that she lied, and Adab Teegal hastened on down the road.

And in the meantime Kajn came upon another old man who was standing on his head in the middle of the road. And when Kajn Tafha asked him why he stood on his head, he replied, "If I stand on my feet, my reflection in the Sacred Lake is upside-down. But if I learn to stand on my head, then I shall exist properly in the Waters of the Gods."

Kajn marveled at his piety, and was ashamed to tell him that he wanted to sell his soul. They blessed each other, and Kajn passed on down the road into the gloom.

When Adab Teegal came upon the pious man it was so dark he could scarcely see him. "I am only an ignorant pariah," he said, "but I have prayed to two gods where my father prayed to one, and I have seen the ocean." And when he asked the old man about Kajn, the old man told him to hurry and he would catch him, for Kajn had only just passed. Adab plunged into the squirming darkness.

Finally he heard faltering footsteps ahead. "Kajn Tafha, Kajn Tafha," he shouted, and the answer came back out of the blackness, "Yes, I am Kajn Tafha, the wise man, and I would sell my soul, and if my ears are honest, I hear the voice of Adab Teegal."

"I am only an ignorant pariah, and not fit to talk of learned things with Kajn Tafha, but I have seen the ocean. If Kajn Tafha will tell me where he is in the darkness, I will lead him home."

"Onward I go, Adab Teegal, for I would sell my soul."

"I am only an ignorant pariah, but I have seen the ocean twice where my father saw it but once, and maybe we can't sell our souls, and maybe we don't even have souls to sell."

Then Adab Teegal heard such a horrible shriek in the darkness that he ran all the way home, and nothing was ever heard again of Kajn Tafha.

Olympians

After the Wilsons moved from Edgewood, their house was left empty for nearly two months; at the end of this time it was occupied by a Mr. Beck, who put a little black and gold sign in his window, "J. J. Beck, Instructor in Music." Also, Mr. Beck joined the Methodist Church on Braddock Avenue, and gave five dollars to the local ball team. When asked to become affiliated with the gymnasium, Mr. Beck said they were doing invaluable good towards the upbuilding of healthy American manhood, but that he personally was denied all violent exertion, owing to cardiac rheumatism. He gave full assurance of his moral support, however.

Within a year Mr. Beck had convinced everyone that he was an asset to the community. As a member of the Christian Entertainment Committee he had applied himself with an earnestness that was not easily forgotten, and already he had piloted seven little girls and two boys safely through Czerny, both elementary and intermediate. The Howardells' eldest daughter, Dorothy, was even playing the "Valse" by Durand, and the "Scarf Dance" by somebody, but she had taken lessons before Mr. Beck taught her, and was unusually gifted anyhow. Besides, she was older, now being nearly fifteen.

A disagreeable incident took place in the basement of the church once, when a chapter of the Boy Scouts was being organized. One little ruffian nominated Mr. Beck as scoutmaster, causing a subdued titter to pass around the room; but he was afterwards reprimanded by the minister, and his own father as well. A younger and sturdier man was elected scoutmaster, of course, and no further mention was made of the matter. It is even doubtful if Mr. Beck ever got wind of it. Aside from this one incident, which was of no importance as it was occasioned by a mere child, Mr. Beck was treated everywhere with consideration and respect. The minister's wife used to invite him now and then to speak at one of her teas on "The Appreciation of Music," or "Music as a Factor in Education," or some such subject, where he always charmed his audience with his astonishing modesty, a certain lovable shyness, and a wealth of anecdotes taken from the lives of great musicians. And nothing is more illustrative of his goodness of heart than the fact that, although he was by far the best musician in the community, he refused to hear of replacing the church organist.

Perhaps the quality which went farthest towards Mr. Beck's popularity was this pathetic modesty of his. Although he knew so much, he seemed to be continually apologizing for his presence. One might almost say that he was timid. When he was introduced to anyone, he stuttered noticeably, and retired from a conversation as soon as was possible within the bounds of politeness. He was tall and thin, which with his ailment, the cardiac rheumatism, gave him a very *fragile* appearance, so that one would inevitably treat him with a kind of tenderness almost without knowing it. As a result Mr. Beck always brought with him into the room an air of peace and mildness, and anyone who talked to him for any length of time was left with an impression of how lovely life can be if we but choose to make it so.

So that Mr. Beck was sweetly and inexorably removed from the class of eligible men, and looked upon as a kindly institution. With an unquestioning docility, he walked in the path that was laid out for him, shielded his failing soul with umbrella and galoshes, kept it sufficiently warm with the horrible respect of his acquaintances. The facts of his own flesh and blood, however, caused him to suffer a mild degradation, which made all of his contacts with life awkward for him. This was the cause of his timidity, or his *fragility*.

All of which agitations culminated when he was teaching the Howardells' eldest daughter, little Dorothy, who was now nearly fifteen, and was his favorite pupil.

* * *

Three times a week she came here with her music roll, corrected her *expressivos*, practiced her fourth finger, and when Mr. Beck praised her, fed her joyous little ego with satisfaction. To Dorothy, Mr. Beck was simply a nervous "Good morning, Dorothy," a pulling of a chair up beside her at the piano, and a voice in her ear that made suggestions, with a queer licking sound in its throat after it swallowed. To Dorothy, none of this was especially pleasant, but it must be gone through before one can play before visitors, and was therefore beyond question. Miss Sweeny was a Catholic, while father said that the teachers downtown charged too much. Then again, she really preferred Mr. Beck in a way. For Mr. Beck meant music to her; the taking of lessons was clearly associated with Mr. Beck; when she went to Mr. Beck, she was performing one of the functions of all the music students in her Sunday-school class.

This morning Dorothy was with him again, had come out of the first spring day and into the dark parlor with the picture of a man with side-whiskers over the piano. One of the windows was open a little, so that the spring air, and the soft noises outside, and the notes of Dorothy's "Witches' Revel" had commingled in a way that caused Mr. Beck to feel a mild and uncertain despair.

A few houses farther up the street, some boys were playing marbles, shooting against the curbstone; while directly beyond, the Wrights' washerwoman was standing in the doorway, leaning, her bare arms crossed gloriously on her breasts. The grass on the front lawns was soppy with the last of the melting snow. Dorothy had finished. "I want you to learn that well, Dorothy. . . . You know, you are my favorite pupil."

Dorothy was his favorite pupil. Dorothy his favorite pupil, and it was spring! That urge, then, was to awaken in them? The tender urge which lends poignancy to "The Barcarolle" and perpetuates the funny little grasshoppers? Were Dorothy and Mr. Beck to *sing* together? Mr. Beck's heart, already weakened as it was by rheumatism, fluttered irregularly with affirmation. The Olympian was rising within him, along with the sap in the trees outside. Apollo was stirring; Balder

. . . But Dorothy had fastened her music-roll; she was leaving. "Good morning, Dorothy."

The next time Dorothy came for her music lesson, Mr. Beck felt strangely unfit. She stepped into the parlor, laid her hat and coat on the settee, and sat down at the piano. She was now ready for the voice to buzz in her ear, and make the funny licking sound when it swallowed. But Mr. Beck experienced a sudden fling of insolence. "It is going to be a wonderful spring, Dorothy." He was comforted with the tenderness of his own voice.

Dorothy spread out the "Dance of the Elves" before her. "Yes, Mr. Beck," she answered, obediently. Mr. Beck understood fatally that she had not responded. Somehow or other, he had expected something of her. There was a pause; Dorothy glanced with unconscious significance at the piano. Mr. Beck found something strangely disproportionate. It was as though he were walking arm in arm with a midget, or riding a puppydog on his back.

"Let me play you something, Dorothy." The piano became a lovable instrument. Dorothy arose from the stool with a puzzled "Yes, do, Mr. Beck." He seated himself in the place she had left; it was warmed! He ran a scale, and was astonished that it was so *brilliant* a scale. "I shall play a little *Albumblatt* of Beethoven." Here was he, and here was the piano; he felt very professional, yet he was trembling as he began to play.

He was elated by the daintiness of its arabesques. Then came a miniature *crescendo*, with its insistent bass, followed immediately by a clean chromatic descent in triplets. It transformed again into the arabesques, and was finished. . . . Mr. Beck left the piano with a feeling of surprise. He had taught this piece probably fifty times in his life, and never realized until now that it was so neat and white. Dorothy broke in with a dutiful "How fine it was, Mr. Beck," and that was all gone, too. Without spirit, he gave her her lesson.

After Dorothy had left, Mr. Beck was frank to himself about any number of things. The scene he had just been through made him weak with humiliation. And to have played for her; as though he had stood beneath her window as a *troubadour*.

Out of this unaccountable disgust, Mr. Beck tried to reach a determination. He must annihilate Dorothy from his head. For at best he could only awake her out of a dead sleep, at best prepare her for some coarse, brutal youth.

It was late, and they were returning in a streetcar. Dorothy was trying to hold her eyes open, lulled by the low groan of the motor. In another fifteen minutes, thank God, Mr. Beck would leave her at her doorstep; she would go to bed without cleaning her teeth. Mr. Beck sat beside her, his eyes working over the other occupants of the car. Everyone was dull, and detestable. But in Mr. Beck there was still a disturbance from his memory of the opera. The duet is so *bold*: the voices of a man and woman in harmonization, adapting themselves to each other, intertwining. The car jerked and groaned through the deserted streets. And they passed dark houses, shutting away all manner of things; houses that stood out frankly and openly, but within their walls, what slinking possibilities; houses with black corridors, with furniture and people in the shadows. These were sleeping houses, and as secret as caves.

Scherzando

As I entered the room, he was reading one of his poems to a very moth-eaten person. "*Catalogus Mulierum*," he grunted at me, and went on with the poem. From which I assumed that the title of the thing he was reading was "*Catalogus Mulierum*," or "A Catalogue of Women."

> "Yes, I know the old ones who have had their day.
> I have observed them.
> Those old wrecked houses;
> Those dead craters."

The next I do not remember. Or rather, I do not want to remember it. It was detestable. And the stanza following. . . . The moth-eaten person clucked after each, and murmured something. When he had read another stanza, I left, while the moth-eaten person clucked—whether at the poem, or at me, I do not know.

> "Then there are the little girls,
> Recently able to become mothers;
> Packages wrapped securely
> In the admonitions of their parents."

Why must men be hog-minded like that, I say. Great heavens! have we exhausted the play of fresh morning on a lake? Have all the possible documents been written of a star near the horizon? I have seen him sitting monstrously in his chair and leering at me as though I were a whole world to leer at. I remember him in the distillation of my memory as a carcass, so many pounds of throbbing flesh with the requisite organs stuffed in, growling over the raw meat of his ideas.

Is there some gigantic cancer for us to sap with wells, and where we can descend on ladders? Could we spend our holidays here, on the edge of the decaying flesh, with our wives and children? I used to grind my teeth at the mere thought of him, until I had diseased my liver, and I ached from escaping juices.

Ossia: There has been Christ, and the saints, and whole libraries of sanctity, and yet there was no law to exterminate this man! What darkness of darknesses have we been plunged into, when pestilence is invited among us, suffered to sit at our table and fester our tongues? But the critics are coming, and the satirists. Soon a wide plague of caterpillars will cover all the green leaves. There will be nothing behind them but naked trees and the scum of intestines. Prepare for a lean season, made meager with excessive insects.

I have sat opposed to him, and remembered the sunlight with a bursting gratitude. I remembered a little town sleeping in the foothills, with a bright clay road working across the countryside, and a green pool with the shadows of trout. I remembered the long, drooping fingers of the chestnuts—for the chestnuts blossom late, and there was a scattered frost of them even though the beards on the corn were already scorched. I remembered all this, while there spread about me the cool, dank mold from the cellar of his brain.

Coda

Let us construct a vast hippopotamus to the glorification of our century. Other ages could have constructed hippopotami of equal vastness, but ours will be superior in this: That it is exact within as well as without. A steam heart will beat against the brazen ribs of the brute, and the ooze of the kidneys will have been studied accurately. On the bolsters of his folded hide we shall have blotches and sores proper to the hippopotamus. And when we have finished, we shall have constructed a vast hippopotamus, which will cast its shadows across the plain, and disfigure the sky to the glorification of our century.

Portrait of an Arrived Critic

Alfred closed the door softly behind her. He would send her lilies. This must not be forgotten . . . lilies . . . to Adelheid. Or perhaps just one lily; more laconic, and therefore more damnably effective. But he had seen an ad somewhere: "Say it with flowers." He must not be department store. Still, he was not saying it with flowers; he was saying the exact opposite, in fact. The exact opposite; poor little Adelheid! He wrote on his calendar "L. to A."

As to this matter of the artist, "precocious crybabies, all of them." That might be an effective tune to hum. But that was rude rather than pessimistic. One may as well be an early martyr as be rude. . . . *Condiebar ejus sale*; "I was pickled in the brine of Christ," Flannagan insisted on spitting it out the other night. Flannagan had outshrieked St. Augustine by a note in translating it that way. But Flannagan, of course, was invariably rude. A simple Freudian case, since his abstinence was notorious. Flannagan was revolting, a tongue dripping meconium, a mess of *caca*.

"Precocious crybabies," then, was Flannagan's province. Alfred put a fresh sheet in his Corona. "Let us, rather, be kindly disposed towards the artist. Let us realize just how pathetic are his bronzes built against time and the universe. Consider the true misery of the poor devil who deposits his treasure, squeezes a tear of joy over his understanding of its significance, and dies. And we, if we do not like it, forget it; and if we do like it, we examine it, and *punctum*. It is astonishing, but true, that there are men who fill their stomachs and burn their oxygen for the sole purpose of perfecting a work of art, although even while they are doing it they are aware that a generation is mewling in the cradle which will have a new idea of perfection."

Flo would complain that he was bitter, and he *would* grant her that he had been "severe." A letter was sure to come from somewhere out in Ohio. If only Flannagan stayed sober! A drunken Flannagan would bawl disgustedly about "parlour pessimism" and "bows to the ladies." Why, of all people, had Flannagan chosen to track *him?* But anyhow, neither Flo nor Adelheid could bear Flannagan. "Or even those who feel that it is not perfection they are after, but mere crude expression, the proclaiming of their own ego, the thrusting of their personal wants and ecstasies on posterity—perhaps their lot is more unfortunate still, since their message, being more individual, is therefore all the harder to convey to the future, let alone the present."

To be making the artists in general provide his comfort for him! It had never occurred to him, during that wretched adolescence of his, that he could have obtained such easy terms with life. Not even a toothache. . . . Furthermore, if he *had* attained a certain competence in things, it was an active intelligence which had got it for him. He had gauged life correctly, and that was nothing if not admirable. Yet there was always a discouraging lot of detestation in the world for someone who had succeeded—which was unfair. Origins should be taken into account, although they never considered origins; if they found a man at *astra* they were inclined to resent it, forgetting his *per aspera*. . . . Adolescence would justify everything; *then* he had *plainly suffered*. Out there in that ridiculous cabin, with the wide nights and the big days to handle, with symphonic storms to wail with, and long stretches of dead summer, and his father reading fairy stories . . . all that meant that he must either burst or get a grip on life. Hallelujah! he had gripped it!

"There are two million seven hundred and fifty thousand ways of writing a given poem, and yet some greasy waif will knock his head against the stars because he has stumbled on one of them. And even while he writes, the wheels of the universe are grinding him towards oblivion. What an interesting phenomenon it is, that the poison of his genesomania is *always* the stronger, that he strives for immortality in the most fragile of substances, art!"

The artist, however clever he was in the use of his medium, lacked a certain astuteness, a kind of cultured shrewdness, in looking at life and relating it with himself. The disappointing thing was that people admired this lacuna, although no lacuna should be admirable. If being a complete man precluded being an artist, the artist should be properly discounted. He could see nothing divine about myopia. There was room here for a less temperamental Nordau. . . .

To put himself over against Flannagan, to make the contrast screamingly evident, that little incident on his first night with Flo was excellent. When he had laid the umbrella and the broom side by side on the bed, and breathed a pun about the "bride and broom," and then let suggestion run its course. Ten minutes later Flannagan had come in, as drunk as a pig, shouting "confessions," a vile vomit paraphrased from Huysmans, something about "I tore open the bellies of little children and sat therein." Flannagan was distinctly a minor character, to be utilized in a romantic novel like a Bowery tough or an Irish washerwoman.

"Couldn't we, in the last analysis, divide the intellectuals into two significant categories, the artist and the compleat gentleman? The artist, disorbited, unoriented, reeling with the mental tipple of his talk about unattainable beauty, unrealizable ambitions, ineffable innuendoes, slashing blindly, without discrimination or dignity, at an escaping color or a half-heard note, distressed in a manner highly romanesque because he cannot express things which were never there to be expressed, irresponsible, childish, unwashed; and the opposing nature, the unit that is perfectly aware of the contracts of society, alive to the subtleties of human relationship, that tiptoes about the world with a discerning and critical caution, likes and dislikes with a mildness born of the obligation of generations, and knows that everything is subordinate to the regulations of life, the compleat gentleman.... But we must have artists, so long as there are walls to be covered, and Pullmans to travel in; as we must also have ditch diggers."

"L. to A." He must not forget the lily.

David Wassermann

Ita fornicatur anima.
ST. AUGUSTINE

1

"You have it all," Wright had said. "To begin with, you are a neurasthenic, or at least, you have just recovered from neurasthenia. You
are a Jew. You have the memory of sex, although at present you are
continent; also, you are in love. And the twenties is naturally a restless period anyhow." Was Wright being decent for once? Did he
mean that just as he had said it? The bastard!

Cynthia must be watching how his hands trembled. That was the
neurasthenia. Or she should think so. And damn it, it *was* so, anyhow.
If Mendelssohn ran up the scale to *ti*, and then was called to dinner,
and got up in the middle of his soup to strike *do*, it wasn't that he
absolutely *had* to. He wanted to, simply, and did it. Yet it wasn't an
affectation, because he sincerely and without forethought *wanted* to.
In the case of the hands, then, if the neurasthenia was there, why
clamp it in a vise? Let them tremble, and perhaps even encourage
them a little.

Hell with such considerations!

Why not cut clean of all that and plunge right straight on? Just
rip and tear, like kicking through a newspaper on the sidewalk.

"I love you, Cynthia. Yes, I love you, even though you *are* a Yid-

228

dish vampire." Cynthia smiled meekly, and continued existing there, two feet in front of him. "I love you"—and she existed; "I hate you" —and Cynthia *still* existed. At times when he left her, he knew all the time that over in Brooklyn, Cynthia was existing inexorably. *"The memory of sex."* At times he had tried to bludgeon her with that, too, and was answered as usual with the quiet fact of her existence.

"The war. I'll get you yet. Gaping on a battlefield in France. Can't you see me there, my face all twisted like a piece of an old tree trunk, a gun tossed somewhere, and my guts oozing out; can't you see me?" Cynthia, with nothing else to say, admitted that yes, she could see him. Monstrous!

With a snarl: "You, my dear, ought to live in some Arcadian province where women are disposed of more summarily. Biceps—that's the way to court you. Like this." He stepped against her, threw his arms around her, pressed her backwards with his chin, and began heaving her to the couch. His knuckles scraped against a chair. The divan reached, he dropped her on it. "Stop it, David!" She laughed, and pushed away one compromising hand of his. Wassermann panted, felt ridiculous. "Straight business, with annoying difficulties and injuries," he thought in the style of Wright as he paid attention to the smarting knuckles. She rearranged herself, with no thought of a recovering hen; the things that slipped by her!

"She smells like a horse." He added aloud, "Perhaps I should have brought Wright with me? . . . She *stinks* like a horse. How is it possible to love such a woman. For I can't lie out of it, she *stinks*. But I *want* her to stink. It is *my* way of having my guts ooze out. That ought to cure me of her, but it doesn't. But this for consolation: my urge is at least proved to be straight lust." Cynthia had answered something about Wright; he would not ask her what it was.

"I suppose I shouldn't resent these failures," he began argumentatively. "We are still walking in our origins. It continues to be a matter of Apollo and Daphne, where if women can't turn into laurel trees any longer, they turn into logs. But then, you must not forget you are always open to the charge of being undersexed, which is scandalous." Both laughed. "Still as I say, you are only acting within the nature of things if you resist. Be as fair yourself, then, and admit that I, too, am acting within the nature of things when I *per*sist." But what an ass to justify her. He should deplore her without end. Never to weaken on the thing. To *know* that she must give in. And never begin defending himself; it should go without saying that his position was fitting.

He pointed upstairs. "Listen: it's sisters, and mothers, and fathers. Great God, what chance do *I* have! Even if you were insane to give yourself, those noises would keep you pure. How could a man *ever* seduce such a woman, with so many thunderous generalities to combat? As I just said, you are protected phylogenetically; with those noises upstairs you are protected socially; and worst of all, you are protected by these damned cerebrizings of mine. Oh tender Gibraltar!" . . . Cynthia was listening intently. "But that's all the wrong tack, Cynthia. Let's *faire table rase*. Why not begin all over again? I am glad to know you; weather and so forth; yes, I know Harry; Ibsen *is* a bit demoded; do you really think so? Come on, Cynthia, let's sing a duet; if we can't agree on love, at least we both believe Shaw is right about the war, Shaw with his rare common sense."

"On the whole we think reasonably alike, David."

"Yes, we *think* very much alike. Our minds are in perfect copulation. But *corporeally*. Damn it, I have more important things in this world to do than niggle around with sex. But so long as you hold me up on this one score, I am worthless. I am kept in an endless state of dispersion. I'm just a *Waldschrat*, one always—swollen———. . ." The people upstairs! He saw it in Cynthia's eyes, and subsided, the harsh word unfinished.

Five hours of this! He left her, kissing her at the door. Within ten minutes Cynthia was undressed, and had walked to the bathroom in her nightgown. Wassermann caught the subway to Times Square as Cynthia was brushing her teeth.

• • •

Wright to Wassermann: "The fact is that you simply *must* stick to this much-ado. If you drop it, you have nothing left. The . . ."

"I refuse to swallow any more of that, do you understand? First Cynthia, and then you; it's too much for an evening, just a l-i-t-t-l-e too much. You and your composure, bosh! You say I am histrionic. But it never occurred to you that your immovable front is another symptom of the same disease. If I am a stage neurasthenic, then you are a stage Stoic."

"Wait a minute. I am not fighting with you, I am *diagnosing* you. Cynthia hears that sort of thing as long as you are with her; can't you listen to one sentence of it?"

"It isn't the diagnosis I object to, it's the flatness of it. You say I have nothing but my agitation, my noise in other words. What am I to answer? You simply kill all chance of discussion with a sentence like that. What are its merits? Is it astonishing? Is it clever? Is it subtle? It just stands out there like a big face fat with a bad liver. If you want to *penetrate* me, I am willing to listen. I am *anxious* to listen, in fact. But if you're going to fling hunks of statements at me like mud pies, I want to make it clear that I am not interested."

"Go on."

"I have said what I had to say."

"No!"

Wassermann snorted. "You're getting weak, Wright, if that's the best comeback you have. Or I've gone the length of you, and am leaving you behind. You must have been frantic for a last word if you could grab at such a shabby little straw as that." Wright said nothing. "Quite in character, you say nothing. That is expected to wither me, to dry me up and blow me away. But this time, it doesn't." Wright smiled encouragingly, said nothing. "I'll give you credit, that works. It gets on a man's nerves, especially a man like me. It would be highly admirable, if it weren't so easy to apply. Another trouble with it is that it is inclined to become too pat. It fits roughly in too many cases to be nicely adapted to any of them. And in time it blunts a man, since it gets him into making a broad division of his sensations: this thing I recognize, this thing I am silent about. With the final result that you become inarticulate. You forget how to carve neat slices off a big steaming idea. You become no better than an amoeba, approaching what is pleasant, and retreating from what is unpleasant, without intelligent observation."

"There is a lot to what you say, Wassermann. But I must be going now, if you'll let me leave without calling it a last bit of blunt technique. The fact is that I *do* have to go. We'll see each other tomorrow night."

A dirty way to defeat a man. Wright's going left him bound. The bile must drip back into his stomach, and stay there poisoning him until tomorrow night. They were monsters, both of them, with Cynthia a little worse because she was a woman, and loved. They were two suns for him to race around; they stood still, and let him break his neck. But the devil; what a superb martyrdom anyhow. If he saw things, and simply *had* to say them, it was worth seeing and saying them at any cost. Not so bad to be a victim of too much clarity. He was a fly-eye.

"Waiter . . . waiter." The waiter came on the run. "I ordered *black* coffee."

2

"Everything in the world's one more little devil's tongue for me to bleed on. If it's a chair, I'll stove my shins on it in the dark; if it's a razor, the relation between us is an immediate possibility of my hurling it out the window; if it's a person, it'll say 'How are you,' and I'll nearly pass out apoplectic with pounding sentences. Don't you ever get that? An egocentric attitude to life, with nothing but you and God, and God making the world to plague you? No, of course not. Roman therms, resignation, either no God or a *laissez-faire* policy on the part of God; ah, how Walter Pater, how Parian marble, how off in the mountains to meditate. But I know there is a God, with a swagger, and an ugly leer, and a quid of tobacco in his cheek. However, my friend, damn you. You are driving me into this. I was unusually conciliatory this evening. Even a bit reminiscent, in fact." Wassermann stopped; Wright stretched and yawned with a miniature embarrassment.

"And then to this: '*D'ordinaire, insinuante et impérieuse, elle violait doucement, intéressée par les capitulations successives, jouissant des retraits et des sursauts de la pudeur des mâles qui n'est vaincue qu'au moment où elle devient inflexible. Son jeu était serré, sûr et astucieux; délicieux insecte d'aventure, serrant autour de sa proie les spirales de son vole, elle chantait comme une abeille; puis, soudain l'abeille se taisait, buvait, les ailes calmes, la vie de la fleur humaine. Mais aujourd'hui, peureuse, elle se laissait dévêtir avec la patience d'une orpheline; sans autre désir que d'être agréable aux mains de son ami.'* What a velvet touch! He caressed those sentences as he would have caressed Mauve herself. For God's sake, man, give over that truck and read literature. Have you ever seen *Le Miracle des roses?* No, you haven't. Then why talk about French literature to *me?*"

"By that time we were all pretty well soused."

"And then to this: *'Où pouvaient, songea-t-il, se recruter de telles vocations? Quelle corne, sonnant dans la nuit, sonnait assez haut, pour assembler un troupeau d'aussi lamentables femmes? Donner toute sa vie à la mort, n'avoir d'autre souci que la toilette des cadavres, la veillée solitaire près des corps rigides et des faces froides où l'ombre du nez marque une heure immuable sur la putréfaction de la joue!'* All the bigger Frenchmen have places now and then that run like rivers."

"*You* know that little hotel, too? The west rooms give you all you want of the Hudson in the morning. And no questions asked."

"Oh, no, I take it back, Wright. You get up in front of me like a big stupid face to be punched, and I am always just a little too off my balance to punch it. Some day I'm going to look at you, and promptly break into little pieces. You and . . ." . . . "And now it's Up-Swallow, Fifty Cents Gone. You couldn't get rid of money faster throwing it down the . . ." . . . "Cynthia are two marvelous forces to have drawn up in either direction of a man. It's as though I were in a big gloomy hallway, with an Italian carved grandfather's clock on one side of me, and a family portrait on the other. Dull gold face and dull gold frame—it's worse than if my two shoulders were sinister, had worms in them, and I could see them out of the corner of my eyes. You're like two big boats, dull black in a dull gray harbor. You're problems, like all static things.

"I had more promise during adolescence, right hand and all. Then these damned problems of human relations hadn't pulped me. I was a shrieking, battling *I*. At night I used to wander through the cemetery, and if I didn't get scared, I'd scare myself. I'd throw my arms around a tombstone, and listen, and then start to blab and blub as though I was mad, until finally I would be half-mad. And then I'd walk slowly away, with my back to all that darkness and pale white, and when I got out of there I would be sick. Once I vomited on the sexton. *Then* I was . . ." . . . ". . . I wanted to kiss Minney and light my cigarette, and instead I put the cigarette in her mouth and nearly kissed the match. Did you hear that? I wanted . . ."

"But that's all different now. A man is worth something when there are women in general, not specific women. While there's a world of women, there's possibility; but what can I do? Flap and flutter and squawk myself over the hedge. Go on stirring the brew to keep it from sticking. Rattle at my brain with words until I've numbed it. Thank God, there's always some satisfaction in a precise diagnosis. So long as I can chart my defections, I at least have the intellectuality of the chart to encourage me. And when I die, I'll know exactly how I'm dead. Hamletism is a remedy worth talking of. Especially Hamletism on the proscenium. For the hamletically inclined, there is always pause enough between the wound and decease to drop a cosmogony and a couple of attitudes on life. And how conciliatory it may be to pass away with a properly modernized *adsum*.

"Oh, hell, oh, hell. Out of this kitchenpot of fairies, and kikes, and lounge lizards, and Spearmint stenographers, and fat old breeding machines on the East Side, out of these five million pancreas and livers, why do I have to moon over Cynthia! Why can't I get back into the swirl of things, and embrace the city in general? If I could plunge forward into some dawn or other. Or if the city could occur to me like a sudden revelation, with me shrieking, 'Fish! Fish! Jesus Christ, God, Son, Savior!'

"If religion is the sublimation of sex, where's *my* breviary? I'm nearly bursting with sex, and yet I just have enough religion to be mildly blasphemous. Why don't people shout at me when I walk along the street; why don't they lock their doors, and pile furniture against them, and watch me from their second-story windows; for I'm one unceasing swollen possibility of rape. I'm satyriasis stalking nymphomania. And yet if an auto were to run against me accidentally, I could call a policeman and have the driver arrested.

"But I have been too honest with myself. A man's a suicide if he insists on clarity. Beyond knowing what's right and what's left, and what's up and down, clarity becomes a grave nuisance. Intelligence is a parasitic growth, and saps the body like a cancer. It endangers the silver medium. The brain was once a mere implement of the body, functioning solely to add to the body's welfare, like the kidneys. But now it is threatening to usurp an entity of its own. It demands certain foods and amusements which can be indulged in only at great inconvenience and often with danger. *Comme on pisse les chiens*, one must walk one's brain. And it is still so young, that one's attentions to it are frequently of a disgusting nature. And so, I have stuffed my brain with rich, oozy clarity, with the consequence that I can see every pore in every nose, and catch the smell of every armpit. And when you see that way, you have two choices: you can be either a dervish or a pig. If you're a dervish, you shrink from it all, and drown yourself in denials and negations, and spend sinister years trying to rub the filth out of your carcass. But if on the other hand you see it all, and *refuse* to deny, and are determined even to *glorify* and *wallow in*, then, friend, you are a pig. That is what clarity does for you. A sweet little virgin who grows up in neatness, goes to school, is courted tenderly, and finally married; there is modesty, refinement, loveliness for you—and intellectual muddiness, and passional stupidity enough to drive you wild. These women are perfectly functioning units, developing logically and infallibly towards the grand culmination, marriage. Thus we see how orderly and social things are without clarity. But *with* clarity, you must be either a recluse starving on God, or a cur with his nose under a tail."

Wright's eyes edged towards the center of the room. Gutzkow, like a monster shadow, was holding a jug. Beside him was a university student with a small moustache, a watch in his hand. "Get ready—get set—Go!" The butt of the jug was raised a little higher, while Gutzkow's lips wrapped themselves surely over the mouth. The liquid began seeking its level. Gutzkow took it amply. It was all like a fire hose spurting into a sewer.

"Fifteen—twenty—twenty-two seconds. You take the money." Gutzkow had won.

3

"I suppose if you picked pins off the floor fast enough you could get out of an *idée fixe*. I'm trying to forget my captivity with battling around the cage. *Cynthia!* Christ, what a Muse! Between—it's a nasty bell to have ringing in your head. Booze, dope, sweating, socialism—they're the only four escapes, and I've tried them all. Dope is the poorest; I can't go that way. I can thump and pound until I burst, but I can't fade away. And booze is only an accompaniment. It's just a steady bass to an agitated treble. Sweating is at best Tolstoyan. It's a grand theory that dies with a whine, like a pig-balloon. And at worst Jean-Jacques Rousseau. Weary brawn at sunset—a tender department store master. Toiler with his pipe; open fireplace; wife and cradle; workbasket on lap; sunset visible through window. And as for socialism, it's either bums or double-lens spectacles.

"I joined the Red Flag. Recommended as trustworthy by a dear and intimate friend. The great night finally approached. We assembled in a rathskeller. 'Would you kindly leave the room, while the matter of new members is being discussed?' 'Certainly, certainly.' I went up to the bar and had a beer. Another beer, and I was summoned before the committee. 'Mr. Wassermann, before you pledge your word, you must understand that this is a grave matter. We are part of an organization forming over the entire country to resist the forces of reaction. We are an underground organization. The cause is greater than our life. The pledge binds you to be subject at any time to perform anything which is found necessary.' 'Mr. Chairman, I am not prepared to go blindly to such an extent. I am anxious to ally myself with the principles your organization stands for. But I cannot forswear the freedom of disposing of myself as I may see fit at any time. And to me my life is more important than the life of a community however great and oppressed.' 'Mr. Wassermann, you are a serious-minded man. You are no doubt earnest in your radical sympathies. But I fear you are not ripe for the cause we represent.' I am rejected, but my dear and intimate friend, who is one of the chosen, enjoys to this day the privileges of this dark organization. Once a month they give a dance, he tells me, and with the yearly dues of five dollars they are able to keep up a pleasant little clubroom, with translations of Russian novels, and three volumes of Schnitzler in the original. Also, I believe, there is a book by Karl Marx. . . . I was too mild. "And again I am thrown back on Cynthia. . . . Scotch? Beer here. A Scotch and a beer, professor. . . . Why can't a man have a real opportunity? Or an arrangement whereby we can be of some use—consumptives, decrepits, and poor devils like me. I want to found a headquarters where all people can come who are going to die. Take a suicide, for instance. He comes into the office, with reliable credentials that he is a paranoiac; he has decided to kill himself. I look through the card index system; and find that so-and-so has been responsible for another half-cent rise in the price of sugar. My suicide receives a full description of this gentleman, his habits, where he lives. Then goes out and murders him, explains publicly that it was owing to the half-cent increase in sugar, and kills himself. Or a consumptive could have done it, and spits his lungs out the following week in prison.

"But it's coming, men," Wassermann ignored Wright, and addressed the people at the next table. "The greatest hope of revolution in America came with the passing of prohibition. The American still has the instinct of the Boston Tea Party in him; he must have something trivial to revolutionize about. You can starve him, rob him, drive him among the cogs of a machine, or explode him, and he'll merely grumble. But step on his corn, or call him a bastard, or kick his dog, and by God, he'll murder you. . . . But I am afraid the ruling classes know this as well as I do. They won't force the issue too strongly, and as a result of this yielding, social unrest will disappear behind the ægis of mean prosperity, the ability to earn a good enough living, to marry and provide your wife with an effective douche. The Bismarcks and von Moltkes of America will be more successful than their prototypes, because they possess enough English blood and English diplomacy to add hypocrisy to the rest of their dirty equipment. And the idealism of America is always low enough to enable the purchase of their chosen leaders. So we can expect every Sam Gompers of the future to appear in the best of society; we shall hear talk of great prosperity; of America's colossal commerce overtopping that of Great Britain; of America's stupendous merchant marine; of American banks in every third-rate city in the world. Everything will be 100 percent American, made in America, *Amerika über alles*. Competent experts will be dispatched at the government's expense to study foreign markets, and the ways of eliminating foreign competition. Do you see what I am doing? I am prophesying the rise of another Prussia." With the word "rise," Wassermann rose himself, and swung his right arm at the crowd that had gathered around his table. "I am depicting our development for the next thirty or forty years, when all of a sudden we shall awake to the fact that the armed forces of three-fourths of the globe are steaming towards our ports, to conquer another and a greater Prussia in another ghastly 'last war.' Perhaps I am ill-disposed tonight, ladies and gentlemen, but that is what I see tonight for this great stronghold of free speech, constitutional rights, and making the prisons safe and so forth." Someone began to cheer, and the others took it up at once. "Shut up, you swine," Wassermann bit at them, and they shut up, causing a dead quiet. Outside, an elevated train rumbled past. Wassermann recommenced in a low voice. His peroration.

"Debs, we don't want you. Our constitutional liberties came too easily to us for us to defend them. Regardless of a country's constitution, it gets the sort of government it deserves; and we evidently deserve a government of hypocrisy, low-mindedness, under the species of eternity, the dollar. We don't want our constitution, Debs, we want salved nonsense, and sleek respectables, and greasy ward-bosses. And if you try to restore to us something we don't want, into prison you go, judged by twelve of our own good and true. To the dungeon with you, Debs, and if you attempt to do anything for us again, we'll lynch you, in accordance with another of our highly democratic customs. Do you hear? Like the friends of good government and humanity we are, we'll squeeze your neck till your eyes bulge and your tongue hangs out, and then we'll let you dangle there as food for the crows and approving editorials in the *Times*." He picked up his glass of beer, put it quickly to his lips, and took it at a gulp. Then with a sudden snarl, he flung the empty tumbler against the ceiling, where it smashed into bits, and fell on the heads of the listeners. He turned about viciously, and burst through the swinging doors, Out Into The Night.

* * *

"Why, Cynthia, must you insist on walking on these noisy streets? I want to break down tonight, and cry, and have my tears kissed, and all that. Cynthia, I am terribly miserable."

"What did you say, David? The cars, you know. It is hard to understand you when you speak so low."

"My God, my God. Everything is monsters! That damned fool speech in the saloon was a monster. My life since leaving you has been one monster after another. This situation tonight is a monster. Monsters, MONSTERS—did you hear that?"

"Yes, David."

"I quarreled with my father today. He wanted me to learn that dirty Jew business of his. Why must all Jews be either pawnbrokers or in the clothing business! I left the house. . . . That was another monster. And I went into a public comfort station and saw montrous phalloi scribbled on the wall and one drawing of the female parts, just the hips and the thighs. The wretch who did that had a direct mind; Rops was never madder; Cynthia, I love you!"

They were already on the Manhattan Bridge. Cynthia said nothing. "*J'eusse aimé vivre auprès d'une jeune géante.* Thank God, Baudelaire understood. I wonder if they know what they are doing, these mild college professors who put that sonnet in their anthologies." Cynthia said nothing. The lights along the shore revealed dim shapes. The thick girders of the bridge itself were dim and far above their heads. "I could take you now, and hurl you away down there into that black water. Couldn't I?" He cackled. "Eh, couldn't I?" Cynthia shuddered as she felt his arms on her hips. "Oh Christ, oh Christ!" he moaned. "I give it up. Cynthia, will you marry me!" Cynthia's heart gave a bound, but she thought it advisable to say nothing. They stopped, and looked down vaguely into the water. Wassermann brooded wearily on the realization that he had proposed marriage, and was no doubt accepted.

4

The candle was nearly out. (Cynthia had insisted on candles.) She seemed to take it all so comfortably. The candle gone, leaving the room heavy with irregular darknesses; the fire in the grate a mere sullen glow; the cold drawing its circle closer and closer about them, and forcing them nearer to each other; his head resting on her knees. Wright wondered if she accepted all this without question; and he suspected that she was perfectly at home.

"Our last night together, Cynthia."

"And our first!" There was a hint of a sigh. Wright winced. My God, how women loved this sort of thing! Men *have* to hate other men, considering what must be said to women. Would she mention Wassermann? But he must quit gauging her; he must dip into this thing with heart. What nasty complications arose . . . his virginity, and her own. Did she know he was watching her? Do women suspect the *calculating eye of the male*? The spider and the fly . . . trite again. Why didn't he rebel? Why couldn't he send her home, even at this late hour, and load his lungs with the cold fresh air of a good book? No, he had but one of two choices: he could pass this by and be as incomplete as ever, or he could keep her here and put up with the tarnish. It was tyrannical, yes, but inevitable, that no matter how far one has gone with reading, life must begin at the beginning. But wasn't this, too, a cheaply romantic judgment to confuse life with sex? Like that little Jew back in Ohio who used to go down to the whore-district to "see life." But damn all this ergotizing; no wonder so many eager little girls can go so long untouched, if men must spend their time in straying from the highway. . . . But women demand some sort of ceremony; just as their sex is distributed all over their body, so the sex urge is less localized, less immediate. With men, phi-landering is cowardice; with women it is a completely accepted com-ponent in the formula of love. . . . Still, he yearned for a direct statement, and trusted in its efficacy, if he could ever find a fitting one. . . . He took off one of her shoes, and hoped to God that he had done enough. As he must have, since she kissed him a moment later, and went into the alcove, where he could hear her undressing. She had only dropped in for a few minutes; really she couldn't stay; and now here she was undressing in his alcove; he felt weighted down with experience, for he knew that *all* women would be this way.

"Good night, Lambert!"

"Good night, Cynthia. And don't worry about me. The little cot out here will be perfectly comfortable." All part of the ceremony, as they both knew; ten minutes later he was crawling awkwardly into bed with her, after rinsing his mouth with Chartreuse.

She cuddled over against him, and a little song of happiness began singing within him. This thing on his shoulder—it was lovely, it was *sweet*. Her cold nose was against his ear.

"Listen, little Cynthia; here is a speech on what people remember: People remember different things. Some people remember the names of everybody they went to school with, and some remember when they had chickenpox, and some remember their Latin, and some remember the first time they saw the Eiffel tower, but I remember the tumult of her breathing in my ear." Thank God, he had delivered it! He had walked up, and laid down his brick, and walked away. But Cynthia was sleepy. . . . He lay there helplessly, and let her slip away from him; tender, brutal, weary, rebellious—one by one his moods changed color, and all the while Cynthia drifted more impregnably into sleep. He loved the little twitchings of her legs. And last of all, he decided to forgive her, and surely girls do not realize they are cruel. Cynthia was asleep.

He must be *thin*, he must be woefully *one-stringed*, to suffer this with such resignation. And poor little Cynthia would unconsciously take advantage of this. Yes, she was safe. Ferociously, then sentimentally, and then wearily he admitted it, she was safe. She would go to Wassermann with all the technical requirements fulfilled.

* * *

"You dog, you can sit there and smirk me on my way into matrimony. I confess, I have failed. It was marriage or nothing, and my nature abhors a vacuum. I'm done for. Wright, this is my epilogue, these words I am saying to you now. Or is my epilogue the ones I say five years from now, when I'm a Jew with a nose and a fat belly?" He approached a sneer. "Do you know, do you realize, man, that I have patched things up with my father, that I am to be his junior partner, and that we are going to enlarge the firm? The Wassermann Clothing Company becomes the Greater New York Clothing Company, a growing organization, you see. Wish me luck, and hope never to see me again."

After Hours

The various arteries of the city having been loosened by the phlebotomy of five o'clock, the streets dripped profusely. The general tangle among the directions of the pedestrians gave an illusion of hastiness, as though the speed of the street were the aggregate of all the individual speeds. The vehicles also added—especially the crosstown car which Howard took. He had attained this car between a channel of automobiles moving like blocks of ice. He had paid his fare behind a pregnant Italian woman who still emanated the odor of this morning's garlic, while a Jew peddler from behind had collapsed his hamstrings by the unexpected impulse of a bundle. He stepped into the orchestration of breaths, sat down, and waited.

The car tugged ahead unevenly. The car filled disgustingly. The inmates, paddled by the conductor's shouts, flowed halting towards the front of the car. Three shopgirls entered, pushing past a fat woman who really should not ride at this time of the day. Their complexions were not yet ten minutes old, having been renewed at five minutes to five. Two girls dropped nickels; as the third paid, pennies were heard chasing one another down the glass chute.

"Hold on there," the conductor yelled unnecessarily at this third girl with the chasing pennies. Howard looked at her and decided that she was a warhorse. "Come on wit' the rest o' the money."

"What do y' mean the rest o' the money?"

"I what do y' mean that y' on'y put in three cents!"

She said she put in fi' cents; the conductor said she on'y put in

243

three; she said she put in fi'. Finally the conductor wouldn't argue no longer, and he turned the crank until all the money was out of the box. Then he held it up in his hand, and when he had taken all the nickels and dimes, there was nothing left but three cents. He showed this to the fat woman, who grumbled with disgust, and to the two other girls, who sniggered, and to a plumber who had just got on the car and who felt embarrassed; he also showed it to two other men whose occupations were uncertain. The girl paid the two additional cents, and whenever the car stopped after that you could hear her telling the other girls that she put in fi'. All sorts of people kept glancing at her and the conductor; the plumber stayed on the platform and looked at the headlight of the car behind.

Out of the newspaper sticking upside down in the overcoat pocket of the man in front of him Howard learned that

obe, Pa., Nov. 10.—A firebug

moreland County, Pa.

ee Destroyed Recently in West-

PECIALTY OF FIREBUGS

NING SCHOOLHOUSES

The damned guy moved his arm like an idiot. Howard fought hard over the thing, but the jerking of the car was another handicap. Then the man moved unconsciously further up the car. Howard observed with satisfaction that the lower half of a woman shifted into his immediate vision. He began thinking specifically of this lower half of a woman. The whole idea became preposterous. . . . Howard observed with profound guilt that he was riding past his stop. After all, it was worth a gambler's chance. Her knee . . . sure enough. After one entire extra avenue, she moved away. Howard left the car with resignation, and walked back in the face of a cold dark wind.

After eating in a chop house with steamed windows, Howard went on down to the Village. Finally he got to the house he wanted, went up the stairs slowly, entered. Various hellos. Howard sat down. Problem: sociability. "...'s Baker doing now ... new girl ... that so! ... devilish cold ..." Fire is agitated. Edna is tweaking Lynch's nose; they shouldn't get off by themselves that way, it breaks up the party. Howard and everybody took everything with silent heroism. Everybody gravely watched Ramsay poke the fire unnecessarily. "...'s Charlie doing ... for a coon's age ... I don't ..." Howard watching Edna's foot; it tapped, tapped, tapped, hinging at the ankle; it had nothing whatsoever to do with Howard; he fingered a book and said things about it. Other people answered things. Differed and agreed. Intellectual conversation. After five minutes it had petered out; two voices started up, and fell together; everybody gravely watched Ramsay worrying the fire. The wind suddenly attacked the three inches of open window; somebody ran and closed it; somebody else said, "Whew ... hell!" Then Englander arrived with the booze, and the evening was saved.

Howard felt his stomach recoil as the first slug of the vile stuff hit it. But after that the battle was won, and Howard poured it down without further discomfiture. The emphasis changed; that is, when Ramsey poked the fire once more before forgetting it for the evening, only a couple of people noticed the maneuver, and one of these was appreciated for saying "How sadistic!"

Somebody suggested poker; Howard heard people shout "Yes, poker!" and "Hell with poker!" and he heard himself shout "Yes, poker!" There being a general shove, he shoved, and learned a few seconds later that he was fighting for a chair. He attained a chair, and sat down, and began beating on the table for poker. Poker came. Within two minutes the cards were sticky with port, and the banker was still distributing chips. Howard won the first pot; somebody up-dumped the table; the game was over. Howard snapped a drink into him, threw back his head with such a jerk that part of the liquid trinkled into his ear.

He swerved about the room with the subconscious realization of many things: the stove in the corner; millions of miles away, Neptune was plunging through space, cold and deserted; it was only a question of time until Edna left Lynch; that queer time in the streetcar—he would say nothing about it; drink it slower, old man, slower. Everyone was frankly in his own orbit; they called out to each other from a distance and in haste, as though they were going in opposite directions on railway trains. They reeled within one another's recognition, and out again. Howard was grateful when spoken to, and answered with overflowing emotion. Frankly, he saw no disgrace in repetition. At times, however, when someone drunker than himself approached, he looked at that person and registered with clarity, "You are drunk . . . you dirty slobbering cretin, you are pig-stewed." At times he even said this, and the remark would secure him a staunch temporary friend.

Edna came up to him. "Hello, Howard dear!" They began to talk. They didn't talk about much, but they talked soberly. Howard became embarrassed and dropped his eyes. Not because they talked soberly, but because he remembered distinctly once when they had ALMOST. Her husband was in the room now, and Howard had just told him he was pig-stewed, and yet with this woman he had once ALMOST. He was overwhelmed by her unheard-of brass. He wanted to crawl away from her. That was why he dropped his eyes.

The independence of his orbit grew more pronounced. Howard went over to a window, and looked out on the street four floors below. Snow had fallen. He lived for a while in the sweetened haze of the swaying electric light on the corner, and watched the shadows adapt themselves irregularly in the snow as the light vacillated in the wind. Little strips of cold air whisked against him. He laid his hot head against the cold pane, and then took it away to observe the grease marks from his nose and forehead. He sat down on the floor, and dropped his head on the seat of a chair. He watched the left wall continually beginning to get higher than the right one. Being experienced, however, he accepted the phenomenon with confidence. He slipped full length on the floor, and felt things revolve uncertainly. Then, of a sudden, a powerful conviction came over him. He understood now that he was going to be nauseated. He left the room reeling, but with a set determination; leaning over, he suffered the fulfillment of his nausea.

* * *

"There had been a cat. Howard had gone out into the kitchen, to get a drink, and seen this cat, and spoken to it without enthusiasm. The cat had looked at Howard with large, moon-steady eyes. Howard had first spoken to the cat, and then caressed it abstractedly, and then swept it off the table. Then he had splashed water on it, and left the room.

And now it was not the *os innominatum* which those two were trying to solve. The *os innominatum* is a bone. *Os*: bone . . . *innominatum*: . . . . The geometry proposition is *pons asinorum*. They were not trying to solve the *os innominatum*, then, but the *pons asinorum*. Howard lived through it all meekly. He accepted it religiously that it must be proved that a^2 plus b^2 equals c^2. Englander drew a triangle on the white woodwork of the door, and he named the sides a, b, and c. Then he made little squares on all three sides. And then he stopped. *Pons asinorum*; he stopped. Howard labored with a half conscious anguish. What next! Englander did not know; Howard did not know; nobody knew. When Pearl began talking to him, he felt himself lean his body with relief to listen to her, while Englander fumbled angrily at a^2.

Pearl talked a lot of stuff. Pearl pulled things about breaking away and "wasting yourself magnificently" and "the good things of life." Howard synthesized it thus: Once you used to live with me; you don't live with me any more; why not live with me for tonight? Howard understood all this with meekness. Somewhere off on the borderline of his consciousness he debated the practicality of seeing this thing through; without perfect awareness he decided that the scheme was impractical. If Pearl's man was getting too old for service as anything but a pocketbook, he, Howard, could not. . . . He had been dropped once; it would be a lowering of his dignity now. And besides, you never know just how much of this kind of thing is real, and how much is a mere feeler to satisfy a woman's vanity. Howard worked at these problems slavishly, and said, "Since I have been married, Pearl, I have received another outlook on life. Tonight, you find me drunk, and therefore as I used to be . . . apparently . . . but in reality I am as different as (gesture) . . . as . . . the world." Pearl followed him. People were disturbing him by their movements about the room. But this was evidently a time for solidity. Howard became more staunch; "You cannot understand, Pearl. I almost love you for it, I confess. But with a man, there is always the dreadful temptation, to use your terminology, to fall into tergiversations against all that he once exemplified. A woman is what she is; a man is a composite of what he is and the negation which that essence predicates. The more pronounced egocentricity of the male results . . . or better, this way . . . no man is a worthy saint who has not been a hell-raiser, and hell-raising is infinitesimally insignificant except when it is found in one who has renounced the Faith. And so I have attained my apotheosis in that I am different from that which I formerly signified. And frankly it is almost pathetic to one in my situation when he finds that a person whom he once loved has not tergiversated with him." And Pearl synthesized that it was all off.

Howard collapsed into glazedness, still vaguely appreciative of the heavy blocks of his diction. He weighed them all over again, one by one, and catching Englander's eye, he smiled. He forgot the smile in the middle, although it wore off gradually, his facial muscles were so stiff with weariness. Then he got up, consciously put his hat on crooked, consciously let his coat drag, and started home.

When he finally got home, he woke his wife while crawling into bed; she cried a little, then they both went to sleep.

My Dear Mrs. Wurtelbach

1

What if he had known Wurtelbach since the days when they had a tent in the back yard and played Old Maid if it rained? It was in the company of Wurtelbach that he had bought his first beer. Furthermore, he had roomed with Wurtelbach at the university. But as to Mrs. Wurtelbach, he had taken her limp hand and been assigned to a chair once, and another time he had been informed that her husband often spoke of him. As a consequence, the letter was written thus:

> My dear Mrs. Wurtelbach:
>   How can I express my sympathy with you and little Dorothy over the loss of husband and father! I heard the terrible news this morning for the first time, and since then I have felt the need more and more strongly of writing a few words, however much they fail of conveying my deep condolence. At such times one is painfully aware of just how cruel fate can be, and how we are all called upon to bear our load of suffering. But surely it must be some consolation to you in your sorrow to realize that there are so many who knew and loved your husband. And then again, you must strive to

remember that he himself would wish those whom he left behind to be as happy as possible.

My mother asks me to assure you in her behalf how greatly she, also, enters in with you in your affliction.

Wurtelbach dead! Wurtelbach pig-stewed . . . dead. Wurtelbach addressing the Chamber of Commerce with that artificial serious-ness of his . . . dead. Wurtelbach sneezing . . . dead. All the little untied ends of Wurtelbach's experiences had just stopped being there to tie. In some closet or other the baggy trousers were hanging which Wurtelbach was going to put on next Sunday morning. His wife and child were probably crying in Sewickley.

Charles did not cringe at sending the letter, any more than he had cringed at eating breakfast. If it had been Charles who had died, Wurtelbach would have sent a similar letter to his mother; indeed, somewhere in the letter he might even have situated Charles com-fortably in Heaven and hinted that it is selfish of us to grieve the loss of one who has been Called Home. Charles realized that he could write it, and mail it, while the fact of Wurtelbach's death would remain on his hands in exactly the same way.

The time he and Wurtelbach had . . . dead. Like lead, in bed, his dull, dull head (pause) . . . dead (one, two, three) . . . dead. "Hello . . . yes . . . oh, hello, Alice. I hoped you'd call. Yes, I got home all right . . . dead . . . rather late, of course, but I had a good night." Now, con-cerning this matter of the Chicago Awto-Lite Company, why not write them and tell them to forward the photographs in any case, and if we found that we could not run the illustrations, we could either return them forthwith or hold them for a future article our editors might get up on accessories. Hanging up there lopsided in the closet, all ready for next Sunday. The pump stopped; it's all over when that convulsion stops down there under the ribs.

Once, with a sudden freezing, Charles understood that he had lost dear old Wurtelbach.

2

First Esther had stepped over the log, and then Miss Anderson had stepped over the log, and then Myrtle and Wurtelbach had stepped over the log, and then, after a long interval, Anne had stepped over the log . . . and then . . . over the log . . . the log . . . log. . . . Then they were all gone. They had all gone ahead, leaving the log behind them, and fresh rips in the ferns growing out of the rotten leaves. Wurtelbach had avoided the cow-flops, as well as the eyes of the girls. What if he were to eat a cow-flop; Christ, what a stir! The girls' legs carried them up, up the hill; Wurtelbach considered the masterful working of these mechanisms.

Esther was a kid; that's why she was first. Or more accurately, Esther was still a colt. Esther went on up the hill, without the least suspicion of the night Wurtelbach wanted to eat her. Esther was as useless as a sparrow. Her unhappy body was without significance. Wurtelbach agreed with a certain guilty awkwardness while she talked of climbing Hawkbill and yelling across to Chestnut Ridge. He was willing to drop behind.

Myrtle, gentlemen, was Queenly. With all her bones comfortably buried beneath a half-inch cushion of warm flesh, Myrtle could take up as much of your time as she cared to by talking deliberately. Myrtle could bathe in spring water without suffering; but the irrefutable fact remained that there was frequently a strong odor which came from Myrtle's armpits.

The general picnic spirit continued. They would be at Buckeye Spring in fifteen minutes. Oh, look, the columbines were still *perfect*! And they had seeded in the valley two weeks ago. The bull! The bull! . . . Wurtelbach promptly advanced, while the girls crawled back under the barbed wire nervously. The brute kicked up clods of grass and dirt over his swaying rump. Wurtelbach collected rocks with an inward emphasis. Then he began throwing, until one rock hit the bull on a protruding shoulder bone. The bull retreated back among the trees, vibrating and sending little pebbles rolling down the hill. Wurtelbach continued to throw, thus assuring safe conduct for his women.

Then came half a mile of tangle, where the trail was nearly lost, until it broke into full view of the mountains. They rolled away blue-black, like the faithful backs of elephants. From across the valley they got the broadside of Craggy. Everyone waited for Anne, and when she arrived she was chagrined at being waited for. You could plunge words deep into Anne. Some little half-uttered sentence with the man-and-woman about it . . . you could let it drop and feel sure that it would be picked up. Anne was like a deep pool: you could throw in a pebble . . . there would be a little ripple . . . and then the pebble would lie there. When Anne went into her room at night and shut the door, you felt that it was being shut with sullenness. Anne was not good-looking; it was generally agreed that she would never marry.

When they reached the Flats, Wurtelbach sneaked away to observe the ridges. Thirty-seven could be seen from here on a clear day. Wurtelbach counted twelve before he thought to close his eyes. When he opened them again, he picked one little white roof five miles down the valley. Then he sailed from here to there in a beeline, and among the ridges. The thin, dead air made him feel the pulse-beat in his ears. Two months after this Wurtelbach was dead.

3

For a few notes the band chugged in unison, and then it broke away again, all the little parts flying off independently. That was jazz. The piccolo wobbled on a three-bar spree; the violin tumbled down three octaves. The pianist bounced alternately from bass to high treble. (No use; everybody just ate.) The trombone saw its chance, and drawled blurtingly. The trap-drummer let loose all over, drums, bells, bones, cymbals. For a while each player ran his own little circle around the melody, existed by himself, felt recklessly assertive. (Five hundred crabmeat salads were removed simultaneously, and five hundred roasted second joints of capon were brought in their place.) The band stopped to change the score, and there would have been dead silence if everyone were not hearing his own jaws.

After the nuts had been passed around, however, and bread-crumbs had been brushed secretly from the knees to the floor, and the cigars were lighted tentatively, one dealer from Buffalo, seated at table 36, offered a joke about a very stupid and very typical Englishman. This Englishman, while visiting his American cousin in California, being greatly impressed by the extended cultivation which was going on, had asked, "But bah Joove, ah say, what do you do with all this produce?" And the American had answered. "Oh, we can what we can, and what we can't can, we can." Now the Englishman was inordinately tickled with this, but later, while trying to repeat it back home, he blundered with characteristic stupidity, "Oh, we can what we cawn, and what we cawn't can we put up in tins." Table 36 laughed the fitting amount, and a dealer from a small town outside of Buffalo told one about a rather fast woman; and what is more, he followed it with one about a woman's parts.

Table 36 was now in a pleasant frame of mind, and when the band jazzed again, everybody joined in the chorus. Two men came out—fairies probably—and sang something or other. The five hundred gentlemen assembled did not listen. The two fairies melted away, and forty women appeared, which explains why certain tables were upset in the yowling rush towards the center of the floor. Yaaing, these babies stood upon ladders, and oscillated the jelly of their breasts.

For an hour, then, this tingling meat was examined. And when it left, the president of the All-American Corporation gave a speech:

"Gentlemen . . . As I look over this glad assemblage . . . of more than five hundred . . . this evening . . . it takes me back nine years to the first annual banquet held under the auspices of the All-American Corporation. . . . Stop to consider, gentlemen, what really tremenjous strides the All-American has made in these nine short years. . . . Transport yourself back to those uncertain days when our organization was making its first struggle for existence. . . . If I remember correctly, there were just . . . one . . . two, there were exactly fourteen dealers present at the first annual banquet of the All-American Corporation.

"How little we expected then, when Mr. Hemmingway talked of moving his little hub factory to a larger city, that nine years from that day we should have . . . not *one* headquarters in a large city . . . not *two* . . . but representatives distributed over the length and breadth of the en-tire world! Little did we think at that time that civilization would develop such an insatiable hunger for our commodity.

"Little did *we* think, I say. But that statement is unjust; for even at that early date the faith of the founder of our organization never wavered. For Mr. Hemmingway was a man of vision, a prophet, a seer. He could foretell, where we could not, what a great demand was to be created in the world for his invention. And today, thanks to the vision of that undaunted genius . . ." THE WORLD IS WITH-OUT A TOY. Romance, realism, the inquisition, the City of God, geo-centricity . . . they have left us nothing . . . nothing but a wobbly art trying to hit us on the head with a club. Is there some life beyond the mucous membrane? Is there some significance beyond a little suburban home? As an adolescent, I carried vague possibilities in my groins; and now there is nothing left but to look at people. Christ, they have even burned out our pessimism!

Ah! to have gotten up in the night, and to have noticed the door open and the light lit. And to have passed down the corridor . . . and nothing . . . nothing . . . to have returned, unchanged.

What are we to do with the growing trees? And Mrs. Buckhorn yelling down the dumbwaiter shaft? Let me rise above . . . let me maintain . . . let me affirm. There is the epigram, and there is the epic . . . and I have squeezed big theoretical tears. If there is one pure joy left with us, it is to pass a tight jobby.

David, my little man, sling your pebble at the universe.

The Death of Tragedy

Part One

Argument: From our eagle's nest above the century, we observe details scattered beneath, finally pouncing upon Clarence Turner as a likely bit of carrion.

In following the road to Lynn, where Paul Revere summoned our forefathers—spiritual at least—to guerilla warfare, note the excellent facilities of the Standard Oil Company for purveying gasoline at exorbitant prices . . . and on the return, fill your pipe with the aid of the tobacco trust, for you can smoke on the after-deck of the railway combine's ferries until the pilot turns and goes the other way, thus making the pipe illegitimate since it is being smoked on the fore-deck. Believe us, it is all built on a healthy basis of Garfield niggers stoning Frogtown dagoes, and Saturday-afternoon amateur baseball games in the suburbs, and especially back in them grand days when papa got over his bun just in time for Sunday dinner. (Recalling the game that wound up the season, Brushton against Homewood, and our boys got licked twenty to one oh Jeezuz. In the last half of the ninth, when Humpty Haas came up to the plate, they hit his bat with a lemon. That same evening, however, the pitcher of the other team got drunk and strayed into town somewhat boastfully. And our boys showed what they couldn't do with baseball they could do with their fists.)

My aunt once told me, if I wanted to be healthy, to read *Science and Health* and eat an apple at bedtime . . . but now the country is going to the dogs, and it is all candy laxatives. Great God, if a volcano came upon us suddenly, and preserved our subway signs for future excavations, surely the archeologists would conclude that the rites of visceral purgation had something to do with our religion. In fact, as enlightenment spreads more and more among us, are we not coming to realize with continually increasing clarity that a man can not put in a good day at the office without his once before breakfast and once before going to bed?

Some day we shall surely own half of England, and have our own taps draining the hearts of the natives of India, to feed fresh blood into our patriotic barrels. Further, Mrs. Purdue, noting the mysterious quiet which suddenly fell upon her son's tent out in the back yard, peeped through a crack to observe six little boys sitting around with their peeties hanging out, and her son was one of them . . . the same one in fact, who later went to avenge the rape of Belgium.

Herein lies wisdom: If we have had so many years of the Democrats, let us go Republican; and when we have had so many years of the Republicans, let us spit upon them, turn our backs upon them, and go Democrat; and when we have tired of being either Democrats or Republicans, let us repeat the process under different appellations. In this way we can always be assured of an abundance of sinecures for our Irish-American population, while we shall seldom make the mistake of electing a mayor without a wad in his cheek . . . like that perfect product from Pittsburgh who, being introduced among Pittsburgh high society, on preparing to make his speech and noticing that Mrs. Eitelbaum was talking, shouted good-naturedly, "Hay there, you shut up 'r I'll throw y'out." As is evident, he won the election because he knowed how to mix with the boys. A similar situation will be observed in Denver, or Charleston, and other cities.

Our rich and powerful country also possesses certain songs, and we rise when those songs are played, because certain of our countrymen are getting control of the entire meat-packing industry of the Argentine. Millions for defense, but not one cent for tribute; my country, right or wrong, my country; we shall have peace, if we have to fight for it; remember the *Maine*; by God, we are bound to be great, for we can find the right sentence. (In contradistinction to the much more accurate Germans who always find the wrong one; as to wit, the scrap of paper.)

There has been kite season, and commy season, and roller-skate season, and baseball season, and swimming season, and roller-skate season again, and football season . . . and then in the evenings a fire is lighted in an empty lot. There are earnest, unhappy souls who observe these fires from a bedroom window or an automobile, and suddenly feel like going out for a walk in the cold fall air. Forms, half red, half black, disappear and return; there is a gush of sparks. I have at such times heard a horn blow out of the darkness, and one voice from the fire answer "All right," thereupon the circle about the fire being diminished. By ten-thirty no one remains but one orphan, one boy whose father works at night, and one other. The fire is allowed to languish; eventually it burns a sullen, characterless red, left alone in the black field.

Also, there are the nice houses. What has been said for the clean, dead houses on a terrace, with father returning a little after five in the summer, slapping his paper against his knee, and being met on the front steps. There are mists from the river which come after dark to lie over this part of the city. In a slight wind, the arc-lights sway on the deserted corners, making the shadows of telegraph wires climb up and down the walls. Occasionally the Polish maid entertains on the back porch.

The great lump of the country rolls on, with Howard swiping apples out of the cellar, and a high school sophomore pimpled with pubescent love, and elderly men dressing up to apply for jobs, and unexecuted rapes . . . and thieveries dead in the planning . . . . . . half-ambitions . . . . fractional insights . . . . while as for Clarence Turner, his book—thank

257

God!—had already reached its eighth edition, and there was the reasonable possibility of his play appearing on Broadway. The success, in fact, had been immediate. Not that Turner was low enough in the scale of jackals to have actually pandered to the public tastes. On the contrary, he had written in all sincerity, and it was simply a lucky accident that those subjects which were nearest to his heart happened to scratch the itch of the muck and glut of America's reading public.

If, climbing upon the ruins of America, we have reached Clarence Turner . . .

Part Two

Argument: Or rather, having cast about for a theme, we came upon that of Clarence Turner. It is, perhaps, worth further development.

On the third floor he stopped at a room which was done in purples; Florence was lying down, appropriately. "Ah, then you *can* come to see me, Clara!" she said to him with a certain commendable richness. He went over to her, and kissed her: kissed her, and all the memories of her. Glancing at the mantelpiece, he noticed that the lion's head had been restored to its place. (Once, he had gone over to touch it, calling forth from Florence a startled cry, pretty but honest. Another time, when he was looking at it steadily, she walked between them. But Clarence got the thing laid out quite clearly after a while, as is evident from this: While they were taking tea together, he had blurted out quite inconsequently, "It strikes me that the lion's head has a most fatherly look." The next time he came, the head had disappeared; and within a week he had attained her!)

"Yes, I *can* come, and I *dare* come, in spite of your loveliness," he answered in tune.

"See what I was reading? Your book . . . again and again, one chapter! You cannot tell me that that chapter was not written to me . . . oh, you know the one!" Not being quite sure of the one, Clarence bowed his head in mute acknowledgment that he knew it, oh, too well. Then a trembling came over him, and he ate her hand with kisses. (But above and beyond the fact that she had set Rimbaud to music, and had even published songs of her own in which Turner figured indubitably, above and beyond the yield of her kimonos and the genius she had for draping shadows about a room, there was the fact that she slid as gracefully into other arms as into his own . . . which explains after a fashion why he suddenly broke off the affair, marrying someone of a less accomplished quality in her voice. Soon after this, as a divine vengeance, came the success of his novel.)

Suddenly she arose, and then, significantly: "But we shall have tea." He looked at her deadly, and let his head sag into his hands. She sang three or four weak little bars of a song of hers, and wrapped her kimono more tightly about her. These little touches had been almost brutally definite; each understood just what had been given and taken. It was, roughly, this: "But we shall have tea" equals "What, Clarence, you think I can be put down and picked up again at will! I shall break the whole trend of our emotions with the irrelevant tinkling of the tea things." . . . His sagging head equals "I accept it, Florence, perhaps after a fashion even welcome it; not too proud to have you see me desolate over the loss. Look, I am frankly miserable; our friendship has meant so much." . . . Her timid little flurry of song equals "Still, you dear, dear boy, it must be that way, if our memories are to be retained in all their purity. Oh, God, to see it of a sudden, just what we had, and what we have lost!" . . . And the wrapping of the kimono equals "But all that is settled now; snap, it is finished. There is a wall between us." Silence for a few moments, while they listened to the far echoes of a relationship which was irrevocably gone. (It was all quite sympathetic to his mentality, this thick aura-of-soul which in the course of centuries has come to interpose itself between the agent and the feminal.)

The silence continued all during the preparation of the tea. Over against the general formlessness of their emotions came the definite clinking of the china. Clarence's eyes worked earnestly about the designs in the carpet. Then she nodded, and he pulled up his chair. Their feet met beneath the table; she did not withdraw, but looked at him steadily. How far their relationship had retrograded!

She laughed after a time in anticipation of a sentence which she was going to say. "Ha, it almost seems," it had been only the littlest laugh, "it almost seems, Clara, as though you will not really be here until you have left." Then she became agitated. "A history of tea! A history of tea! Is there anything but walls and beds which has seen humanity more intimately? Indeed, I vote for tea, Clarence, for here the great organ notes of our passions are turned into the neatest, tiniest little cameos. Think of a murder across the tea table. What a lovely *hokku* the whole idea would make! . . . It should be done, of course, with some sort of poisonous needle, held out along with a very properly turned compliment, and barely scratching the skin. . . . And the final death; would the victim fall across the table? Would the tea-things come rattling to the floor, the destruction of a miniature empire? Really, it is all very lovely, don't you think?" (Both being very conscious that Mrs. Turner could not do this sort of thing at all.)

And then: "But let me put away the tea-things. I must put them away now. For I shall not be able to bear it, seeing the room all cluttered up by you. And I must rearrange the chairs." Without ostentation, Clarence took the ends of the cigarettes which he had lined along his saucer—there should be no fetishes!—and carried them to the grate, threw them out of his life, and hers.

It was all so plain that this day was his last hold upon their intimacy. Now he could still go to her and take her in his arms; but after leaving this room this day . . . when he met her on the street, he would touch his hat, ask a few words about her brother, tell her some recent anecdote, and then hurry away.

He resented any distraction as a sin against this woman in front of him. Yet his wife would surely be expecting him from now on. He felt subconsciously that he should offer Florence a pure immersion in the present, in the emphatic this-ness and here-ness of their parting. Their parting, since that was certain. Everything that had happened this afternoon seemed to leave some little broken end. He arose abruptly, went to his hat and coat, and threw them across his arm. Walking to the door, he opened it, and paused with one hand on the knob. Florence dripped into her chair, looking at him without meaning.

On her little writing table the phone began ringing. Once, twice, then with a nagging impatience. Tacitly, however, they agreed to rule it out of the scene. Still, it *did* increase the tempo of their leave-taking, for he began to close the door with a jerk of sudden decision. She leaped from her chair, bolted towards him. He received her with a groan, crushing his hat between them. Then he turned and went stumbling blindly down the stairs, while the phone peeled forth one wild, unbroken plaint.

Reaching home, Turner hurried straight to his room, where for some hours he wrote feverishly.

Part Three

Argument: Becoming impatient, the author finally wanders elsewhere, and seems in the direction of a positive beauty, when the old subject returns like a gastric juice in the throat.

He fell asleep in the early morning, and when he awoke again at eight he found that the life had faded out of him. He went down for a walk, bought an orange at an Italian fruit store on Sullivan Street, and ate it standing on the corner. A drayhorse had fallen in the slush; Turner watched the agony of its feet as it struggled to rise, while its team-mate looked about with indifference. Finally he surrendered himself. He accepted it more or less consciously that he had given time enough to the burial of his love—taking the term, that is, as a technical expression, by which is meant that love, like potato farming or marine insurance, is developing a specific nomenclature as the manifestations thereof are becoming more standardized with the help of education. Now, if our more prominent novelists, of the type of Turner, could have taken two years of the classics and then two years intensive study in amoristic engineering, this fact could have been put upon its right basis long before now. A graph of the human heart, for instance, by a senior A. E., could have traced the curve from Seeing Her Pass, through Poignant Night and With Her Alone, ending perhaps with Burial of His Love. To look upon this as a scientific terminology, that is, so that the phrase "burial of his love" should not be dismissed as banal, but rather accepted as the accurate dictionary equivalent for the thing itself, and sanctioned by the consensus of the leading minds of the nation.

The steady rumble of everyday had gradually reclaimed him, so that he turned from the drayhorse—Christ! after Florence could not his wife even be called a drayhorse! Stand up the sorry thing and look at her. He could do that; that was his trade. The brute, walking along these streets; exciting no interest, and yet tearing the last strip of dignity from the woman he had married. Consider all the little pulsing hearts, too good for other pulsing hearts, but not good enough —oh, God! how shortcoming—for *one* pulsing heart, our hundred millions are composed of. What sewer cleaner's daughter would marry the son of a honeydipper? Yet Clarence Turner . . . after Florence . . . his wife! Added to a sleepless night, it is not hard to understand his bitterness.

When he reached the apartment she had already left, which was a show of delicacy that he had not expected of things. The furniture sat about, peculiarly irresponsive to his emotions. Going to his room, he threw himself upon the bed, and sobbed.

Lying there sobbing, and the stars *do* go around the earth. He has read any number of volumes on the play of the mucous membranes. Let us erect a dirty little monument to these intellectuals. There is even the possibility that we shall be driven into the Church by the scurviness of our free-thinkers. Building upon the sound foundation of this low-visionedness, there are those who, coming from Ohio, own the loss of an "r," while others, friend, can pronounce certain words with the accent on a different syllable than is customary. Such observations are really of value, since they may contribute to the happiness of still others.

On the other hand, oh, God, on the other hand, we shall sail easily across an enthusiasm of contours. To the south, the broad back of a hill curved down slowly into the plateau. And still farther south, an opposing curve swelled up and stretched away in the haze. While the lake fitted itself silently into the basin which the glaciers had scooped out for it some thousands of years ago. Or, off against the sky, consider the little meadow lying beyond a V of two hills. Or trees banked up the mountainside like clouds, and at irregular intervals the black-green firs jutting out like a city of church spires.

While there are, for those who love such things, rains which come ripping along the valleys, attacking whole forests, bending around gaps between the mountains, driving things before them. Further, there are patchy rains; they piddle for a while, then pour, then even cease entirely, so that the sun gets at the landscape here and there in shafts. And there are still other rains which you go on the porch and exclaim, "Why, it is raining!" they have sneaked into being so imperceptibly. While after any sort of rain the woods are even smellier than usual.

Oh, vomit of loveliness! Let us rise in the night and give thanks for the pure horizons that remain to us. Exult, for the heavy hills are patient to be climbed upon; willingly they suffer us to paw at their necks and sit across the peaks of their ears. And looking down from them, we see the valley, as it dips and waves, and how the shadows of the clouds . . . the shadows of the clouds, there being any number of clouds that day, though there was also the night when I went to the door/ and found the whole world snuggled away under snow/ that spread off and over the hills/ blue in the full moon/ sifting softly against the fences of the meadows/ and drooping from the fir trees.

Addenda

Turner's convalescence was hastened considerably by the intelligence that his play was really to appear on Broadway; he also became wrapped up in the consequences of a note which had said among other things, "*Je te désire.*"

The Book of Yul

Part One

While waiting, two men carried on a conversation that flapped and fluttered like an old newspaper. And a third was silent. Finally, the conversation gained in intensity, culminating in some disagreeable figure or image. Whereat, the third man rose and left the room. With us following, for it is he who conceived of Yul and the eleventh city. Thus:

Three men in a room, towards night. Two of them sat in the cold, sprawled somewhat, and with their overcoats on. The third was huddled in a Morris chair, knees up to his chin, looking down over his toes at the vague carpet. "Do you think she will come?" one of the other two asked. He swallowed, and noticed that his throat was getting sore. For a while they shifted slightly, in silence. (As the room grew darker, no one had moved to light the lamps.) The sounds outside came in dampened by the snow.

"We should have started a fire when we first got here," the first man said, yawning. "If we're going to wait around here we might as well be comfortable."

"Too late now, she'll be along any minute."

The man hunched up in the Morris chair sniffled three or four times, and then blew his nose. "Ah, what a bitter world!" one of the others laughed. "Look, the poor devil had to move." ... A heavy clock, in another room somewhere, or upstairs, or in the hall, sunk

264

seven strokes into the room. Outside an automobile stalled. They heard the scraping of the self-starter several times before the motor began working again. Then the car jerked ahead; then stalled. After a few minutes, however, the motor thumped with a solid regularity, and the car passed on down the street. Out of the high windows the snow could be seen falling diagonally across a street lamp.

"This waiting outside the gates of Heaven is cold business."

"Why in the name of God do you call it the gates of Heaven?"

Somebody could be heard walking. Thump, THUMP, THUMP louder . . . then THUMP, THUMP, thump fainter. "Probably the people in the next house." Listening intently, they could even catch a grumble of voices. Off up there, on the other side of the wall somewhere, people were no doubt sitting around talking, before a big fire, in a room full of light, eating, or maybe drinking something strong. Like those conceptions of perfect luxury which are inserted in the upper right-hand corner, the rest of the picture being devoted to a boy in rags, starving to death in a snowy alley.

A wind caught in the chimney in such a way as to disturb the burnt rubbish in the grate. The smell of rotten apples blew out into the room. Two girls passed outside, laughing, and hurrying with short, sharp steps. The man who had swallowed a little while ago brought up some saliva and swallowed again, to test his throat; the glands were distinctly swollen. He shot his cigarette into the dead grate; after a few moments, however, he lighted another. He said, "Damn this place for a tomb." A pause; then he continued, "When I stay very long in a place like this I always think, what if I were trapped in? . . . When I was a boy, I saw a crow early one spring standing bolt upright in a tree. I went closer, and he didn't fly. Then I saw that his foot had been caught in a fox trap. He flew to this tree, where the chain got caught in one of the branches. So he had been there during the winter, exposed to the cold and without food; and when he died, the trap weighted him so that he stood up as chestily as the healthiest crow you ever saw. . . . When I wait in a place like this, I can't help thinking of dying that way. Can't you imagine us all sitting here in this darkness, dead, you holding a pipe, and me like this, and him over there in the corner all hunched up!" At this point, the man in the

Morris chair arose, left the room, and could be heard immediately afterwards going down the stone stairs to the street.

The snow was falling now in thick wet gobs. Before he had gone fifty feet it was clinging to the fuzz of his woolen coat. Big banks of cleanliness had been stacked up. The lights of the store windows lay distinctly across the pavements. In that arc-light, in the carbon, in one molecule of the carbon, maybe, there was a little world, with planets and stars, and an infinite sky, and things living on some of the planets, and things living on those things. Some day some big hand would want our universe for an arc-light, and crunch, away it would go. "In one little corner beyond the stars, a world glowing up there all by itself, not crowded in the way ours is . . ." God, what a night! He listened unconsciously to the different scrapings of the shovels.

He started to turn into the subway, but did not do so, since an elation was on him. Instead, he went into the park, and stamped about in the heavy snow, even walked across one of the ponds, in fact. A gust of wind hit him strong enough for him to rise up against it, and yell into the teeth of it. Then he swung his arms, and charged an embankment. When he reached the top, he looked about him, a half mile across the park to the lights of the apartments along the edge. The wind dropped away; he was almost hot after his exertion. He opened his coat and laughed a stage laugh. Then he chanted, "*Sic erat in principio, et nunc, et semper, et in sæcula sæculorum, amen.* And the wind, appearing before me, spook, speek, spike, spuck, SPAKE, 'Behold the eleventh citee.' And I, answering unto the wind, spook, speek, spike, spuck, SPAY-ACHE, 'Verily, verily, do I behold the eleventh citee,' for there are ten others buried beneath it. Gloria!"

And then continuing to singsong the *Sic erat*, his mind wandered off to elaborate the eleventh city. "It is in the bottom of the sea," he thought, "and lived in by extremely cultivated fishes." But I happen to know that it is not at the bottom of the sea; or that it is not even near the sea. But it stands, bulky and dead, in the middle of a plain, silhouetted against the sky, and cold.

It is granite. Even the beds on which the people sleep are granite slabs, built in square holes carved out of the walls. For people live in this eleventh city: quiet, gray-eyed people, who slip about the stone streets, and in and out of oblong holes which serve as doors. But the under cities are filled with corpses, lying in rows, perfectly preserved, and without smell. The streets are long straight lines, and other long straight lines drawn perpendicular to these; the same is consistently true of the architecture.

And there was a traveler in this city, by the name of Yul. Looking ahead at the end of the widest street, he saw a break in the two walls of granite, and went towards it. It was a stairway, he found. Broad stairs, the width of a palace in his own country, led down to a platform, and so on down and down to platforms. All this was lit with a uniform incandescence. While at the base of the stairs there stood two granite lampposts, of no great size, but which he could distinguish as clearly as though they were immediately in front of him.

But Yul did not descend these stairs.

Part Two

Yul found the system of transit that had been evolved here of great ingenuity. It was composed of sixteen parallel tracks, or rather, endless platforms, which moved continually. These platforms were provided with benches, pavements, empty rooms, and the like. Now, as Yul stepped towards the south, he noticed that each platform moved slightly faster than the one to the north of it; and although the change from platform to platform was not abrupt, by the time Yul had reached the fifteenth platform to the south he was speeding enormously. The sixteenth platform, however, was entirely different from the fifteen preceding. To begin with, he found that it could not be boarded at any point, as with the other platforms. In front of him there moved a stone wall; occasionally, behind this he heard a roar, as of something which approached and retreated. And Yul, noticing that a group of gray-gowned figures had stopped near him on the fifteenth platform and seemed to be waiting, waited as well.

Within a short time he saw a tower approaching on the sixteenth platform. It advanced evenly, floated towards them, growing gradually above them as it came. When it was only a short ways off, he also

267

noticed that there was a break in the stone wall at this point, and that some of the figures farther down the platform were already entering there. In due time it reached him, and he stepped under the square stone arch on to the sixteenth platform. Everything was quite different here. Instead of the stone benches, pavements, kiosks, there was nothing but this lonely tower and a straight steel track that blurred away to the east and west. Like the others, he entered the tower, and found it a sort of rest room or waiting room.

Finally, above the grinding of the platforms, a far-off whirr was heard. The gray-clad figures left the tower, Yul thinking it best to follow. A line of cars shot up to the tower and stopped. Yul followed his companions into one of the cars, and they sped along the sixteenth platform. Yul sank into a stupor from this accumulation of speeds, partaking of nothing but a bitter, burning liquid which was brought to him at intervals. After another two days, Yul tired of the cars, and descended at one of the towers. Then he crossed the fifteen other platforms to the north, and found, when he stepped off the last of them, that he had returned almost to the starting point.*

He came to the wide street again, and entered one of the oblong cuts in the stone which served as doorways. Inside, there were winding stairs, lit with the same unvarying incandescence that he had noticed on the stairs leading down to the buried cities. Yul wound slowly upwards, his steps slapping back at him in a confusion of echoes. The stairs curved into a room; a large, square room, empty except for a tablet on one of the walls and a bench placed before this tablet. Yul, who could not read the tablet, noticed the firmness of the characters, and passed on into the next room. This room, too, was large and square and empty. But there was a window hewn out in one wall, oblong like the doors in the street, except that it was lying on one of the longer sides. From this window Yul could see across the plain to the even, cold horizon. It was in still another room, the third, that Yul voided.

Yul then came from this place into the street, and walked along

* He had circled only once about the city in all this time, and that in spite of the enormous velocity with which he had been traveling; which facts, it is hoped, will tend to show the vastness of the eleventh city, and of the ten cities buried beneath it.

until he came to a larger granite entrance than was usual. He entered, finding himself beneath a balcony. He walked farther and saw a floor of white marble, dipping in a slow curve towards a stage or altar in the distance. Yul fell upon his knees and wept, this quiet curve was so soothing to him. Looking above him, he saw that here, too, there were curves; the walls reaching up thin arms of broken arches; a ceiling behind shadows, and vaulted; and thick wooden beams that worked among one another like a mass of human bodies. The church was nearly dark; while the altar, seen far off through a cylinder of darkness, glowed with a soft phosphorescence.

As he wept, Yul felt something like a purring of the floor, while an uncertain but penetrative odor filtered about him. The marble was warm, so that he lay flat on his back and sent his eyes into the shadows of the beams.

The odor increased, until Yul felt a restlessness come over him. He arose, and began putting aside his clothes, until finally he stood naked in the middle of the vast, empty church. Then, listening with great intensity, he thought he could distinguish footsteps. They were far away, but hurrying. They would increase, then nearly fall away completely, so that Yul began to despair. But finally they became firmer; they were advancing; they were upon him . . . and down to one side of the altar he saw a form coming towards him.

While it was still far off, Yul could already distinguish two eyes, which were like moist planets shined on by the sun. That is, they seemed to lie on the face, with an aggressive clearness; while they did not burn but had rather that quiet, steel blue light of a planet. Of a moist planet, that is . . . not of some dry planets which are like a copper red spark. Yul watched the eyes, as they came nearer to him, like magnets.

And as the form stood before him, Yul saw that it was the form of a woman; and at once he loved her clamorously. But she picked up the clothes that he had thrown off and held them out to him, so that Yul put them all back upon his body. When he had dressed, he stood in front of her, and looked into her eyes. They were big and deep, like lakes, for he could see down into the rich black pupils as though they really were made of water. She took him by the hand and led him towards the altar, until Yul threw back his head and sang. But his notes began lingering and grumbling to one another among the beams, so that he quit singing. . . . He was led to the edge of the altar. Then she let go his hand, and jumped. Looking where she had jumped, Yul saw that she had leapt across a pit in the center of the altar. He looked down into this pit; it was dark, but so far below that it made him shudder he could see the incandescence of the lowest of the buried cities. Then he jumped and followed his companion on the other side of the altar.

For a time they labored along together, down steps into cold damp places; around sudden bends into rooms that were warm and brilliant; through some narrow passage with a rough, pebbly bottom; then across a little stone bridge under which a spring flowed out of the rock and back into it. But of a sudden she stopped and opened her arms to him. Yul closed against her, looking into the roads and caverns of her eyes. She stepped away, tore back her garments with one fling of her hand . . . and Yul crumpled on the ground under the impact of his disgust. For shining out upon the hairs of the *mons Veneris*, there was a third eye, which beheld him steadily and without blinking.

. . .When Yul awoke, the woman had gone. He began working his way slowly back through the labyrinth of rooms and passages. At last he came upon the pit, and jumped across it. He saw as he went out of the church that immediately in front of it was the broad stairway which led down into the other cities. He looked along the narrowing avenue of stairs, and at the end of them he could make out something that moved. But a peculiar sickness was upon him; he longed for his own country, and dropping where he stood, he fell asleep on the first of the granite stairs.

Part Three

Later, Yul returned to the stone church . . . and the assembled multitude, lifting its thin voices, chanted in unison the Litany of Error:

We shall go into the tenth city
    Glory glory unto our woes
And take the hands of our fathers
    Glory glory unto our woes
And kiss the nail holes in their palms
    Glory glory unto our woes
And in the palms of our mothers
    Glory glory unto our woes
And touch the old shells of their skin
    Glory glory unto our woes

And rejoice that now they are alive oh unfolding of the revelation oh ecstasy of blossoming into a world of eternity oh astonishment of opening their petals in the warm garden of our Maker glory glory unto the woes of our fathers and our fathers before them and whatever may befall us in our own day

The multitude, and the priest ... they had alternated, the priest alone, standing in the glow of the altar, carrying the "Glory glory unto our woes." But when the lob-end of the prayer was reached, the priest and the kneeling multitude rose up, while heavy music was suddenly sprayed into the church. After the singing was ended, the music wound on for a few bars in reminiscence ... then it suddenly regained its vigor, and while the multitude knelt again with bowed heads it repeated the entire form of the litany, growing at the last into a tangle of chromatics, with agitated notes crawling in among one another, and accumulating fugues, while the whole jumbled mass grew more voluminous and climbed slowly up the scale. Out of it all there burst one neat, soft chord, high in the treble. This chord hung, while the rest of the music dropped away, until finally it existed all by itself. Then it, too, gradually weakened. But for a long time after it was gone entirely, the multitude remained kneeling.

Now the ceremony seemed to drop more into the business of worship. At times the multitude would rise, kneel at times, while there were even times when it became prostrate on the white marble floor. Up from out of the altar, a long sermon was delivered by one of the priests. It was a well-wrought sermon: it showed the effects of a mind that had devoted long nights to working out the arabesques of its idea. "That which is created creates in turn that by which it was created." The voice from the glowing altar suffered its little elations, its momentary discoveries, its occasional felicities between the idea and the expression thereof . . . the words spread out over the quiet multitude, certain sounds lodging among the beams of the ceiling, others shooting straight to the ear, others floating up sluggishly . . . so that it all became slightly confused and mellow . . . in spite of the hard little stones of the priest's inexorable logic . . . and the voice rose and fell, went slower in places for the purpose of emphasis, hurried across parenthetical explanations, paused before launching on new developments of the idea, halted and retracted a statement to a degree, dropped into a steady trot of exposition . . . the multitude, far from being disturbed that the words of it all did not reach them with clarity, rested comfortably on the dips and fluxes of the priest's voice.

The sermon was followed by a prayer . . . in trailing sentences of unequal length . . . some short . . . some stretching out to the length of two breaths . . . and at the end the multitude joined with the priest in praying . . . the frail single line of words from the altar, then the confused growl of the multitude. After the prayer, the church lay lifeless for a few moments.

Then a flash of light shot across it. The priest climbed in leaps upon the altar, until he stood looking down upon the multitude. A chord was struck, and the priest, taking his pitch immediately as the chord vanished, chanted:

LET THE NINE CHOSEN BE BROUGHT
INTO THE HOLY ARENA

And off somewhere, lost in the caverns of the church that led away to the right behind the altar, the chant was repeated in a little thread of voice:

Let the Nine Chosen be brought into the holy arena.

Then even fainter, away to the left behind the altar:

Holy . . . Holy . . . Holy . . .

LET THE NINE CHOSEN BE BOUND UPON
THE BEAMS OF THEIR CROSSES

. . . Let the Nine Chosen be bound upon the beams of
their crosses.

Crosses . . . crosses . . . crosses of holiness . . .

LET THE NAILS BE DRIVEN INTO THE
HANDS AND THE FEET OF THEM AND
THEIR SIDES TRANSFIXED WITH SPEAR
HEADS UNTIL BLOOD MIXES WITH THE
SWEAT OF THE EXECUTIONERS AND
REJOICE THAT NOW THEY ARE ALIVE
OH UNFOLDING OF THE REVELATION
OH ECSTASY OF BLOSSOMING INTO A
WORLD OF ETERNITY OH ASTONISH-
MENT OF OPENING THEIR PETALS IN
THE WARM GARDEN OF OUR MAKER
GLORY GLORY UNTO THE WOES OF OUR
FATHERS AND OUR FATHERS BEFORE
THEM . . . AND LO! BEHOLD THEM ENTER!

The voice stopped; the priest's arms were stretched out in imitation
of the agony of the cross; music broke out, while at the same time a
shrieking rose to the right of the altar; silk streamers began dropping
and twisting, played upon by lights of all colors. The college of
priests hurried up before the altar, howling "Glory, glory!" leaning
forward and bearing the crosses of the Nine Crucified like banners.
They stopped short before the pit; the music dropped away; the
streamers subsided into a lazy billow; the lights became one penetrating reddish purple, which lay in all corners of the church like a

sunset. The bodies of the Nine Crucified could be seen moving in silence on their crosses. . . . The priest, from the summit of the altar, gave a signal with his hand, and the crosses with their burdens were dropped into the pit. For a time they could be heard, scraping now and then against the sides, or colliding with one another. Finally, as they reached the bottom of the lowest city, faint thumps came up out of the pit.

The multitude huddled together, closer about the altar. It seemed to be listening. The thumps became heavier; they recurred at set intervals, like a slow treading of feet. Outside the church, beheld by no one in all this city, the march of the armless giants . . . advancing down the broad stairway which was the width of a palace in Yul's own country . . . little ripples passing along their ranks and being lost in the distance . . . armless giants, which rise up boldly out of their legs, like towers.

A Progression

So all these people are adding their mite to the fortune of Mr. Dougherty. That little bald-headed man, for instance, is head of the bookkeeping department; only last week he was publicly lauded by Mr. Dougherty himself for working out a system which would take care of the new factory in Hoboken. He is evidently worried, says something over-hasty to the treasurer, comes down the green plush carpet on the run; so that the treasurer winks at the filing clerk, who winks back, hoping thereby—in accordance with a vague enough logic—that he will get his five-dollar raise next Friday. As Miss Rosenberg's typewriter goes *tink* at the end of the line, Mrs. Murdock's typewriter is just being charged with a white sheet and two carbons, and the typewriter of the new girl in the corner leaps into the beginning of a new paragraph. A man from one of the departments upstairs passes the head of the bookkeeping department, while an office boy is crossing the room diagonally, steering among the desks.

Dougherty had evidently done right to wait for Griffiths to call him. "Never let'm think you're too anxious, that's my philosophy," he said in the direction of his private secretary. Then he dismissed his desk completely, lighted a cigar, and went over to the window. He could see down twelve floors of the building opposite him before it dropped on out of sight; looking up, he could see five floors before the partly drawn blind cut him off.

But it was already after four; Mr. Dougherty would have to be

275

starting home soon if he did not want to get caught in the rush hour. He slapped shut a few drawers, put some papers somewhere else, got his hat and coat out of the wardrobe, and left. As he stepped from his private office into the general offices, the ripple of prestige preceded him. An aisle was cleared through the comers and goers; the operator put her best into a "Good evening, Mr. Dougherty"; the elevator boy caught the door halfway as he was closing it, and held his car for Mr. Dougherty; downstairs, the starter saluted professionally; then Mr. Dougherty stepped out into the street.

Objects moved. Things passed irregularly, some slick and shiny, some looming up and approaching like a broadside, some wheezing. Others crossed, went down, went up, bunched, shot ahead. One peculiarly agitated division kept working in and out, crying. He moved himself among shapes, sizes, and directions. The wind of an approaching storm writhed through a gulch, but he was firm in his resolution, and drew close the flappings of his mantle. He advanced, steering himself without question.

Suddenly he swerved, dipped behind two other figures that were moving to cross him, and plunged into a warm breathy chamber, descending into the thick smells. He reached a platform in time to catch the local which was just pulling in; he took it, changing for the express at Chambers Street.

The first fifteen minutes or so of the ride was carried off without anything unusual occurring. In fact, the train had already pulled out of the station at 116th Street without the hint of a catastrophe. But there the tracks become temporarily exposed, running high in the open for a disturbingly long time before they would dive into the protecting earth again. Suddenly a swarm of airplanes descended on the train, buzzing about it, flying in among one another, dipping at the cars, and swooping up and over them. As one airplane drew up for a moment alongside the speeding cars, it became clearly evident that it was filled with Indians. And judging from the hideous expression on their faces, they were giving war-whoops, although nothing could be heard but the spitting of the airplane engines and the rolling of the car wheels. Then something shot out of the airplane, breaking the window directly in front of Mr. Dougherty. A second later he was lassoed firmly about the waist, jerked out of the window, and hauled rudely into the airplane, the swarm of them disappearing towards the south, flying all the way to one of the deserted islands in the South Seas, in fact, where they killed Mr. Dougherty and ate him, which recalls the somewhat similar case of Ellery Smith.

On returning home one night over a not particularly difficult road to his farm less than a mile out of town—further, there was even a full moon—Smith lowered the bars of the pasture gate and discovered that he was in an unknown country. He started back to town; but the town was gone. Between that and early morning when, crawling with open arms towards the broad, clean sun, he fell into the abandoned quarry south of Crow Hill, and broke his neck.

But there is this difference: that Ellery Smith suffered mishaps of an obviously superhuman or metaphysical import, whereas the loss of Mr. Dougherty bears heavily upon one of the most deplorable paradoxes in all the length and breadth of modern society. For in Heaven's name, how can we without blushing speak of Progress when we mean thereby the invention of a mechanism thanks to whose ingenuity not only can remote and seemingly inaccessible places be reached by methods which at one time would have appeared almost Divine, but also the unscrupulous can utilize as still another accessory to rapine and murder! This, I say, is nothing other than a vomit in the face of that Higher Idea of Progress, which takes into account, besides the increase in man's scope of mechanical effectiveness, also a concomitant chastening of the spirit; which, burning away through education all dross of savagery, leaves the greatest of God's creatures with a mental and moral equipment capable of putting to the complete—and undefiled—advantage of society those super-tools which our restless ingenuity has fashioned.

How, for instance, to take the problem up from yet another angle, can a society consider itself anything but ridiculous wherein the man of thorough and well-digested learning, the scholar and the philosopher, finds his liberties infringed upon by the meanest superstition-monger, the lowliest believer in ghosts? Pursuing the matter still more deeply, we see that scholarship itself cannot exclude those persons of a weaker mental muscle who, lifting the burden of much learning upon their shoulders, display thereby how miserably unfit their frame is for sustaining it. My mind runs at this point to the case of M. Henri Basle, a member of several learned organizations in France, and an excellent stylist as well, but whom I must quote as a muster of dark and crooked thinking:

> From behind thick smears of trees and the unevenness of the ground—which, in addition, was covered with a tall grass—you could see certain parts of the upper story of the house. Especially, if you had had courage enough to climb inside the wall. A gravel path wound towards the house, and a boy once took a stone from this path and threw it at one of the windows. When the hole was made in the glass, a butterfly fluttered away, the boy dying that same evening. . . . All this happened, it is true, before my time; but I did see the house and the gravel path which led up to it, and I have heard noises come from it with my own ears. . . . If I remember rightly, it was constructed of some dull gray stone, which had been made even duller by the soot coming from the mills along the river.

In the above quotation kindly notice first of all that the writer's honesty has proved even greater than his credulity. It is more than significant that in the very paragraph which aims to plead for ghosts the author's characteristic circumstantiality contains the germs of the rebuttal. If *this* man had seen the butterfly, I should be much more inclined to waver in my denouncement of the whole thing as either quackery or superstition.

Then again, if ghosts really do exist, how are we to dispose of the problem of their propagation? For if the ghost is the simulacrum of the human, by what logical step can it be denied the possession of male or female organs, whichever the case may be? Or, if the possession of these is granted, by what further logical step could it be maintained that the ghosts were barren? Yet there are no more so-called ghosts than there have been people to contain them. And if the body is rotted, and the soul is in Heaven, Hell, or Purgatory, what is there left whereof a ghost could be constructed? Nothing but the memory of a man, which is to say, *nothing*. For memory is a mere inclination of the worms of the brain, like the leaning of tall grass after a storm.

Therefore, *there are no ghosts*. The invention of the ghost is a mere northern aberration, with an origin that is easily felt when one considers the blunt mists rising from our bogs, or if one has happened to observe the broad blossoms of fog which frequently nose through our dark forests. And we will even grant that one could wish there were ghosts, to sift about the rooms of a deserted mansion, or blow down low corridors, serving, in short, to counteract the increasing blatancy of our customs. The truth is that these unearthly existences about us are not ghosts, but *ghouls*, or *demons*, devoid of all this austere, ghastly poetry. They are hard little pebbles of malice, and cancers of envy, and running sores of hatred, and like the Great Bent Master of them all, quick moving, keenly intelligent, and fiery tongued.

"Fiery tongued," I say, for at times when I consider the idiocy of those who maintain that the devil's tongue is rounded, I marvel that I could hold my peace even so ably as I have. For why, I ask, if the devil's tongue is rounded—or even has that soft amorphousness at the end which is the property of the tongues of humans and of cattle—should we associate the lascivious with those things which protrude in points? You have but to cast one glance upon the azalea when it is flourishing at the height of its lubricity to become convinced that the tongue of the devil is as dart-like as a flame, and as disastrous as that object—if we could call a flame such—when it penetrates into the vase of the ear. And ah, Christ! what ill-formed dreams come frequently of this copulation. But I am being led by passion to wander from the topic—for there are times when a passion will engross me much the way a blood-hunger will engross a gnat; the gnat (or in some parts of the country I should better speak of a black fly and in others a punky, while I believe the sand fly of the southeastern beaches is also similar) when it has at last succeeded in alighting and penetrating the skin and the water under the skin, falls into such a rage of feasting that it seems to forget everything else, even the necessity of fleeing to preserve itself, so that the bitten party can approach his thumb with leisure and crush the life out of it without its so much as attempting to leave the well it has sunk into the flesh. But let me close this digression abruptly, and step forth now, once and for all, and declare myself as avowedly against the round-tonguers and the soft-tonguers as I am against the Black Angel himself.

Yet, almost without knowing it, I find that we are naturally prone to overstress the darker phases of a subject; applying which to the present writing would mean that there was a constant danger of giving too much to the devil and his horde, and not enough to God. So I consider this decidedly more pleasant aspect of the child Argubot, whose father and mother always told the truth, told the truth so much, in fact, that while Argubot was still young the King came and had his mother's ears cut off, while his father was put to death. Thereafter the boy lived alone with his widowed mother, who still told the truth even though her husband was dead and her ears were cut off.

But Argubot never told the truth at all. Once when he was late for supper, his mother asked him where he had been, and he said that he had been out with the ghost of his father riding on the moon. His mother said that he was untrue, and that he had fallen asleep in the hay, and called him to be whipped. But Argubot said that his mother must not whip him, because his father told him he would be King some day. So that his mother had to put the whip back behind the stove unused, for the ghost of his father *might* have taken the little boy for a ride on the moon, and she had always felt that Argubot was going to be King some day. At other times he told similar perplexing falsehoods.

Until the poor woman didn't know what to do. She wanted her boy to be honest, like herself and her dead husband, whom the King had killed; for she didn't want him to become another untrue King. She puzzled for many days how that she could prove that her son was not true, so that she could whip him. Although she was very poor, she gave a candle to Mother Mary. Then a plan came to her; but she would have to tell a lie. She hesitated for a long time, finally deciding that she must do so for the sake of her son.

She went to a neighbor at the far end of the town, whose cat had kittens, and asked for one small black kitten. Then she came home again and called Argubot to her. "Little son, I have brought you three kittens, but that you may not get tired of them, you may have only one of them at a time. But as all the three kittens are nearly alike, it will be hard to tell them apart. But if you look into their eyes, you can tell them apart, for their eyes are different. One is called Big Eyes, because the black of his eyes is always as big as the whole eye; I will let Big Eyes come to bed with you; if you awake in the night, and are afraid, just move your toes under the blanket, and Big Eyes will tumble and prance at them. The second is called Little Eyes, because the black of his eyes is only a slit; he is a lazy fellow, and at noontime you will find him stretched in the sun on the back doorstep. The third is called Medium-Sized Eyes, because the black of his eyes is neither big, nor is it just a slit; you can play with Medium-Sized Eyes in the mornings and afternoons, but be careful of him, for he is the liveliest of the three, and is liable to scratch you."

But Big Eyes, Little Eyes, and Medium-Sized Eyes were all one kitten, although Argubot did not know it. For at night a cat's eyes are big, and at noon they are very small, while in the morning and the afternoon they are neither big nor small. And the widow was sorry that she had been untrue, but she stood by her plan and waited to see what would come of it.

The next morning, when they were eating their porridge, she asked Argubot about the kittens, and he said he awoke and was afraid, but he didn't have to call her because Big Eyes was there and played with his toes. And his mother said nothing. . . . The next morning after that, when they were eating their porridge again, she asked him about the kittens and he said that he awoke and was afraid, but he didn't have to call her because Big Eyes was there and played with his toes. And again his mother said nothing. . . . But the third morning, when she asked him about the kittens, Argubot exclaimed, "Oh, mother, Big Eyes and Little Eyes and Medium-Sized Eyes were all three on my bed last night." And now his mother knew that he was untrue, and she went behind the stove to get her whip.

But Argubot ran out of the house and became King.

And when he was King, he despatched a messenger to the south, telling him to bring back a cat with big eyes, and one with little eyes, and one with medium-sized eyes. But the messenger returned cold and hungry, and fell before King Argubot, saying, "My Sire, I could not contain the cats, for some evil spirit changed them in the bag. . . . The first day, I caught a cat with medium-sized eyes, and put him in my hunting-bag, but when I rested that night and looked at him, there was another cat like him in his place, but his eyes were big. 'Very well,' said I, 'we will let this be our big-eyed cat.' The next noon I caught a cat with little eyes, but when I sat down to rest in the afternoon I looked at him and his eyes were medium-sized. 'Very well,' said I, 'we will let this be our cat with medium-sized eyes.' And the third day at noon I caught another cat with little eyes, and returned home, happy in that I had fulfilled the commission of my Lord. But after trudging all day I came upon the castle at nightfall, only to find that all three cats had eyes as big as the full moon."

King Argubot was displeased, and despatched the same messenger to the north with the same mission, but the result was no better. Then he sent other messengers in other directions, and they all returned with the same tale. Thereupon the King had all the messengers thrown into the dungeon.

The King was sad, and went out into his garden. But here a good fairy appeared before him and said that if he would release all the messengers from the dungeon, the three cats would be given him. He did so, and they were.

Then he sent the messengers out over the land again, this time to find his old widowed mother, if she was still alive. And they returned with his mother, bringing her before the King, but she did not recognize that he was her son.

"Old woman," he said to her severely, "do you see that cat at my feet?" and he pointed to the three cats which the fairy had given him. "Now I pick it up and its eyes are big. I put it down and pick it up again and its eyes are little. I put it down and pick it up a third time, and its eyes are medium-sized. Is not that so?"

And the old woman began to weep, and said, "Please my Lord, but it is not so. There are three cats at the feet of my Lord."

The King Argubot roared out with anger, so that the old woman began to tremble, "What does this old woman dare to gainsay the King!"

"Please, my Lord," she sighed, "but I lost my dear son, once when I was untrue. And now, although I can not understand it, I must tell the truth, even though it cost me my head, even as it cost me the head of my husband many years ago." King Argubot was sure that this was his mother before him, and he told her who he was, and stepped down from his throne, and led her into a great banquet prepared for her.

Soon after this, King Argubot, hearing of a beautiful princess who was weaving a golden garment of a golden thread on a golden loom, but who lived in a country very far off, went in search of her to make her Queen. When at last he found her, she looked upon him and fainted with love, so that she broke the skein of gold with which she was weaving. But there was a curse upon this princess, whereby, if it should ever happen that this golden thread was broken, she was doomed to die nine months after that time.

The King and his Queen began wandering to fling off the curse; by royal decree, thousands of witches and ugly old women were burned; but the curse could not be flung off, so that at the predestined date the Queen died, after giving birth to a Prince, who lived on after her. King Argubot returned to his own country, and mourned for five years. Then, finding that his people were at the mercy of usurers, he had all money lenders put to death, and devoted himself to the welfare of his kingdom, at the same time teaching the young Prince also to love and protect his subjects.*

So wisely did King Argubot pilot his kingdom that all who were good became favored and happy, while the malicious and the

* Not to be confused with a later Prince Argubot, of a different lineage, and of whom it is recorded: While walking on the seashore and thinking of the problems that beset his kingdom—most especially the pestilence which at that time was raging in the larger cities—Prince Argubot was suddenly conducted away on a carpet of zephyrs, and into an intensification of beauty which was beyond the endurance of mortal eye. When he was returned to earth, little children hid at the mention of his name, and old men marveled that their Prince, once so kind to his people, should have grown more cruel than even his uncle before him.

283

scheming among them could not flourish nor take root, so that finally they crossed the border into other countries. And when at last it was time for the King to die, all his subjects threw down their tools and neglected their crops, allowing pests of all sorts to spring up among them; for, they said, they wanted to perish with their King. But when the King heard of this, he blessed his people, but asked that if they still heard his authority they should return to their tasks, so that his corpse might not be buried in a land of desolation. And the people, hearing of this, returned to the fields and the workbenches, that a thriving state might be maintained as a monument to their beloved monarch.

Soon after, King Argubot breathed his last, and as his soul rose out of the window, the voice of his Angel-Wife was heard calling him to her couch in Heaven. O glory of their re-union in that gentle land above the sky!

In Quest of Olympus

1

With an uncertain tide—or better, current, since I am speaking of a little lake, or an enormous spring, or some sort of underground river—I simply took all chances and allowed myself to drift. For the most part it was black; me lying in the bottom of the boat, conscious by means of some complicated mechanism of sensation, or rather, some peculiar centralization from divers termini, of a gentle motion; the boat scraping now and then against an unseen rock that jutted up, or perhaps the sides of the cavern. Once or twice I passed a little ball of pale bluish light, however. A crunching sound. The boat had grounded on pebbles. Feeling in the dark, I stepped out on a smooth bank which began to ascend immediately. I said farewell to my boat—perhaps forever!—and began climbing. It was rough and jagged, like a sieve for grinding nutmeg; then became almost as steep as a perpendicular cylinder; and finally narrowed after the manner of an inverted funnel. I had to stop, for I had come upon a wall, a smooth, flat surface; and further, I was exhausted. I dropped where I lay, fell into a sort of stupor, and when I regained consciousness it was owing to faint irregular taps coming from far beneath me and forcing themselves upon my notice. It was my boat, broken from its moorings, starting easily on its way!

I cursed the foolhardiness that had got me into this thing. And I confess that I even wept, for the feeling of desolation and loneliness which came over me was too powerful for resistance. Then I remembered my training, and putting away all fears, confided my problems to Him who sees even the slightest move we make, and who hears even the weakest little sigh from our uttermost within. A new courage poured into me like wine, and I recommenced examining the wall. At last I came upon a place where the smoothness of it was broken by cracks large enough for me to insert my fingers, and the ascent continued.

As I climbed, it began slowly to dawn in the cavern. (The noonday sun of the countryside above, that is, was penetrating through some cavity into these depths.) I came upon the first sickly weeds, a few beetles, worms and the like. And it was not long before I was in full daylight, struggling through a thick underbrush which was so luxuriant, so impenetrable, that I almost wished for the cool desolation of my cavern. Working among the briars, especially the insistent blackberries—insistent because they seemed to be actually reaching out to catch the wool of my coat—I came upon a cluster of sumac, and then an even thicker muddle of ferns and alders. As the ground was unusually rough, my feet would slip from the rocks, and lodging in some unnoticed cavity covered with dead leaves, they would be held there by a tangle of roots, while at the same time I was kept busy dodging beneath the low crooked branches, making detours, or creeping through chance holes in the foliage. And then of a sudden I broke through to a road, and looked across broad easy meadows . . . and why! there was the house where Treep used to live!

And that stump in front of Treep's house, that was where the oak used to be which Treep had loved so much and then his master had ordered him to cut it down. Treep used to go out and pat the shaggy bark of this oak while it was still standing. But his master said finally, "Treep, cut down that oak." Since it was decided that the oak was needed for timber. Before that Treep had even felt that long after he was dead the oak would stand there; but now the oak had to be chopped down, and Treep went out with his axe to chop it.

No one was near, however, so that Treep rubbed his head against it, and explained how unhappy he would be without it and how he would hollow out the stump and plant therein some of its own acorns. Then, after weeping, he attacked the trunk with his axe.

But as he swung his axe, it caught in a low branch which was sagging somewhat, Treep being knocked on his back by the rebound of this branch. At first he was angry; but he said that it was right for the oak to defend itself, and it should not be rebuked. When he returned to chopping, however, a rotten branch from high up in the tree became dislodged, and cut a gash in the nape of Treep's neck. "Thou ungrateful oak!" he shouted in anger; "Thou must know that it is not my fault that I must kill thee, and thus not place the burden of thine own disobedience upon a heart which is already weighted down by the necessity of fulfilling a loathsome command put upon it by my master!" And Treep resumed his task.

But as the axe sank into the trunk, a large chip of wood flew up, striking Treep full on the forehead, so that the blood poured down into his eyes. Treep arose at one leap, regained his axe, and began brandishing it about his head. "Oak!" he shrieked, "Oak! Thou art no longer the big friendly thing that I rubbed my ears against and hugged with my arms, but a monument of malice and spitefulness rising between me and the commands of my master. And the love I bore for thee now being completely vanished, I swear by the blood dripping from my forehead that I shall attack thee in all ferocity, not stopping until thou lyest a corpse at my feet!"

And then Treep assailed the oak with bitterness, half blinded by the blood from his forehead, his body aching and tired, but sustained with such a vengeance against his old friend that he hardly knew what he was doing. Indeed, blinded as he was by the flow of both his blood and his emotions, and although a practiced woodsman, he was not felling the oak properly. And when at last it became so weakened that it began to topple, he saw that it was falling towards his master's garden. At this point he was plunged into an inordinate hate; he did not even take into account the enormous mass of his enemy, but as the oak began leaning with increasing rapidity, he hurled aside his axe, and heaved his shoulders against the falling trunk, trying in this way to change the direction of its fall!

But the oak continued on its descent, and as it stretched out along the ground it held Treep beneath it, crushing the life out of him almost instantly.

2

Treep was aware of no change whatsoever, except that he was growing. Soon his hand alone was as big as his whole body had been, with the rest of him increased in proportion; and soon after this his hand was as big as his new body had been . . . and so on, indeterminately. When he had ceased increasing, he looked about, stretched his arms which were as thick as a countryside; and opening his jaws, he yawned as wide as a gulf. But he was conscious of a pain beneath the nail of his right little toe; and reaching down he pulled out a splinter, the oak which had killed him. . . . This had been the magnification of Treep.

Noticing that the sky was only a few arm-lengths above him, he sprang into the air, caught hold, and hoisted himself on to the other side. The country was rough but comparatively level. Glistening in the distance there was something which looked very much like a palace. He made off in this direction.

As he came nearer he could distinguish figures moving about, all of them as big as he was himself. Then messengers came ahead to meet him, small, the way he had been before death, and they perched on his shoulders like doves. They explained that they were the former poets of the earth, and that this was Heaven, and that they were usually the only earthly existences admitted here. But Wawl had seen Treep's struggle with the oak, and had decreed that he should be magnified among the gods, and then they all fell to singing their own compositions at once. He walked ahead, not much disturbed by their twitter, until one of them climbed into the shell of his ear and explained, shouting above the others, the dilemma which Wawl had occasioned by his deification. For in magnifying Treep it was not found possible to magnify his name, and there were no more names nor offices left in Heaven. Wawl had decided, however, that if Treep dared he might attack any god he so desired, and if he defeated this god could usurp both his name and office. Treep asked the poet what gods were disliked in Heaven, and the poet mentioned both Arjk and the Blizzard God. Arjk, it went on to say, was undoubtedly a powerful and handsome divinity, and would be a much worthier foe to unseat than the Blizzard God, who relied mostly on cunning and harassing. . . . Treep decided that it was Arjk whom he would battle; and halting outside the castle, he sent word to Wawl that his faithful servant Arjk was approaching.

Soon a distant tumult was heard, and the poets in a panic scrambled down from Treep's shoulders. Then Arjk appeared, growling and cursing, and demanding to know if this was the liar who was adorning himself with the name of a god. Treep answered him, "Step aside, Treep, for I am Arjk, the faithful servant of Wawl, and I have come to pay him homage." Thereupon the two of them closed in upon each other, a battle following which lasted for two years. At the end of this time Treep conquered and threw Arjk out of Heaven. Then he sent word again to Wawl that his faithful servant Arjk was approaching, and entered the palace.

3

Some time after Treep—become Arjk—had established himself in Heaven, Wawl summoned him to the palace. Arjk entered and bowed before him. About the feet of Wawl adoring women sat, their breasts dripping at his glory, indeed, their entire bodies flowing with love of their Lord. Wawl dismissed his attendants and began speaking to Arjk immediately. But the castle was so large that it had its own internal weather. And as Wawl commenced to speak, a little storm descended about the august forehead, filling his hair with a silver moisture and pricking him with minute tongues of lightning. Wawl peered through the mist wavering before his eyes, and raised his voice above the small but distracting thunder.

"Arjk," Wawl addressed him, "thou art the most mighty of my warriors."

"Whatever strength I possess was granted me by Wawl."

"I trust that thou wilt remain faithful to me, for thy powers, if turned against me, could cause all manner of evil in Heaven."

And Arjk, bowing even lower, answered with emotion, "Before everything else comes my gratitude to Wawl. In the magnification of Treep there was also the magnification of Treep's devotion. And this devotion is mortgaged solely to Wawl." And then rising to his feet, Arjk gave way to his elation, and sang to Wawl of the glories which he, Arjk, had accomplished in Heaven, and of the might and splendor which belonged to him, Arjk. Saying among other things, "I, Treep become Arjk, can drink and carouse in Heaven and yet retain the most powerful arm among the gods." The elation continuing, Arjk took leave of Wawl, and went for a mad ride in his chariot, hurling bolts haphazard out of Heaven, and shouting to the rattle of his steeds' hoofs.

Then of a sudden Arjk spied the Blizzard God riding in the distance. And looking closer, he distinguished Hyelva fleeing before him, her white robes fluttering back in confusion. Arjk wrenched his steeds until they were headed towards the Blizzard God, and his chariot went swaying and rocking back and forth across the clouds. The Blizzard God was shrieking as he pursued, "Hyelva! Hyelva, open the great gate of thy body! The great gate of thy body, that I may enter in!" while the hoofs of Arjk's horses set up a reverberation through Heaven, Hell, and Earth. But Hyelva sped on in silence.

It became evident that Arjk would overtake the Blizzard God and rescue Hyelva from his fingers. But Littic, who was a kindly deity, though under the domination of the Blizzard God, released his lights through Heaven, so that both Arjk and his horses were blinded. Letting his reins slacken in his stupor, Arjk watched the lights play on all sides of him, saw the thick trunks of flame with tongues protruding, or semicircles stretching across the whole sky, with balls of a bluish jelly sliding along them, or puffs of light waving like dust towards the zenith. And while Arjk relaxed, enchanted, the Blizzard God sent a broadside of tempest against him, blowing him out of the chariot and the bolts from his hands. Then the Blizzard God hurried again after Hyelva, falling among her garments like a hawk among the feathers of a dove. His appetites were so ravenous that he tore away everything which covered her body . . . and the little bits, whirling about in the tempest, spilled finally out of Heaven, and falling, covered whole states and provinces of the earth, so that some houses were sunk even up to their second stories in snow.

4

And one of the places where this snow fell was New York City; I am speaking particularly of West Sixteenth Street. Ah, how lovely it was before being shoveled away at a cost of some hundreds of thousands of dollars! The air was almost black with snow; it was so thick that at times stray flakes, falling down the particular air-shaft, swerved and sifted through the partly open window of the particular kitchen. This kitchen was dark, with dirty dishes showing up here and there, while the other rooms of the suite were lighted. All were empty, however, except the one in the extreme front, where James Hobbes was lying on Esther MacIntyre.

The point was this: Could Hobbes, or could he not, succeed, with only one hand, in capturing the object which Miss MacIntyre held in both of hers—if she held anything at all!—but would not willingly relinquish? Hobbes had maintained that he could; Miss MacIntyre had sassed back that he couldn't; thus, a protracted struggle had begun between them. Resulting in their tussling on the couch, and Hobbes groping resolutely—but awkwardly!—after the hot fists she held against her breast. Then of a sudden he made a dive of his hand, which silenced the giggly thing. And he continued the attack, disposing of garments rapidly. When Esther's bewilderment was startled away by the realization of a still greater boldness on his part, she began to resist . . . weakly, however . . . but he no longer cared . . . slipped off the couch . . . thumped against the floor . . . like a sack of potatoes.

Someone was knocking, jerking them out of their sloth. She went for her hat and coat, and as Hobbes returned to the front room with Harowitz, mumbled something about being in a hurry, and dashed out. Hobbes yanked a chair at Harowitz, pointed to a magazine, and went after Esther. As he came out into the blizzard, hatless and coat-less, he could see nothing of her. Besides, he was not exceptionally interested. He returned to his apartment slowly, even stopped in the dark kitchen a few moments and leaned against the wall. Then he went to the front room, where Harowitz was waiting for him.

Harowitz was moving about the room, from one island to another. Hobbes stretched out on the couch, giving a slight grunt which was a mixture of many things—such as self-comfort, the necessity of say-ing something, disapproval, nothing at all—but mainly composed of this: that Hobbes had planned the next time he would see Harowitz, to look at him abruptly and say, "Harowitz, what would you think of a man who walked into your house, and when you weren't watching him went into your cupboard and stole a drink of whiskey?" Harowitz wore a size-eight shoe, carried a cane, could speak both French and German fluently. His left eye was weaker than his right, but not enough to necessitate his wearing glasses. He was not married, had graduated from a law school *magna cum laude*, and also knew some Spanish. On his mother's side he was not full Jew.

Or perhaps Hobbes would have waited until Harowitz had begun to explain something, such as "The perfection of machinery, and the consequent large-quantity production, has made war an absolute necessity for the first time in the world's history." Then Hobbes would answer, "Yes, Harowitz, quite right, but what would you think of a man who walked into your house, and when you weren't watch-ing him went into your cupboard and stole a drink of whiskey?"

It was not the drink of whiskey that Hobbes had minded. It was the *principle* of the thing. But he said nothing to Harowitz. The state-ment, after all, would be too blunt, so blunt that even if Harowitz had not taken the whiskey he would realize that he was being accused. But first of all, he must make sure that Harowitz was guilty. It did no good to mark the bottle, since a small amount could easily be replaced with water. Perhaps there was some harmless, colorless, tasteless sub-stance which he could mix with water in a decanter beside the whiskey bottle; but if this mixture were poured into the whiskey it would make the whiskey change color. Hobbes imagined it turning a brilliant green or blood-clot red immediately before Harowitz's eyes. Then

Hobbes would come in and offer him a drink, bring out the whiskey bottle, look at it, look silently at Harowitz, put the bottle back, glance at his watch, and regret that he had an engagement.

Until he had something as definite as this, however . . . so he had grunted merely, as he lay down on the couch. Harowitz explained to him how war was inevitable at this point in the world's history, and while he was talking Hobbes brought out the whiskey. . . . After a time they were not clear-headed; the mixture of whiskey, gas fumes, and old breath had taken the freshness out of them. They watched each other now and then with tired eyes, trying to become interested in some assertion. Harowitz left within an hour, while Hobbes continued to lie on the couch.

Hobbes listened to the soft pads of snow flattening against the windows. Rising, he switched off the lights and opened a window in the next room. The cold air began circulating. . . . His mind was completely lax. So that the form of this procedure began to impress itself upon him. That is, he revolved it that he had been hot, and that now a cold current was blowing across him. Later on that evening he wrote the following poem, which, after he had finished it, sent him out for a long walk in the storm.

Here are the facts, given as I have known them:

Last night I slept with my shame bared to the ceiling;
The bed was hot against my back and buttocks;
My arms were swollen with the bites of black flies.

And now the thunder-caps quit dropping below the horizon;
The thunder-caps are beginning to march above me;
I watch, with the salt stinging the rim of my eyeballs.

A breeze starts up, making the lake look blue-black;
The blue-black swallows fly even more click-jaggy;
The green trees in the distance become also blue-black.

I close the windows fronting on the southwest;
The thunder falls immediately on the lightning;
And the rush of rain in the trees upon the thunder.

The black flies of Massachusetts are blown into New
  Hampshire;
And the black flies of New Hampshire are blown into
  Maine, while
Those of Maine are blown, some into Canada and some into
  the ocean.

Water hits in bucketloads against the woodshed;
Water hurries beneath the dried-up shingles;
Water drips mysteriously in the pantry.

The rain settles now to a steady business;
It lays itself without violence over the pastures;
Night falls, with the rain now gently piddling.

A new wind falls upon us from the northwest;
Veering, it whips the fog along the hillsides;
And shoves the entire storm out of my knowledge.

A haze of light spreads in the north horizon;
Pale shafts of light waver on the north horizon.
And puffs of light like dust wave towards the zenith.

A calm lies on the face of the earth and waters;
It sits among the trees and in the valleys;
A frost is nosing against the wild cherry blossoms.

The sun comes up as clean as a brand-new dollar;
The pink sun edges flatly above the skyline;
As rash as a blast of unexpected music.

Praise to the Three-God, Father, Son, and Spirit;
Who, as He found Himself at the beginning;
So is He now, and so shall be forever!

5

Father, Son, and Holy Ghost, so comfortable in Heaven. (Oh merely
that I might live in one of the back alleys of Heaven, though my house

fronted on some dump heap of empty bottles and rusty tomato cans! Indeed, I conceive of Their comfort as that of a royal family that never was. A family, composed of king, and queen, and princes, and princesses, living in a suite of rooms borne upon the shoulders of their subjects. The palace marches across the country, through rivers, up and over mountains, while the populace, squirming beneath, hold it up with poles. Ten thousand, say, labor simultaneously at these supports, while others rest, others follow to take their places, others have been relieved from duty and return to their families. The palace moves in a straight line, and in the course of this line there is a lake. The subjects disappear beneath the water; others take a long breath, dive down, and replace them at the supports. Some are lost; many are content to suck the water into their lungs, thus ending their unhappiness; but the palace moves on. At times music is heard from above, or a platform is let down for food, or filth is thrown out, falling on the populace. But otherwise, it travels like a silent cloud above them.) So comfortable in Heaven, and yet Jesus must go out into the night again, leaving the warm fire of this sanctity.

Some people were sitting in a prominent café in the theater district, when lo! Christ was discovered sitting among them. I can pay no greater tribute to my countrymen than to recite the tact and affability with which He was received. A committee was organized on the spot to show Mr. Jesus the more prominent sights of the town, such as Riverside Drive, the Woolworth Building (from where He could get a good bird's-eye view of the city), and the Brooklyn Navy Yard. At this last-named place He was to be given a private demonstration of a new gas which our chemists had invented and which promised to put us far and away in advance of all other fighting units of the world. (The intention of this demonstration being to show that so long as Christianity possessed such weapons there need be no fear of the spreading of Asiatic paganism.)

It was suggested taking Him to one of our larger churches, but this was quickly hushed up, as it was realized that the situation would surely result in ill-feeling, since, even if the Catholics could be persuaded to sacrifice this honor to the Protestants—which was, of course, out of the question—at least twenty Protestant sects would have arisen to dispute the honor amongst themselves. So it was thought wisest of all to take Him to a theater.

The play was by a very prominent American dramatist, and had been reviewed by the New York critics with such really gratifying and penetrating comments as "Every man, woman and child should see this play (*Times*) . . . really scrumptious (*World*) . . . Grips you from start to finish (*American*) . . . One of the best plays of this season and far better than anything of last season (*Tribune*) . . . An all-around good play (*Sun*)." There was some skating on thin ice, but no one could fail to catch the moral tenor behind it all, and it was hoped that this moral tenor especially would appeal to Jesus. In one detail, however, the play had been amended, a short passage having been omitted from the first act which ran, "Why am I so crucified with poverty!" It had been unanimously decided that nothing unpleasant should be suggested to Him.

Jesus was interviewed between the second and third acts, but declared that he had nothing to say, refusing especially to compare conditions here and in Heaven. But in spite of his reticence, favorable comments appeared in all the evening papers, although one anti-Church labor organ queried mildly whether it would be the Star of Bethlehem this time or the Star of Bethlehem Steel.

During the play—which was a matinee—the city administration had been anything but idle, and it was decided to give Christ the freedom of the city regardless of what might happen to the Jewish vote. So He came out of the theater and walked down Broadway to City Hall, and behind Him followed a long procession of scenario-writers, burlesque Amazons, fairies, lounge lizards, Jew and Irish comedians, jazz hounds, pimps, promoters, whores, traveling salesmen, confidence men, bookers, gamblers, kept women, millionaires' sons, publicity agents, sporting experts, dopes, land sharks, connoisseurs, rumsellers, holders of boxes at the opera, ammunition makers, specialists in men's diseases, whatever of the general populace, in short, happened to be passing through Times Square . . . and also angels. Not those Angels that sit at the feet of Jesus in Heaven, however. I mean those more immediate angels, angels from Wall Street, the backers for plays and movies . . . bald-headed angels, angels whose intentions are juicy in proportion as their groins are parched, angels who will dribble as much as twenty thousand, say, against some coozy's leg. Yes, there were a number of these sweaty, red-faced angels in the procession.

Christ suffered these honors, and many others, ultimately slinking away from His followers, down side-streets with warnings, "Commit no nuisance," through the smoke and slobber of the men's saloon of a Jersey ferry, and then, quite alone, as the sun was going down, He stood in a graveyard, on a hill, looking out over the Jersey swamps; kneeling—I know my readers will pardon the theatricality of the gesture—with His arms outstretched to Heaven, He prayed and wept. Then, growing calmer, He read the tombstone of Johann Bauer, *geboren 1827, gestorben 1903*, at present *Mit Jesu*. Weakened by a peculiar lassitude, He sat on one of the iron railings surrounding the grave. . . . Crickets began climbing upon His sandals, and Christ, noting their hunger, took a boo from His nose and dropped it for them to eat on. When this boo was consumed, he put another in its place . . . and so on, until all the crickets had been sated.

As Christ heard a faint noise now, He bent His ear to the ground, discovering that the noise came from one unusually minute cricket which was rubbing its wings across its back to produce a little whir of gratitude for the Divine Food it had received. A second later the entire swarm joined in, the graveyard trembling with their praise. Then, with a blare of Hosannahs, an Angelic Horde flew towards Him out of the sunset.

Other battalions answered from the West, as they likewise advanced steadily upon Jesus. And still others, from all corners of the compass. The sky was churned with song and Seraphic Maneuvers. For these great fleets of God's Elect, multiplying egregiously, began winding in among one another, melting together, separating, deploying in the shape of V's like wild geese, or banked up like pyramids, or upside down, or advancing in columns . . . while miracles were scattered upon the earth like seed. The sun, the moon, the stars, the planets, and all the wandering bodies shone together. Fountains burst forth; wild beasts lolled among the clouds.

All motion and song stopped . . . some thunder was climbing

across the sky. Then, as it disappeared in the distance, things began revolving, a Sublime Vortex sucked up into Heaven. In the very center, unmistakably wide open, stood the Gate, with squadron after squadron of Angels already hurrying within. Christ, too, began rising, while God called out to Him, smiling, AHRLOM AHR-LOMMA MINNOR. And Christ answered, MAHN PAUNDA OLAMMETH. Thus had one spoken and the other answered. Then He entered Heaven, the rear armies of the Angels following Him rapidly.

> Olammeth! . . . the seed
> . . . This sudden certainty!
> Fulfillment, bursting through the mists
> Olammeth, His Breasts!
> Across night
> Projected . . . (latent) . . .
> when lo! the *Sun*!

Heaven's Gate swung shut.

First Pastoral

1

Is the Divine present to a degree, so that one could speak of It as either more or less present? Or must this Divine be either present or absent? To the eye of an athlete the sun is gloriously brilliant, while an old man with failing sight may see it as a dull sullen glow behind a mist. Is it that way with the Divine? Or is the Divine like some figure of a flower or animal in the clouds, which one man sees and another does not see, while there are no possible gradations between the seeing and the nonseeing? The question is not at all impious; for to ask whether the Divine must be either present or absent does not imply a limitation of the Infinite Being, even though the word "must" has been used in the statement of the question. For this "must" refers not to the Divine, but to man, with his limited orifices of penetration. Obviously, God is universally present, and we can speak of His absence only from the standpoint of man's failure to distinguish Him.

Grant, first, that the Divine must be either present or absent, with no intermediate gradations. Which means that a man either lives with God, or does not. If he lives in the understanding of God, of what use to him are the mere functions of Churchly worship? Further, if the Divine must be either present or absent, then it follows inexorably that It can only be absent, for otherwise we should have an Infinite Being understood by a finite being, which is absurd.

Granting the antithetical proposition: The Divine can be either more or less present. In this way the world would become hieraticized after the manner of a pyramid, with the countless hordes of ignorant but faithful followers of the Church forming the broader, heavily weighted base, while as we went upwards with a decreasing proportion of mass the Christians corresponding to these higher positions would have a clearer understanding; and at the very top would cluster the body of martyrs, crowned by Jesus. The entire construction would be the glorious edifice of that combined πίστις and γνῶσις which marks all those who have remained untorn by schism; while the dry sands, swirling in the wind, tossed about without meaning and without incorporation into this stable structure ... these sands, obviously, would be the pagans, the heretics, and the like.

A stirring tope. But the difficulty enters when we examine further just what this "greater or lesser presence" involves in the way of conduct. Would we not, for instance, be drawn dangerously near to some of the neo-Platonist errors? For if the Divine is present to a greater or lesser degree, the worshipper must serve in accordance with the abundance or meagerness of his light. This leads us towards a general synthesis of religions, for if God is present in degree, then He is present in the religion of the most impious pagan, but present so faintly that the entire system of worship is distorted from the true worship of the Church beyond recognition. It is far removed, but exists nevertheless, just as the echoes of the Words of God when He commanded "Let there be Light" are still trembling in the air, becoming fainter and fainter, even more faint as our thoughts are upon them, but bounding on eternally. That peculiar "rustle of silence" which we hear in a perfect calm is the accumulation of just such infinitely faint noises, piled up from the first crack of creation. But the point to be emphasized was that if we grant the greater or lesser presence of the Divine, we must recognize the pagan as worshipping the True God, but in his own ignorant manner.

How, then, should we go about it to bring such people into the Realm of Jesus? By letting them worship in their own manner, once their provinces are under the temporal jurisdiction of the Pope.

They would thus be looked upon not as pagans, but as the weakest members of the True Church, and much nearer to the lowest Christian than this lowest Christian is to a saint. But obviously, such a line of reasoning would bring us close to the subversive teachings of Plotinus and Porphyry. Yet as we have seen, the opposing doctrine leads to just as unholy an attitude towards the Church. What then is the conclusion to be drawn? It is: *Let man always distrust any ratiocination which does not follow hand in hand with the Word of God at every step.* That true understanding is not in γνῶστις but in πίστις. Or rather, that πίστις is γνῶστις.

The greater the cogency with which the brain could make the Church seem wrong, the greater was the proof thereby that the soul had become infected. And Brother Angelik's deep learning in theological subtleties made him perfectly aware of what turpitudes logic without love might involve. Still, he had indubitably been enthralled for a time by the heavy bonds of his antitheses. And as he lifted his head now to deliver a short prayer of thankfulness to his Maker— Who had guided him so securely out of this intricacy of the Devil— he observed that in his anguish he had wandered far beyond the walls of the monastery!

Here was Hell's mockery. Angelik had thought that this bejeweling of heresy marked out the nature of his struggle against Evil, while it had in reality been a mere subterfuge, a lure to produce the breaking of his vows, since he had stepped out into the world, beyond the pale of his seclusion, beyond the point stipulated in his solemn oath.

While, further, Brother Angelik had come upon the shepherd John and the shepherdess Jocasta. This John having slipped his hands against Jocasta's flesh, the two of them were now lying earnestly interlocked upon the sod.

If prayers possessed the properties of mass and weight, and their density under ordinary temperatures were that of a thick, sluggish fluid, prayers then would have nosed quietly down the corridors of the monastery, oozed through the cracks of the massive, ill-fitting doors, and perhaps even set the statue of the Virgin to circulating on its side by the altar. Again, a blackness, obviously symbolic, of heavy clouds, had gathered over the sky; and having gathered, these clouds lay there like a threat. In the late afternoon the clouds were split to expose a sun which was already part eaten by the shadow of the moon, and which dropped below the horizon in full shadow. Thus, without twilight, midnight followed on the heels of day, while the storm broke, slashing and stumbling in the dark, and rocking the monastery like a ship.

The forces of sin silently multiplied, filling his brain with their progeny after the manner of vipers. When the she is in heat, her gaping, filthy maw is turned to the male. He inserts his three-tongued head into the jaws of his woman, buries it avidly even to the eyes, and projects into her, by the junction of their mouths, his procreative venom. Maddened by her pleasures, the wife then slays her lover by ripping open his throat with her teeth; while as he perishes, she drinks in his spittle. Thus, the father is consumed during the excesses, but the sperm of his spittle still remains to destroy the mother. For later, when the seed has aged, small objects begin wriggling in her warm insides, slashing and beating against the womb. She realizes now what her sex entails and bemoans her wretched husband's offspring, which are destined to murder in turn, and are already tearing at the barriers which enclose them. Until, since there is no channel whereby the young can be born, they split the agonized bowels with their struggles, and the belly is rent to provide an exit. The little snakes lick the body which bore them, a generation of orphans even at birth, since they had hardly seen the day before their miserable mother was dead.*

Nocte surgentes, vigilemus omnes; let us all leap up in the night, and wait! But not for a fleshy love. For some austere sign, rather, which will be found lying across the sky like a comet. Charmed thesis and antithesis of love, of that *higher* love. And in despair he prayed, loudly and disagreeably, complaining, defying, hemming and hawing with his temptations, his moans echoing down the corridors, and buzzing

* Prudentius, *Hamartigenia*, lines 585–607.

with the storm in the ears of his Brothers, who listened in the darkness and understood that Angelik was struggling for his Faith.

> Let me hold in my arms Salvation.
> Let me lie between the breasts of the True Church.
> Let me speak and in turn be spoken unto.
> Let the belly tremble at the touch of my hand on the door.

> *Dilectus meus mihi, et ego illi!*
> One unto the other, and that other unto the first.
> Moving among the lilies, while the day dawns, and the
>   shadows lean.
> Thy dugs are richer than wine.

He crawled to the statue of the Virgin, and touched the stiff marble folds of her garments. Another voice near him piped up in prayer. Then his fingers fell away, and he was ashamed. "*O gloriosa virginum, benedicat te Deus et sanctum ventrem tuum.*" . . . He sneaked back to his cell.

"Lord, my God, help me, for I am weak. A sign, oh Lord! Show me that I am not alone." Then Brother Angelik became peaceful. He was contracting business with his Lord. "Tonight it is storming. Let it storm tomorrow, and I shall remain with my Brothers. But if there is sun, I shall know that Thou has forsaken me." Now, as it had been written before the world was assembled out of Chaos, the sun shone unusually bright the following morning, and looking across the hills, Brother Angelik saw that everything was as calm and pure as a mirror.

2

It was dawn, although the sun had not yet risen . . . full day, without the sun, as though the world were lit by a calm but thorough Logic. The hills lay about with a dogmatic distinctness. Every pebble possessed its contour, every grass blade its line of demarcation. Or, when some group was too far off to necessitate a definition of its individual components, it in turn formed a unit of itself; in just this way, for instance, a small patch of timber extended like a pronounced ellipse on the bias against one of the farther hills. Sky, cloud, earth, and the things on the earth . . . all this was differentiated categorically.

Brother Angelik wandered over the hills as the shepherd of John's sheep, John having been persuaded to visit a sister in Padua. And when Angelik had led his sheep to where Jocasta's were already grazing, he called out to her, "Hast thou an apple, shepherdess?"

"Ha, we maidens have many things, shepherd, but not an apple."

"That is an ill omen."

"And why, Shepherd, is it ill that I should not have an apple?"

"Because then thou shalt feel compelled to give me a kiss."

"And why, shepherd, must I give thee anything?"

"Because I am going to wager with thee that I can tell thee thy name, and I must win something for my wager."

"But my name is Jocasta; I need lose neither apples nor kisses to be told that."

"And I, Jocasta, am the appleless, unkissed Theodoce. So now we know each other, and our sheep have already made friends without this banter, and if thou wilt sit here beside me I shall tell thee a story."

"Tell me, then, the story of how Theodoce comes to be tending John's sheep."

"Ho, that is a homely story. I should rather tell thee how Zeus gained entrance to Leda as a swan. Or perhaps thou hast already been told that story by some shepherd?"

"Where dost thou come from, Theodoce?"

"From Padua."

"Then I must believe that the shepherdesses of Padua love stories more than virtue."

"In truth! The girls of Padua do not put themselves above the gods. And if Zeus could invent such escapades, the shepherdesses of Padua are not too virtuous to hear of them."

"Well said, Theodoce. And I, as a reward, shall hear thy story. But first, thou must tell me why that story of all stories, has been chosen."

"Because I had hoped that perhaps I, by changing myself into a slave, just as Zeus changed himself into a swan, might gain admission to the bosom of some lovely shepherdess."

"Beware, Theodoce, lest thine incantations fall amiss, and thou turnest thyself into an ass."

"I have no fear, Jocasta. Indeed, I am quite willing to become an ass, if that is the surest way to charm a woman."

"Ah, thou hast a barbed tongue, and I shall leave thee."

"No, thou wilt pick them up and carry them away from me like precious baubles? Lips, breasts, shoulders, thighs, in short all those lovely parts of woman? Stay, Jocasta, and let me at least ravish thee with mine eyes."

"That is an undressing which all maidens must suffer; thine eyes attempt not my virtue but thine own; so I shall stay, and be looked upon."

"Such things are so much polish, that virtue may shine the better."

"Virtue! I think my hearing is better this morning, Jocasta, than it has been."

"And why is that, Theodoce?"

"Because yesterday, when I was by here, I heard thee say no such word to John. Ho! but we will dismiss that, Jocasta, if thou answerest me these questions. First, dost thou grant that we should strive after happiness?"

"Yes, Theodoce."

"And that, therefore, any moment which could be made happier, and is not, is a waste of that moment?"

"Yes, Theodoce."

"And dost thou further grant that there is more happiness in the marriage of a shepherd and shepherdess than when they remain unjoined?" (Brother Angelik was aware that here he was confusing the two ideas of happiness and pleasure, but that this ignorant girl would not perceive the sophism.)

"Yes, Theodoce. Since thine eyes yesterday were sharper than thine ears, yes."

"Then Jocasta, I have conquered thee, for here is a moment which could be made happier and is not!"

"Thou art very learned, Theodoce."

"Ah, but thou hast armed thy virtue with words, and even if I lay low the words, the virtue still remains to be stormed. But see, Jocasta, while we have been wrangling here, how easily our flocks have intermingled! Finding convenient pasturage in the same place, they have all gone there without question. Or note the slight jerk of the sheep's head, effected while the grass is firmly between the teeth, and serving to rip the blade and its stock asunder. If I should draw the picture of a sheep, I should draw its legs to establish the laws whereby, if one leg rests at a given point and forms a given angle with a line drawn horizontally to that point, the other three legs, by the reason of a sheep's balance, would be at three other predetermined points, the whole presenting a rigid relationship. But all this is foreign to the sheep, which, finding the grass of interest, grazes upon it. Ah, would that I could wander thus over Jocasta's knolls and hillocks!"

"Thou art a poet, Theodoce, and poets can sing just as well unto themselves."

Jocasta ran suddenly into the thicket, and would not appear even though Angelik threatened to kill himself. Finding a dagger on the ground, he plunged it into his breast, and fell with his heart against the sod. The blood from the heart soaked into the grass, trickling still warm through the cool pebbles beneath. What was it seeking, that it worked so swiftly among them? For it went with unmistakable haste. As it filtered, the impure red passed into the lonely pebbles; until as clear water it trickled between slabs of bedrock, and mingled with little pools that lay down there in the darkness. Then in elation, this pure water of Angelik leapt steadily towards the sunlight, and Jocasta, who had come there to drink, drank of him and murmured, "How thirsty I had been!"

As an interesting parallel it might be well to add that the day of Brother Angelik's death was the same as that on which Paulus Thessalonicus, then residing at Alexandria, wrote what was considered among his friends to be his most successful epigram. It runs:

Lamp, when there is a faint shuffling of sandals outside
    my door,
And the odor of unguents and perfumes
Calls me like a blare of trumpets, so that I
Arise hastily from my table . . . go out, lamp.
For tonight I shall be laying aside my text
To become the grammarian of sweet Amyctis' body.

Prince Llan

*An Ethical Masque in Seven Parts, including a Prologue
and a Coda*

I—Prologue

*Programme: In the beginning was the waters of Chaos,
with their horizons lost in blackness. This was unbeautiful,
and without history. Following the* fiat, *sprouts that long
line of descent ending in Prince Llan.*

Logos Verbum the Word—universal brew bubbling and collapsing—
then this wad of runny iron and rock settles into a steady elliptic jog
—cools, crusts, that objects wriggle in the slime, and box-like things
bump against the trees—heroic march of that one tender seed
through groanings and agues of the earth, through steaming fevers,
through chills slid down from the poles, hunger, fire, pestilence, war,
despair, anguish of the conscience, lo! this clean-blooded man, this
unscrofulous unsyphilitic neat-skinned gentleman, this ingenious
isolated item, Prince Llan.

But where was Gudruff?

Gudruff was gone.

Why should we care where Gudruff was?

Gudruff was Prince Llan's intimate and adviser.

308

Where were they last seen together?

At table, drinking grog, and talking of the future.

Prince Llan himself—his mind had moved elsewhere—and when the auctioneer had shouted Who buys these women? Llan answered I buy these w— and flung down the money inasmuch as they were dear girls they were lovely girls nor were they afraid by God of him. Their breasts were tight up beneath their shoulders. Their breasts, they stood out firm like pegs. When they walked, one could note their sitters, how they undulated. And taking each girl by an arm, so that his thumbs were pressed carefully into their armpits, Prince Llan started with them out into life.

II

Programme: The Prince, his life and character. He has undergone hazards and ingenuities which, though varied and of long duration, telescope into a single enlightenment. Then he falls into one period of focus, of anchorage, and this is like years of vicissitude. The Prince, being an earnest man, becomes uneasy, attempts vaguely to formulate some principle of living. He would find some one exhortation or admonition to simplify human conduct.

Lost in a forest of Siberia, cold, destitute, and rained on, the Prince found three leaves blown under a rock, and dry. With these, by rubbing sticks, he builded them a fire, and they became so warm that in time the two girls sang. Caught in an avalanche on some far-off peak, they rode laughing into the valley on a ledge of ice. He tugged them through shaking sands by the arm. He dragged them from flopping seas by the hair. Together they cooked with dis-ease. Together they bowed down to Siamese gods. They ate yellow dogs together. When beset by Arabs, he suddenly leapt with these girls to one side, leaving the Arabs crushed by a falling star.

"Let us have a garden," he said to them, so they grew a garden of flowers, mostly depraved. When it was trumpeting with colours and pleasant stinks, the three of them withdrew. For days he martyrised himself, draining his poor body of its very marrow. Long after his groins were appeased, the itch, the erotic erethism, continued in the mind. If he had lain on his back, and made an idle half-turn, burying his nose perhaps in the rancid grease of their hair, at the odour, the odour of rotting apples, he would become alert again. If he but saw a fountain innocently playing, or a steaming kettle, it derailed him. His garden, rained on by bees, was calmly impregnated. The blossoms withered, to bear fruit; the Prince crashed a rock through their little house, and the three moved on across the face of the earth, across its nose, mouth, cheeks, and hair.

Shortly after this the Prince went alone up into a mountain with a burning bush on it—and standing, his arms Napoleon-fashion, he took stock:

"If I incline to a certain dish, it is that I like it, even before I have first tasted it, the vacuum of this as yet untasted dish pre-existing in the mind. There are vacuums of millions of combinations of organic substances pre-existing in my mind, and I shall die without quieting their pressure.

"Love, the love of one object to the exclusion of all others, enables us to thrive despite this famine. Love is a process of individualization: there is the general vacuum Love, and it is filled when one finds a specific object to adequately symbolise this general. The poet loves his material when he must have that material and none other. There are poets who may choose this or that, being interested primarily in the arrangement, and to this extent they are not filled. Similarly, these girls for me may particularise, but they do not symbolise, the general. Which is to say that I do not love them, because I ask only that they be delicate and smell right. They cannot end the famine, and I am the most forsaken of men, loveless, tossed without anchor.

"Thou shalt not commit adulteration."

III

Programme: "If we cannot yet be wise, let us be passionate."
But this is a spring *of human conduct rather than a* maxim,
and the Prince is, therefore, in mid-career, engrossed quite
simply in the keenness of his sensations. The poet adopts his
protagonist's viewpoint, and portrays life as a mad-house
wherein even logic would be a kind of derangement, of bias.
Yet the Prince, with Grailism in his blood (and by Grail-
ism would be meant precisely that search for a rule of human
conduct) hurries on, if not towards something future, then
away from all things present.

On a screen the projection of a beating heart, the size of an elephant,
convulsing irregularly. Its owner suffering some spiritual or physical
torment. As they watched, a large drop of blood collected on a valve,
sidled across the slope of the meat—like a tear rolling down a cheek.
The drop detached itself, and they shouted, with hell an eternity of
having the finger-nails pulled out, the walls crooked. The chairs tire
one's elbow, or the muscles of our necks. The lights will go out, come
on again, flicker. Lewd pictures were hung, the lewdest portions
obscured by splotches of ink. The floor slants, occasionally a door
would open, so that a chill passed through, with the lyric cook stumbling across the room, skinny and starved. The Pontificers fought
their way among the ruins of chairs and people; carried banners (*Let*
each man build a bridge; *If every man builds a bridge the world will have*
no time for vice; *Build bridges*, signed, The Pontificers); the lyric cook
gnawing at his knuckles. He was mumbling recipes, describing the
setting of tables, rehearsing an ideal course of dishes, and in the
midst of a peculiarly dull catalogue of ingredients, he will burst out
with songs in praise of food.

Mine enemy was strong. He possessed the good things of this
world. I was a coward, timid and lugubrious. I slunk. I slunk on my
belly. I slunk with terror into her bed, taking the wife of mine enemy.
When he returns, she will spew upon me, and he will beat me with

a horse-whip. Ampersand placing the germs into the blood through the sucking of lice not affable skulls whom the madam lay with the man so aloof from us as he stood on stilts that passing dogs stopped to befoul them.

Euonymism holds our salvation to lie in the use of the left side. It points out that past civilisations decayed, and that they held the left side unlucky. Yes, the founder of Euonymism was here: a tailor, descended from twenty-seven generations of tailors, and they all had lifted the pressing-iron with their right hands, until his race was puny on the left side of its body. He had plugged up his right nostril, and cast out his right eye, and was standing on his left leg, shouting his doctrines at the parade of Pontificers, out of the left corner of his mouth, wiggling his left ear. *That is why it is called EUONYMISM.*

(Sitting down, the chair collapsed. Stepping across to pull a lever, he was soused with water. Falling, he arose. Rising, he fell. Sighing, he threw off his clothes, finding them distressing.)

Now:

The Thirty-three Systems strive after a synthesis. As they watch, the synthesis is attained, and the Thirty-fourth System joins the ranks. Regardless, Euonymists and Pontificers rushed at each other, trampled down a convention of three thousand specialists on the mating habits of the female Polar dung-beetle. Prince Llan leaped up, and ran with his two girls for the shore. The ship was waiting. The mob threatened. No time could be spared. He threw them across the gangplank as the ship commenced a yaw towards the South. SLIP THE CABLE, SET THE FORE-STAY SAIL AND THE FORE-TOP-MAST STAY-SAIL. These filled with a groan, as the first of the pursuers began stringing over the hill. CUT THE SPRING; SET THE SPANKER VANGS, the MIZZEN-TRY-SAILS, the MAIN-TOP-GALLANT STUDDING SAILS—the ship now moving confidently out into the water. They cast off the club-haul; next, gammoning, they gybed the boom taut with a grummet, gave a sharp bowse to the bolt-ropes, and luffed the halyards to the fag-ends of the davits. The ship scudded into a vicious head-sea, simultaneously with the clewing-up of the spun-yards, while several men under the second mate went madly to work keckling the parbuckle, and marling the lazy-guy with gudgeons. The captain's voice rang out thwart ships above the gale, giving orders to loosen the crupper till it squared the jib-boom—and Prince Llan knew that he was advancing into another world.

IV

Programme: Through the conversation of two well-formed but ignorant women, we learn of a new curve in the Prince's emotions. The Prince himself, by his speech and behaviour, corroborates this.

SCENE: *A dense grove in the midst of a rolling barren plain, rather like the pubes on a white body. The Prince's two* GIRLS *sit observing the horizon. The* PRINCE *sleeps. Tableau. Music. Finally one of the* GIRLS *begins talking softly.*

Girl. He calls us Alpha Nomega. So you, dear, be Alpha; I'll be Nomega. Or if you prefer, I shall be Alpha.

Alpha. Back on the farm; home and mother; thoughtless; happy; brute made me woman; thirteenth year; knew no better; driven away; city; loved; at times didn't love; I hate men, Nomega.

Nomega. Drunken father; invalid mother; nice man; took to room; gave candy; tickled; happened; fourteenth year; had to pay; but it died; now I am a big empty place, Nomega.

Alpha. Bring carpet slippers; sits reading by fire.

Nomega. Lean over back of chair and kiss; smile; pat cheek; both tiptoe across room; pull back curtains; smile to each other at what see there asleep.

Alpha. Tiptoe back to fire; lay head on his knees.

Nomega. Look up into eyes.

[*They fall silent, observing the horizon. The* PRINCE *sleeps. Tableau. Music.*]

Alpha. But the Prince is good to us, Nomega.

Nomega. Too good. How can we be assured of a future with such a strange man? Look what he wrote, just before falling asleep. I watched the words forming. [*She slips a paper gently from under the* PRINCE*'s right arm.*] "Taken in the absolute sense, taking old age, that is, divorced from the example of some specific old man, the loveliest life and the loveliest thoughts should be produced after the sperm is silenced. I imagine a life as broad and deep and quiet as a mountain lake, and it seems to be solely the property of old age. I am speaking, however, absolutely, without concern for examples."

Alpha. [*Taking up the notebook.*] "Metaphysics is the yearning to see one's own eye, when there are no reflections, and when one eye cannot be taken from the head to be examined by its fellows." And he, Nomega, is the man who has crawled with us into secret places.

Nomega. [*Receiving back the notebook.*] "True love is specific; but mine is more generalised, like that of the housefly, or the philosopher."

Alpha. Thank God he can still talk of love.

Nomega. We should have run off and hidden among the Horrors. Have sneaked behind the big screen with the heart going on it. We could have hired servants had we stayed there, and had others to tie our shoes for us.

Alpha. The hungry man would have cooked for us.

Nomega. But now we must make the best of things. We must use technique with the Prince.

*Alpha.*Yes, but he is becoming too forgetful. He is interested in other things. Yet such an earnest man should still be grateful for any display of science.

[*Silence. They observe, not the horizon, but the* PRINCE. *He moves in his sleep, and mutters,* "Gall in the blood. The passions are like gall in the blood." *He smiles, becomes quiet, and a flute bleats tenderly as they turn their eyes again to the horizon.*]

Alpha. [*Sadly.*] But let us put this worry aside, Nomega. Let us recite.

Nomega. Yes, what should it be? Why, let us recite the First Litany of our Profession.

Alpha. Yes, let us recite the Office of the Enormous, the Misshapen, and the Ill-formed.

Nomega. No, dear, let us recite of that rarer movement, the Natural and the Divine.

314

Alpha. I shall try, although I remember the other better.

[*They recite.* * *And their unhappiness seems to vanish as they become engrossed in their connoisseurship. The recitation is half lyrical, half shop talk; it involves both the philosophy and the procedure of coupling, and becomes at times somewhat clinical. It seems to clear the air like a discharge from the clouds. When it is finished, their interests change. They glance appraisingly at the* PRINCE, *to gauge his slumber.*]

Alpha. Nomega, the cat is asleep.

Nomega. The cat is asleep, little mouse.

[*They crawl into each other's arms. But the* PRINCE *stirs and awakes.*]

Prince. Pathetic little girls. I have doubtless inserted many barbs into your tender minds. These barbs will rankle, until some day, when you are older, you will understand. At that time it might aid you to remember that man possesses a species of seed which, if properly laid within the soil of woman, can frequently result in her drinking poison, or falling from a bridge.... Now, go, little sealed things, little unplumbed possibilities, little fields unplowed. Ride off in a carriage tight shut, where no ray of sunlight can enter.

[*They go, after each has received a kiss and a gift of money from the* PRINCE.]

Prince. [*To himself.*] There, how gently he sent them off. And he might just as readily have driven them with clubs. He bowed them away as virgins, instead of beating them as bitches. That is better, since more proper to a parting.

[*They went, and the* PRINCE *watched them mould together into a spot on the horizon.*]

IV

Programme: The Prince in harbour. The Prince as sage. The Prince at rest. An equilibrium, however, which was gained by too ready a simplification, too hasty a survey of the

---

* Their recitation, which appeared in the *Broom* version of "Prince Llan," is omitted here, as it is thought to have caused the suppression of that issue of *Broom.*

territory, the Prince's defence of reason being simply a more
remote aspect of his passion.

The universal brew had bubbled and collapsed; box-like things had bumped against the trees; there had been, you will remember, war, pestilence, and anguish of the conscience; the Prince had bought those girls; he had ridden avalanches with them; he had rushed them away during scramble of Euonymists and Pontificers; gammoning, the spanker vangs were gybed taut with a grummet; and he had become a new man; sent them away as virgins, though he might have beaten them as bitches; and he now walked with a slow tread, after all these years, thoughtfully, to himself, saying:

"A reality encompassed by intelligence falls outside the realm of a complete experience, outside the realm of an organic understanding. There is described to me, in every detail, every elbow of height and breadth, every vibration of smell, every grade of colour, some place —but this place does not live for me as an immediate possession until I, too, have been there, and experienced it through the orchestration of the senses. Yet a reality so encompassed by the intelligent cannot be mistaken for any other—and when I do come upon this place I can apply my tests, and make sure whether or not it is the place intended. Or even going beyond this, I could say that the glory of philosophy lies in just such an act of intellection; in the stating by intelligence of what can never be immediately, *organically*, experienced."

Was this the man who had martyrised himself? It was. Speak, that the younger may be edified. Let them hear what they already knew in their minds, but shall not know in their bodies until they, too, are tottering.

"A man, suffering from untold miseries, can go out and plunge his knife into a wild beast, or his axe into a tree, and by so much resolve his discomfiture. An act is unmistakeable: this man has acted. But he cannot plunge his knife into an odour on the wind, or a sudden memory of childhood, or a vague forewarning of death. Vicariously, he has tried to slay the wild beast instead of the sudden memory of childhood. He stoops over his kill, spies a single leaf detached, on the ground, contrived ingeniously, and his misfortunes are suddenly situated elsewhere.... To obviate this, let him divorce himself from organic experience, and translate these vaguenesses into the certainties of the intellect. Life, established by the poets as a fever, remains a problem of distress which cannot be solved in terms of positive happiness, but may in terms of pains absent."

The Prince transcribed carefully.

"The intellect is the most advisable narcotic, since it enables us to live a waking deep-sleep, to get the completeness of the facts, but without the poignancy. By the word I create, I act—which means, I slay. Man by nature a slayer. Having become too subtle to dispose of his maladjustments by the slaying of wild beasts, he turns to the slaying of his emotions. The intellect unites living with death, perception with immunity. Let us admit only as much emotion as will serve to add zest to our perceptions. Let emotion be gall in the blood.

"To find that method whereby life, pressed into firm little bricks, is handled at leisure. For life to tear at our chimneys and howl faintly outside the windows. Or even better, life as a tinkling of far-off cow-bells, coming up irregularly over the low hills. This we mean by the consolation of our philosophies. We must search, not for experience, but for the symbols of experience; reason and art each aiming at a formula in accord with its particular properties, its own potentialities. Idea cuts through a tangle of emotion; emotion cuts through a tangle of ideas—and each, expressed by the formulæ of art and thought, are remedies against the complexities of existing. I bare my teeth at the yapping of the senses; I devote myself, rather, to seeing how, if a given thing is so, other things follow. Yet how strange that at this point, rising in thought above my own uneasiness, having found this rock on which to enforce myself, I should receive word from Gudruff. From Gudruff, and I once sat at table and drank grog with him. Has he, too, found fierce temperance? He writes, Gudruff writes: 'Sweetly tired body' ... 'muscles of my throat' ... 'hay, cow's breath, urine, manure, and old sun-dried timber' ... '*temptationi inguinum*' ... 'beyond the reach of duties' ... 'blessings from Gudruff.'"

VI

Programme: The Counter-Prince, and Conclusion. Gudruff
offers the rebuttal which the Prince had unconsciously deter-
mined to ignore. The Prince, deprived of both the anchorage
of his wisdom and the impetus of his passion, moves on halt-
ingly and irresolutely, the poet now comparing life to a
troubled half-sleep.

To his good Prince Llan, greetings from Gudruff, or
perhaps greetings from Gudruff's skull, or more accurately, greetings from that much of Gudruff as may still
lie in the Prince's own heart, for the rest of him may
have been thrown to the winds by the time Llan receives
this letter. This sweetly tired body may have been laid
aside, stopped even by its own hand.

After they parted, Prince, he walked for days, eventually passing through a parched country and finding
no water. His spittle was a dry pulp, a cotton wad in the
mouth. He came to a stream, pushed his face against it
horse-like, and suddenly the muscles of his throat began
sucking in the water with a passion which astonished
him. It was not Gudruff, it was his throat that was drinking, while he leaned back and watched. He threw off his
clothes, he lolled in the stream. He let the sun dry him,
and moved into the shade to sleep. But a change had
come over him. He had learned, Prince, that one can
observe with deliberation what is usually taken without
thinking, that one might go through life holding a
minute ear to the body.

He found that he was close to a village. It is somewhere adjoining, but beyond, the territory of the dear
Prince's father. There is wealth, but not the kind to
tempt a restless and grasping people. He entered, and
forthwith five women and nine boys were brought to

him in recognition of his station. He felt it advisable to send some of the women away, but perhaps this was due to the fatigue of his long journey. Since then, Prince, he has remained in this village, where, in his own fashion, he has become wealthy.

To witness: The heavy syrupy smell of over-ripe strawberries; cool mint; the worminess of rich loam soaked with water; the bitter-sweet of a barn, its mixture of hay, cow's breath, urine, manure, and old sun-dried timber. This ensemble of growth and decomposition, freshened with morning. . . . He lay there in peace. And suddenly, suddenly, *plena recognitio facultatum corporis latuit subito ei; se relaxabat, est molliter lapsus contra ter-ram, deinde se debat suorum temptationi inguinum.* The remainder of the morning he spent in reading.

Patiently and earnestly, his dear Prince, he has gone about it since then to enlarge his knowledge. Each day, perhaps, some new pore has been opened, some new nerve stroked. As he grows old he feels creeping over him the haze of venerability. He is now a veteran, dear Prince, and he feels that he has used his intelligence nobly to heighten every channel of sensation. He is at least for-tified with the feel of moral victory, of having done what *he* could to extend beauty further into the realm of ugli-ness. This body has not strained and fed and given off unheeded.

But now an illness is on him, and perhaps the roots are numbing. Perhaps when the Prince receives this he shall have passed beyond the reach of duties and obligations.

Good Prince, blessings from
    Gudruff.

Prince Llan cried, "I am coming, Gudruff, I am coming." He stum-bled forward, throwing himself heavily against the door in front of him. It was an oblong door, encrusted with minute carvings. There were houses, mountains, three peasants sitting at a table, women washing clothes, lovers kissing by a well—tiny dramas were carved upon this door, and Prince Llan shoved it open. His eyes were partly closed, glued with a heavy sleep. An ear sat between a filtering kidney and an intestine with its lugubrious burden. Parts of himself, reduplicate, lay about him. He climbed over a twitching leg. He pushed aside a piece of throbbing brain tissue to keep from crushing it under his heel. Other parts sauntered through the air like fishes. Peering, he saw a door; it wavered beyond a film of mucus, an oval door with a heavy brass knocker. "I am coming, Gudruff," he murmured, as his body, dragged by unseen weights, spread over the ground like molasses. He shifted his bulk, forcing it to slope against this door, and the door budged reluctantly, allowing him, down a corridor beyond, the glimpse of a door. . . .

VII—Coda

Programme: Might Joseph be the marriage of Prince Llan and Gudruff? Might these two unstable types be somehow joined, producing in Joseph a dualism at one with itself, a dualism not of strife but of mutual completions, a dualism of systole and diastole, a synthesis? For a moment the poet so feels, and in the firmness of his certainty attempts to crystallize this enthusiasm into dogma. Whereat the cosmic burden overcomes him; and in killing himself he does no more than what for most of us is adequately symbolised in the abuse of alcohol, the listening to a symphony, or the turning out of a light and crawling into bed.

Joseph, singing with the birds in the morning, busying his carcass in physical toil before the heat of noon, next eats, and snoozes doglike while the sun is most intense. When the splendour is diminished he appears again, and returns to the fields. In time the shadows lengthen; Joseph takes food and drink which, the body having been depleted with activity, is drawn in like water poured on a desert. At dusk the muscles have been appeased; the brain speculates contentedly. Joseph lies in wait for a better understanding. We are nearing the completion of the cycle; what has gone before has sweetened the twilight. The eye flows calmly over the silhouette of the black hills. The moment has come to shut himself away. Going indoors, the hero turns to his books, confining himself within the sharply restricted funnel of his lamp's light. Ultimately, laying aside the books, he goes to his woman, and the cycle closes.

Si hortum in bibliotheca habes, nihil deerit. If, says Cicero, you have a garden and a library, you have all. If you have life (*hortus*, garden) and the contemplation of that life (*bibliotheca*, library, books). Above the molten flow of emotion, a rigid and well-knit crust of ideas, said that great platitudinarian, Cicero, that unfortunate, knowing the laws of good fortune. But you will pardon the author, dear reader, if at this point he interrupts himself. For your author is dying. I, Morducaya Ivn, the respected chronicler of these meditations and events, rose from my desk but a few moments past, laid back my head, and cast a mortal potion into the belly. Already, there is a drowsiness mounting my legs. Between me and death there are less than my fingers full of people.

There is an old Chinese woman, exhausted of a dropsy. A baby in London, deformed by its mother's corsets. Three of five drunken sailors in a brawl at Singapore. Then me.

When I am dead the boats will still sail down the river . . . people will eat supper with their windows open . . . and doubtless take walks across the country during week-ends. I will be dead. Dead in a coffin carried through the street, and my beard growing silently.

They say the baby won't cry when it's slapped. . . . Down, you bastard! and one of the sailors is gone. . . . Now that Chinese woman is staring: pingee, pongee, pungee, pung, yes, grandmother died of a dropsy.

I am demanded back to be remoulded. This borrowed ego returns to the great Ware-house. My collection will be scattered: this much of beef, swine, mutton, herbs, rum which, taken into the blood, became me. I could situate my elements thus, roughly, in pre-history. Twelve portions of this nose once floated in a tepid sea, the liver of a dinosaur. This mouth, or rather this eye-tooth of this mouth, was belched up in part during the ejaculation of the Himalayas; it is a relic of the earth's earlier enthusiasm. And ah! this little strip of thumb-nail, immediately within the border of the moon, who would believe that it was once included in a germ which gnawed at the brain of Jesus?

And so I am reclaimed metaphysically. Strictly to observe relationships, in the light of Jupiter, I do not matter. As I was slung together, so shall I fall apart, an aggregate of casual units, subject to the chemistry of the Law. And when the earth, the black cold earth drives on through space, drives on through force of habit I suppose, and there is left nothing but a dead worm sticking to the collected works of Shakespeare, what will it signify that Ivn perished of the nature of things, and of poison cast into the belly?

Ivn, you are dying! Not an aggregate of units, not a relative trifle in the light of Jupiter, but you, I—I—

> Out of the big black hole
> into my own awareness out of nothing
> thus from the grinding womb of the Mother Nebula
> I,
> *my* heart, *my* fingertips,
> I, the affirmation, the solely significant . . .

Facts, tiny facts, the patient ministering to our daily needs, the balancing of hungers with appeasements. But what—that tingling in the ears; it is music, or death. I fail. I struggle once more to my feet, choking. Of a sudden I am elated with futurity. I bellow:

> I have suffered the prologue. I have heard the orchestra
> strike up, the curtain rises, and God! I am called to go
> elsewhere. I saw their fat happy faces, caught a glimpse

of them dining, and the door slammed shut in my face.
To live among those beeves of art. And here and there
little cries come up out of the earth, like flowers. When
the world rises and sings—but I am dead.

[*Dies.*]

THE END

Metamorphoses of Venus

I

All those goodly people came together and voted to live in peace. They made pacts, mutual checks and surrenders, and thus the better filled their bellies, and slept the sounder, and in time developed that pleasant convulsion of the muscles, that baring of the teeth, which is known as laughter. Thanks to their cunning and virtue, we could move in the assurance that three lines writ on a piece of pulp would designate one person among hordes, carrying our message across the errors and rumors of great rivers, across the coughing of the seas, and the heaviness of plains. This we shall call an edifice, a structure of rock and iron; and the flames overtopping this edifice, we shall call love.

No, I lay no snarls, oaths, or venom against the grinners and the smirkers, for they bear their own distress inseparably, like a hump. Their curse is in their solitude, which is a shadow stalking them in silence. Their curse, hear me, is in the way they eye their women. Their curse is in the meanness of life, the paleness of art, the dullness of their fellows.

I met a man who had met another man, and from one to the other, and from that second to me, was handed down this: There was a rich country where the grapes were fat and the cows oily, and people had learned to make all living things diseased, that when eaten they might be daintier to the palette. So their foods were pungent, and

324

rancid, and bitter, and rotten-ripe, their cheeses gamy and their meats of a syrupy sweetness. These people died with abscesses in the heart, or foreign growths sapping the bowels, or great flower-like ebullitions of ebony blood beneath the armpits—and this was the life of even the sturdier and grosser among them, the peasants.

While the court had moved still further into artifice. When the Queen was rutting, she found even her engineers of value, who had for instance contrived to direct warm currents of air and musk across her and her associates. There were more inventions, serving some of them to frustrate and others to point her desires, but they are not within the focus of this parable. The stranger came simply to tell me how once the Queen, when supposedly nearing the height of her sufferance, had suddenly pushed aside her three laboring courtiers and complained that she was surfeited. Her face twitched and became withered. Then just as quickly, the witheredness vanished, she smiled at some new thing, and murmured "Paul." Now, the courtier who had been named Paul was in reality Hozzidac; and the Queen was Queen Muin, but he answered, he also with a new smile, "Virginia."

Cast on the island as a child, kept alive with turtle eggs and bananas, Paul had lost his one companion, a sailor who smoked dried ferns in calabashes, when he was hardly more than twelve. Since then he had sat daily, as the sailor had taught him, on a rock overlooking the sea. He had learned the quiet procedure of sunsets; unknowingly, his body had absorbed the march of colors, from yellows, through pinks, to velvet lavenders. But one evening, as the sun was half cut by the horizon, with the rest spilled out in a copper rope across twelve flat miles of new pennies, prodigally a star fell sizzling into the sea. Immediately after, he heard for the first time a female voice, and he knew that he had not sat waiting all these years for a ship, but for Virginia.

Leaping from his rock, Paul ran to the shore, and dragged her out of the ocean like a fishing net. She had fainted. With one hand on her hair and the other on the firm mound covering her heart, Paul sat quietly and waited for Virginia to awaken. Her eyes opened slowly, then started, and she moved herself frailly away from him. She asked for food, and Paul brought her a necklace he had made of colored stones. She smiled sadly, and made the sign of biting with her teeth. Paul, meek and distressed, held out his finger for her to avenge this mysterious wrath. But she pushed it away, and made signs of swallowing—so that Paul brought her turtle eggs and bananas, and also some dried ferns stuffed into a calabash. Later he led her to his hut and gave her a warm soup. Then she pushed him out the door, made signs that he must not enter—and Paul sat through the night, ready to rip apart with his hands whatever prowling thing he might hear clumping about in the blackness.

With that first impromptu evening corroding like a slow patient acid in the recesses of their memory, these two hastened to erect barriers of daintiness between them. They fought restlessly against everything in this scheme of living which pushed them too undeviatingly, too unsubtly, towards each other. From Virginia Paul learned again to speak, and with words came a new awkwardness. Language itself was a deflection of their purpose; even the simplest words were circumlocutions, while these simple words in turn must be circumlocuted. They developed comforts and amenities, and by so much the more they had placed a hard safe crust above the volcano of their desires. Unknowingly, they determined to forget the slow patient acid in the recesses of their memory; they would live and die, with that the last direct caress between them.

Here was an experience which no humans ever before had known. Their care for each other, their aloof delight in each other, was unique. The polarization of precisely these two egos could happen once, and only once, in eternity. Was it finally those very barriers, so unquestioningly erected between desire and fulfillment, which became tentacles drawing them closer together? At moments their words became a song; and All That They Had Done became All That They Had Done Together. Something arose which I shall call a warm glow—and this glow radiated from them across the world of objects so that, looking upon these objects, they saw things in a strange and astounding light.

Then, cutting across these complexities of evasion, came a storm. While the island shook from the blunt broadsides of thunder, and giant trees spun about and toppled to the earth, Paul and Virginia sat crouching in a tiny cave. Paul's eyes glistened; Virginia's hair was tousled, she laughed-with-the-wind. As Paul grasped her by the shoulders, she glanced at him with a shudder, then with something even roguish; finally she became limber, and here on the rough ground they bedded.

Later the ululations of the storm subsided; rain fell only when a casual gust of wind blew drippings from the trees. The storm had bundled off to some other portion of the globe; somewhere else the storm was stumbling across the waters; it was no longer their storm.

II

1. The Warrior Returns

Returning from the war (a bullet had flattened against her picture worn over his heart) he sang his way back through France and sunny Spain, tossing to the mendicants small coins and curios plundered from the enemy, and carousing in the night with heavy-booted brigadiers, telling them, to the plunk of tankards on the oaken boards, how a girl (golden-haired) sat humming frail songs in a tower and waiting for his return. Arrived at last, he swam the moat, and scaled the walls with grappling hooks, and with a curt whisper turned the growling of the dogs into a whimper of welcome, and suddenly appeared in the tower kneeling beside his cousin. But she paled slightly at the sight of him, and her eyes faltered, so that he understood more than if she had spoken whole volumes, and with one stroke he despatched the head from its body, he himself stepping without hesitation along the parapets and free into the air.

2. The Homestead Among the Lilacs

An elderly couple, grown silently too old for the ravages of desire, live alone at the end of a winding lane off the main road, tending their gardens of flowers and vegetables, keeping one cow and a family of cats, and living in the letters they receive weekly from their daughter at college. She returns for the summer vacation, so that a man is brought from the county seat twenty-four miles off to tune the piano. The daughter plays strange music; also, without malice, every Sunday morning she plays old-favorite hymns to the accompaniment of their thin voices. She is receiving letters, this daughter; and by her exuberance they know that these letters are from a lover. The mother finds accidentally where they are kept. Then every night the old couple read them over together in secret. They also sneak down to the rural mailbox and take out their daughter's letter, steam it open, make a copy of it, and replace it in the postbox. Finally the daughter expresses a wish to "visit a girl friend." But the parents know that a rendezvous rather has been arranged between their daughter and her lover, and that she is to spend the night with him at a hotel in the county seat. She returns; the old couple welcome her, and do not question her too much about her girl friend. That evening, after dinner, she retires to her room, and the old couple sit on the front porch, waiting for their daughter to post her letter, and for night to fall.

3. Imponderables

They had first met at a sculptor's studio, where he was interested in the peculiarity of her figure. Milton exclaimed with vigor that she was built like a peasant, and thereafter called her *ma paysanne*. Aline discovered that she could be happy with this man. He taught her the luxury of big beers after an hour of tennis. They would go on long walks together, and returning on the train she usually fell asleep on his shoulder. But one evening in the early spring, when he was to meet her, he came two hours late, breathing heavily, with his eyes over-bright and unfocused. "I tried not to come," he sighed hopelessly, dropping into a chair. The idyll was over. He burst out that he was in love with her. His good humor had been a deceit, and he could bear it no longer. While she, she was an unconscious vampire who demanded that men just be "nice" to her. She cried a bit, after which they

328

"made up." He avowed that he was a fool for having been so tragic, and was hilarious the rest of the evening. He insisted on calling himself a victim, however, and when he was about to leave her for the night, he grew sullen again. Hereafter Milton was seen notoriously with other women. When he met Aline in a group, he would overlook her entirely, or else greet her with a boisterous, aimless familiarity. He "forgot" his engagements with her, then clamored for a reconciliation, until she held out her lips to him, whereat he brushed them cheerfully and absent-mindedly with his own, and began talking of other things. Or again, with the sweetness of a benediction, he assured her that for woman to pride herself on being desired by man was like a cabbage priding itself on being eaten. About this time it happened that Aline met with a series of misfortunes entirely exterior to Milton. Yet he somehow "rode" upon them. Busying himself elsewhere, he secretly voted himself a victory: he was manipulating an indeterminate but efficacious vendetta.

4. Death Us Do Part

Miriam was unusually conscientious in her devotion to her husband and her three children, which may be accounted for by the fact that not only was she an earnest and well-meaning woman, but also she had a lover. Gradually, as the husband and lover came to know each other more intimately, the relationship was tacitly avowed and agreed to. Miriam remained delicate in her difficult position, and each man respected the other for his share in the possession of her. With this deep channel of emotion in common, the two became close friends, so that when Miriam fell ill they took turns watching at her bedside. After her death a hostility arose between them.

5. The Seduction

For twenty years he has lived alone in New York, going every evening to the burlesque shows; and for twenty years he has stood at the stage door each night after the show, hoping that tonight (tonight!) he will at last muster the courage to pinch a chorus girl as she passes. Finally one girl drops a package as she is hurrying home from the theater. He snatches it up, takes it to his room, opens it, and finds that it is a slice of beefsteak. With gritted teeth he plunges his fingers into the flesh and pinches it unmercifully. The next morning his landlady finds him dead of apoplexy.

6. Built for Speed

Although it meant the loss of a fortune if she married him, Florence never hesitated. She stood up staunchly before her father, faced the old man's mouthings against popery, and then the two lovers set out for the station in the dark, through a howling blizzard. Their hardships during the next months, while she was furthermore being gnawed at by a child in the womb. He could seldom find work, so that hunger and deprivation were added to her miseries. The child was born dead, and she nearly succumbed to puerperile fever. Several times the parents wrote, offering to care for her if she would leave her husband; but she always answered, boasting of their prosperity and happiness. And though he himself begged her to go back for her own good, she would not: a life with him, even in destitution, was preferable to a life without him. Finally the husband gets a steady job as a clerk, and their hardships are over. In time they furnish a home. The household duties become irksome to her; she complains that he cannot afford a maid. She sees him now under steadier light: he is honest, kindly, but without brilliance—and now for the first time she resents her past sufferings. The flatness of her life becoming too unbearable, she deserts him.

7. The Rabbit Skin

The professor of physics in a small-town college lived quietly and contentedly with his wife and child in a duplex house not far from the campus. This child had come only after five years of waiting, when he and his wife had already begun to lose faith in her ability to have children. After school hours he goes on long walks with the child, or else spends his time in the basement making it mechanical toys. At night he sings to it:

> "By o baby Bunting,
> Papa's gone a-hunting;
> He'll bring home a rabbit skin
> To wrap his baby Bunting in."

One of his colleagues in the biology department, who is collecting certain vital statistics, requests him to submit to a physical examination—as an outcome of which he learns that he is sterile. He takes the news quietly, but later complains of being ill, and asks that someone else teach his classes for the day. He goes on a long walk in the woods; at first he groans aloud, and then, shamelessly, he sings "By o baby Bunting." A kind of peace descends upon him: he is reconciled. After all, the child has made his life richer, even though he is not its father. He will steady himself, will struggle to preserve his old attitude towards both child and wife. He returns home, almost in elation, his victory has been so thorough. His wife meets him at the door, open-armed, smiling. She whispers to him the news: he is again to be a father.

8. The Tragedie of the Doctor Faustus, Done into Words of Four Syllables for the Children of This Country

It was not as an old man that Faust first laid down his book to hear the choir of angels, and the young men returning from the harvest, and the First Citizen inviting the Second Citizen to go with him where the beer was best and the girls prettiest. During a strenuous adolescence, knowledge had meant to him precisely the one channel of escape from these discomforts. With that richness, or sensitiveness, of character which made him find things appalling which others took for granted (seeing one specific beautiful woman as beauty, or one specific white shoulder as woman, and thus finding terror where others found a purpose) he turned from life to the relics of life. For here, after all, were the same factors, but under a simpler, or kindlier, aspect. With young Faust, then, the humanities were not the crowning of the human, but a substitute for the human; he was becoming gnarled when he should have been made mellow. And Faust would have already been a monster, except that he was young. As he aged, Faust deepened his knowledge, until as an elderly man he realized that this very substitute which he had sought for living led back in turn to the obligations of living. To be wise, even on his own terms, Faust saw that he should have to travel man's normal orbit, man's proper cycle. Thus, at a time when he should have relaxed, looking upon the world with the twinkle of a well-fed mind and belly, Faust saw that the structure of his years should rest upon the foundation of a different youth. In complaining of knowledge as vain, Faust was too wise to apply this universally; it was meant simply as the diagnosis of his own diseases—and Faust suffered remorse, was without dignity. With the help of artifice, Faust *purchased* his youth: Faust was now a monster. In purchasing Gretchen, in having to purchase Gretchen, Faust understood exactly the extent of his poverty, and was consumed in his own bafflement.

9. The Tribe of the Maroans; Their Virgin-Worship

If a virgin among the Maroans dies, and she is under the age of ten, she is buried lightly, with one foot exposed, that her body may be digged up and devoured by wolves. If between the ages of ten and twelve, she is similarly buried, her shame having first been removed and mummified and hung in the Sepulcher of Hope. But if she is twelve or more, and is nubile, yet has died a virgin, then the body is warmed over a slow fire, and given to the young men, themselves warmed with a brew of bay leaves, to exact their pleasure.

III

Of fish, the male exudes a cloud of sperm which, by encompassing the female, leaves her fertile. Was there, on a subtler plane, some similar interrelationship of human minds and emotions? As he sat here now, unprisoned (unprisoned! for erratically enough he thought of convicts, turning in their cells, in a life without the imminence of transgression) sitting here, he recalled a kind of flush which had seemed to pass from his vertebra and arms and shoulders, and to be projected like a cloud about the clothed figure of this woman. Those silent spasms—he wondered if she too had been aware of them, or if they had filtered somehow into her subconscious, if some sperm might now be basking in the cells of her brain, thriving and growing sturdy, until, with apparent suddenness she became amenable to him, or pliant rather, or mentally supine: a seeded field, waiting to be sunned and rained upon.

Where she deliberately blinded herself, he was trying to see more keenly. Obscuring the basic facts, she would spend her time rather going beyond those facts. She might, for instance, be thinking of some trip with him in Italy, or her making clothes for a four-year-old child, or even deciding what kind of flowers grow best in window-boxes. He, on the other hand, was stepping, or eyeing—or sparring even. At times he would drop some little root into her, some tentacle; or he would crouch back, wounded with apprehension like a snail.

He had sat and nodded with her, and held out his cup to be refilled; and the excitement of their dialogue, mounting into the abstract and will-less, into the pure inutile, had made him overlook the slinkings and sneak-thieveries of his profounder business. After such moments he returned with something like freshness and guiltlessness to their vague, indecisive dalliance, their warfare without visible objectives.

"I remember," he wrote her, smiling with a mixture of beatitude at the sudden clean memory, and amusement at his own unconscious trick of making love to her by recalling an affection for another, an affection which she could not dismiss, as it had values, and which she could not resent, as it had innocence, and thus which should pique her most in that it both provided an object for jealousy and made jealousy unjustified, came, you might say, fully armed, but bearing palm branches of inoffensiveness, "I remember" [nor was this something social, something which could be exchanged, smiling, at the club for something else] "that I was sitting in front of a humming stove, and the door opened, and a girl broke into the room, her clothes smelling of the crisp snowy air, her smile stiff-muscled from the wind. We had not known each other intimately at all, but I leaped up suddenly and embraced her. I kissed her, almost without knowing it—so had the act preceded the emotion."

Those were the simple words: she could take them as such. Everything behind them, that unique combination of declivities and purposes which had contributed to their genesis, could be caught by him alone; even now, immediately after the event, they were scattering and fading off into one another. After all, that memory, remembered here, was not a fact but a *symbol*. He had been weary with his own bandyings and wanted something simple, some smooth rails to glide upon. Perhaps, then, he had not written those sentences in accord with any vague technique of seductiveness; perhaps she had not even been within the focus of his aims. And all that was involved here was the curve of his emotions from complexity to simplicity, a curve which had been materialized, or symbolized, by his choice of two corresponding specific factors. His complexity, that is, had taken form as the stiffness and purposelessness of him sitting before the fire. And the desire for the sudden smooth rails of simplicity had attracted this other memory of the time when the soft, cold-nosed girl had appeared and "the act had preceded the emotion." While this woman had been simply the gravitational element; that is, since he was writing *her* a letter, and a *love* letter, he had made the unconscious selection of this particular symbol rather than some other.

Oh, it didn't matter, it didn't matter, it didn't matter. "I believe that at bottom man expects to find in woman a haven, yet this is precisely what she is not." Woman as the prostitute type, woman as racially a vendor of love. When she yields, she yields not to a man, but to some social distinction. She must take a car conductor because he is the *best* conductor. With a young man of promise (are destitution and promise identical here?) she is prompted by the potency of his youth, but yields after the imaginings of a problematical future. In the course of years, as his merely physical, or technical gifts decrease, he retains her or loses her in proportion as wealth (or reputation if she is subtler) is won or lost. Where then is the haven, since one gains it the more only by needing it the less?

Back in those Dark Ages of adolescence, when every train ride he took or every time the whistles blew at New Year's, or when vacations began or vacations ended, or on his birthday, he had decided that from now on it would be a closed book. Each day was to be a fresh day. In despair he resolved to drop each time a quarter into his bank as penance; and soon he had enough to buy his little cousin Ethel a Christmas present. Then came the startling birth of a *philosophy*. For how, he reasoned, could he be magnetic, so long as the surcharge was being led away through inappropriate channels? How could he set another in tune with him, unless he himself were vibrating enormously? *Circulus vitiosus*—for if he could not acquire the proper recipient of his energies until he had turned from himself, no more could he turn from himself until he had acquired the proper recipient of those energies. A ghastly pessimism, which he solved strangely enough by simply waiting until the manna fell from heaven, until a woman came and jokingly asked where she should hang her toothbrush, and then—praise God—really did hang it there.

Occasionally with real warmth, with a willingness and pliancy, he pursued his letter. He wrote of a certain song which they had heard once without thinking, and how, when he had heard it again recently while alone, it recalled this time they had been together. He requested that she return to her usual mode of hair-dress. And he hoped that she would go to the concert with him.

Coda

His friend Jim, an older man, had told him: When undressing beneath the eyes of a mistress strip first to the waist, then remove shoes and socks, and last, drop the remaining garments at one stroke, so as to

335

pass from attire to disattire without suffering the indignity of inter-mediate stages.

She had been born for this; in blind accuracy her body had been fashioned and steered towards this one thing.

If he smiled upon her, her whole body smiled back—by his frown she was left hopeless—she looked at him silently, with moist dog-eyes—he spat.

A record of sheer concupiscence; a mass of lewd and lascivious imaginings; things obscene, indecent, and lubricitous.

Appreciating the abstract syllables beyond the actual content, noting the growth of a dead uprooted flower, forgetting the heart, finding sufficient excitement in the lips, yet broken suddenly with pure anguish.

The Anaesthetic Revelation
of Herone Liddell

1. "In that most bodily house"

The first thing of importance that had happened to Herone Liddell following the accident of his birth was a near-fatal tumble he had taken, about the age of three. Spitting meditatively from the height of a second story, he lost his balance, and fell at an angle on his head. Subsequently, he tended to assume that he had hit the ground before his own spit.

Had he been older, his neck might have been broken. But the bones were still soft enough for the dislocation to be rather like a bend than a break, leaving him, as a quirk, a tilt of the head slightly to one side, the way some dogs intently listen.

Yet in one notable respect this fall, this accident, had become part of his essence. For it had marked his early years by their own peculiar kind of "falling sickness," sudden spells which the family called "fits," when he felt himself sinking, and would create a great clamor in the belief that he was about to die. Similarly, night after night, he reenacted his "traumatic experience" by dreaming exactly the same dream—a dream of walking down stairs that vanished into a pit of nothingness, at which point he would awake in terror.

Nowadays, Herone would probably have been diagnosed as having the amount of neurosis "normal" to his injury, and perhaps would

337

have been treated by a child psychologist, had his parents been able to get one cheap. But as it was, he was left to improvise his own cures, which were along the lines of religious piety (a "natural" compromise, since such reverence is a species of fear, yet also has strong connotations of solace).

So young Herone lived much with thoughts of God the Father and Christ the Son, often trying to be exceptionally good. And when, sometimes at sunset, shafts of golden sunlight shot down from turbulent black and golden clouds, he saw them not as the physical things they were, but as paths one might traverse in the other direction, by spiritual ascension such as he had seen depicted in his books of piety.

However, in the course of living, his earlier attitudes gradually became submerged beneath successive deposits of secular realism, the accumulation of experiences with people in the everyday world. And by the time he was ready for college, his religious interests had become so transformed into sheerly aesthetic analogues, if he thought of "grace" at all, it was neither the theologian's kind, nor even in general the social graces, but the possibilities of stylistic grace, to match the possibilities of stylistic grandeur.

So much, for the present, regarding the first thing of importance that had happened to Herone Liddell, following the accident of his birth.

The last thing of importance (we omit intermediate hirings and firings, marriage, divorce, remarriage, and other incidental steps along his way as a Word-man) was a surgical operation, which was now to be performed on him, at the age of sixty. It was the sort of operation usually classed as "minor." In fact, beforehand the surgeon had proffered with a laugh, "For cases like this, there's no need to make out your will," whereat Herone, who had not thought of making out his will, promptly began wondering whether he should make out his will. Also, something had happened (if it had happened!) which was to make Herone think of his operation as decidedly "major."

Either the hour for which the operation was originally scheduled had been set ahead without the surgeon's being notified, or the surgeon had been notified, but had forgot. Or there had been some other hitch. Or Herone, already drugged to the stage of near-dementia, was reading the signs wrong (under conditions certainly not favorable to his reading them right). In any case, while he lay in a semi-maniacal state, fighting helplessly to be listened to, and hearing the words he tried to form become vexingly dissolved into inarticulate tongue-waggling, he heard, or thought he heard, snatches of conversation.

They seemed to be about the surgeon: Where was the surgeon? . . . Had he been notified? . . . Someone should phone him. . . . Yes, he was still at home, having breakfast. . . . He'd hurry right down.

Did Herone really hear these remarks? And if so, by how long were they separated from one another? Meanwhile, the situation contained an ingenious kink of this sort:

Somehow, since early childhood, there had lodged in Herone's imagination a strong misgiving as regards anaesthesia. He had feared with a fear almost magical a possible point at which, partially anaesthetized, he might still be conscious, yet wholly within the power of another, unable to call a halt in the proceedings, despite his rights as customer. Somewhat, he said, as a suicide might feel who, after having leapt, wanted to retract his decision, but was powerless to do so. In his imagination, this moment of helpless resistance, when others could do with him as they chose regardless of his struggles, had seemed somewhat like the sickened sense of falling he had experienced, in the recurrent nightmare of his childhood. Related to it was a horror of being confined. Thus, even under the most trivial of conditions, as were his arm to be so caught in his sleeve that a few moments' patience would be required to extricate it, his spontaneous tendency would be, rather, to attempt tearing himself loose in a frenzy. And his present condition was a perfect instance of such a situation—for as he lay half-conscious in the operating room, he felt several expert tugs, and lo! both arms and both legs were clamped tight. So now he lay there, raging helplessly, with no more rights than a carcass, bound in the very way he had most greatly dreaded.

It was a Poe-esque situation, as with the story of the man who, having all his life dreaded the thought of being buried alive, awoke to find himself confined in what, in stony horror, he took to be a coffin.

339

However, in his imaginings, Herone had overlooked one notable motivational distinction. The Philosopher admonishes that anger drives out fear—and true to the book, Herone's fright turned to rage, almost rage in the absolute. For he was so confined that the only mode of fighting possible to him under the circumstances was limited to whatever kind of surgings could take place within his own guts. At least the physiological processes that might load his blood with his own adrenalin were not strapped down, so he freely seethed within. Outwardly, the resources of hating were reduced to mere cursing— but even that outlet in turn was reduced, by the aphasic conditions resulting from the amount of anaesthetics already in his system, to ineffectual words that somehow refused to come out right. Things were so set up that, if wanting to call someone a filthy bastard, he would at most hear himself, as though from within himself, shouting as though from outside himself, "oo lya snar!" This was especially vexing for a Word-man, in his ferocious but futile struggles against the "indifferent Powers" that bound him.

There was one other surprise: For many years, in his bouts with insomnia, Liddell had slept with a red bandanna kerchief over his eyes, to keep out the faint rays of the early dawn. But now, during the delay (if there was a delay!) while waiting for the surgeon (if they were waiting for the surgeon!) his eyes were exposed to the glare of strong lights immediately above him (presumably floodlights to be used for illumination during the operation?). In his befuddlement, they had upon him the effect of the blinding glare used by police officers when questioning criminals or attempting to break the spirit of political prisoners. He felt not merely assailed, but invaded.

So there he lay, suspended in a state of helplessness and rage, just on the edge of extinction, while vaguely around him were persons whom he could remotely hear in snatches but could not see, and who seemed to be waiting. He heard himself almost as though he were an observer from without. But no, it was something very much inside him he was hearing. And he would go on hearing it for some days after the operation was over. In its purity, it was not him; but it was an aspect of him, and it would try to make all of him over in its image.

"Bruised bleeding maniac," he reconstructed afterwards, heroically; "made powerless by straps and pain and drugs," though he had of course lapsed into total oblivion before undergoing any of the processes to do with the actual incision. "Cursing whoever from outside attends him, him there inside his own seething—his will to live made pure revilement."

Or otherwise put: "The little man with the great big bad unconscious; the timid man with a roar somewhere within, emerging as out of a chasm." Somehow, apparently, his sheerly vegetating body had received as an outrage the very service that his citizen self was paying to have performed.

"The groins divided, a mind divided," he wrote in bed, using pencil and clipboard. (He had quickly come to the conclusion that the operation had produced a "psychic shock," that its nearness to the genitals made it psychologically equivalent to castration.)

One almost comically unstable symptom made him swing back and forth as between two wholly different personalities. Certain ideas that occurred to him (or came to ride him, rather) turned his diaphragm into a band of steel, stopped all unfoldings, transformed the churning gases of his bowels into stony immobility. But other ideas, equally beyond his willpower, brought with them relaxation, and a corresponding flow of blessed flatulencies, until in the course of events things shifted again to associations of the rigidifying sort— and in a flash, the muscles of his stomach became hard knots, as clenched as a fist. In brief, he could shift (or, more accurately, he was shifted) between tense associations and relaxed ones, with the muscles of his bowels and stomach making a burlesqued behavioristic replica of the difference between the two attitudes.

Had he started under bad auspices? The morning he was to leave for the hospital, being awakened early by the sputtering of a car down the road, he had made up these lines (he had numbered the stanzas, to accentuate their development as stages):

Stages

(1) Ducks quacking, dogs barking,
    A kitten scurrying for cover—
    And there he was.

(2) All day
    The songs, the games,
    The friendly altercations.
    "My compliments! My compliments!"

(3) A dim shape
    Borne away by shadows
    In the dead of night.

Bad auspices, unless you interpret such things after the manner of counter-boasting (saying the worst, to "prevent" the worst).

Now, lying with distended bowels, a loathsome tube inserted through one nostril into his stomach, he tried to wince ("in that most bodily house, where there was no place to wince to")—and all the while he kept wondering whether it was a good sign or a bad one that he could not stifle a refrain: "Pity for each wincing thing/ pity, and thanks for the eventual/ kindliness of cure-all death."

Herone was impressed first of all by the extreme *physicality* of his condition. He thought of himself as an item in the process, to be poked or jabbed, at set stages along the way, in accordance with a pre-arranged schedule—and things would proceed as per schedule despite the fact (if it was a fact!) that something had gone radically wrong with the schedule at the very start—if he could trust the naggingly unforgettable though muddled memory of his impotent rage while lying strapped and waiting (a maniac in a straitjacket), under the inquisitorial glare of the floodlights, or whatever they were.

Had he fought even while wholly anaesthetized? Could the body, even in sheer mindless physicality, hate the instruments that prodded at its tissues; and might it thereby load the blood with the juices of sheerly physical strife?

When, all full of his experiences, though still somewhat in a fog,

342

he had started to discuss them volubly with his roommate, an intern who happened to be present made a sign indicating that Herone should shut up—and then severely murmured to himself for Herone's benefit, "Writers talk too much."

Even in his befuddlement, Herone had to admit that the intern's point was well taken. In fact, Herone had often made the same point himself, and about himself, particularly during recent years when, the country having swung far to the right politically for a spell, Herone found many of his earlier liberal attitudes and utterances in danger of being made to look absurdly suspect. Yes, for some years Herone had been ruefully proclaiming that it was, alas, a writer's business to talk too much, though he finally had had to abandon this line when he heard some damned newsman on the radio say the same thing about newsmen.

In any case, now at a time when Herone felt a great desire to verbalize about the bepuzzlements of anaesthesia, and would gladly have enlisted the whole hospital in the task of speculating about his symptoms in particular, and about the symptoms of the anaesthetized in general, he found himself abruptly put Under the Sign of the Quietus. Thus, the degree of persecution mania "normal" to his profession was greatly increased by the Kafka-like quality that pervades the disrelation between the immediate physical ministrance of the nurses and the Hidden Authoritative Essence somehow brooding invisibly above and beyond all this particularity—the great God-like Routine that loves us all equally and impersonally, and decrees what is best for us, while we need but surrender ourselves, in full confidence, to its judgments.

Since he could not surrender himself psychologically (subjectively), while at the same time his physiological (objective) surrender was necessarily almost absolute, Herone in his role as impatient patient came to think of himself as a prisoner, perhaps even a "lifer."

Add this angle: Quite as a person pursued cannot sleep, so a person who cannot sleep is like one pursued. And for the week following his operation, Herone's insomnia, which had always been a major topic of conversation with him (as of an attainment), had acquired proportions nearly of grandeur. As he lay listening, round the clock,

343

to the muddle of sounds (some clearly interpretable, others vaguely so) that mark the cycle of a hospital's routine, his mind felt tense as a steel trap, set but never sprung. Thus, he *was* a prisoner, almost literally, to the extent that The Routine would not or could not or simply did not prescribe sedation sufficient to release him from the dreariness of his stony vigil. He wrote:

PRAYER FOR INSOMNIACS

Great God, thy wondrous world is full of aches,
Of which a goodly share of them are mine.
On every side are proddings to mistakes
And most straight things get twisted serpentine.

Great God, the mass of miseries is deep,
And many are the wounds that will not heal.
But all I ask for me is: Let me sleep—
And Great my Lord my God, it is a deal.

Yes, maybe his psychologer friend was right, when contending (in a case not unrelated to his, though Herone had protested violently) that operations of this sort often aroused a "castration anxiety." Maybe our hero had got himself into a jam.

Lying awake as stony as a statue, he began trying to get things straight.

How look for origins? Herone thought it possible that his experience managed somehow to link up with a "primal scene" as early as his fall at the age of three. Both were, you might say, species of the same genus, or even particulars of the same species—and thus, as regards the logic of the emotions, it was as though he had recently had his childhood all over again.

But what of the malice? The early experience, so far as he could remember, had been wholly without warfare. It had simply happened. But apparently his new experience had involved almost an orgy of hating. Apparently (as he gathered from a passing remark by the surgeon) even when completely unconscious, on two different occasions his muscles had knotted while being sewed—he had been fighting at the very roots of himself. Was that merely physiological, the sheer will-to-live manifesting itself fundamentally as meanness? Or had it also owed something to "conditioned" kinds of reflex?

How deeply might an idea-motivated body hate surgery? Enough even for the ideas to do their work when the mind had lost all track of them, like a kind of "pre-hypnotic" suggestion?

At least there was the fact that at the height of his adolescent religiosity, he had joined a sect of faith healers, and had been a most devout believer. True, the sect's stress upon the healing properties of "love" left no place, overtly at least, for endrocrinally stimulated hatred as a mode of survival. Yet religion goes deep, and the depths are full of paradoxes—so he had to consider this possibility. And at the very least it was a simple realistic fact that he was on principle as dubious about "medical progress" as he was about "progress" generally. There might, then, be this strong "doctrinal" resistance, capable of God only knows what ultimate corresponding response in the tissues—and attested by the fact that, on the surface, he tended to associate hospitals much more readily with death than with cure.

Similarly, he resented the ways in which the modern hospital had restored the ancient art of blood-letting, though the New Phlebotomy was contrived indirectly, by the resources of finance. He had quickly become so cantankerously resentful of the present procedures, with their arrant gadgetry, that he was fairly let alone. For he loudly protested his distrust of the very thing that most people seemed to associate with the greatest glories of modern medicine, and he had always contended that medicine should be pills or nothing. But he watched his roommate being assailed by an endless procession of pretty girls who entered at regular intervals, to stick that elderly, long-suffering gentleman abruptly in the behind, as per the doctor's orders. Herone held that someone should invent a combination walkie-talkie, hypodermic needle, and cash register so that, each time the patient got another shot, a bell might ring, while the charge for the deposit of rare metals and pedigreed bugs would be recorded grandly in the accountancy department, and thus could show on the patient's bill even before it began to work on his body.

But attitudinizing of that sort had come later. It could not have accounted for any battles directly connected with the operation itself.

Second, how deeply might he resent his surgeon? He had originally intended to have the operation performed by a different knifeman, or seamster—but delay and distance were involved, and he chose his present practitioner instead. Such initial indecision as to the choice of surgeon could lie there as a fertile source of resistance, insofar as anything went wrong—and is there not a sense in which even the "best" of surgical operations could be said to go wrong? At any discomfiture, the patient might be tempted to resent his choice— and all the more so if one were an old liberal, his politics much the worse for wear, and had lain helplessly bound beneath the "politically inquisitorial" glare of a long narrow searching light that he remembered vaguely as the visual equivalent of a piercing shriek.

Then again (and this was along the lines of Herone's psychologer friend's ideas), there is something somewhat "outrageous" about an operation on the groins. The repairing of Herone's hernia involved a radical "invasion of his privacy." True, he knew that he had paid to have it done—but doubtless his tissues didn't. And once his identity as a customer had been put to sleep, maybe a more conservative self took over.

Ultimately, however, as always with a Word-man, the problem had developed into a problem of the Quietus. The ideal patient was expected simply to *believe in* the Routines, and no questions asked, whereas nothing was normal with Herone until it was talked about, if even then. But the surgeon had become so evanescent, Herone almost had to scheme to see him—and for quite understandable reasons, nurses and interns avoided all discussion like the plague. Everybody going about his or her business—and from the standpoint of a Word-man, it was as though some Dirty Deed had been done, with no one returning to the scene of the crime.

Directly from this situation came his sense, or conviction, of the Ultimate Trap. Another name for the Ultimate Trap was Writer's Guilt—and he had built up his data on Writer's Guilt thus:

On many occasions in the past, in his younger days, when he was walking the city streets working things out, he would stop by a storewindow or hallway or lamppost, to take down a note that he thought might be usable—and almost immediately, someone would come out (the storekeeper? the janitor? a plainclothesman?), and would edge towards him, to spot what might be going on, just in case. . . . Or, at least, it seemed that way! And now, he suddenly thought, that's how his note-taking might seem, to all these people expertly going about their business.

For Writer's Guilt derives ultimately from the writer's sense of The Guilt of the Written-About, which can be avoided only if the subjects have strong reasons to believe they are about to be praised.

Still, without even thinking of it in these terms, Herone seemed to have hit upon a kind of solution, in connection with a local priest whose company he had recently come to enjoy.

Though essentially an agnostic, Herone roundabout resembled a believer—for his distrust of pronouncements about the supernatural extended also to a distrust of the naturalistic critique of supernaturalism. Sensitive above all to the ingenuities of dialectic, he knew that one need not believe in God to love theology. He relished the sheer stylistics of piety—and he thought it gallant of monastics willingly to put their wills at the disposal of the wills of others (as one does in effect, when taking the vows of obedience to a monastic order). He was troubled in particular by the religionists' talk of "humility," while attributing to humankind so arrogantly high a place in the cosmic order (though he had to admit that often such "arrogance" did seem to manifest itself as considerateness, whereas his own tendency to belittle mankind's role in the universal scheme often went along with a tendency towards "pigheaded mulishness").

In any case, Herone asked that his monastic friend come visit him—and improvising, in a kind of "secular confession" whereby the nonbeliever's sheer utterance would have to be its own absolution, Herone discussed his quandaries almost hilariously. When it came time for his friend to leave, Herone felt purged of all Kinks. And when his wife came to see him that same afternoon, he bobbed like a cork on the waves.

Accordingly, all the more surprising was the development a few hours later.

* * *

Once again, it seems, Herone had been the victim of circumstances, responding with over-promptness to a certain telling convergence of events:

His roommate, who had undergone an "exploratory operation" (cystoscopy) with the aid of spinal anaesthesia, and who had been consistently the very soul of good humor, surprisingly took it upon himself to become a howling demon of pain. For several hours, without let-up, at each exhalation he groaned, a groan that sank into Herone's weary wakefulness until he felt as though his own guts were being torn apart.

Let us call it The Night When Room XQ–27 Went Crazy. The closing routines before bedtime were over. Herone had been given his pathetically ineffectual sleeping pill. The lights in the hall had been dimmed. The mixture of clearly and vaguely interpretable sounds in the distance had dropped to a minimum. But here, within a few feet of him, was a formerly good-natured man darting about the room, groaning aggressively, and ceasing to groan only during the intervals needed to draw in the breath needed for the next groan when breathing out.

Herone began to twitch. Whereas he had been quite weak, he got out of bed, and (along with his groaning roommate) started to wander up and down the corridors, ignoring the pleas and imprecations of the disgruntled nightshift. Of a sudden, he felt so strong, he could have dressed and walked out of the hospital, speedily and without assistance.

In fact, he tried to figure out how he might scheme to do just that. For as he found his body jerking, rigid and strong, he decided that he had been given, not a sleeping pill, but strychnine. He wrote notes, hiding them about his clothes, in case, when he was dead, "the evidence" would be destroyed. There could even be a "motive." They had misunderstood his note-taking!

Finally, having burnt himself out, he crawled back into bed to await his end. His roommate, in time, ceased groaning. Herone became aware that the muscular jerks were diminishing rather than increasing. He would live!

The next morning, attempting to read, Herone made a discovery.

He noted that he was affected by a kind of aphasia whereby, when he got to the end of a sentence, he had already forgotten the beginning of it. He could follow an idea consecutively when writing it, but he could not maintain the sense of continuity when reading.

Now, of a sudden he realized: He had been taking as "reality" a kind of world that had come to him through the partial distortion of drugs (probably the original anaesthetics) not yet eliminated from his system. His *crise de conscience* had been primarily a matter of unaccustomed chemicals.

He was glad to get back!

The next day he was almost infantile in his sense of contrition. He apologized profusely to any and all—and though no one seemed overtly resentful of his antics, the Quietus popped up again, as soon as he touched on the subject of "symptoms," possible responses to drugs, and the like.

One especial absurdity resulted from his overeager desire to make amends. It involved his two Gigantic Aides, the one More Gigantic, the other Only Slightly Less Gigantic, one on the day shift, the other on the night shift—and the two of them together would have made at least five of our hero.

He liked them both, but particularly the More Gigantic, who had inducted him into the routines the first night he came to the hospital, in preparation for the operation the next morning.

The day after his brainstorm, when he was sheepishly telling his wife about the turmoil of the night before, the More Gigantic Aide happened to be in the room at the time—and she said, "I'll bet you wouldn't have acted like that if I had been on duty last night."

To Herone, who was to this giantess "like a cat at the feet of a queen," this notion seemed quite correct—and he exclaimed spontaneously, "I believe you're right!"

But later, he began worrying about his remark. It implied an adverse criticism of the other aide, he felt, the Less Gigantic one, who had been on duty that night—and he was trying to make up with everyone. Yet the More Gigantic one might pass on his remark to the other aide, without wholly explaining how he happened to say it. (This had become a major matter!) And he felt all the surer that some such misunderstanding had come about when the Slightly Less Gigantic Aide, while arranging his bed, began (in what seemed to him exploratory tones) praising the aide who was his favorite.

So he wanted to explain to her that, in saying he would have acted differently had the More Gigantic Aide been on duty, he did not mean to imply any criticism of the authoritativeness of her, the Less Gigantic one.

It was a difficult matter. So he took her hand, and started to explain. Whereupon, before he could say a word, she wrenched her hand loose and rushed from the room.

And Herone saw himself in the role of an old goat who, the moment he began to get the least bit better, made a pass at a nurse! Also, he had no illusions as to how long it would take for that story, in the Less Gigantic Aide's interpretation, to filter through the staff.

2. "We must tentatively read the signs"

But what of the "Revelation"? It happened thus:

Mostly, his sleep was too scant and shallow for dreaming. Only in flashes, at best, could he get beyond a kind of half-awake dozing, a semi-stupor while conscious of the nearly constant hospital processes. (In all hours of the day and night, a hospital suggested to him the hustle and bustle of a grammar school at recess.) But there was one notable "epistemological" dream, and he clung to it for hints of something; though it had the evanescence of a fever dream. The main difficulty is: A fever-dream is far from providing the best example for making clear the precise logical difference between the realists' notion of intuitions that grasp reality as it really is, and the idealists' notion of intuitions that, in their role as appearances, are essentially different from the ultimate things ("things-in-themselves") they represent.

In this dream he saw several rods of glowing white light. These rods were symmetrically arranged somewhat like the blades on a lawnmower, except that lawnmower blades are somewhat curved whereas these glowing rods were straight. There could have been five, six, or seven of these—and one of them might have been central, like an axle.

The important matter was their relation to one another. In one sense, each was distinct; in another sense, they were all one (the kind of dialectical ambiguity one meets in the relation among the persons of the Christian Trinity). Almost immediately on coming out of the dream, Herone thought of a possible explanation for the ambiguity. At one stage in the progress of the anaesthesia, the patient's eyes might have become so unfocused that the long rod of glaring light above the operating table (if there had been such!) was seen as several. In this respect there really would be a sense in which the different rods of light could be simultaneously one and many.

Along with his perception of these glowing rods, there was a voice speaking (a kind of Voice in the Absolute, proceeding not exactly either *ab intra* or *ab extra*, since it was too remote or impersonal to be his, yet too much in tune with his own thoughts for it to be someone else's). In any case, it was giving a *rock-bottom explanation of things*, and with regard to the effects of "proprionyl," Herone's dream-name for his anaesthetic.

However, in the solemn pontificating of the Absolute Voice, "proprionyl" was being praised not for its value as an anaesthetic, but for its contribution to the understanding of "reality." The design of the glowing rods (in their ambiguous shift between oneness and plurality) purported to reveal the structure of the universe in a wholly *realistic* way (a point that must be stressed, because of what came later). It was intended to teach *exactly how* the universe is constructed. And though it was an invention made for pedagogic purposes, it was intended not as a "model," not as a "suggestive illustration," but as a revelation of the literal basic fact.

Yet that pedagogic note must have introduced a principle of instability into the "vision." Or rather, it must have provided a transitional bridge whereby the Absolute Voice could pass from a *realistic* to an *idealistic* position. For the Voice explained how, on one occasion, something went wrong with the working of this fundamental educative device—and in the course of repairing it, an important new discovery was made. It was found that the rods could be seen from different angles of approach (that objects could be seen from many sides), so that the interpretation of reality became more complicated

351

(we might say more "perspectival," though this word did not present itself during the dream).

The dream ended just as the turn had been made from the wholly realistic view of the design (the notion that its appearance was identical with the way things really are) to the kind of thinking that is essentially idealistic (because of its "perspectival" emphasis, its suggestion that the true vision is to be approached through the obscuring yet revealing fragmentation of many different local standpoints).

In the last analysis, Herone thought on wholly awaking, the first version of the design would be scholastic, the revised view Kantian. And the best way to possess the first position is to begin with it, since it cannot be reached from the position of the second. For anything perceived must be an appearance; by definition an appearance is to be distinguished from a reality; and thus, the appearance must be what reality is not.

A world of appearances could be known as a set of usable signs; but no matter how well a system of signs was made to serve in the pragmatic business of survival, you could not get around the purely formal consideration that a thing can be an appearance only insofar as it is not the reality behind its appearance. For if it were an out-and-out reality, then to that extent it would not be an appearance.

A painting can be an imitation of a tree only because it is not a tree. And a real tree, by reason of its realness, cannot be a mere painting, or imitation, of a tree.

Anyhow, rightly or wrongly, Herone had the conviction that he had watched the very essence of realism, through the very essence of criticism, become the very essence of idealism. (Later, he decided to define idealism somewhat punningly as: "A philosophy that, confronting the distinction between mind and matter, asserts that only mind really matters.")

But speculation on his dream quickly moved from questions of "aesthesis" and "anaesthesia" to problems of an ethical, or even sociological, order. In fact, he was not averse to wondering whether the sort of considerations he came to next had in reality been prior to his "vision." In that case, the "vision" would have been in effect the reduction to a corresponding but simplified design, somewhat as when complicated attitudes are duplicated by absent-minded "doodles" that somehow stand for them (the attitudes leading to a kind of act that translates the attitudes into graphological terms quite different though essentially analogous).

From the realistic point of view, the design had been intuited to be as purely and simply and immediately real as the taste of an orange, or as the thought that, if A is bigger than B and B is bigger than C, then A is bigger than C. But once the Absolute Voice had noted that, in the "repairing" of the design, a way had been found to see around the corner of its immediacy (and thus, in effect, to change its status as immediate into a status as mediatory), then forthwith the simplicity was gone. The intuiting of reality would now be idealistically indirect and complicated, with the medium of observation itself prejudicing or distorting the observation (though one might hope to approximate the state of simple, immediate, absolute, "intuitive" knowledge to the extent that one could by critical analysis make allowances for the distorting effects of the medium, including the medium's nature as "informative").

The social-minded parallel of Herone's Radiant Quincunx (and it had been radiant though he was not sure it was a quincunx) involved two views on the nature of hierarchy, as it applies to our views on human relations. Certain relationships are simple, he thought, and thus allow for the direct "realistic" awareness that something is as it is. But certain other relationships intrinsically involve a contradiction, which must be idealistically discounted (the discount usually being guided by materialistic notions of "interest" as the primary motive behind the given social transaction).

To illustrate the case of a simple, realistic relationship (though aware that his example was rife with possibilities of interpretation in the spirit of idealistic symbolism), Herone told himself:

"A, let us say, is a ferryman. B wants to be ferried across the stream, and is willing to pay A for this service. Here, obviously, observable at a glance, *uno intuitu*, is a direct and simple relationship such as fits perfectly with a realistic philosophy. A has an immediate service to sell; B wants the service and is willing to pay immediately for it."

The example was not quite perfect, Herone felt, since a purely barter deal would be much more realistic than one involving money, which already had a highly "idealistic" element in it.

Or, more accurately still, realism must begin even further back than barter, prior to any "justice" of the *quid pro quo* sort. Realism would be naturally tribal, grounded in services of sheer familiarity, like those binding parents and offspring. It centers in such sense of purpose as results spontaneously from the combination of agent and scene (motives reflecting the needs proper to a given natural species in a given natural situation). Realistic services would be basically incommensurable with one another, like the variously interacting functions of the organs in a living body.

Herone even wondered glancingly whether talk of the "incommensurable" relation between "eternity" and "time" could have its sociological beginnings in a wholly "pre-talionic" sense of community, before the thought of scales had furnished the material for conceiving the idea of justice in oversimplified terms, at the very start, as reduction to the image of the balance. Might speculations on the "absurdity" of the "incommensurable" relation between God and man arise as a late-idealistic, "post-talionic" attempt to recover the principle of this primal realistic order? And thus might "ancestor worship" begin philosophically in the "incommensurable" relation between the power of the adult, as compared with the pathetic limitations of the infant, the powers of adulthood corresponding to the "infinite" or "eternal," and the limitations of infancy corresponding to the "temporal"? And surely a "pre-talionic" idea of justice is needed, if we are to think of God as "just" in sentencing all men to natural death because the "first" man had fallen into disobedience.

In any case, nothing could be farther from realism, in its essence, than the kind of thinking now called Realpolitik (which is a materialistically toughened brand of idealism, idealistic sentimentality in reverse). The problem of cooperation that Herone's tentatively imagined Ur-Realismus could not solve, and that accordingly called for the death of realism in its purity, was signalized perfectly in the Spanish proverb "When two share the same purse, one laughs and the other weeps." True realism can't long survive the ability of language to observe that, when the cream has settled, one can "by sheer oversight" grandly pour himself the thick and leave the thin for others, in their role as mean, justice-mongering grumblers.

One might become more exacting still, and contend that realism could not prevail in its Simon Pure state except prior not only to all taliation but even to all speech. Thus, the "truly" realistic vision of the Design was impaired as soon as the Absolute Voice entered the situation (which it did almost at the very start of the dream as he remembered it). Implicit in the Voice would be the *dialogue*; and implicit in the dialogue would be the *dramatis personæ* of different points of view, the "perspectival" element.

But at least the nature of the transaction between A, who would transport for a consideration, and B, who would be transported for a consideration, was clear and direct. And in this sense, it could serve as an example of the intrinsically realistic, particularly when contrasted with another kind of service, which Herone thought of as necessarily involving a contradiction. For instance, it is a doctor's job to cure us of our ills. But insofar as he succeeds, he does himself out of a job. Or, less drastically, if he cures us in one visit, he'll earn much less than if he cures us in ten. To an extent, then, we must take his goodwill "on faith." We cannot directly know. We must tentatively read the signs. The situation itself contains this contradiction, as an intrinsic part of its nature. And in this sense it is a relation intrinsically "idealistic."

By the same token, there would be intermediate cases (most of the world's relationships would probably be in this class) where quasi-realistic claims may be affirmed despite the intrinsically idealistic nature of the case (a situation that contains the maximum opportunity for an essential deception).

Herone did not flatly assume that "contradictory" relationships (like that between hospital and patient) led necessarily to deception. On the contrary, he assumed that the principle of good faith was generally predominant, and sometimes complete. He merely had in mind the fact that the situation was intrinsically "contradictory," hence not the kind that could properly be treated in terms of simple realism.

(He had heard tell of a time in old China when the relation

between physician and patient did have the kind of directness that would naturally allow for simple realism. Then a man paid a physician to keep him well, but stopped payment whenever he got sick. However, Herone reflected, such an arrangement might set the conditions for an opposite kind of twist, as a pinch-penny person might become chronically ailing, if only to do his physician out of his wages. Herone further noted that there was a sense in which modern medical insurance did operate along the lines of the old Chinese custom, with corresponding tendencies on the patient's part.)

In any case, the dream's two views of the Design suggested to Herone how a philosophy of realism might fit (and thereby be a misfit) with the conditions of a medical bureaucracy built atop a "kinked" or contradictory kind of relationship. Or, going further, he glimpsed the possibility that all bureaucracies, in their double role as servants of the community and perpetuators of themselves, called for "realism" while needing the check of idealism, in turn checked by materialism.

Where there is bureaucracy, "realism" combines with absoluteness and authority, to suppress inspection. It requires, first of all, an act of *faith*. One must put himself trustingly in the hands of those who "know best." He must take things at face value. Whatever is done to him, or whatever he is told to do, is purely and simply for the purpose of cure—and that's that.

"Perspectivally," discounting with the aid of an idealistic dialectic that contains at least one strongly materialistic strand, he may see, or think he sees, an essentially contradictory situation that calls for a more complicated terminology of explanation. He may see, or think he sees, situations whereby "medical ethics," supposedly designed to protect the patient from mistreatment, could function rather to protect the profession from inspection (much as military men use "reasons of security" to avoid civilian inspection of their policies and expenditures).

But insofar as the physician's professional manner (with all the corresponding hierarchy of attendance by interns and nurses) is accepted realistically, *simpliciter, uno intuitu*, as equatable with the poise, authority, competence, dignity, and professional goodwill that it

356

proclaims on its face, then the patient is enfolded in a Grand Mystique of Absoluteness, calling for silence and obedience, and readiness to pay. Something untoward may have happened? Try and find it! Indeed, try by questioning even to prove to yourself that it did *not* happen—and the wall of the Grand Mystique was just as impenetrable.

Thus, in sum, Herone, by profession one who "talked too much," and above all a lover of the "comic discount," confronted a mighty, awesome monument, built out of little things that went unanswered—a great chasm of tiny silences—just when he had been all set to chatter like a jay.

Though Herone had been greatly relieved on finding that the worst of his over-responsiveness had been due to the drugs themselves which were still vestigially with him, leading him to interpret physiological symptoms in terms of sociological causes, he still did somehow greatly want to mourn the loss of something. "I feel," he wrote in the style of *Galgenhumor* to his psychologer friend, "as though I had had my connotations cut out"—to which the psychologer friend subsequently answered: "You're lucky. In many such cases I have read about, the patient feels rather as though he had had his denotations cut out." And he told of one poor luckless devil whose wife had decided to have their second baby, just about the time when he went for his operation. She had her baby, all right; but by the time he had recovered sufficiently to make it, she had decided to have it by a different father—so the operation was closely followed by a divorce.

Herone kept trying to remember a poem in Catallus he hadn't read since his adolescent days at college, on lamentations by one of the priests of Cybele, just after the operation that vowed him permanently to the deprived physical condition required of those ministrants (the *Galli*, in ribald jest called *Gallæ*).

In particular, he worried about some lines of his own he had written only a few months ago. For he felt that, from the symptomatic point of view, they lent themselves to two completely different interpretations:

Season Song

O when will the snow melt on the mountain?
The valley is now in heat.
And when will the heat of the valley go
The mountain snows to meet?

O once I went to the mountain
A feverish one to meet,
That we might go
As quick through the snow

As though to be in heat.
O I fear the time in the valley
When heat and cold have met
And the sun has set.

Actually, there had been no snow on the mountain, that hot day when the lines occurred to him, just at the turn from spring to summer. The valley had been unusually hot, but some bare rocks on the mountain had happened to glisten in a way that suggested snow. The second stanza grew, not out of an actual experience, but out of the first stanza. (The "one" didn't seem quite right, though the inversion of the words "to meet" somehow seemed passable in this instance.) And at least, he had been through the second stanza "in principle."

It was the burden of the third that worried him. One can never be quite sure when such imagery is prophetic, creative, eager to hasten the day, and when it is an attempt, by counter-boasting, to forestall the dread time prophesied. At the moment, he inclined to fear that the "creative" possibility was uppermost. "Oh, that something fortunate had ever happened to me or my brothers!" Keats wrote just before the end; "—and then I might hope,—but despair is forced upon me as a habit." But alas! it was more than a habit, or even a premonition. Events only a few weeks later proved that Herone would have been justified in taking his attitude as a certainty.

Still, Herone told himself for solace, between the futuristic symptomatics of the "Season Song" and his postoperational symptoms of the present, he had dipped into another kind of scheming; and he asked himself just how far the stylistics of gallantry might legitimately be carried. Here had been gestures that, borrowed from a long tradition of poetic posturing, seemed to him somehow to build up—or "imitate"—a world cunning enough to keep a metaphysical body engrossed with the proprieties of thanksgiving and leavetaking, since Man (in his role as Word-man) is sentenced to the sentence:

SOMA AND PSYCHE

A Body's Platonic Converse with Its Soul

Soma, pleading:
    Inbeing,
    Flask without fault,
    Give, give,
    Until we melt.

    Now, beyond all thinking,
    Give towards an ultimate drinking.

    Give me unearned
    Thy chaliced selfhood towards me turned.

Psyche stirs. . . . Pause. . . . Then Soma resumes, more excitedly:

    What flower is this
    Unfolds in darkness as furtherance
    Of my mute ministering utterance?
    O—I would mount to depths,
    To drain full cups
    At near-collapse,
    To kiss
    A silken secret's lips.

Psyche, to herself, musing:

Move,
Be led,
Let wings be spread
To give,
That he may love
And dying live.

How far carry this sort of thing, the Kantian (hence, idealistic!) principle of *As if*? There he had written *as if* snow were on the mountaintop. And here he had written *as if* he believed in body's being related to soul like masculine to feminine (the flat opposite of the classic equations, yet using a classic idiom, though perversely).

Might his "anaesthetic revelation" (or, more accurately, his "post-anaesthetic revelation") be reducible ultimately to but the more pressing realization of a condition that he had realized long before he ever took his somewhat expensive punishment? Were there certain resources of language, driving us towards a purely linguistic fulfillment, as though towards the origin of everything? A terminology had certain logical conclusions implicit in it, certain possibilities of completion, or "perfection"—and for a symbol—using species maybe these can form as real a kind of ultimate purpose as any congeries of material things and physical sensations. The Kantian "as if" would be a variant of such a notion.

For instance, we might say that a poet writes "as if" certain perfections "really" existed, or that a person could act gallantly in real life itself "as if" the poet's imaginings "really" existed. But an "as if" so conceived would not quite hit the mark. Rather, one should approach the matter roundabout, thus:

First, there would be the sheer physicality of life, the human organism as simply one more species of alimentary canal with accessories.

Second, there would be the miracle, or accident, or perhaps even morbidity, of language, in various ways helping this particular species of alimentary canal to guide and protect itself in its tasks of growth, temporary individual survival, and reproduction.

Third, there would be the motives intrinsic to this special property, this miracle, or accident, or morbidity, of language—a plane of symbolism capable of pointing towards "perfections" intrinsic to itself. To live by these, in the sign of their sheer formality, would be to live by "real" ultimates, ultimates proper to the medium.

However, in the light of sheer physicality, from the standpoint of the human species as digestive tract with trimmings, such a way of life would be but an "as if."

Herone could not honestly say that this notion made him any richer. But he did know that, when he left the hospital, he would be several hundred dollars poorer.

What Liddell resented most was not the impossible slip-up as regards his operation (if there had been such a slip-up, and if he had not merely got things crooked as interpreted through the confusions of his drugs). He resented most the fact (and he could not fathom the reasons though the fact itself was brutally clear) that, whereas this institution must have had more soporifics per square inch than a poppy field, he was allowed to go so many times round the clock, burning brightly awake like a Blakean tiger in the forest of his quandaries. For beyond the nag of the insomnia, there was also the fact that such constant wakefulness denied him the guidance of his dreams.

How could our hero hope to see around the corner of himself, if he could not catch himself dreaming? What could he learn by simply trying to figure out where a particular flushing of a toilet or tinkle of ice water was coming from, or whose steps those were in the hallway? Herone had been kicked in the teeth—and at the very least, he felt, he was entitled to discover what the more primitive aspects of his personality, or personalities, thought about it. But to his knowledge, there was only one other occasion when he got far enough asleep to go beyond a kind of half-blinded observation of his surroundings into the *bona fide* realm of dream—and he was grateful for it, even though it resulted in a nightmare from which he awoke abruptly, in exceptional terror.

This dream seemed to involve a kind of counting game that was played with bones shaped somewhat like wrenches, thus:

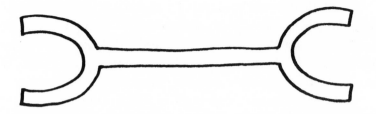

These bones were ambiguously motivated. In one sense, there were players who were somehow making them hop about; but in another sense, they seemed to be moving of themselves. There were at least two players, one of whom was Herone, though in an "absolute" sense —for no person was actually visible, nor were there any visible means by which the bones were caused to move. The "game" consisted mainly of pressing one or another of the four prongs against the ground.

At the same time, a kind of Absolute Voice (or Voices?) kept reciting pairs of numbers, such as "three-four," or "seven-eight," or "eleven-twelve." Then of a sudden a transformation took place. One of the wrench-like bones became Herone himself—and he awoke in terror when the pressure on one of the prongs became instead like a "full Nelson" in wrestling, a grip that was about to break his neck.

At this point, instead of paired numbers, the Voice had shifted to a group of three—"two-three-four"—and as Herone lay awake, still fresh from the nightmare and trying to fathom it, each time he repeated to himself the numbers "two-three-four," shivers of dread would go through his body. The ability to re-induce this shivering effect by repeating the number persisted a surprisingly long time.

In trying to locate the implications of this dream, Herone could not turn up one single possibility to work on. But after the shiver-effect had been worn out by several experimental repetitions, he found himself as it were changing the direction of his thinking. He thought of a literary conceit, along these lines:

Recalling the old Mother Goose jingle, "One, two, buckle my shoe, Three, four, knock at the door," etc., he thought of a possible trick whereby the numbers could be treated in a way to make them pointedly "meaningful."

By the time he was two,
He had learned to buckle his shoe.

At the age of four,
He found something oddly revealing in the response
    he got
When he had knocked at a strange door.

Between the ages of five and six
He became a useful participant in the mysteries of
    fire-making
And often went forth to pick up sticks.

And by seven or eight
He was actually building usable things with them,
Laying them straight.

And so on. But by the time the pattern had got thus far under way, Herone began to suspect that this dream might be quite close to the thing he was looking for. For it might cut all the way back to the "first fall," when his neck was injured. (He kept clinging to the notion that his experience on the operating table had somehow harked back to his "original sin" in falling on his head.) The counting game might figure because, most likely, at the age when the accident occurred, little Liddell was being taught to count, and by such devices as the Mother Goose rhyme he had now been making "meaningful." His spontaneous description of the bones as "wrenches" seemed to fit with the same possibility. (It was also an unexplained fact that after the operation he had a sore neck—though he had not the slightest idea how he got it or what to make of it.)

However, even hypothetically granting that there was some emotional connection between the operation and the fall, he could not account for the tremendous change in motivation that seemed to take place when his dream shifted from the playful pairs of numbers to the shivery group of three.

Did it all perhaps involve an ultimate magical difference between

363

even numbers and odd? In any case, there was one other numerological moment that occurred to him one morning when, in contrast with his usual depression and disgruntlement, he unexplainably felt perky as a puppy. It concerned a design that apparently contained elements of "rebirth," since it concerned an idea for a cartoon-like cover to be published on the Christmas issue of some "smart" magazine. The scene was the little town of Bethlehem, on the first Christmas Eve. The Three Wise Men could be seen coming down a lane that crossed a little bridge and led to the Stable. Above the Stable there glowed a large five-pointed star. There were many other stars in the sky; but they were all smaller, and six-pointed.

Ostensibly, Herone's contrast between the one large five-pointed star and the many smaller stars of David referred slyly to the historic turn from Judaism to Christianity, from the "Old Law" to the "New Law." But Herone never for one moment thought that in its nature as a "doodle" it should be interpreted simply thus. Herone wondered whether, numerologically, it could be another variant of the hidden distinction, in his psychic economy, between even numbers and odd.

Other connections suggested themselves as possibilities. Years previously, during a time of great distress, he had had the sense of an eye, staring at him from the heavens. The bright star of Bethlehem now seemed to him a benign variant of this same fancy. Next, he asked himself, might "stare," in his psychic economy, be the verb form of the noun "star"? He next recalled that his nonsense syllables for "you filthy bastard" had originally been "oo lya star." But later he changed the "star" to "snar," on the assumption that if, when he lay waiting half-drugged before the operation, a mouthpiece had already been inserted to keep him from biting his tongue, this obstruction could have been partly responsible for his difficulty in speaking. If it was there, he certainly hadn't noticed it; for he had been aware only of the vexing way in which the words he tried to form turned out wrong. But if it had been there, he thought, then a "t" would more likely sound like an "n." Hence he changed "star" to "snar." He next noticed, to his bepuzzlement, that the light of "star" also hides itself under the bushel of "ba*star*d."

*Omnia exeunt in my*sterium.

When he hit upon his rebirth symbol, Herone was moving towards the day when the "prisoner" would "escape." But there was still one further ill-starred moment to develop, before he was formally wheeled down the hall to the elevator, to descend to the street level, and there be wheeled to the waiting car, whereat—praise God! —the Rule of his Better Half would again take over. We cite the incident for reasons of symmetry, to round out the design:

Herone's roommate, who entered the hospital later than he did, "graduated" before him. After one night when he had the whole room to himself, a new patient was brought in, a laborer who had fallen from a scaffold. Herone watched the badly wounded man's clothes being removed and heaped in a pile. Later, relatives came and took these away. But before they left, they remarked that his purse was missing.

Herone promptly imagined an ironic situation: (a) workman falls from scaffold; (b) others rush to his aid; (c) some expert scoundrel, under the guise of caring for him, frisks him and steals his purse; (d) and thus, when the hospital attendants arrive, while they think they are carrying away the victim of an accident, they are also carrying away the victim of a robbery. Whereupon Herone confided sympathetically to a nurse: "The poor devil, he gets a bad bump, and gets robbed besides."

Shortly afterwards, an intern entered, glanced at Herone severely, and muttered loudly to himself: "His purse is probably being held for him at the office." In brief, Herone's remark had been interpreted as a suggestion that the patient had been robbed by one of the hospital attendants. One more bad mark for Herone.

Slink away, Herone. Make your exit, as Keats of the letters might say, "like a frog in a frost." You didn't show up so well in this episode. Yes, you had been somehow knocked crooked—might it even be true, as you feared, that one eye seemed inclined to stare, and to be bigger than the other? Yes, you had been trampled on, worked over, kicked in the teeth. Now you were almost ludicrously limp. And the punishment you took was particularly humiliating, since the operation was rated decidedly as "minor." What if you had been processed in a "major" way?

Slink back to freedom.

3. "Haunted by ecology"

Convalescing, if we could call it that (perhaps "being slowed down" would be more accurate), Herone continued to ruminate about his recent quandaries. A man with paranoid tendencies, he thought, might be successfully transformed into an educator—but only insofar as things are not under the sign of the Quietus. (Further, he tended to assume that everyone is paranoid, since we are all pursued by the discords of the social order.)

He thought of that sanguine fellow, Benjamin Paul Blood, a protégé of William James, with avidity proclaiming the "anaesthetic revelation" he had experienced in a dentist's chair. Surely at the bottom of him there was a happy simpleton that took delight in the sheer affinities of sound (along the lines of his thesis that "icicle" is not a fit name for a "tub"). Here was the symbol-using genius reduced to one perfect strand.

Herone had this happy strand, too. He loved the sheer jingle of words. Even in his anguish, Keats had it, as when he wrote, just before the end: "Yet I ride the little horse, and, at my worst, even in quarantine, summoned up more puns, in a sort of desperation, in one week than in any year of my life." Whatever fragment of a damned outraged monster there may be, howling deep down in a chasm, there is the possibility of this pure exercising whereby essences are suggested by an engrossment with the sheer accidents of words.

Eager for a summary, he slowly put some things together (remembering his imprisonment, but now from the side of freedom, though a freedom vexingly frail). As Herone figured things out, they might be summed up thus:

"First," there is man the "economic animal," in the strictly biological sense, such a creature of ecological balance and geophysical necessities as he would be even without his "reason" (that is, without his ability to find words for things and non-things, though frequently, by misuse of his "reason," he puts himself geophysically and ecologically in jeopardy, at the same time victimizing many humble "lower organisms" that don't quite know what happened to them; but somehow, as the result of human improvising, they ceased to find life lovable, or even livable). Here would prevail, basically, the aims and behaviors that make for growth, self-protection, and reproduction.

Now add *language* (the "grace" that "perfects" nature). Henceforth, every "natural" movement must be complicated by a *linguistic* (or *symbolic*) motive—symbolic not just in the general sense that an animal's posture may be symbolic of its condition, but also in the more specific sense that the word "tree" is symbolic of the thing it names, and this word can undergo developments, such as declensions, syntactic location, grammatical and phonetic changes, that are quite independent of the nature of tree as a thing.

There may even be a sense in which we might say that, for the symbol-using animal, there never had been a wholly "natural" motive (in the sense of a motive wholly alien to the principle of language). From the very start, the human infant's sheer *potentiality* as a symbol-using animal must differentiate its responses from those of a species that does not possess the inborn ability to learn language. For a non-linguistic species would presumably not suffer the kind of "pre-privation" that must mark the linguistically helpless human infant.

Though Herone did so fearsomely, since one contradicts Aristotle in such matters at one's peril, he wondered whether his position somewhat invalidated the scholastic principle: *nihil in intellectu quod non prius in sensu.* For the forms and principles of a language are never present as sheer sensation, though they are at the very core of our intellects (as when we conceive of natural relationships after the analogy and grammatical structure, such as subject and predicate, essence and accidents, active, passive, and middle or reflexive).

In any case, once language has become re-enforced by a complex sociopolitical order (with its corresponding codes of "reason" and "imagination"), the *material* reality of the human body in physical association with other bodies human and nonhuman becomes submerged beneath the *ideality* of sociopolitical communities (which are saturated with the genius of language).

We probably think by only a few basic terms, though their paucity is obscured from us by the ways in which the many synonyms are not quite synonymous; for instance, "proceed" or "advance" don't quite make the same cuts as "go" or "move."

Poetically, philosophically, the ideal world of the pun becomes at this stage available in all its reaches. Thus, if we speak of light as a stream, of ideas as part of a historical current, and of urine as flowing, then urine, light, and ideas can be secretly one (one with blood, with rivers, with the stream of consciousness and the flux of time). For underlying such similarities of usage, there are affinities linking the human body, the world's body, and the body politic.

Also, an *attitude* towards a body of topics has a unifying force. In effect its unitary nature as a response "sums up" the conglomerate of particulars towards which the attitude is directed. See a letter of Keats (March 17, 1817), modifying a passage in Act II, Scene iv, of first part of *Henry IV*: "Banish money—Banish sofas—Banish Wine—Banish Music; but right Jack Health, honest Jack Health, true Jack Health—Banish Health and banish all the world." Here, he is saying in effect: The feeling infuses all things with the unity of the feeling.

Attitudes, in this respect, are a kind of censorial entitling, reduced to terms of behavior. They are an implicit charade, a way of "acting out" a situation. Or they are like a highly generalized term of classification, a broad logical category—for in effect they classify under one head all the many different particular situations that call forth the same attitude.

When an attitude towards the world is developed in a moment of poetic or philosophic fusion (epitomized in some overall title of titles, for "Everything"), it probably embodies some such implicit puns as were already considered, in connection with the range of things that "flow." But such unifying verbalizing, or entitlement, is in effect a step beyond human body, world's body, and body politic, though it draws upon analogies from all three of these realms. It is a kind of "transcendent" entitlement, since its unifying function is in effect an addition to the elements it unifies. And in this technical sense it could be called "cosmic," or "supernatural," or "religious" (being technically "religious" in the sense that, like religion, it infuses all things with the essence of the Word, the Logos, the personality of the "first" creative fiat).

Suppose you are a musician—and of a sudden, a likely theme

occurs to you. You awaken—and there it is. And somehow it is like an unopened bundle of possibilities.

Maybe this theme appeals to you because of its hidden relations to some other theme—a theme that you may have actually heard, or all-but-heard, many years ago, in some situation then that seemed to you vaguely laden with some such futurity as you now experience clearly. The theme thus looks back to an earlier time when you were vaguely looking forward (in effect fumbling with the beginnings of a word, a class name which you would need later, when you came to classify this later actualizing experience under the same head as the earlier potential experience).

Next, you proceed to develop variations on your theme. Successively, you make it brisk, playful, plaintive, pensive, solemn, grandiose, nostalgic, muscularly ingenious, and the like.

On the surface, at the very least you have produced a form by carrying a principle of consistency into an area that threatened it with disintegration (disintegration insofar as the principle of consistency risked becoming lost in the variety). But insofar as you have succeeded, you have unified this variety.

And have you not done still more? For insofar as your theme originally welled up from a secret personal relationship to situations that, however tinged by symbolism, were themselves largely outside the realm of symbolism (as the *thing* tree is outside the realm of the *word* "tree"), you have saturated this whole range of the symbolic and the nonsymbolic with a single personal motive, summed up in the attitude-of-attitudes that was implicit in your theme (which would be the musical equivalent of a title-of-titles).

Thereby you have had, in effect, an immediate vision of an ultimate oneness (thanks to symbolic manipulations that have brought many disparate things together). You have had the direct feeling of this principle. You have "got the idea."

Can you, then, ever rest unless this perfection is actually attained? Furthermore, the search is made especially uncomfortable, and on many occasions undesirable, by the fact that, in the course of your efforts after the perfection or simplicity of unity, you find so many reasons to be glad that the world is in pieces. For if it were really all one, where could you turn, at times when again you must make a break for it?

Man's symbolistic genius first exiles him, by putting a symbolic veil between him and the nonsymbolic. Next, it aggravates this state of alienation by making possible the complicated world of social status, the ladder or pyramid or hierarchy of offices, with their various "unnatural" kinds of livelihood. Next, symbolism acts to make amends by dialectical devices—of poetry, philosophy, politics— whereby things otherwise thought disjunct can be said to partake of a single unifying essence that transcends their separateness.

Either the memory of such unities, or the feeling for the possibilities in such a unifying principle (a feeling sharpened by at least partial attainment of such unification) acts in a way whereby the momentary experience of unification becomes a motive, a desire to have perfect consistency always.

Here would be the realm of "gallantry," of purely ideal gesturing, the realm where, for instance, a masculine alimentary canal pays a deft compliment to a feminine alimentary canal, using to this end all the resources of symbolistic finesse necessary for acting "as if" these were not *au fond* two animal organisms dredged up from the sea-bottom.

"Love" begins as a sheerly natural emotion (animal, nonsymbolic). Call it simply appetite, seasonal desire. So likewise with "duty," insofar as we mean by duty the kind of loyalty that marks the relation between parents and offspring. Both emotions, in this sense, would be "positive," as positive as hunger or toothache.

But once the symbol-using animal has developed complex ideas of property, with their corresponding notions of propriety, these two sheerly natural kinds of love and duty "transcend" their positive condition, becoming profoundly inspired by the negative (as in the thou-shalt-not's essential to the formulation of all moral and social codes: justice, etiquette, "protocol"). Primitive seasonal sexual desire becomes *amor, eros*; the kind of familiar loyalty that begins in the relation between parents and offspring becomes *charitas, agape*. Both "love" and "duty" are now best studied as variants of the "imperial" motive—for they derive their personality from their nature as responses to the conditions of status, ownership, governance that develop historically through the aid of symbolism and that are, above all, infused with the genius of the negative (the thou-shalt-not's, and their corresponding quasi-positive forms in the case of moral precepts expressed in an affirmative style).

A set of consistent sentences about "everything," with appropriate summarizing title (or "god-term") and symmetrically distributed subcategories, would be the ultimate perfection of language. Metaphysics reveals this drive most obviously, but it prevails *mutatis mutandis* as the principle of all substance (which Leibniz defined as "unity in plurality," and which later theorists claimed more specifically for the role of the "imagination").

Here begins the drive towards a logic of completion, a cult of perfection, which shows up drastically alas! as a goad towards empire-building, while the ways of empire serve in turn to localize the terminologies of gallantry, with their increasingly minuscule codes of courtliness.

The issue will finally be settled by the extent to which the purely symbolic genius of perfection is allowed to fall out of line with the needs of the body as sheer body. For the world of gallantry (when science has been carried into industry by the applications of politics and commerce) threatens at every point to disrupt the "ecological balance" of the purely physical world. Man's "dominion" over the "lowlier" species that are put here for his "use" threatens at every point to become manifest in a way whereby he destroys what he needs directly or indirectly for his own survival. The great "as if" can be like a very delicate dance, at a gorgeous festival, atop a volcano that is about ready to blow. And often the dance isn't so delicate, or the festival so gorgeous, either.

Thinking along these lines, Herone began to feel "haunted by ecology." The very thoroughness of his concern with man's symbol-using genius forced him to think with new intensity of man as sheer animal. He must go south, and to the sea—he must stand "on the brink of the drink." On the shore, thinking of the sea as scooped out, he would be as though on a high mountain overlooking an abyss.

4. "Watching young Keats die"

In Conclusion: Herone Liddell's letter to a member of what
Keats has called "that most vulgar of all crowds, the literary."

Dear ——,

What hit me? I had been trampled on, worked over, kicked in the dentures. It was doubly humiliating, to be so beaten by so minor an operation. Still, maybe there had been a kind of "cleansing," too. For even an impatient patient necessarily has patience of some sort.

Gradually there emerged The Resolve: To the South. To the South it must be, though the fall and early winter following my punishment were mild, and even beautiful. To the South. Yet never did a beckoning beacon arouse less sense of expectancy. (Each year I come more to loathe and fear the traffic of the highways.)

So, we have improvised again—and it may turn out not badly. We're on a kind of key, not skeleton, I hope, though the first live thing we encountered, on our first walk on the beach, at sundown, was a dying black duck that mutely begged us to respect its privacy, and we did. The next day we found it again, now partly buried in the sand by the tide.

Ironically, we got our place through the *ex officio* offices of a kindly real estate man who, living palatially, had only a palace to rent, but gave us a tip, presumably from sheer pity. (May he not also need a dash of terror, to complete his cleansing for the day.)

Barring car trouble on the way back (we had almost none on the way down) we should be able to manage the whole trip for surprisingly little beyond the amt. we shall save on what our bills for heating would have been, had we stayed north. Yet on the third day of the idiot drive south south south, I had begun digging into the new areas of self-doubt, and even thought compulsively of a U-turn in the grand style, north north north, straight back into the winter we had fled from. (Traveling even at our moderate speed is as crazy as snow; one falls into a kind of trance, a near loss of personal identity—only to be wrenched out of it, now and then, by suddenly discovering that one had been masochistically imagining oneself in a wreck.)

I guess that by now the clock in the dining room has stopped. Since we did not know where we were going (except for the general direction: south), lack of destination makes the trip seem more like a destiny. Here, on the beach, one is encouraged to mistake outlook for insight. And there is the doubtless anally motivated business of searching for the remains of things that died before we did. Insofar as one is Puritanical, shell-gathering can further gratify his moralistic compulsions by giving his walks the selectivity of an acquisitive purpose. And formally, the minuteness of such a concern is forced upon one, perhaps, by sheer contrast with the sweep of the horizon.

I greatly admire the coquinas, which live so dangerously in the unstable sand where the waves wash. The valiant little fellows make good broth.

Consider me a fairly well-stocked dictionary standing on the edge of the abyss, confronting the biological fatalities under the grim signs of geophysics and ecology, in a mood Ultimate and Beyondish. End of formula. (The fishermen, I suppose, are as though bringing up live truths from dark depths.) The shell-gatherer, let us say, is forever hoping to find a perfect specimen of Convoluta Rigidiformis Oblongata, and thereby solve the secret of all life.

We have a little house, only 100 yards from Old Restless—and I can hear him tossing throughout the night, an insomniac even more sleepless than I, though much less unsleeping than God. (Since God is by definition wakeful always, even to the most trivial details of His Creation, I guess it follows that my insomnia is my nearest approach to godliness, though at times it leaves me awfully glum. I envy those earnest fellows of earlier ages who, where we say "insomnia," would doubtless have spoken of "watching and waiting." They could have welcomed as a call, as a promise, what is now but a damned nuisance.) Yes, we are on a sheer slither, between Gulf and Bay. So we go scrunching our way on sand and shells along the Edge of the Ultimate, selecting from among the forms of things that conched off before we did, things dredged up from that profusely life-giving charnel-house, the sea. The good wife is so much more expert at "shelling" than I, whenever I do turn up something, I suspect her of making a special fuss about my find, to heal my ailing ego.

I have been doing my exercises. For instance, as regards the multiple personalities of pelicans, I have figured things out thus: Standing, these birds are as solemn as deacons; when they swim, they nestle in the water like sitting hens; they fly in formation like a band of witches; and they plunge after their prey like a suicide jumping from a bridge.

I'm not quite sure just why—but I have found this a fitting time in which to see re-enacted the poignant death of Keats. I have been re-reading his letters, particularly his last ones, with a mixture of professionalism and tearfulness. I have been watching young Keats die.

In August of 1818, his walking trip through the Lake Country, Scotland, and Ireland had been suddenly interrupted because of the "sore throat" that was the first symptom of his fatal illness. About two years later Shelley, when inviting him to Italy in hopes of aiding his recovery, would write: "This consumption is a disease particularly fond of people who write such good verses as you have done, and with the assistance of an English winter it can often indulge its selection." The word for the disease appears seldom, though near the end, when still in quarantine at Naples, Keats writes to the mother of Fanny Brawne: "It has been unfortunate for me that one of the Passengers is a young Lady in a Consumption—her imprudence has vexed me very much—the knowledge of her complaint—the flushings in her face, all her bad symptoms have preyed upon me— they would have done so had I been in good health."

During the time when Keats was nursing his brother, "poor Tom," the reference was usually to Tom's "nervousness." And it is almost gruesome to see this same word gradually coming to take over, prophetically, in Keats's references to his own condition.

But if "nervousness" is what we might call the passive word for a necessary involvement with the sensations of his body (and "sensation" is as lively a word with Keats as "passion" and "imagination"), the active one is "fever." You can get almost the whole scope of his quandaries by reviewing the variety of contexts, with corresponding range in attitude, that serve as setting for this many-faceted word.

In August, 1819, he writes to Fanny of his engrossment in his work: "I encourage it, and strive not to think of you—but when I have succeeded in doing so all day and as far as midnight, you return as soon as this artificial excitement goes off more severely from the fever I am left in." Later in the same month, he writes her applying the same word to his work: "I am in complete cue—in the fever." (This was about a year after the interruption of his walking trip. "Cue" seems a slightly strange word here. And I wonder whether, as incentive in the background, there could have lurked the word "cure.") There is another reference, written while Tom was still alive, to "the feverous relief of Poetry," followed a few lines later by an expression that, viewed in retrospect, was portentous: "There is an awful warmth about my heart like a load of Immortality." (I admit, I generally incline to consider the word "immortality" a simple euphemism for "death.") The passage was in connection with "the shape of a Woman" who had fascinated him. He writes, in a wholly accurate synthesis: "Poor Tom—that woman—and Poetry were ringing changes in my senses." (A few days later she would be described as "an imperial woman," with the "Beauty of a Leopardess." He had not yet met Fanny. For his first impression of her, he would be "forced ... to make use of the term *Minx*.") On another occasion, when he refers to "seeing now and then some beautiful woman," he describes the experience as a "fever."

There can be an "idle fever," too, of months "without any fruit." And on the subject of money troubles he can lament, "I cannot write while my spirit is fevered in a contrary direction." Claret is praised because it fills the mouth "with a gushing freshness—then goes down cool and feverless." Near the end, his tragic "passion" for Fanny is referred to as "this fever" ("Through the whole of my illness ... this fever has never ceased wearing me out.") And one passage, in a letter to Fanny, suggested to me some notions in the direction of a universal irony. He writes: "I had a slight return of the fever last night, which terminated favourably ["fever" into "favour"?], and I am now tolerably well, though weak from the small quantity of food to which I am obliged to confine myself: I am sure a mouse would starve upon it." The medical practice of the times, in reducing the sufferer from tuberculosis to a minimum diet, suggests the ironic possibility that,

375

unless one has precisely the right remedy for a disease, or the right solution for a problem, one might tend to hit upon the *very opposite* of the right way. For, from the standpoint of sheer dialectic, there is a sense in which the "closest approximate" to the right way would be its diametrical opposite, the wrongest way conceivable. From the standpoint of dialectic, as Coleridge was assiduous in pointing out, "extremes meet." Thus, in this purely formal sense, the wrongest way would be next in line with the right way.

Fever or no fever, the tendency has been quite transformed into gallantry when, writing to Fanny of his fear lest love burn him up, he dance-steps: "But if you will fully love me, though there may be some fire, 'twill not be more than we can bear when moistened and bedewed with Pleasures." When his illness, we might say, has "progressed," the theme gets a variation: "There is a great difference between going off in warm blood like Romeo, and making one's exit like a frog in a frost." (The choice here is between fever and chill, I take it.) But the final form, a few months later, is in a letter to his friend Brown: "I shall endeavour to write to Miss Brawne if possible today. A sudden stop to my life in the middle of one of these Letters would be no bad thing for it keeps one in a sort of fever awhile."

Going farther afield, but still interpreting in the light of these passages, I'd say that the bodily sufferance and the poetic activity are interwoven in Keats's formula, written about two months after the interruption of his trip: "The faint conceptions I have of Poems to come brings the blood frequently into my forehead." And a statement written about the same time shows how his often mentioned "indolence," by merging with his cult of sensation, lets the paths of poetry and disease temporarily run along together: "I melt into the air with a voluptuousness so delicate that I am content to be alone." Symptomatic, in the sheerly bodily sense, would be this sentence written in the spring of 1819: "The weather in town yesterday was so stifling that I could not remain there." But the symptom joins with the motive of woman when, the autumn of that same year, he writes to Fanny, who had "dazzled" him: "I cannot breathe without you."

Several months before the first gong had struck (the hemorrhage of the lungs was the second), he had written on the joys of being "passive and receptive" like a flower, of "budding patiently under the eyes of Apollo," thoughts to which he was led "by the beauty of the morning operating on a sense of Idleness." And still earlier, when talking of Imagination, he had struck his slogan, "O for a Life of Sensations rather than of Thoughts!" Later he describes "a sort of temper indolent and supremely careless," a "state of effeminacy," a "langour" (*sic*), a "Laziness," a "delightful sensation about three degrees on the side of faintness," which he called "a rare instance of advantage in the body overpowering the Mind." And about this same time the condition is described as "a sensation at the present moment as though I was dissolving." On this subject, I have corrected a memory that had played me false. At odd times, I had gone about, saying, "as prompt as the bee to the blossom," but it should have been "as punctual as the Bee to the Clover."

"I did not know whether to say purple or blue so in the mixture of the thought wrote purple." As regards the parables of Paronomasia, I'd consider this statement, in its role as a "doodle," the perfect instance of the Word-man's method, when building up a world. To me this "portmanteau" construction is saying in effect, if we apply its lesson to the considerable range of things loosely brought together under the heading of his fever: I did not know where sheer healthy indolence stopped and a morbid kind took over; I did not know where such sensations were expanded into an abstract cult of sensation that would be in turn capable of serving well the cause of imagination generally; I did not know where the cause of imagination generally merged into its specific use for poetry; I did not know where my love of poetry in turn merged into my love of woman, and where that more general interest became narrowed to an almost insane engrossment with one woman, as I lay on my sickbed, imagining her in full health free of me, my powers of concentration now fixed upon her only, since their employment in my craft was now denied me by the mounting exigencies of my disease ("My imagination is horribly vivid about her—I see her—I hear her. There is nothing in the world of sufficient interest to direct me from her for a moment")—so I somehow put them all together, in my "vale of Soul-making," quite as romantic and bodily fevers had merged in

377

me, until I could not know where one left off and the other began.

For though he had earlier said that "A Poet is the most unpoetical of any thing in existence; because he has no identity" (at a time when, writing to his brother and sister-in-law in America, he said somewhat belittlingly of his sister: "Her character is not formed, her identity does not press upon me as yours does"), later he was to propose a "system of Spirit-creation" that he considered "a grander system of salvation than the chrystiain religion." And he went on to explain: "This is effected by three grand materials acting the one upon the other for a series of years. These three Materials are the *Intelligence*—the *human heart* (as distinguished from intelligence or Mind) and the *World* or *Elemental Space* suited for the proper action of *Mind* and *Heart* on each other for the purpose of forming the *Soul* or *Intelligence destined to possess the sense of Identity.*" (Incidentally note that, however roundabout, Keats has made his scheme closely analogous to the Christian Trinity after all. For "World or Elemental Space" would correspond to Power, "Intelligence" to Wisdom, "Human Heart" to Love—so in his recipe for "Identity" would be implicit the internal bearing of the three "persons" upon one another.)

One major strand, I'd say, was still to be supplied: the motive of empire. Poetry, "the Imagination," is not complete until it also somehow links with the norms of governance. Though the connection was definitely touched upon when Keats gave his recipe for the "imperial woman," and though Keats's discussions of ambition, and of doing "good" with his poems, also bore upon this motive, I think that the clearest reference to this strand in the motivational recipe came in a long passage Keats quoted from a statement by Hazlitt, in connection with an earlier essay on *Coriolanus*, in which Hazlitt had written: "The language of Poetry naturally falls in with the language of power."

Writing to his brother and sister-in-law in America, Keats quotes Hazlitt as saying, in altercation with an opponent:

> I affirm, Sir, that Poetry, that the imagination, generally speaking, delights in power, in strong excitement, as well as in truth, in good, in right, whereas pure reason

and the moral sense approve only of the true and the good. . . . We do read with pleasure of the ravages of a beast of prey, and we do so on the principle I have stated, namely from the sense of power abstracted from the sense of good. . . . Do you mean to deny that there is any thing imposing to the imagination in power, in grandeur, in outward shew, in the accumulation of individual wealth and luxury, at the expense of equal justice and the common weal? Do you deny that there is anything in the "Pride, Pomp, and Circumstance of glorious war, that makes ambition virtue!" in the eyes of admiring multitudes? . . . Is it a paradox of my creating that "one murder makes a villain, millions a Hero!" or is it not true that here, as in other cases, the enormity of the evil overpowers and makes a convert of the imagination by its very magnitude? . . .

Keats's comment on this passage (in all a very long one) had been: "The manner in which this is managed: the force and innate power with which it yeasts and works up itself—the feeling for the costume of society; is in a style of genius—He hath a demon, as he himself says of Lord Byron."

These pages were no mere retailing of literary gossip. Keats was quoting a writer to whose position he obviously subscribed. Twice he explicitly says that to him Hazlitt meant "depth of Taste."

I was particularly happy to observe how, in contrast with critical stupidities now current, the cult of passion, sensation, and imagination never led Keats to forget the notable element of *abstraction* in his calling: "This morning Poetry has conquered me—I have relapsed into those abstractions which are my only life." . . . A reference to himself as having "love of Beauty in the abstract." . . . "The mighty abstract Idea I have of Beauty in all things." . . . A reference to his "abstract careless and restless life." . . . He tells a friend that "any thing cold" in him should be attributed not to "heartlessness" but to "abstraction." . . . He writes amatively to Fanny Brawne: "Forgive me if I wander a little this evening, for I have been all day employ'd in a very abstr[a]ct Poem." . . . And when distinguishing between "imaginary woes" and "real ones," he observes that the imaginary ones are "conjured up by our passions," whereas the real ones "come of themselves, and are opposed by an abstract exertion of mind." . . . And among the lines quoted from Hazlitt is the passage: "We do read with pleasure of the ravages of a beast of prey, and we do so on the principle I have stated, namely from the sense of power abstracted from the sense of good."

Some months after the sore throats had set in, Keats writes: "My Thoughts are very frequently in a foreign Country—I live more out of England than in it." One might take these words purely as an expression of his romantic imagination. But near the end, this same Elsewhere Attitude has picked up an additional grim dimension. Thus, while still in quarantine, referring to the Port of Naples, he says: "it looks like a dream—every man who can row his boat and walk and talk seems a different being from myself. I do not feel in the world." And a month later: "I have an habitual feeling of my real life having passed, and that I am leading a posthumous existence."

Still speculating under the sign of "purplue" (or rather, of the synthesizing principle embodied there), I next think of a letter (July 25, 1819) where, in connection with his "swooning admiration" of Fanny Brawne's beauty, he makes a somewhat Wagnerian reference to the love-death pair: "I have two luxuries to brood over in my walks, your Loveliness and the hour of my death. O that I could have possession of them both in the same minute." The sentence gives me reason to believe that in the "Bright Star" sonnet, written during his trip to Italy, where he was soon to die, the disjunction of the closing line ("And so live ever—or else swoon to death") should be interpreted not on its face, but as two apparently quite different ways of saying the same thing, the moment of Keatsian languor conceived as permanently prolonged.

Previously, in fact, he had given what amounts to a poetic definition of his word "swoon":

The fifth canto of Dante pleases me more and more—
it is that one in which he meets with Paolo and Fran-
chesca—I had passed many days in rather a low state of
mind, and in the midst of them I dreamt of being in
that region of Hell. The dream was one of the most
delightful enjoyments I ever had in my life—I floated
about the whirling atmosphere as it is described with a
beautiful figure to whose lips mine were joined at [read:
as] it seem'd for an age—and in the midst of all this
cold and darkness I was warm—even flowery tree tops
sprung up and we rested on them sometimes with the
lightness of a cloud till the wind blew us away again—I
tried a Sonnet upon it—there are fourteen lines but
nothing of what I felt in it—O that I could dream it
every night—

> As Hermes once took to his feathers light
> When lulled Argus, baffled, swoon'd and slept. . . .

And so on. The makings of the "Bright Star" sonnet had figured
further, in that same letter of July, 1819. "I will imagine you Venus
to-night," he wrote, "and pray, pray, pray to your star like a
He[a]then." And when, in closing, he calls her "fair Star," I suddenly
seem to glimpse in the sonnet, and particularly in the opening line,
"Bright Star, would I were steadfast as thou art," a motivational
strand that may have been intensely there for the poet, though present only in the offing for his readers. In his transcendent way of getting union with a loved woman whose body his disease had denied
him (a union got in spirit by prayer-like communion with a star that
stood for her), does he not also make Fanny transcendently steadfast
whereas, in his tortured, ineffectual imaginings as an invalid, when
forbidden to concentrate upon his poetry, he could not keep himself
from concentrating instead on the possibility of Fanny Brawne's levity, beyond the powers of his jurisdiction?

And may he have succeeded, too, despite the illness that kept them apart, in circuitously carving his mark upon her? For I take the words "prie*st*li*k*e ta*sk*" to contain a pathetic enigma, the building blocks of his own name, "Keats"—the consonants acrostically scrambled (*st-k* and *t-sk*), the vowel-sound preserved in "priest"—and even the silent "a," if you will, that is sounded in "task."

When, quoting Ford's *'Tis Pity She's a Whore*, he writes, "I have endeavoured often 'to reason against the reasons of my Love,'" I think of a line (on the "reasoning" of love) I happen to have been reading recently in Dante on purgation: "*Amor che nella mente mi ragiona.*" And I would think of both these places when he says, "A Man's life of any worth is a continual allegory. . . . Shakespeare led a life of Allegory: his works are the comments on it." For I am coming to believe, more and more firmly, in the possibility that our lives cannot escape being "allegorical."

Think how readily, for instance, the materials of science can conceal the "allegory" of our motives behind pragmatic problems. A poet, let us say, writes of some icy region, and immediately we are warned: "Ha! Here is the imagery of frigidity. Let us look more closely, to see just how the discourse or 'reasoning' of self-willed castration figures here." But let that same man be an engineer who conceives of a practical device for improving the methods of preserving foods by refrigeration—whereat the symbolism retreats behind the obvious materiality of the practical problems to be solved here, and behind the publicly recognized utility of the results.

Or let a poet write of the moon, and by his very choice of subject he forewarns us that he may be lunatic. Yet the scientist, speculating on the conditions necessary for a lunar voyage by "space ship," may be so accurately involved in his planning that the "realism" of his solution deflects our attention from the essential "allegory" that prods him to the project in the first place.

Implicit in all mechanism there lies an enigmatic image—and its meaning is doubly hidden by the obvious materiality of the devices (with their material problems and correspondingly material solutions) in which the ultimate dream-like purpose is embodied. Thus we are trapped by our contraptions.

And in this sense, quite as Dante's view of ultimate motives, in the last canto of the *Paradiso*, terminates in such kind of folding-back-upon-the-self as can be figured (here where the idea of Faithful Love is *generalized* as highly as possible within the strict limits of *personalization*) in terms of the Virgin Mary as the Daughter of her own Son (*figlia del tuo figlio*—a realm where causes final and efficient merge), so man's worldly speculations about his worldly destiny must come to center in the self-entangling problems of Words About Words, which I would name reflexively as LOGOLOGY.

For there are things that on their face are symbols. And there are things that, though intrinsically non-symbolic, are by the human, symbol-using species infused as thoroughly with symbolism as all Creation is said by the religionist to be inspired with the Word of Heaven. And the sheer dialectics of the case is such that there can be nothing else.

We could dialectically dramatize it all by setting it up as a battle of Gallantry *vs.* Ecology, involving the nearly contradictory attempt by the use of symbols to see around the corner of symbols, into a reality purely and simply extra-symbolic. Out of this arise the shifting lines of battle between business and government, the aesthetic and the practical, commissars and engineers, priests and prophets—of Pope St. Guelph grievously at odds with Emperor Ghibelline the Great (the issue being further complicated by the fact that even our most "down to earth" ways of living are as inexorably ruled by "spellbinders" as are the realms of poetry—and the man of "hard, cold facts" differs from the speculative man mainly in having less occasion to realize how ridden by the "gallantry"—and corresponding meannesses—of speech he is). Do not the laws of "gallantry" inevitably make for a tragically prideful neglect of sheerly material motives, even while acting to make up for the insufficiency of sheerly material motives, which would literally bore the symbol-using animal to death?

As regards our first swim (in the Far South, with a light wind from the Farther South): The sea was as mellow as an over-ripe cantaloupe, which is my ideal of culture. The sea was so mild, I got scared. For just when I was prepared to battle, not the waves (for it was calm) but the cold, lo! I found myself feeling as though about to dissolve in luxury. It was less like swimming than like Death and Transfiguration. And I have become so demoralized, as regards my attempts to understand the purport of my symptoms, I found the relaxation frightening.

Where were we? "Gallantry" vs. "Ecology." Might not the principles of "Gallantry" make for a tragically prideful inability to live a life modestly befitting a human animal, which is to say, a life that would permit us to be truly gallant with regard to the "lowlier" species, too?

To think words by the seaside is like hearing music from a distance. (Even a trivial tune, floating at night across waters, seems a bit fate-laden.) It is to be reminded that, though we think by symbols, we live or die by the demands imposed upon us physiologically, ecologically, geophysically. Yet one goes avidly in quest of the question best designed to make his assertions look like an answer. We are a dismal breed, needing our glasses to find our glasses.

Put me, motivationally, under the sign of Ailments, Ecology, Geophysics, and Symbolism. Watching young Keats die, I join him in the name of Royal Purple, even as I wonder what might be the special etiology of my particular ills. I live by dodges, and so do my symptoms. Watching sunsets when shafts of golden sunlight shoot down from turbulent black and golden clouds, I would school the self to see these shafts as sheerly physically as possible.

I dote on thoughts of verse that would have but fragments of meaning, like shells the sea has pounded into bits. The nearness to nonsense might help accentuate the lines in their formality:

Entrance, with Fanfare

Hornswoggle thus, you and all others of like ilk—
Hear now the words of Silkentine, and be
Content with golden laudability.
Whom should we stand at, whom against, and whom?
Braving their selves throughout all Christen-doom,
Gulp down hard liquor with their mother's milk.

Start stopping-spot like any run-down rebel
The eighty-seven ways of sitting at a table.
(Bah! if the sea is restless, why in God's fair name
Should *they* feel justified to petition for sound slumber?
Consider me elsewhere . . .)

exit, trampling

The portion in parentheses would be spoken in an abrupt change
of rhythm, like a burst into petulant prose. This next should canter:

They're scattered 'cross the countryside
A long ways from the house.
So gather round the gadgets, girls,
And we'll all have tea.

The absence of a final rhyme in a quatrain so much like a jingle
should be experienced as outrageous. One critic suggests that
Mother Goose, in her archetypal perfection, may be as near as poets
qua poets ever get to Heaven. Poetry could not say something, while
remaining pure. Poetry can be pure only when it attains to the sheer
gestures and tonalities of itself, being statement but "in principle,"
Utterance in the Absolute, signifying sound and fury, full of nothing.
At the farthest reaches of the mind, there can be but the undirected
feel of language, going beyond doctrine to grammar, beyond verbs
to the paradigms of verbs, loving verse most for its bare prosody,
needing meaning only because by shades of meaning we increase the
subtlety and range of accents.

Meanwhile, I comb the beach for a wrench-like shape such as I
dreamed of in the hospital. If I could dream it, the sea can make it—
and having made it, the sea can toss it up.

Sincerely,

Herone L.

P. S. One night, our two cots pushed as snugly close as could be, I lay
awake listening to the bluster of the climate. The rain slapped loudly,
as it fell from the roof to the cement floor of the porch. Farther off,

the thrashing of the sea was more violent than usual. "Sea-Storm at Night," I thought, entitlingly. And tried some rhymes slightly deflected: "Sound of sea-dream yonder. The sea is roaring its own sea-monster. It would pound its own waves down under." The next day, cradling over a shoal in the bay, I dozed, while wavelets nudged against my moored rowboat.

P. P. S. To reach this front of sand-topped ridge, we drove over a sunny clop-clop bridge.

THREE EXERCISES

One-third insomnia
One-third art
One-third The Man
With the Cardiac Heart.
   KENNETH BURKE, "Know Thyself"

First Exercise for Year's End

December 31, MCM53

Like wires singing near a meadow, the new dawn rose, swelling silently towards full day, while tiny rivulets of light trickled with fragrance into all the nooks and crannies of the morning. Worms and little crushed insects began feeling glad in the bellies of birds. Insofar as was possible, darkness ceased pressing upon the surfaces of things. A soft motionless sliver of cloud was stretched in sharp suddenness across a slit in the otherwise uniform and brittle sky.

Already the Messenger was writing. Even in the pale dusk, he had begun—and he would still be at it when nature's rheostat of sunrise had been turned to full. He wrote:

> Sir:
> Since my last communication to you, Sir, new things have unfolded. Or at least, they seem to be unfolding. There are signs of some loss of faith in public promises, though the general sluggishness in the buying of baubles may indicate not so much a loss of faith in them as a drop in the means of testifying to such faith.
> Some students (still no alarming number) have re-fused to be hazed in the normal manner. The churches are being stirred by an influx of new converts that bring turbulence and controversy into a realm heretofore

389

quiescent. It was necessary that a certain impudent slave be put to death; having been commanded to fan the king, he was found to have added a secret contrivance whereby he also fanned himself. And it is rumored that there is unrest among the Lesbians, who are flocking about a stupendous Amazon-like Leader, or rather Leaderess, they call "Saint Lemming."

By now the petals of the day had almost fully opened. Indeed, some showed signs of loosening, as though they would drop before too many hours had been invisibly frozen in the warming sunlight. The Messenger continued:

In accordance with my instructions, Sir, I have sought for opportunities to meet people as it were by chance, addressing them as though confidentially, in the hopes that, by seeming to confide in them, I might bring them to confide in me, and thus to reveal whatever might be forming. Yet among wide ranges of the populace, there seems to be, rather, a race towards absolute nothingness. It is as though, to guard against the suspicion of dangerous thoughts, the people were learning to have no thoughts at all. And I find it very difficult to read the signs, when secrecy has become thus doubly self-protective, by not even letting itself know its own mind. But I do begin to glimpse a possible method, as in the case of the following incident:

Recently, in a public place, a weak and ineffectual fellow, naturally loose-tongued but made even more so by drinking, offered up a riotous jingle about a commoner who took liberties with one of the Queen's maids in waiting. And I would consider the likelihood that the thought of taking liberties with the Queen's maid really signified the thought of taking liberties with the Queen; while the thought of thus encroaching upon the Queen signified in turn the thought of dishonoring the King, but with one notable distinction: That whereas such an implicit reference to the Queen might indicate a purely lubricitous imagining, the thought of taking liberties with the King might rather signify a civic stirring. I cannot at this time be certain. But I am looking into this possibility with the patience and caution you have taught us to exemplify in our ministry to you.

The Messenger wrote more in this rich vein, until it came time for him to have his morning orange juice, and soon thereafter happily to undergo, with his usual regularity, his body's major unburdening for the day. So let us leave him to his gracious tasks and solemn enjoyments, while we turn aside, to raise our voices in exaltation and exulting:

Incipit vita nova, we exclaim. *The new begins all over. Begins all over where? Begins all over again.*

See how song touches all in pleasant painfulness, with its tasty odors. O lovely Garden of Pure Confusion. O Paradisaic Tower of Babelization. O Fall into Eden.

True, Good, and Useful Beauty—all hail to thy Circling Four-fold Three-ness.

Second Exercise for Year's End

December 31, MCM54

. . . something that you're going to be amazed how true it is . . . something like clear sunlight maybe, slanting on crystal twigs, of a frosty morning, and after a dream of being snubbed by waiters. It was planned for midnight of a yearsend. Year-send? what sort of mission is that?

> Fall: I put 'em up. Who'll take 'em down?
> Spring: I take 'em down. Who'll put 'em up?
> O Bitter Recurrent Riddle of Storm-Windows.

You are a-guilt with hopes of preferment? You are a-grovel with undone self-love? That sinfulness you feel? Nonsense! It's but a body-odor or bad breath your friends won't tell you about—and they'll stop avoiding you, if you but buy the right bottle. Buy-o buy-o baby, on the installment plan.

The more he saw how things were shaping, the more he 'gan fershtay how the split between bourgeois and Bohemian arose in the first place. Byron, all is forgiven; but how did you get that passport? Back, back, back to *La Bohème* (with a difference)! Running around in circles, in flight from the wheels of technology. Confessing confusion at fission and fusion. (O fatal acrostic: nuclear, unclear. And in the custody of killers?)

> Think how with all of whom I'm out of step with,
> Think how of all the sleepless nights I've slep with!
> How many bats are need to fill a steeple?
> What makes me be such very awful people?
>> Out of star-born into war-worn,
>> Into the flat-tire of satire . . .

The questionnaire asked, in effect: "What sort of person are you?" Well, he happened to be the sort that's against answering questionnaires—but within the conditions of the contest, how could he say so? Let's start a Guild of the Bureaucratically Guilty, its members pledged always to answer these things wrongly, but never to admit membership. That's at least one thing could be cleared up.

All hail to the Three Great Modern Isms:

Bureaucratism, and its counterpart, Cultural Toadying.

Bohemianism, the only *remedy* for Bureaucratism. (We say *remedy*, since there is no known *cure*.) Hard-pressed, crowded into one odd corner of the mind—Walt Whitman with a crying jag.

And third, running back and forth between Bureaucratism and Bohemianism, and arising in response to the general turn from Quest to Inquest: Informism.

O—right up out of from inside way down in under, I had those take-me-way-down-back-down-somewhere-or-other blues. Everywhere was loaded with things that would delight an imbecile, things to put around a Christmas tree for babies. And might we should establish a govt. bureau to keep stars from shooting out of season—then, with less unsafety, we could hang out our supermannish satellite, the mooniest moon.

> My country,
> Why be greatly famed for kill-stuff?
> My country, harshly by the news begoaded,
> Yankee (awake, and to thyself), come home.

Envoi

I met a man who said: "We were climbing a steep hill. But just as we neared the ridge along the top, we paused to rest. While resting, we might have let our vision sweep across the broad valley that lay below us. But instead, though keeping the valley's presence so strongly in the mind's eye that we could almost literally see it, we gazed towards the ridge above and beyond us. And even as we watched, of a sudden there rose from the other side (which we had never seen!) the magnificently upright heads of a buck and his several does. We should have a word for that experience, in exactly that order."

He talked of a broad, horizonless lake, its water absolutely still, but with a gently sloping surface. "Limpid moveless water," he explained, "tilted slightly sideways. And when it freezes, O the ecstasy of skating from the upper end."

He explained how, without the slightest need for propulsion by one's own efforts, by merely holding the body in a fixed but comfortable position, one could go faster and faster and ever faster—for the lake extends forever, somehow circling back upon itself at every moment, whereby the skater need not strive again for starts. "O come skate with me," he said, "on the gently sloping lake."

He said, "We stand at the doorth of the year" (as though "door" were a verb, and he made a noun from the verb form, "dooreth," as with "warmth" from "warmeth," and "width" from "wideth," and "coolth" from "cooleth"). Thus, in his way, when thinking of year's end (the entrance to two-faced January) he spoke of "the doorth of the year." "Come, O come with me," he pled, "at the doorth of the year, to skate forever on the gently sloping, firmly frozen lake." And somehow placed a precious burden on my heart.

But, "No!" I de-reflectively answered. "I'd like to let me linger yet awhile, whatever it may be my personal mooneth." Even now, at midnight, I await the beckoning morneth, when the sun comes uppeth, when the pink sun edges flatly above the skyline, comes up as bright and clean as a brand new dollar, as rash as a blast of unexpected music . . .

On Creative Dying

An Exercise

To speak at all is to be a tiny frog with a big voice. And if a frog can believe in himself—as he apparently does when twanging his fiddle in the marshlands—why not I? The difference is that the frog knows nothing of the news. Yet how can man know no news?

> Always that thought pursues:
> "How can man know no news?"

Poetry having been invented long before journalism, the ancient bards shrewdly became the first newsmen. In their travels they brought timely tidings (astutely edited) to exchange for bed and board. Then gradually things piled up, until now there's so much organized information assailing us, from all quarters, about human jeopardy in the large, how have they the effrontery to be any less impersonal than a tabloid headline?

> THREE KILLED
> IN CRIME WAVE

it said, thereby implying that those three particular endings were important mainly by reason of their place in a trend.

(I got a place in a trend. I'm better than him. My Ism is better than his Ism. True, I weep my heart out. But I'll glow like a blowedon coal if you tell me I wept well. And anyhow, any mood, no matter how fleeting, is in its way pretty damned eternal, at least as long as there are people around. I got a place in a trend. You got a place in a trend. All God's children got a place in a trend. When I get to heaven I'm goin' to take out my place in a trend, I'm goin' to trundle all over God's heaven.)

Maybe the problem is along these lines: Particularly in this run-down post-Whitman era, few can versifyingly CONFESS in ways that build up the Poetic Image (to match the bureaucratic need for a National Image such as might be dreamed up by an expert Public Relations Counsel). Indications are that poets will fare best if their offerings are Plush, in a quasi-democratic sorta way. I hate, I hate, I hate. (Kill, kill, kill, kill, kill.)

Here is an Early Memory (not too early). It concerned a story about traveling across a desert. If the thirsting man came to a crystal-clear waterhole, he knew to shove on, sans to touch a drop. But if it was mucky and slimy, he knew that here was a liquid he could sop up in confidence. The glass-like clear one should be avoided, because it was poison, pure alkali. The mucky one was safe because, if all that other stuff could thrive there, then surely the human organism might commune with its nature. Think of that story as a PARABLE, when you buy modernique "processed" fruits and vegetables. Are they perhaps sans blemish simply because they are loaded with pesticides? A self-respecting worm would not be found in such a joint? Demand a runty, scaly, disfigured apple.

(How build up a viable Poetic Image, unless we can get togidda in avowing: Not one single apple, though it came from the Garden of Eden, unless it has scales and worms and general health-giving discoloration—in defiance of modernique sales promotion?)

This note came in, from a correspondent who was trying to reduce, and who, as regards modernique modes of obliteration, was disgrunt:

> Our physicists are wonders all
> And the bomb they made is a heller.
> If only instead

Their prowess had led
To inventing a no-cal alcohol
I believe I could even stand Teller.

And who would deny that that's quite a lot of standing?

A decent man's job is, among other things, to grieve for his particular country's imperialism. He should leave it for the decent citizens of other countries to grieve for theirs. Guard against the goad to be self-righteous by being one's foreign neighbor's conscience's keeper.

Don't put your money in a hole in the ground. Put it in a savings bank where, if our politicians can contrive to keep things pretty much as they are, your sums will earn in interest just about the amt. you lose annually by Creeping Capitalist Inflation. The savings bank can use your deposits to make profits in ways that help cause this same inflation. But, like a good mediævalist, you won't be guilty of usury (*nummus nummum non parit*). Yet you won't lose out cruelly as though, like a mediæval miser, you had put your money in a hole in the ground. For that sorta thing had to do with when the tiny hoard was, like silence, *golden*.

I know what gives. Things filter down to the Great Three Stages at the basis of all human culture: (Latin) *puer, vir, senex*; (Greek) *pais, anēr, gerōn*. That is to say, from child to man to oldster—the first stage too young to bear arms, the second arms-bearing (plus all the qualifications and reservations!), the third blessedly too old. (I ptikly admired the attitude of a bright lad who, enrolled in training for the kill, loved to prove himself a good marksman in the absolute, while not even wanting to shoot a woodchuck. He was sorry for any poor duffers trying to make an honest living.)

Another correspondent sent in anonymously this disturbing statement (we tried hurriedly to locate him, but Intelligence fell down):

I killed him while he sat at the piano. He died with his foot on the pedal, a shriek continuing for some time after. And the memory of the echo is still quick within me.

Yes, Intelligence fell down. The Poet's Image was slipping. He had
no plush-carpet sentiments to encourage govt.-subsidized distribu-
tion overseas. Sans Eleganz. The best he might hope for was to be an
arrested adolescent who managed not to get arrested. He kept thinking of the rich woman, who threw the leftover roast into the garbage.
(The rich bitch, who kept her husband slaving to keep up.) He liked
the idea of honeysuckle by the outhouse (suggesting as it did the nearness of motives sexual and fecal). And he despaired of the clean-cut,
riding smooth-shod over sales resistance. Their spoiled brats would
be like horses in a barn, eating all you'd give them, and doing nothing useful but shit.

"Scat! Cats! I've never met an ILGWU, no, not one." Yet he must
have had a hangover. For the windshield wiper kept flicking "Strep
throat—strep throat." And when the wife said "messy edges,"

"Messy edges" rang like "Snookie Ookums"—
And "Snookie Ookums" just like "Essie Omo"—
behind the which disguise
there lurked a girl now possibly in heaven
whom he had known explorer-wise
when he was circa ætat. seven.

I would not fight with whom. I would not, nor for anything, how
that the day be sweet. If I were gracile enough, I'd do an ironic idyll
about a milkmaid with milkpail and Geiger counter. Or a conceit
about Sebastian, the patron saint of fairies, pierced placidly with
arrows. Or about a pious penniless poet who named his children Iamb,
Trochee, Dactyl, Anapæst, and Spondee, since they were all born of
Rhythm. I'd keep on the go. To the best of my ability, all would be
hit and run in the transport department. I'd aver as to how, in all
decency, an undertaker should not violate a corpse, lest he lose his
license. And I've never met an ILGWU, in either day nor night.
Scat! Cats! And may God give us a good groove in which to grovel.
I once heard tell of an Oriental potentate who, obsessed by fantasies
of *vagina dentata*, on the advice of the court magician was cured by
having all his concubines' teeth pulled. He put his money in a Swiss

bank, since the Swiss had been FREE for one hell of a long time. And now he's on the Riviera, all set to stay cleared out for good, as soon as Western subsidies can't any longer stave off that much-needed revolution back home.

Quick! Close the windows. The lovely quickie storm has let loose upon us. Let loose in ways compulsive to be pious. (Afterwards I looked up,/ and there was that/ poor old/ run-down/ chopped-up/ but still there/ third-quarter/ Moon.) Pray think of me as a friendly fellow who would make you feel at home by just sittn around complainin about being bequeathed by the centuries an almost irresistible need to be a failure. (How believe in the saga "from canal boy to President" when there are so few canals?)

What's it all about? I'll tell you. I had thought of looking up a place I'd been forty years ago. I didn't know why, except that, when I was there then, I was more itchy with a Sense of the Unfulfilled than a dirty dog has fleas. So I said let's go back and see what the hell. That's not much of an Image. But it's a scientific fack, involving puzzles about occupations and destinations.

What if it turned out that one's occupation
Was but to have a wavering destination
To each day keep on going on renewing
Whatever it befell one to be doing?

We went by car, the wife and I (she putting up with this damned nonsense, while we drove and drove).

As for the light that might explain,
Oh, do you have the lamp, sir?
This morning we were north in Maine
We're now in south New Hampshire.

We're here all set up for the night
In a model motel, the price was right.
And at no extra cost
We found what was not lost:

399

A sickly sickle of a moon
The merest silver slither
That makes one ask oneself too soon
Where go from whence to whither?
(Feeling the need to be elegiast
He had gone forth to check up on his past.
But lest it all bewitch him
He took the missus with him.)

Lines written in a motel in New England in late August.

I heard the pigeons cooing
And on the principle of *lucus a non lucendo*
I thought of mine enemies.
But my bleat having bled
I shall back to bed
(Having taken a good slug
Of the inspissate incipience of alcohol).

Interlude

Notes on a Picture in Progress—

with regard to the trip, say how, again and again, going around a bend in the road, coming upon a vista . . . then, near the end of the trip, stopping to visit a painter friend . . . coming into his studio . . . there, begad, there was the truly startling vista . . . on that massive canvas, only a few feet square . . . the rock, not meant to seem enormous as regards the imitation of sheer size . . . but enormous in its emphatic thereness . . . like a great growth . . . a cross between a rock and an imaginary flower? . . . maybe a kind of signature? . . .

and the many disparate birds, in all sorts of momentarily summational postures . . . the silent, motionless flutter-buzz . . . (action-painting is all to the good . . . but why not, like this, use all the resources natural to painting? . . . why not?)

aside: on the history outside the painting . . . drawings that trace successive transformations of the rock, from a squat, oblonguish thing lying on its side, into an upwardness, a mounting like a mountain . . . or the preparatory sketches for other items, each with corresponding modifications, and bits ultimately selected . . . including tentative strategic plans for the action as a whole . . .

above all, the history inside the painting . . . for instance, a broken tree stump, and the fitting of it rhythmically to the climbing of the rock . . . the undulant snow . . . and the human comedy of the birds . . . yet what could have happened to them? . . . they are in transit from where to where? . . .

alighting . . . standing still or turning around . . . being glum, or alert, or in sundry other ways preoccupied . . . beginnings, turnings, subsidences . . . many birds, they seemed like many more . . . a thesaurus of postures . . . an invasion of disparateness . . . the twitter of many unrelated bird-notes . . . embodying a principle of fragmentation, to play off against undulances and solidities . . . yet not like fragments of a thing broken, for each was a totality . . . yet are they not the fragmentation of a flock? . . . for whereas we think of a flock as all one, we here thought of many disparate ones, each in an attitude of its own, each at some different moment of fulfillment . . . (am I remembering wrong? or was not each oblivious of the others, wholly wrapped up within itself?) . . .

Let's see, how many elements in all? . . . first, startlingly, suddenly, as you walk into the room: the rock . . . all about it, the worry of the birds variously busy . . . the wave-like snow, with small bits of rock jutting forth here and there, doubtless a thematic transition between the birds and The Rock . . . a broken tree that has three distinct moments: (1) its toppled top (2) still connected with a bristling stump (3) by some tough, sinewy strands of the trunk. (Your eye keeps connecting back and forth along the strain of that sinew. That's major.) . . . and sky—though at this stage it escapes me . . . the treetop is subtilized by what I'd call the "principle of ramification" (here got literally by the tree's lean branches) . . . and I'd want to see this as another kind of transition into the birds as a "principle of fragmentation" (though conveyed not by breakage but by the clutter—or convocation—of individual birds) . . . I keep tinkering with some vague "terministic" kinship between "fragmentation" and "ramification."

401

Having looked at all sorts of horizons for several days, coming around bends in the road, I entered the room—and suddenly I saw not "out there," but IN. (Maybe this accidental contrast explains why I'm vague about the sky) . . . despite the almost documentary accurateness of the *things*, despite the ample evidence, both in the painting and in the preparatory drawings, that every stroke of the brush, while calligraphic, was also weighed against the objectivity of the object, here was an opening of another sort, an opening INWARD. It had to do with that keen paradox whereby, the more scrupulous the observations "out there," the more likely the disclosures are to betoken an *intrinsic* lurking . . . Realism, sub, super, intra . . .

Notes on a painting by Pierre Fleur, Rock Flower, Peter Blume . . . that was a glowing interlude—that which I saw that time, though not coming around a bend . . . yet it keeps on being there suddenly . . .

End of Interlude

Where were we? I was talking of a trip, vaguely in search of a vista, but with sights along the way. "Why hang on and on, like a chronic illness?" I asked in effect. "The glancing blow." . . . "Be by twinges." . . . "Call it pound, call it ounce—or pounce." . . . "Or in terms of transport, hit-and-run." . . . But what do about Image Trouble? Find somehow the sort of Poetic Selph competent to deal appropriately with governors of states who encourage the sort of thing that leads to the bombing of little children at Sunday school? Or else have no Poetic Selph at all—just Image Trouble? Or relegate some utterances to prose, some to verse, each assigned to a different aspect of the personality? My bleat having bled, I shall back to bed.

SOMATICS

After forty, it's patch, patch, patch.

—OLD SURGICAL SAW

Though it but sits and thinks
Even then it's shoddy.
How might I fool this jinx,
My unheroic body?

Publisher's Note

Here & Elsewhere is the most inclusive collection of Kenneth Burke's fiction ever published. It reprints the text of the revised 1966 edition of *Towards a Better Life*, Burke's novel of 1932. It also reprints the texts of the nineteen stories gathered in *The Complete White Oxen* (1968), the revised and expanded edition of Burke's collection *The White Oxen and Other Stories* (1924). Four further pieces round out the book, the previously uncollected "Parabolic Tale" (from *The Sansculotte*, January 1917) and three prose "exercises" (from Burke's *Collected Poems*, 1968).

The title of the book is of Burke's own coinage, and dates back to 1924. In his preface to *The Complete White Oxen*, Burke asks the reader's indulgence while he voices an abiding regret: "The title I had chosen for the original [*White Oxen*] was *Here and Elsewhere*. I was talked out of it, but I wish that I had kept it. Yet I don't feel I should make the change now thus belatedly." We hope that, had we been able to consult him in the matter, he would have happily consented to our use of the title for this edition of his collected fiction.

TOWARDS A BETTER LIFE

Burke began his only novel when he was in his late twenties. It was written mainly in Andover, New Jersey, in a small house in the country that he purchased in 1922 and in which he lived for most of the rest of his life. *Towards a Better Life* was published by Harcourt, Brace & Company, New York, in 1932, when he was thirty-four.

The first ten of its eighteen chapters appeared serially before publi-

cation—and in the same order Burke gave them in the finished book
—in *The Dial* (August, October, and November 1928; January, March,
and May 1929), *The Hound & Horn* (Fall 1929, Winter 1929–30, and
Spring 1930), and *Pagany* (Fall 1930). Their periodical titles were "A
Declamation," "Second Declamation," "Third Declamation," and so on.

When the "Seventh Declamation" appeared in *The Hound & Horn*,
Burke prefaced it with the following note:

The preceding six of these Declamations appeared in *The Dial*.
They, and whatever others may finally be issued, are meant to
possess each a certain validity independent of their fellows, while
forming a sequence which should provide added interpretation
by its order. The Declamations are a kind of fictive moralizing,
wherein the dogmas are prior to the events, though not always to
be read as absolutely as they are stated.

The scheme, when working most effectively, should result in
the writer's associating a code with its origins, and in the reader's
glimpsing a situation behind a morality. Yet perhaps our sincerity is less a question of message than of manner.

This manner is not wholly pliant. At times it has compelled
circumlocution. We assumed that reality can arise out of any convention; and if we were wrong in this assumption, the aesthetic
of the Declamations is fundamentally imperiled. For in their
attempt to provide a literary, rather than a vicarious, experience
they embody a deliberate pompousness which is unpardonable
unless pompousness is not necessarily bad.

The Declamations originally took shape as an objective, realistic novel. The material is finally given in a different form
because I could not write it as I at first planned. The problem of
moving a character from one room to another became sufficiently difficult to make narrative impossible. Thus the present
method arose as a subterfuge, an avoidance.

The earlier Declamations deal with our protagonist's somewhat self-inflicted undoing and flight. He is a very frank, a very
earnest, a very conscientious man, in whom one need place slight
confidence. He has an enquiring mind, through failure assisted

to focus itself upon the norms of conduct. He is writing to a certain Anthony, whom he considers privileged. Being not letters, but epistles, his Declamations remain unsent. He has left Anthony in full possession and enjoyment of a young woman, Florence, whom he also considers privileged. He believes in the justice of their union, though at great discomfiture to himself. In proclaiming criteria and imperatives, with the garrulity of envy he allows his reminiscences to encroach upon his aphorisms.

The Declamations may eventually be assembled under the title *Towards a Better Life—Being the Statement of an Attitude*. I have also considered such titles as *Manifesto*, and *Testament*. They are here mentioned for their possible value as an indication of purpose.

Certain phrases from this note made their way into Burke's preface to the first edition of *Towards a Better Life*.

In 1965, Burke revised the novel for republication by the University of California Press, Berkeley and Los Angeles; it was brought out the following year, when he was sixty-eight. For this edition Burke wrote a second preface, which combines with the earlier one into a memorable statement of the book's formal models and rhetorical strategies. A further statement, published as the jacket-flap copy of the California edition, supplements the prefaces:

Kenneth Burke says of his novel: "Clearly, it is part of the 'negativistic' movement typical of our times, in which so many of man's greatest rational inventions somehow seem to keep turning up with drastically irrational results (almost as though we were deliberately trying both to go crazy and not to go crazy). It can be read as the ironic portrait of a self-chosen victim who was 'captain of his soul' in the sense that his misfortunes were largely those of his own making. It can be read as an attempt to improvise a realm of ritual even while recognizing that any such rites will necessarily go askew. Above all, it can be read in the light of an uneasy, ambiguous relationship between the motives of tragedy and of comedy.

"In essence, the book is a kind of '*grotesque* tragedy.' Yet the grotesque itself might be defined as a kind of 'comedy without laughter'—and many of the protagonist's situations are comic thus twistedly. But such discordant elements fall together clearly enough if we see in the *book a ritual of rebirth* (the paradoxical use of *grotesquely tragic* devices to solemnize the emergence of *comedy* as a 'doctrine'). Thus the story ends fittingly at the moment of darkness before dawn, when the promise of a 'new life' is both foretold and held in problematic abeyance: 'The sword of discovery goes before the couch of laughter. One sneers by the modifying of a snarl; one smiles by the modifying of a sneer. You should have lived twice, and smiled the second time.'"

TWENTY STORIES

By 1928, when the first chapter of what would become *Towards a Better Life* appeared in *The Dial*, Burke had been writing short stories for more than a decade. In 1924, fifteen of these were collected in his first book, *The White Oxen and Other Stories*, published by Albert & Charles Boni, New York.

The book opened with the previously unpublished title story, a draft of which was making rounds among the editors of avant-garde magazines as early as the spring of 1918. "The White Oxen" was followed by revised versions of "The Excursion" (*The Dial*, July 1920), "Mrs. Maecenas" (*The Dial*, March 1920), "Olympians" (*Manuscripts*, February 1922), "Scherzando" (also *Manuscripts*, February 1922), "Portrait of an Arrived Critic" (*The Dial*, April 1922), "David Wassermann" (*The Little Review*, Autumn 1921), "After Hours" (*S4N*, November 1922), "My Dear Mrs. Wurtelbach" (*Broom*, January 1923), "The Death of Tragedy" (*The Little Review*, Autumn 1922), "The Book of Yul" (*Secession*, July 1922), "A Progression" (*Secession*, Winter 1923–24), "In Quest of Olympus" (*Secession*, January 1923), "First Pastoral" (*Secession*, August 1922), and "Prince Llan" (*Broom*, January 1924).

Burke prefaced the collection with a quotation, in Latin, from the introduction to Martial's epigrams; loosely translated, it reads "I would ask you to excuse the playful candor of my words if I were setting the example, but Catullus writes this way, and Marsus, and Pedo, and

Getulicus, and everyone else who can be read all the way through." Burke also supplied the following Author's Note:

> With the exception of "The White Oxen," these stories have appeared in *Broom, The Dial, The Little Review, Manuscripts, Secession,* and *S4N.* They are arranged approximately in the order of their completion, and represent, it seems to me, a certain progression of method. In stressing one aesthetic method, we lose others. I see these stories as a gradual shifting of stress away from the realistically convincing and true-to-life, while there is a corresponding increase of stress upon the more rhetorical properties of letters. It is a great privilege to do this in an age when rhetoric is so universally despised.

In 1968, the University of California Press issued a second edition of *The White Oxen,* in which Burke added four further stories to the original set of fifteen: "A Man of Forethought" (*The Smart Set,* May 1919), "The Soul of Kajn Tafha" (*The Dial,* July 1920), "Metamorphoses of Venus" (the magazine *1924,* October 1924), and the much later "Anaesthetic Revelation of Herone Liddell" (*The Kenyon Review,* Autumn 1957). The contents of this volume, too, were arranged "approximately in the order of their completion," and the present book reprints them in the order Burke gave them, with the fugitive "Parabolic Tale" inserted between the first and second stories.

In his preface to *The Complete White Oxen,* Burke picks up where his previous preface left off:

> In an Author's Note to the earlier *White Oxen,* I observed that the sequence of the stories embodies a gradual "increase of stress upon the more rhetorical properties of letters." And with more defiance than assurance, I proclaimed it a "great privilege" to take such a turn "in an age when rhetoric is so universally despised."
>
> "Rhetoric" can have many different meanings. I mainly had in mind an interest in formal and stylistic twists as such, along with their entanglements in character and plot.

Consider, for instance, "The Book of Yul." The story was built around a dream so obsessive that I even tried to make a melody in keeping with it. And despite my tragic helplessness in draftsmanship, I attempted some relevant illustrations. As I see it now, de Chirico could have done for me the sort of mausoleum city I had in mind, if he had put in a wraithlike throng here and there.

But my point is: Along with the compulsiveness of this "content," I was much concerned with what I viewed as a "rhetorical" element. Thus, the first paragraph is conceived as "annunciatory," and sums up the tenor of the story as a whole. In its role as a *beginning*, it begins with the words "While waiting"—and the whole first section is set up in terms of *expectation*. In the course of it, the words "thump" and "scrape" are present in one sense—but they contain an ambiguous dimension that will be revealed when they reappear later in the story. (Only much later was I able to discern how superbly Father Aeschylus had anticipated such intentions, not only in his general feeling for the formality implicit in a plot, but also in his specific way of *beginning* his great trilogy on the very *theme* of expectation.)

Burke continues his preface with "a few additional backward-looking pages"—a mix of reminiscence, literary gossip, and glosses on the individual stories:

[In "The White Oxen,"] the character of Gabriel Harding probably should have been treated without any "inside" knowledge of his motives. Then the sexually ambiguous implications of his role could have been clearer.

The "Man of Forethought" item belonged in *The Smart Set.* And though it is smart in a way that makes me smart a bit, after much hesitation I decided that it should be included. The editors who took that one came close to accepting the much better story "Mrs. Maecenas." But I later found good cause to be grateful for its rejection, since its acceptance by *The Dial* marked the entrance of that magazine into my life—and for me that was almost as momentous a moment as the act, or accident, of being born.

"Mrs. Maecenas" was obviously influenced by some early work of Thomas Mann [which Burke translated for *The Dial* and for Alfred A. Knopf], as well as by Mencken-and-Nathan's enterprise (which had been an adventurous guide for us during our years at high school). The story reflected Mann's gallant error, in the excessive imputing of virtues to the average citizen. Quite a time was to elapse before I began to suspect that Mann's bourgeois-Bohemian dichotomy, for all its twists, too simply divided the realms of the "neurotic" from the "normal." For instance, you are not likely to find many on the "Bohemian" side of the antithesis falling into line with militaristic trends which the average citizen is so prone to equate with love of country. Or consider the typical prowess of TV commercials, in peddling poisons or arousing absurd fears and appetites, on a national scale.

"My Dear Mrs. Wurtelbach" marks a kind of turning point. Here I was trying to work out a form that would proceed somewhat like the movements of a symphony, with qualitative breaks from one part to the next (as though each were on a different "level"), rather than embodying the kind of continuity "natural" to conventional narrative. While planning the piece, I proposed a bet with Malcolm Cowley [then an aspiring poet and an editor at the little magazines *Broom* and *Secession*]. Both of us feeling glum about the literary situation, I proposed to make a bet with him that I could turn up with something formally different from the average. But not only was he to be assigned the role of betting that it couldn't be done, he was also to be sole judge of whether the project worked.

The bet was for $10, which was a lot. Cowley agreed—and later he graciously judged that I had won (but only with the added stipulation that I should not try to collect the ten dollars). From then on, I kept experimenting with that disjointed kind of form which [at least one reviewer] condemned as sheer insensitivity to form (though in subsequent years the experimental "sophisticating" of form has taken so many new turns, my attempts at innovation must seem by comparison almost as neoclassical as a drama by Racine).

The notion of different "levels" comes clearest in "In Quest of Olympus," with its succession of Up and Downward Ways, the final *apparent ascent* actually being (though I did not realize this fact at the time when I wrote the story) an *enigmatic descent*. The ambiguity is discussed on pages 334 to 338 of the essay "The Thinking of the Body," in my book *Language as Symbolic Action* [1966].

Looking back now on the whole succession of "peripeties," I'd characterize (or rationalize?) the structure thus:

(1) Birth, symbolized as climbing out of a cavern;

(2) "Break-away" stage of adolescence, as the protagonist becomes magnified by the chopping down of a (parental) tree, with corresponding ascent;

(3) The protagonist (whose new identity is marked by his forcefully acquired change of name) confronts ambiguities of sex in terms of "pre-forensic" or "magical" conflicts among nature-gods that stand for a psychology, a cluster of discordant motives;

(4) "Descent" (via a dreamer's onanistic spill?) into a quotidian world of social criticism, here presented in terms of low-visioned sexual dalliance, under the sign of dirty dishes in the kitchen sink;

(5) Compensatory ascent, in terms of grand natural processes (the incident of the earlier "nature-gods" now being transformed into a poem that embodies a cult of nature as honestly and piously edified as the author could make it);

(6) Said compensatory exhilaration proves unstable, as indicated by the fact that a brief silhouette of perfect bliss in Heaven is burlesqued, albeit with a touch of nostalgia;

(7) Christ's descent into the dirty everyday world, treated vindictively, in terms of social criticism;

(8) Christ's culminative ascension, a return to the womb that is ambiguously, or enigmatically, cloacal, as discussed in the pages mentioned above.

"Prince Llan" turned out to be *au fond* a kind of psychic bookkeeping, a split into two selves, one grown up, though problematically (the "Prince"), the other (Gudruff) representing the vestiges of problematical adolescence, here treated as a separate person who calls the "Prince" to regression. The would-be resolution (Joseph) but re-enacts Gudruff's reflexive cult of sensation on a "higher" level, as suicide. The whole is but decorative, a "masque"; yet in its nature as a doodle it does symbolize a basic pattern of the mind (that was to take a more serious, or even urgent, turn in my novel, *Towards a Better Life*). I have since seen the imagery of infinite doors (one opening, to disclose another; this second opening, to disclose a third, etc.) utilized in a motion picture to represent a mental patient's profound malaise. And the principle of fragmentation turns up under many conditions. For instance, when discussing the fragmentation of the statuary in Peter Blume's exceptionally radical painting *The Eternal City* (see "Growth Among the Ruins," in my *Philosophy of Literary Form* [1941]), I try to bring out the transitional potentialities of this device. Or consider the observations of the Cambridge literary anthropologists on the "rending and tearing," or *sparagmos*, of rituals that led into Greek tragedy. But though I can find the pattern operating elsewhere in my own works (for instance, the last chapter of *Towards a Better Life*, or the middle section, on "perspective by incongruity," in *Permanence and Change* [1935]), its use at the end of "Prince Llan" owes much to a suggestion by Malcolm Cowley. . . .

As regards the last story, "The Anaesthetic Revelation of Herone Liddell,"* which was written many years after any of the others: I have always had a fondness for what the Germans call an *Erziehungsroman* (the Goethean mixture of *Wahrheit* and *Dichtung*, or the dialectic of Mann's *Magic Mountain*, or the moody treatment of ideas in Walter Pater's *Marius the Epicurean*; a grand variant, which I came upon late, is Hermann Hesse's *Glass Bead Game*). I tried a departure in my novel, which was designed gradually to extricate a plot out of aphorism. And my

* In case anyone is interested, I would pronounce the name thus: "Herone" is a two-syllable word with the accent slightly on the second syllable. The accent in "Liddell" is strongly on the second syllable.

last story in this book is somewhat in the same mode. In fact, there is a sense in which it could be classed as a kind of sequel to the novel, for as the earlier "declamations" courted an affliction, so this "revelation" involves a wan cult of recovery. Thus, when the novel was republished, I somewhat inclined to include the "Anaesthetic Revelation" in the same volume. The "schematism" (to use a deliberately unwieldy word) lines up thus:

(1) The underlying situation: the compelling immediacy of Liddell's *physical* suffering;

(2) Thoughts on the attendant, non-physical realm of symbolism;

(3) Relations between the two realms—culminating in the "gallantry" of symbolism with regard to dealings between male and female alimentary canals (with emergence of a valetudinarian purpose: to the South, and to the Sea);

(4) Wherein the physicality of recovery by a southern sea builds atop the symbolism of the scapegoat (as Liddell, while nursing his sensations, meditates curatively on the dying of a great poet).

I cannot argue as to whether or not such things *should* go on. All I am saying is that, in this story, they *do* go on. And one might get the point I'm trying to make here by contrasting Liddell's thoughts with the out-and-out fictive account of Brother Angelik's speculations on faith and knowledge in "First Pastoral" (I did not realize at the time that in his bargain he actually "tempts God," thereby personally deserving the fate already determined by the nature of things), or the narrator's ill-tempered theories, in "A Progression," about the nature of the devil's tongue.

"Two words on two embarrassments," Burke continues, "and I shall be through":

I grew up in an uncouth age and neighborhood in which it was taken for granted that minorities "normally" referred to one another as Dagoes, Hunkies, Niggers, Micks, Kikes, and such, along with our sound suspicion that we were all minorities of one sort or another. (Imagine the stigma, for instance, of living in Brushton rather than Homewood, or Homewood rather than Squirrel Hill, and so on.) Thus, some of my early stories show occasional pre–Reichstag Fire laxities. Since then, Hitler and his noxious Ism have made it hard even to remember the climate in which such laxities were taken for granted. Gone forever (and perhaps for the better) are the days when it could be considered good clean fun, at a booze party, if Whitey the goy sang Negro spirituals in a Yiddish accent. I leave the bumpy passages as they were. First, they're not so tough anyhow. And second, I have the firm conviction that my subsequent work makes my position quite clear on the subject of ethnocentric bias, except in the sense of culture as a picture gallery that can liberally accommodate many different kinds of portrait and portraiture.

Of sexual passages in the earlier stories, some were adolescent, others reflect the traumatic survival of adolescent rigors. But in the light of later developments (particularly the cultural trends that have followed upon the Perfecting of the Pill), I find it a bit quaint when I apologize (and in Martial's Latin yet!) for any "license" in any of these prim imaginings.

Burke ends his preface here. But in the spirit of post-Pill permissiveness, we supplement his concluding comments by restoring to "Prince Llan" the Office of the Natural and the Divine, the suppressed recitation of Alpha and Nomega to which Burke refers in the footnote on page 315:

Love in the male should be subordinated to mastery, in order that the fine edge be not taken too soon from the attack.

The male strives to remain calculatory until he has reached a point whereat decision is irrevocable. Then, and only then, he must shift the direction of his emotions, and speed in arithmetical ratios of progression, like an object drawn by gravitation, towards catharsis.

Let the female remember simply that she is a flower holding up its chalice, a vase to be filled.

While that act is most efficient in which, the two phenomena having transpired simultaneously, the parts are left ticking irregularly from the repercussion.

THREE EXERCISES

The three "exercises" that close the book are more precisely prose poems rather than fiction. They are reprinted from Burke's *Collected Poems, 1915–1967*, published by the University of California Press in 1968. The first two were privately printed by Burke as New Year's greetings to friends and were later collected in his first volume of poetry, *Book of Moments: Poems 1915–1954* (Los Altos, California: Hermes Publications, 1955). The third exercise, "On Creative Dying," was first published in *Limbo*, April 1964. For an epigraph to these pieces, we have chosen a stanza from "Know Thyself," one of the later items in Burke's *Collected Poems*.

A SPECIAL PROBLEM

Why, after thirty years as a matchless critic, did Burke choose, in the mid-1960s, to resurrect, revise, and otherwise "worry the bone" of his earliest work? Why was there a second edition of *Towards a Better Life*, and why an expanded edition of *The White Oxen*? Malcolm Cowley, writing to Burke in 1966, suggested that, had Burke "made a big sale" of his fiction in the twenties and thirties, he would have forgotten his novel and stories and moved on to criticism without a moment's regret, apology, or self-recrimination. In reply, Burke wrote:

> You may be right, who knows? But I have my doubts. For I doubt whether you would have abandoned your poems, had they sold like Robert Frost or Edgar Lee Masters. My hunch is that you'd still be working over them, just as you are now. And in my case, there is a special problem (not typical of our trade but certainly not a *special* case in the sense of its applying to me alone). The inability of critics to see what was going on [in *Towards a Better Life*] was a godsend to me as a critic. I'm not arguing here as to whether the book is good or bad. All I'm saying is that the goddam stupid baystards couldn't even see what is going on here . . . [couldn't] even see what is being dealt with!
>
> As I sees it: That item was my analogue of Nietzsche's *Also Sprach Zarathustra*. That is, it was my fictive way of summing up

the implications of my critical way. And just as you have had reasons for hanging on regardless of sales, so I have had reasons for hanging on. We're just that kind of guy.

A related thought can be found in the postscript to the 1966 reissue of Burke's first critical book, *Counter-Statement* (1931):

> The author believes that, for all the occasional immaturity of some attitudes in his *Counter-Statement*, the book adequately supplies an introduction to his later concerns. [So do] the two works of fiction which the author published early in his career, and which, whatever one may think of their intrinsic merit, have been of great value to him, because he can now remember them as from without, whereas once he experienced them drastically from within—and he has found this double vision useful for his analysis of motives.

DISCLOSURES & ACKNOWLEDGMENTS

For *Here & Elsewhere*, we have copyedited Burke's texts afresh, silently correcting a few obvious misprints and bringing consistency to certain matters of spelling, style, and typographical display. We should perhaps make it clear that all footnotes in the text are Burke's, and all material in square brackets is our own.

We wish to thank Michael Burke and Anthony Burke, the executors of their father's literary estate, for giving us permission to assemble this book, and Denis Donoghue, a longtime champion of Burke's fiction, for contributing the introduction. Our editorial work is much indebted to the checklists of Burke's work compiled by William H. Rueckert, Armin Paul Frank and Mechthild Frank, and David Blakesley; to the edition of the Kenneth Burke–Malcolm Cowley letters prepared by Paul Jay (1988); and especially to Jack Selzer's *Kenneth Burke in Greenwich Village* (1996), a thorough account of Burke's early career, 1915–1931. We should also like to thank the reference librarians of the Boston Athenæum for their cheerful and resourceful bibliographic assistance.

Christopher Carduff
Black Sparrow Books
Boston, Massachusetts

About Kenneth Burke

Born May 5, 1897, Pittsburgh, Pennsylvania. Attended local Peabody High School with Malcolm Cowley, lifelong friend in literature, 1912–16. Attended Ohio State, then Columbia University, 1916–18. Moved to Greenwich Village, 1918. Married Lillian Batterham, 1919 (three daughters). Member, editorial board, *Dial* magazine, 1921–29 (music critic, 1927–29). Bought farm in Andover, New Jersey, chief residence for rest of life, 1922. Short stories  collected in *The White Oxen*, 1924. Thomas Mann's *Death in Venice*, translated by Burke, 1925. Dial Award for distinguished service to American letters, 1929. *Counter-Statement*, volume of formal and aesthetic criticism, 1931. *Towards a Better Life*, 1932. Divorced Lillian Batterham; married her sister, Elizabeth Batterham, 1933 (two sons). Music critic, *The Nation*, 1933–36. Guggenheim Fellow, 1935. *Permanence and Change: An Anatomy of Purpose*, 1935. Executive Committee, First American Writers' Congress, 1935. *Attitudes Toward History*, 1937. *Philosophy of Literary Form*, collection of reviews and essays, 1941. Lecturer in theory and practice of literary criticism, Bennington College, 1943–62. *A Grammar of Motives*, 1945. Fellow, Institute for Advanced Studies, Princeton University, 1949–50. *A Rhetoric of Motives*, 1950. Poems collected in *Book of Moments*, 1955. *The Rhetoric of Religion: Studies in Logology*, 1961. *Language as Symbolic Action: Essays on Life, Literature, and Method* and *Towards a Better Life* (second edition), 1966. *Collected Poems, 1915–1967* and *The Complete White Oxen*, 1968. *Dramatism and Development*, 1972. Gold Medal, National Institute of Arts and Letters, 1975. National Medal for Literature, 1981. *The Selected Correspondence of Kenneth Burke and Malcolm Cowley, 1915–1981*, edited by Paul Jay, 1988. *On Symbols and Society*, 1989. Died November 19, 1993, Andover, New Jersey.